"A quiet gut-punch of a debut... Absorbing and alive, the kind of novel that swallows you whole."

—Kirkus, starred review

"Naima Coster is definitely a writer to watch. Her clear-eyed writing interrogates race, class, and family in a refreshing and thoroughly engaging way. A lovely and thoughtful book."

—Jacqueline Woodson, author of *Brown Girl Dreaming* and *Another Brooklyn*

"This is the story of a family—which means it's the story of imperfect and vulnerable creatures—failing at love no matter their efforts. In *Halsey Street*, Naima Coster shows us one young woman's tangled efforts to return home and repair the intimacies we can hardly live without. It's a poignant, moving book, written with deep empathy and sophistication."

—Ben Marcus, author of *Leaving the Sea* and *The Flame Alphabet*

"In this lovely novel, Naima Coster captures, with depth and nuance, the yearnings, ambivalence, and insecurities of a woman on the brink of adulthood. In the process of healing old wounds, Penelope Grand must mend complex fractures in relationships with her estranged mother in the Dominican Republic and her father in Brooklyn."

—Christina Baker Kline, *New York Times* bestselling author of *The Orphan Train* and *A Piece of the World*

"With this debut, Naima Coster has established herself as a major new talent of literary realism. A tale of what happens when your own past is rendered as unknowable as your future, this family story looks at all the different ways loss defines us. Brooklyn is under trial for Coster's Grand family in a way any New Yorker can recognize, but Coster goes the additional mile to investigate the nuances of the gentrified and the gentrifiers. Race, ethnicity, and class are masterfully challenged in this narrative of self-discovery and the quest to preserve one's heritage while honoring lifesaving transformation. A brilliant debut."

—Porochista Khakpour, author of *Sons and Other Flammable Objects* and *The Last Illusion*

"Naima Coster's first novel is rich and flavorsome, a portrait of a Brooklyn neighborhood in decline and renewal and of a young woman—a risk-taker, fierce yet loving. First novels rarely come as skilled, touching, and real as *Halsey Street*."

—John Crowley, author of *Ka* and *Little, Big*

"Coster's absorbing and beautifully written novel, *Halsey Street*, haunts me still. Set in two cities I love, Pittsburgh and New York, it's both lucidly familiar and emotionally unpredictable. It's a novel that faces head-on the complicated ways women are split between their duty to their families and their personal passions. In this deeply profound and moving story, Penelope *es* tremenda!"

—Angie Cruz, author of *Soledad* and *Let It Rain Coffee*

"How does one gifted young woman find her life? Through a deep journey of mind, body, and spirit across cultures, classes, and city blocks. Coster's Penelope rises and falls, flies and stumbles, and goes straight to the heart in this beauty of a debut. Get to *Halsey Street* as fast as you can."

—Stacey D'Erasmo, author of *Wonderland*

"*Halsey Street* introduces Naima Coster as an important new voice, wise, elegant, and utterly engaging. Her protagonist, Penelope, is a fierce yet tender heroine who must navigate modern-day Brooklyn, must learn to move between classes and countries. Coster captures the ache and longing of living life as an outsider, while also illuminating the force of history and family. A remarkable, heartbreaking debut."

—Rebecca Godfrey, author of *The Torn Skirt* and *Under the Bridge*

"A poignant and absorbing Brooklyn elegy, told by a young woman lost in the no-man's-land between gentrifier and gentrified."

—Johanna Lane, author of *Black Lake*

"In her stunning debut novel, Coster remarkably renders the complexities of people and their many relationships as well as the tricky interplay of past and present. Alternately delivered from the perspective of Penelope and Mirella (with a little Spanish mixed in), Coster's realistic depictions of these two hurt and angry women and the broken man who connects them will haunt readers while making them flinch, gasp, and quite possibly cry. Wow. Powerful, unforgettable, and not to be missed."

—*Library Journal* (starred review)

"In her perceptive, memorable debut, Coster reveals the personal toll that gentrification takes on one damaged Bed-Stuy family . . . Penelope's status as both an insider and an outsider in her childhood home affords Coster an acute perspective from which to consider the repercussions of gentrification, as well as a family's legacy of self-destruction."

—*Publishers Weekly*

"But where *Halsey Street* most impresses is in its sharp and sophisticated moral sense. Take the issue of gentrification. In lesser hands, this could become—in many works of contemporary literary fiction, does become—ham-fisted or preachy. Coster's treatment, though, is always gracefully done. We don't get a fictional 'take' on gentrification. Rather, we get a story that makes the phenomenon meaningful through its narrative integration . . . *Halsey Street* regularly rejects simplicity for complexity. Like Woolf said of *Middlemarch* this is a novel written for grown-up people—the most surprising and satisfying element in a continually surprising and satisfying debut."

—*San Francisco Chronicle*

"*Halsey Street* pays careful, detailed attention to the ways family ties can splinter and fester and ache, and the way a neighborhood that used to be familiar but no longer is creates a feeling of isolation . . . And [it] offers the same attentiveness to the changing landscape of Brooklyn, and to a Bed-Stuy that is rapidly becoming unrecognizable. It's a detailed portrait that's almost a love letter."

—Vox

"Active erasure shows up strongly in Naima Coster's beautiful debut novel, *Halsey Street* . . . In her portrayal of a borough that's lost its identity, Coster paints a vivid image of a broken family that isn't clear how to move forward, but knows that it must in order to survive. We become who we must be, particularly in times of turmoil. Brooklyn is not what it used to be, so what will it become? *Halsey Street* grapples with that question."

—Bitch Media

"A meditation on family, love, gentrification, and home."

—*The Millions*

"*Halsey Street* tackles big issues like race, gentrification, and immigration but what's most beautiful about Coster's novel is that it is primarily about two women coming home and navigating the bewildering territory of their adult relationships with each other, with their pasts, and with their homes. Coster gives her characters of color permission to just be people—messy, hurt, sometimes hurtful, generally-mystified-by-life human people—liberating them (and thereby all her grateful women of color readers) from having to always be all of the demographic identities that precede them in a world that considers them first an aberration and a problem."

—Bustle

"This moving yarn gives us enchanting heroine Penelope Grand. She's dealing with her suddenly gentrified neighborhood, which presents unwelcome surprises."

—*Essence*

"*Halsey Street* takes on gentrification, focusing on the relationship between a mother leaving home and a millennial daughter returning home. Forgiveness and empathy are central themes to this piece of authentic fiction, in which Coster takes on intergenerational multiculturalism."

—PEN America

HALSEY STREET

NAIMA COSTER

Text copyright © 2017 by Naima Coster
All rights reserved.

No part of this work may be reproduced, or stored in a retrieval system, or transmitted in any form or by any means, electronic, mechanical, photocopying, recording, or otherwise, without express written permission of the publisher.

Published by Little A, New York

www.apub.com

Amazon, the Amazon logo, and Little A are trademarks of Amazon.com, Inc., or its affiliates.

ISBN-13: 9781503941175 (hardcover)
ISBN-10: 1503941175 (hardcover)
ISBN-13: 9781503941168 (paperback)
ISBN-10: 1503941167 (paperback)

Cover design by PEPE *nymi*

Printed in the United States of America

First edition

For Jonathan

Is there anyone among you who, if your child asks for bread, will give a stone?
Or if the child asks for fish, will give a snake?

—Matthew 7:9

Porque la piedra
en esta mano pesa más
que lo que aguanta
tu corazón.

—Li Yun Alvarado, "Adiós"

1

Pittsburgh

The bar was two stories below street level, its wooden walls curved to resemble the bow of a ship. The amber glow inside was artificial and dim, the hurricane lanterns hung so low that patrons sometimes walked right into the unlit lamps. Penelope had no trouble navigating the darkness. She knew her way around the Anchor by memory, slid into the back room easily, and sat in her usual leather armchair, her drink cold and tall on her lap.

The back was nearly empty, quieter than the bar, where revelers shouted orders across the counter and fell over each other, scrounging up quarters to pay for the jukebox. Back here, the light was blue, and it was even harder to see. The blue light was meant to be starlight, this whole back room the deck of the ship. The night sky and dark sea floated on the wallpaper, and a cratered aluminum moon revolved overhead. Penelope liked the way drinking back here could feel for a while like living inside a bad art installation. However cheap it was, she liked the immersion. The bartender knew to give her extra-long shots of the gin she liked best, and sometimes, in gratitude, she kept him company while he worked. Other times, she sat back here and waited to take him home after his shift. But tonight she wasn't planning on spending the night with him, although he was generous and fine to talk to. Tonight, she wanted to be alone. It was her father's birthday, and she was celebrating. He had made it to sixty-three.

She had sent flowers and a copy of *Stormy Weather*, an old black-and-white musical they had watched together when she was a girl. She had called him three times over the course of the day to sing to him and tell him she loved him. On one call, he held the phone up to the air so she could hear the record he was playing. Penelope recognized the song by the lyrics: "Lush Life" by Coltrane and Hartman. They had listened together for a while. His neighbor, Miss Beckett, had plans to go over and share dinner with him that night, which Penelope thought would be festive enough. There was nothing else that she would ask for, not even to be nearer to him for the day. It was sufficient that he was alive, and he wasn't alone.

Happy birthday, Pop.

Penelope toasted the dark and drank. Her gin was clean and fragrant—cardamom, cucumber, juniper. She inhaled its perfume. The table beside her was covered in knickknacks: a ceramic starfish, a bronze whale, bits of coral. She picked them up and rearranged them, then stared at the ocean murals on the wall. It required no effort for her to slide outside herself and into the blue of the room.

Her eyes were closed when she felt a tap on her shoulder. A man crouched down beside her—some goon who couldn't believe she had come to the bar to sip her gin and be left alone. He had a funny row of bangs across his forehead and eyes that shone green in the strange light of the room. He grinned at her and gave a little wave, and she was ready to tell him to fuck off, until she saw the tiny button pinned to the breast pocket of his shirt. She squinted and made out the orange letters in the dark. He offered to buy her a drink.

"After this one," she said, still fixed on the button. They had the same alma mater, or they almost could have.

The boy looked a bit younger, maybe twenty-four or twenty-five, so they wouldn't have overlapped at school, even if Penelope had stayed all four years. She sized him up, as if he were some radical alternate version of herself—boyish, white, light-eyed, further along. He wore his plaid shirt unbuttoned over a T-shirt in an attempt to look casual, like a workingman and not an aesthete, in a bar filled with servers and bartenders and cooks from across the city. His loafers gave him away: they were boxy, made of slick leather. She wouldn't have looked at him twice, if not for the button.

She asked if he was an artist. He said yes, a sculptor, and asked about her.

"I was," Penelope said, and the man laughed.

"Aren't you a bit young for the past tense?"

"I'm not," Penelope said, and he went to go buy her the second drink to smooth things over. When he returned, he didn't ask her to explain. He went on about himself, which was fine. Penelope wanted to know.

He had finished school in Providence not long ago, and in a few days, he'd be starting a grad program in sculpture. For his funding, he would teach a class on spatial dynamics. Penelope mentioned she was a substitute art teacher for the Pittsburgh public schools, but she hardly ever got called in because it was easier for the schools to just cancel the class. She told him about the art festival by the rivers each summer, and the galleries worth visiting, and it felt good to be able to tell him something that he didn't yet know. After a while, she ordered him to bring her another drink, and when he returned with the wrong kind of tonic, she sent him back to the bar.

His name was Bernie or Bryce or Blake—she couldn't remember—and when he asked her how long she'd been in Pittsburgh, she said, "Always," although it had been only five years. It was a half-truth. Her life hadn't started, really, until she was on her own here. The city had been good to her. Even her father seemed to have good days when he came to visit her. He got away from that empty house, and she took him to dinners at her bar in Squirrel Hill, where he ate for free, while she worked just half a shift. He liked being out someplace, people watching and drinking coffee. They made plans every time to watch a game at Heinz Field, but they never made it to the stadium. It would be too hard for Ralph to get to his seat in the upper deck, where Penelope could afford tickets, and neither of them wanted to endure the trouble. Instead she rented cars and they went for long drives over the Allegheny and the Monongahela, all the way up to Mount Washington to watch the city flicker on at twilight. They listened to tapes he had brought along with him—Marvin Gaye and the Moments. They could do it all sitting down. They found a rhythm that helped Penelope believe it had always been just the two of them; they lived in Pittsburgh; Ralph had never been married; she had no mother; there was no woman named Mirella.

"Drink this."

The green-eyed kid interrupted her, handing over a fluorescent yellow shot. He held another for himself and he beamed at her, as if they were having a terrific time and might leave together soon. Penelope had planned only to celebrate her father for a few hours, alone, and if she wanted to take someone home, it should have been the bartender. He had beautiful hands and knew how a night with her would work— a few rounds of good hard drinks, the laughter and plain talk of an easy friendship, and then ecstatic, rapid sex, before one last drink, and good-bye. Penelope didn't think the green-eyed boy could offer her any of that. He was gawky and young, and he looked at her as if he were thinking about asking her to prom. But he was pretty and much further along in his art than she would ever be, which made them even, in a way, at least for tonight.

Penelope drained her glass, her eyes on the sculptor as she tilted her head back.

"Your turn," she said, and he mimicked her, pounding the center of his chest afterward to dull the burn of the shot.

"Let's leave," she said. "I want to show you something."

Penelope took his hand and left the blue sanctuary of the back room. By the bar, old seafaring songs were playing overhead, and the regulars were singing and swaying along. Penelope laid a fan of bills flat on the counter for her bartender. She didn't trust the grad student to tip well, and she knew the bartender needed it—the gas was always turned down too low at his place. He winked at her and waved good-bye, and Penelope said she'd stop by to see him some other time.

They rose out of the belly of the Anchor onto the sidewalk. Water Street was swollen with drunken college kids, back in town for the semester. The city was undoubtedly better when they were away. They started to walk uphill toward Penelope's apartment, and Bernie or Ernie or Blake tried to put his arm around her. She kept toward the other end of the sidewalk, and eventually he gave up.

The squat buildings along the Slopes were unlit and quiet, their Easter-egg colors obscured by the dark. After a while, the grad-boy was panting from the steepness of the streets, but Penelope didn't slow down. She was used to the incline. Between breaths, he spoke loudly, his voice slicing through the night. He was babbling on about the year he had spent in Berlin on a fellowship, how he rode a bicycle to his workspace. Penelope shushed him and said, "We're almost there."

At the door to her loft, Penelope turned on all the lights so the sculptor could take in the apartment. The floors were polished black wood, the walls unpainted brick. Large cement pillars held up the ceiling and gave the loft the look of a maze. She kept her easel against the wall facing the eastern windows, which brought in a blinding light each morning, even in winter.

Before the sculptor could ask how she afforded the place, she told him she made good tips and few people wanted to walk this far up the hill. She poured them two more drinks, although her body was already rocking inwardly, as if they truly had been on board a ship. The grad-boy, a lightweight, was already slurring his words. He made a great effort to enunciate, as if he still had to win her over. Couldn't he tell she'd already made up her mind?

They sat on Penelope's bed, one of the few pieces of furniture in the loft. She had bought it years ago with nearly all of her first paycheck from the bar. After a month of sleeping on a bundle of sweaters and a rug, the bed had been proof that leaving New York was worth all this solitude, this space. She missed her father, but life with him would have made her feeble, plastic; here she had her bones.

They drank, and Penelope showed the green-eyed boy her portfolio, the one with her most recent drawings.

"Is this what you wanted to show me?" he said. "You hardly use any color."

He flipped through quickly, barely admiring her sketches of the bridge to Herrs Island, a half-dozen bottles aglow on a table in late after-noon, watches and hats and fountain pens in the lost and found box at her bar, Josephine Street under snow, pairs of pedestrians huddled close.

He paused at a drawing of a brick building on a shady street. The awning couldn't be read, the letters smudged and faded. Light reflected off the glass door and windows, so nothing inside could be seen. A crack split the pavement in the foreground.

"This one is waiting for something," he said. "Maybe inside, or in front. Along the sides. Something else."

"That's all there is," Penelope said, and she knew the defense would never have held in a critique, the thin idea that since it was drawn from life, she didn't have to change anything. He told her she should go back to the building and observe it again. "It doesn't exist anymore," she said and slid the drawing back into the portfolio.

"You're no beginner," the grad-boy said. "You should stop doing these object studies." He went on to say Penelope should come to the colloquia at the university this fall—they were free and open to the public, although the public didn't seem to care. She could come and learn even while she worked at the bar. There was really *something to be said* for studying art, but he didn't say what. He offered these solutions for her life, fixing problems she had not named, so Penelope began to unbutton her shirt. She slipped off her skirt and her boots, her too-small underwear. The grad-boy shut up quick.

He was attentive, if a bit delicate, and she came first, which was more than she had expected. He was sweating and smiling when they were through, his hair mussed and his face proud. He kissed her and asked for another drink. When she returned with two old jam jars filled with gin, the boy was already asleep. Penelope sat beside him, her limbs splayed apart so the cool apartment air could dry her skin. He had left his wallet on the nightstand, so she rifled through: his university ID, his health insurance card, and a tattered picture of a big dog, maybe his when he was younger, maybe dead now. He was already a card-holding member of at least three coffee shops over in Lawrenceville. On his license, she saw that he was from Oregon, an organ donor, born in December. She checked his birthdate again and did the math. He was twenty-one.

Penelope sipped her drink and wondered whether to ask him to leave. She figured it was too late, they had already slept together, and she could let him sober up for a few hours. He was right when he said her drawings were all object studies. He hadn't lied to win her over, which she appreciated. What he hadn't understood was that she didn't have to do more. She wasn't working toward a class or a show. The drawing was an exercise, as much a part of her routine as evening tea, morning runs, these sips of gin. The sketches kept her muscles working; they tempered her moods. She had no fellowship to Berlin, but these object studies, they were hers.

Penelope picked up the sculptor's plaid shirt from the floor, turned it over in her hands. She fingered the little white button still pinned to the pocket. She took off the button and slipped it inside her portfolio, along with her drawings. Penelope finished the two jam jars of gin and choked down a few aspirin from the nightstand to offset a hangover. She lay down with the blue-ink-and-white drawing of her father's store still in her head. Before she drifted off, she saw the crack in the pavement deepening, wide enough for a man to fall in.

The alarm went off too soon, and Penelope slapped the top of the clock. It didn't quiet, and the boy beside her moaned. She heard him rustle, turn onto his side. She thought, *He's going to vomit all over my black beautiful floors,* but she couldn't move to bring him a bucket. Her ears and eyes were stuffed full of steel wool, her mouth too dry to speak. She slapped and slapped the alarm clock, until she realized it was her phone ringing. She forced her eyes open and saw the phone lit up on the nightstand. It was a call from a 718 number she didn't recognize.

Pop.

Penelope sprang upright in bed, still woozy, but her thoughts suddenly, dreadfully clear. *My father is dead,* she thought. *He has fallen down the stairs in that house again, and this time he's dead.*

"Hello?" Penelope shouted into the phone. The green-eyed boy groaned, and Penelope swatted at him violently. She repeated into the phone, "Hello, hello?"

A man on the other end asked for Penelope Grand, and when Penelope answered that she was Penelope Grand, the terrible anthem started beating in her head again—*He's dead, he's dead, my father's dead. It's his birthday, and now he's dead.*

"Are you the daughter of a man named Ralph?"

The man's voice was even and low, as if he had called to inquire about an overdue library book and not to announce an emergency.

"Jesus Christ, what's happened? Put my father on the phone."

"He's pretty out of it right now. I have him here, on the corner of Franklin Avenue. He's refusing to go to the hospital."

Penelope had not forgotten how it felt to receive a call like this, although it had been over a year since the last. That first phone call came rushing back to her, as if no time had passed at all. Ralph's accident had happened yesterday, this morning, a few hours ago. He had never been safe. She had always been waiting for this second call. When she asked what was wrong, the man said Ralph had too much to drink and then took a fall. He was bleeding from the head.

"Why are you calling me? He needs an ambulance."

"We found your number in his wallet."

Penelope began to curse.

"Honestly, it doesn't look like more than a scrape. He probably just needs to go home and sleep it off. Put some ice on that eye."

"But he's bleeding."

"I only called because I noticed he can't really walk. I'm the manager at the bar up the block—"

"Sheckley's?"

"So you know where we are. I'll stay with him until you get here."

Penelope told the manager she couldn't pick Ralph up, and when he asked her why, the shame nearly swallowed her voice.

"I'm far away," she said.

The manager started going on about how he couldn't wait outside with Ralph all night. He had a business to run, had to get back to the bar, and the only reason he was being nice was because her father was so old and couldn't walk right. Penelope pinched her thigh to keep herself from cursing at him. "I know someone who can help," she said. "Stay where you are."

Penelope hung up and called Miss Beckett. She told her Ralph was bleeding outside Sheckley's, and she had to go to him as fast as she could. She asked the old woman to call as soon as Ralph was back at home. Miss Beckett agreed and hung up in a panic. Penelope was left with nothing to do but wait.

She thought briefly of crying, but told herself there wasn't any need to—Ralph was fine. A head scrape, a hangover, a little blood. Nothing else.

The green-eyed sculptor was sitting up in bed now, rubbing her back. He squinted at her in the dark, his short hair sticking straight up. He asked her if everything was all right, and he opened his arms for her. She rested against his lanky body, and he brushed his lips across her forehead, her shoulders. He made all the motions of a longtime lover, and it was nice to feel that he knew her, that they were steeling themselves for bad news they would bear together. It was beautiful, the vise of his arms, his measured breath, and she made a great effort to shut her eyes against the picture, forming and re-forming in her head, of her father, his face slashed open. The phone call had come and gone, and, still, he was alive. He was newly sixty-three.

Penelope woke to the sun in her eyes. It was after six, and no one had called. Her alarm hadn't gone off either. She rose from the bed, and the sculptor didn't notice her slip away. She sat naked on the floor and dialed her father.

"Good morning. Grand residence."

"Una, is that you? Where's my father?"

"Morning, Penelope. He's fine. I gave him some tea and some bread last night, and the bleeding had nearly all stopped by the time I put him to bed. I don't think he'll be needing stitches. The worst part was getting him up those stairs. It wasn't easy, I'll tell you that."

"What happened?"

The sky outside her windows was a cobalt blue and lightening. Penelope watched the exquisite change in colors while Miss Beckett told the whole story. It was a terrible film, unspooling in her head.

"I came by before, like I said I would, to bring him dinner and make a pot of tea. He seemed a little sad, playing 'Alabama' and going on about how much he missed Lionel, how Lionel would never live to be sixty-three, how he wished he could go have a drink at Lionel's bar. He talked about the times he used to go to Sheckley's, with you and with your mother. How he used to have a family on days like this.

"By the time I got to Sheckley's, that manager was getting impatient. A mean-looking white boy, tattoos everywhere, on his neck and his hands. He said Ralph had been in there for hours, just drinking and not saying a word, until he got up and they could see the kind of trouble he has—that he was unsteady on his feet, and it wasn't just the beers. So they went with him to make sure he got outside all right. Something about liability—they didn't want him to fall inside the bar. And when they got to the curb, somehow they dropped him, and Ralph still had the bottle in his hand."

"You should have taken him to the hospital."

Miss Beckett snorted. "Force Ralph Grand to do something he doesn't want to do? Impossible, and you know it."

"Put him on the phone. I'll convince him."

"He's fine now, Penny."

"You promised you'd call as soon as you got him home."

"Call you for what? Hmm? What were you going to do from all the way out there?"

"He's my father. You should have told me whether he was all right."

"I had my hands full with him! He might be all skinny now, but he's still a grown man. I had to get him up the stairs and change his clothes and get him in the bed all by myself! I thought my strength was going to go out on me, that we were both going to fall down those stairs and die, and here you are, telling me I should have called—"

"All right, all right. That's enough," Penelope said. The women sat in silence on the line. "Will he have a scar?"

Ralph already had a crisscross of scars along his spine from the surgery after his first fall, but no one could see those. He wouldn't be able to hide a scar on his face, not even from himself.

Miss Beckett sighed. "I'll take a look when he gets up."

Penelope tried to imagine the chronology of the night, what she had been doing while her father was gearing up for another fall. She sat down in the armchair at the Anchor; Ralph sipped the last of his tea with rum in the living room. The green-eyed boy squatted beside her; Ralph lifted the needle off a record, squirmed into his coat. She and the green-eyed boy walked up the Slopes; Ralph tumbled into a car that would take him to Sheckley's. She entered the loft; he entered the bar; she fucked the boy; he drained his beer; she drifted off to sleep; he smacked his head on the pavement; the bottle broke.

Penelope thanked the old woman, and Miss Beckett huffed.

"You know, this is the kind of thing that family usually does."

"I'm grateful, Una. Just let me know, will you, if he needs anything else?"

"You know what he needs."

"I have my life here."

"Everybody's got a life someplace else! You've got yours there, your mother has hers wherever she is. Everybody's got a life, it seems, except your daddy!"

Miss Beckett hung up, and Penelope sat motionless on the floor, her bare legs and bottom cold, her breath short. She was used to the old woman's meddling but not her anger. But Ralph had never been injured and alone—the first time he fell, her mother, Mirella, had been there.

Penelope had received that first call at the bar, just over a year ago. Her boss said someone was on the line from New York. It was her father's old friend, Freddie Elias. Dr. Elias told her about the fall and calmly recounted Ralph's injuries—broken fingers, knuckles, an eye-socket fracture, a bruised hip, likely concussion, and a few slipped discs in his spine, *but he was fine*. Penelope made it to the break room before her feet went out from under her, and Una and Freddie had done their best to calm her down from where they were. Freddie had even suggested putting Mirella on the phone, although he knew they hadn't spoken in years, not since Penelope left for Pittsburgh. Penelope had shouted that no, she didn't want to speak to Mirella, especially not now, not ever again. She had hung up, resolved to call back when her father was awake.

She had told herself that if her mother weren't there, she would have flown to see Ralph, but then Mirella left for good, and still Penelope couldn't bring herself to fly back. Instead she called every day and sent flowers and chocolates. When Ralph was out of his temporary wheelchair, she flew him out to Pittsburgh and saw with her own two eyes that he had survived one disaster and then another. The sight of him sealed up some of the guilt inside her. She kept flying him out, whenever she could afford a ticket, and Ralph looked a little feebler every time but never as awful as that first time, when his back was hunched and his fingers gnarled, and he was quieter, as if the fall had cleared away a part of his brain, too. He had recovered, and it was Miss Beckett who gave her reasons to worry—she called to say Ralph was moody, or Ralph was crying, or getting thinner, or Ralph was stuck inside because there was no one to shovel ice off the stoop. Her father never told her these things himself, but she had assumed he was safe, even if he had lost things. A person could live with misery.

But now Penelope could see his blood; she could picture blood crusted onto Ralph's forehead. An idea she had managed to submerge since that first accident began to rise up in her; it settled on the rim of her conscience: her father could die while she was away.

Penelope stood, her head still clogged from the drinks, and she found her clothes. She dressed again in her fake leather skirt and brown boots, her T-shirt the faded color of wine. The sculptor was still asleep, and she couldn't remember his name, so she called him, "Hey, hey."

She shook him awake. He smiled at her, as if she were rousing him for another round.

She handed him his shirt and his underwear, said there had been a family emergency and she had to fly home.

"I thought you were from here," he said. "A steel girl through and through?"

"I'm not," Penelope said. "You need to leave."

He stood to dress, and Penelope started to strip the sheets off the bed. She would need to buy boxes. Her boss wouldn't be awake for a few hours, but she would call him then and let him know she was quitting, but that she'd need at least two weeks of double shifts to make enough for the move. The grad-boy quietly lifted Penelope's phone off the floor and tapped in his number.

He interrupted her rolling things up and tossing them in piles to give her a hug. He kissed her on the cheek and breathed in her ear, but it didn't charm her. They said good-bye and he lingered in the doorway, as if he were afraid to leave her. She ignored him and flashed around the apartment. She closed her easel, carried the empty jam jars to the sink, lifted out a mass of dried gym clothes from the machine. These were the many things that had kept her away from Ralph, these petty, little loads.

The grad-boy asked her whether she really had to leave so soon, and Penelope laughed.

"Why should I stay any longer?" she said. "To go another round with you?"

He blinked hard, as if she had struck him, and Penelope saw then that his eyes weren't green at all—they were brown, like hers, the color of rosewood. She turned away, back into the apartment. She didn't owe him anything.

"Where is home anyway?" he asked, as if the more kindly he spoke to her, the greater his chance at making her stay.

Penelope didn't look up when she answered. "Bed-Stuy."

2

HOMECOMING

Penelope arrived in Brooklyn on a Sunday morning. She went straight from the airport to the room she was renting on Greene Avenue, a few blocks from her father's house. The mustard-yellow brownstone was in better repair than her father's house had ever been. Vines fell delicately over the edges of the concrete window boxes; potted mums lined either side of the stoop. None of the original sandstone was visible through the brilliant yellow paint, unlike the other houses on the block, which stood in grim shades of brown.

The landlady was waiting for her on the stoop like a picture out of a catalogue. She had pale blond hair, lifting in the morning breeze, and she wore a black-and-white polka-dot dress with a collar, a pair of little red sandals with a heel. She was round faced and pretty, a white woman who smelled of perfume and an air-conditioned summer.

"I'm Samantha," she said. "Welcome."

Penelope had guessed she would be much older, since she was already married, a lawyer, the owner of this house, but she didn't seem very far from her in age. The women shook hands, and Samantha unlocked the door behind her, the knob and then the deadbolt. Penelope thought it unusual that she had turned all the locks since she had been standing right on the stoop.

The layout of the first floor was exactly the same as her father's house, but the interior of the house was immaculate. As Samantha led her up the stairs, she pointed out the original nineteenth-century medallions on the ceiling, the refinished, cream-colored moldings.

"The houses where I grew up in California are hardly ever this beautiful. The designs are so garish and cold. But there's so much history in these brownstones. It must have been a magical place to grow up."

Penelope nodded at her, certain there had been no magic in her growing up. She followed the landlady across the polished floors and empty landings. Every door was shut on every floor, until they reached the attic, which looked as if it were the point of a cathedral, expansive and light-filled for a single room, its walls forming a peak at the ceiling. Her boxes had arrived, and they were stacked neatly beneath the only window in the attic, a porthole, rimmed with white wood, large enough to offer a clear view of the street below. It was the picture of the window that had made her bookmark the ad, call, and say she wanted the place. It wasn't as much light as her Pittsburgh studio, but it would do, and the price was decent, a bit less than the other rooms she had seen online. Penelope wondered now why they had been willing to rent the room for under market value. Maybe they had paid for the house in cash and didn't need the money at all; maybe they wanted to imagine themselves magnanimous for renting to someone like Penelope; maybe they had plans to hike up the rent later. Penelope decided to ask why they had searched for a tenant.

"It's a little embarrassing," the landlady said. "But our daughter's convinced a ghost lives up here. We thought having a real person in the attic would make her less afraid. And you sounded just perfect—you're a schoolteacher, aren't you?"

Penelope mmhmmed. On the phone it had seemed a better idea to mention the substitute teaching than the bartending. She wasn't sure yet what kind of white people Samantha and her husband would be. Penelope handed her a check for the first month's rent, and the landlady gave her a ring of keys.

"I forgot to mention that the pipes sometimes bang at night, but you must be used to that. These old houses." Samantha smiled at her as if they were fast friends.

The landlady said she was off to meet her husband and their daughter in the city. They were headed to a playground then brunch with another pair of parents they knew from law school. She wished Penelope a good day and left the attic, her heels hardly making a sound.

Later, Penelope heard a car pull up to the front of the house. She looked out the window and saw Samantha climb into it, wearing sunglasses and carrying a red purse to match her shoes.

Penelope set down her suitcase and pulled out her old radio, tuned it to the Motown station. She could have called her father, but she decided to unpack, to give herself time to work up the nerve to walk over to Halsey Street. She opened the window, lit a cigarette, and settled into the familiar late-August heat.

She didn't have much to arrange. She assembled a wooden breakfast table by the china sink, hung scarves from the wall to give the room some color: gold, sky blue, pine green. She plugged in a toaster and a hotpot for tea, lined her bottles of gin in a row underneath the table. The ad had explained she wouldn't have access to the kitchen, which wasn't a problem for Penelope since it had likely saved her money on rent. She could use the bathroom one flight below on the fourth floor, and she would have it all to herself. Surely, they had enough bathrooms for the three of them on all the other floors of the house.

After she put together her four-post bed, Penelope was drenched in sweat and smoke. She sat on the bed to tack photographs of Pittsburgh overhead. The black-and-white squares covered the sloped ceiling as high up as she could reach. She hoped they would offer her some kind of comfort, a reminder that she had left, she had been away for five years. Her life in Brooklyn hadn't been her only life.

She unpacked her easel last, opening it before the porthole window. She looked down on the street and saw how similar the block looked to the one she had grown up on, although it was quieter than Penelope remembered. There were about as many trees, tall London planes, with brown bark peeling off in strips. The branches spread over the block, forming a canopy of shade. A few old folks sat on their stoops. Children in stiff church clothes skipped down the block. It was afternoon now, and a few white women worked in the little gardens in front of their houses. Their children rode bicycles to the corner and back.

Penelope gathered her new set of keys from the floor and left to see her father. The house was just a few blocks over, and Penelope wanted to see if the other streets were as quaint as Greene and Bedford. Ralph had narrated the changes in the neighborhood to her over the phone, five years' worth of losses. His store wasn't the only one that had closed. Lionel Sheckley wasn't the only friend who had died. Almost everyone was gone, he said. He hardly recognized Bed-Stuy.

Penelope didn't run into anyone she knew on the street, but the crowds on Nostrand Avenue seemed the same. She had to weave through the packs of people, talking and laughing, fanning themselves in the heat. Soca blared out of a beauty supply shop; the glare off the glass storefronts was blinding. The avenue was the Brooklyn she remembered; the side streets were stranger, quieter, emptier.

She found the old mud-colored house easily and climbed up the stoop to ring the doorbell like a guest. It would be a few minutes before Ralph made it down the stairs. Penelope took in the rusting iron of the rail on the stoop, the peeling paint above the threshold. The pavement in front of the house, down at the garden level, was cracked. Somehow the hydrangea bush seemed to be thriving: dusty blue, it grew in a plot of dirt, just inside the iron fence that separated the house from the street and the two brownstones on either side. The fence was rusted, too.

Penelope heard Ralph before she saw him. A heavy step, the scrape of one leg behind him. Another step. He swept aside the lace curtains on the door and peered onto the stoop. He fumbled for the doorknob and spoke to her through the glass.

"There's my Penny," he said. He jerked the door open and threw out his arms. "There's my girl."

Ralph crushed Penelope to his chest, and he felt so light against her, his arms bony and limp. Penelope let her face sink into the collar of his shirt. His back was stooped, and they were the same height now. He smelled like soap and tobacco, his mineral hair tonic. He wore his hair in a soft gray fro on most days; the tonic was for special occasions, to comb his hair over, wet and flat, with a part on the side. Penelope felt the creased skin of his cheek, velvety against hers.

Ralph stepped back into the doorway, and she could finally see his face. The cut curved from his temple to the inner corner of his eye. He wasn't squinting, but the skin beneath his eye was puffed up and purple. The gash gleamed yellow-red under the bacitracin he must have slathered on that morning.

Penelope refused to stare.

"I've been waiting for you," he said and clamped his hand on her shoulder. He gave it a squeeze and then turned back inside.

Penelope entered the house and felt her former life heaped upon her. The doors to the parlor were pushed open, and she saw the dirt coagulated on the mantels and the mirror, the fireplace clogged with bricks. She had sat beside Ralph on the day he filled up the fireplace with bricks; Mirella had gone out to the stoop in protest. She had left the door open so she could turn around once in a while and yell that Ralph was ruining the house, that all she had wanted was a room where she could light fires in the wintertime. Ralph had explained to Penelope that a fireplace was a disaster waiting to happen, too big of a risk given their investment in the house. He ignored Mirella and laid the bricks down in a row. He showed Penelope how to use the trowel. She had spread the mortar.

Ralph rested one hand on the open parlor door, the other on her shoulder. He leaned on her hard.

"She took all the furniture from down here when she left."

The empty parlor smelled of mildew, and the sour scent went to Penelope's head. She had forgotten her morning eye-opener, and she needed to sit down.

"Let's go upstairs, Pop," she said, and Ralph led the way.

He dragged his left leg behind him as they climbed the stairs. Penelope paused on each step, waiting until Ralph made his way up to the next. He heaved his body up, gripping the banister with one hand, pressing against the wall with the other. Penelope hadn't seen the stairs since she left for Pittsburgh, and she felt a yoke close around her neck as she counted the steps between the first floor and the second. Had he hit each one? Or had he plummeted down, no impact until he reached the bottom? Penelope shook her head and coughed to clear her lungs. There was no reason to worry; it was over now. She was here, and they were fine.

Ralph was panting when they reached the second floor. He shuffled into the living room and fell back onto the beaten-up olive sofa. Penelope softly set herself down next to him. The arms of the sofa were stained with ink from when Penelope used to leave her drawing pens uncapped, and they would bleed onto the cushions.

Flowerpots stood on every flat surface in the room: the windowsill, the top of the television set, above the fireplace, the coffee table, and the lamp stands. Mirella's plants had once made a green perimeter around the room, but the pots were all empty now, filled with chalky dirt. The room stank of stale coffee and ash. Penelope was glad she had gone to her attic first instead of here.

Ralph reached for her hand across the sofa and looked at her as if he wanted something.

"I made up your old room."

Penelope started to speak, but he raised his voice over hers. "I know you're a woman and all that and you need your space, but there's plenty of space here."

Penelope pictured Ralph tripping around her old bedroom, trying to fix the sheets and dust, as if a clean room could convince her to live again the way she had as a girl.

"I'll think about it, Pop."

Ralph nodded and crossed one leg over the other, using his hands to lift his left leg at the ankle and lay it over his right. He was handsome in his blue pinstripe shirt, his white chest hairs sprouting over the collar.

"You're skinnier than you were at Easter," he said. "Don't they have rice and beans in Pittsburgh?"

Penelope explained that she had been running a lot, more, actually, ever since he fell outside Sheckley's, but she didn't say that.

"Careful now," Ralph said, his gray eyes watery and sincere. "You wouldn't want to hurt yourself and wind up like me."

Penelope slid across the sofa to examine the cut. He had been lucky, she thought, that the glass didn't enter his pupil or slice open more of his face. It was healing slowly. In two weeks, Penelope had uprooted her life in Pittsburgh and returned to Brooklyn, and Ralph's skin hadn't managed to close around the wound. Penelope touched her father's cheek.

Ralph pushed her hand away.

"Pfsh!" he exhaled. "It looks worse than it feels. Don't you worry, Penny. Everything is gonna be all right now that you're back. Una thinks you're going to get that job at the elementary school. It's a sign—everything falling into place so quick! It was time for you to come back. Now, I had always imagined your mother would be here, too, when you came home."

Ralph lifted his pipe out of the ashtray on the table, struck a match and held it in the chamber until the tobacco lit up. He puffed smoke into the space between them, and the room seemed to shrink.

Penelope got up and hauled open the window, but the air that flooded in was warm and damp. She stuck her head out. The backyard below was overgrown with weeds. Three lawn chairs, streaked by rain, pointed in different directions. Someone else's orange cat sat on one of them sunning itself. The old lanterns strung from the back of the house to the far end of the wooden fence bobbed uselessly in the breeze. The shed, where Mirella had kept her gardening tools, was boarded up.

She knew her mother must have taken her old seeds and supplies with her. It was unlike Mirella to leave anything of hers behind. It surprised Penelope that the flowerpots were still there.

"What's in the shed?" she asked, without turning back toward the room.

"Old things from the shop. Signs, the cash register, the records we still had on the day we closed. The ones we couldn't sell even after we put them on clearance. Your mother thought it would be better to keep it all out there."

"Doesn't that shed still leak?"

"As bad as the ceiling on the fourth floor."

"Mami never understood the shop."

"Not like we did."

Penelope turned to face her father. The dust motes floated between them, and Penelope wanted to ask him to come and stand beside her at the window. Sitting down, he looked fine, as if he could have hoisted himself up and strode over to put his arm around her and look out on the yard. Penelope might not have ever left if she knew she would miss the final years of seeing her father strong. She could have found other ways to avoid her mother. She could have lived in another neighborhood. She could have met him sometimes at the shop. She could have left the house, this life, without leaving him.

"Maybe I'll buy you some curtains," she said. "It's too bright up here."

"All right."

"And maybe I can help you move a few things down to the first floor. That way you don't have to worry about climbing down those stairs, as well as the stoop, if you want to go outside."

Ralph held his pipe in his hand and looked at Penelope as if she had suggested something obscene. "Go outside to where? Sheckley's was a onetime thing. It was my birthday."

"Maybe now that I'm here, you can get out more—"

"We've always lived on the second floor."

"Pop, you're living in a museum, everything arranged just like it used to be. Why don't you move downstairs?"

Ralph bit down on his pipe and crossed his arms. He made a grunt she was meant to understand as his answer. He was as defiant as a little boy, and Penelope knew she would get nowhere by pleading. She spoke as sternly as she could.

"You can't keep waiting for her, Pop. Mami isn't coming back."

"Pfsh! You think I don't know that?" Ralph began to shake his head as if he couldn't believe Penelope wasn't smarter. "I'm the one who married her—I know how stubborn she is. I'll never see her again. Not in this lifetime. But that doesn't change a thing."

Penelope crossed the room to sit beside him and make peace, but Ralph didn't acknowledge her. He tilted his head back and stared up at the ceiling. Ralph didn't like to argue, and he would stop a disagreement dead as soon as he could. When he could still walk, and Penelope and Mirella would start to fight, he would tear out of the room, huffing loudly but not speaking. He didn't want to hear. Looking up was his new way of leaving a room.

"Come on, Pop."

He kept puffing on the pipe, holding it upright between his teeth. She put her head on his shoulder, and he didn't move, just kept exhaling smoke into the room. She waited.

"Forget I said anything at all."

Ralph lowered his chin onto her forehead, and she knew it meant he had forgiven her, that he would, in fact, forget. She wrapped his hand in hers, and they stayed like that for a long time, the traffic growing louder outside on Halsey Street, the day passing away from them. The light retracted slowly over the floorboards, as if it were trying to escape through the window.

When Penelope returned to Greene, the activity on the block had died down. Most people were inside their homes for the evening, and the ones who were outside were on their stoops, watching the sun go down. Inside the yellow house the lights were off. The landlady and her family were still in the city, and the house felt as vacant as her father's in the darkness. Penelope felt her way up four flights of stairs in the dark, crossing the landings quickly, to the top of the house.

She turned on the light and took in the smallness of the attic, the way her entire life had fit into this single room. She had everything with her now, except her art, which she had shipped off just yesterday, when she was still in Pittsburgh. She had double wrapped everything in Bubble Wrap and cardboard, all her paintings from art school. She had kept the paintings because they were proof that she had once thought art would be her whole life, and not one habit of many.

Penelope started the pot for tea and wondered what to do with her night. As a girl, she'd had no places of her own in Bed-Stuy; she had followed her father around to his haunts, and when she was old enough she set out for the city to drink and meet men. She could try to find a bar, but there would be no point in drinking if she had to sit in sick awareness of herself, surrounded by well-off white people, new to the neighborhood, blind to her, or worse. She drank her tea and started to feel restless, an itching in her soles. She decided to run.

She would do one of her old loops to survey the neighborhood— the concrete and intersections would be the same, and she could run off the dull feeling she had caught from being back in the old house, seeing her father, and, somehow, her mother, too.

Penelope left the house just as the evening heat broke into a soft rain. She chose to run along Bedford because the avenue seemed to stretch indefinitely in both directions, as if she could reach Pittsburgh if she kept running west. She went east instead, and then south, crossing the streets as quickly as she could. There were as many liquor stores as ever, and she picked up her speed every time she passed one so she wouldn't hear what the men loitering under the awnings muttered at her. She passed the same half-dozen murals—for ODB, for Rosa Parks, for a young father shot and killed before reaching thirty.

The streets were a mix of run-down apartment buildings with eroding fire escapes, and regal brownstones clustered in blocks of colors: a row of tan houses, then red, then chocolate brown, once in a while a house painted bubblegum pink or mint green. Penelope ran past the apartment building on Marcy where they had lived when she was younger, a few games of chess being played in Tompkins Park, and the empty bleachers. She saw an abandoned building on Flushing, most of the windows boarded up with planks of wood, the others gaping like cavities in the gutted house. Bottles and black bags of trash formed hills inside an empty lot, closed off by a chain-link fence. An elderly woman sat on a lawn chair, having a beer in the front yard she had covered in Astroturf. She seemed unbothered by the rain. An American flag hung motionless from a pole behind her chair, the Stars and Stripes collecting water.

Penelope headed back south, intending to return to Greene, since the rain was picking up, but instead her body propelled her to Lewis Avenue, past a gourmet pizzeria, a one-room bookstore, and a wine bar where the Puerto Rican deli used to be. She stopped to stretch on the corner, right across from the health food store. She'd never seen it before, but, of course, she knew how to find it.

The shop glowed behind a hedge of skinny ginkgo trees. The awning was a deep brown, the color of fertile soil, and above the entrance was the shop name: "SPROUT" in block letters, the *T* curling into the leaves of a green shoot. It was like any small upscale supermarket, with aisles of canned food and broth in boxes. The produce was arranged in crates under soft spotlights at the front of the shop: bunches of purple kale and rhubarb, blood oranges, and swollen avocados. Customers crowded around the produce and stood in lines before the dry-food dispensers, which looked like gumball machines filled with grains and beans and nuts.

They stood in lines with their Tupperware, occasionally sampling what they were buying, stealing a hazelnut or a handful of muesli. The shop was so bright she could see the colors of their painted nails, the patterns of their short-sleeved blouses, the glint of the eyeglasses on the men and women. The crack still parted the sidewalk in front of the store. No one had bothered to fill it in.

They had painted over the exterior so that it was lime green now. Penelope wondered if the new owners had seen her initials there: *PSG*, Penelope Sofia Grand, carved into the brick, beside the *RAG*, for Ralph Arnold Grand, and the *M* that was all Mirella left behind. Had the green paint been enough to cover them?

The rain started to fall more heavily, and Penelope watched the customers open their umbrellas when they left the store, and the people who were already on the street rushed for cover—a mother pushing her toddler in a stroller, a man mean-mugging at the bus stop and hugging his arms to his chest, two older schoolgirls in YMCA camp uniforms, lifting their backpacks over their heads and slurping violent-purple quarter waters as they exited the bodega, their teeth stained.

Penelope could have crossed the street and stood under the awning of Sprout, searching for the letters they had carved and waiting for the shower to pass. She could have seen if the etchings were still there; she could have felt them under her fingers. She decided to run on instead.

3

The Harpers

Principal Pine was waiting for Penelope on the front steps of the elementary school. She was a slender black woman with her hair in twists, her face touched by an array of colors: gold, pink, bronze, black. She smelled of immaculate makeup, sweet oil on her scalp. Gold earrings in the shape of Africa dangled from her ears. Penelope was sweating, the blazer she wore too heavy for the warm weather. She extended her hand to Mrs. Pine, who gave her a hug instead.

The principal led Penelope through the hallways back to her office. The school was empty, except for the teachers in the classrooms for professional development. They were squashed into too-small chairs, but they still managed to look official with collared shirts and yellow notepads. Besides the teachers she did not recognize, the school looked nearly the same. It still had an antiseptic smell, as if every surface had been scrubbed with bleach. The walls were covered in cork bulletin boards and grimy subway tile. Enormous barred windows faced the yard.

As they entered the office, Penelope geared up to make her pitch for the position. She was ready to sell the idea of teaching art where she first learned to paint; she would talk about giving back to the neighborhood, finding freedom in creativity. The principal sat behind her desk, and before Penelope could speak, she said, "I've solved our little problem."

Principal Pine explained that she couldn't offer Penelope the job since she didn't have the right degree to teach full time in a New York City public school, but she could bring her on as a substitute and never hire anyone else.

"We've had so many issues with the budget, I don't expect anyone will be in a rush to hire a full-time art teacher anytime soon. I can make this fly on my end, at least until the end of the school year—how's that sound to you?"

Penelope wondered whether to unlatch her portfolio and show Principal Pine that she had, at least, some credentials.

"Una speaks very highly of you," Principal Pine said. "She was here for forty years, long before I came in. She says you're up for the job, and that's really all I need to know."

Penelope nodded and said the bits she had rehearsed just so that she could feel she had earned the job in some way: *grateful, community, creativity, empower*. It was easy enough to say, although she was indifferent about teaching children. She could have made her money another way, but she owed it to her father, now that she was back in Brooklyn, to live somewhat more respectably. He had never put her through the kind of speech he would have been justified to give: two parents, art school, city college, a big house, and she had never done anything besides mix drinks, wait tables, and shelve books at the library. Principal Pine was merciful and didn't ask to see her résumé.

"I'll give you a rundown of the school these days," she said, and Penelope pulled out her sketchbook and attempted to take notes. There was a mold problem on the third floor, and they had spent the summer removing asbestos. They had a standing old guard of teachers who preceded Principal Pine in their tenure at the school, and there were the young white teachers who stayed for a few years before going off to grad school or getting married and returning to whatever town it was they came from. Most of the students had lived in the neighborhood their whole lives; the school had lost a few kids whose parents moved farther out in Brooklyn because they could no longer afford their rent. A few had been evicted midway through the year. There was a growing number of white children at school, some whose parents had bought brownstones in the neighborhood, others who belonged to a different zone school but whose parents had petitioned for them to attend PS 23. The school was becoming more popular, in part, because of the jazz band and the new community garden. Principal Pine had started both programs. The students learned to play the trumpet and trombone, the clarinet and saxophone, and someday soon, the tuba. In the garden, they caught water in rain barrels and collected compost; they picked vegetables and sent them over to the food pantry down the block.

"Plant a garden and the white folks come running," Mrs. Pine said. "I figure if they're going to live here, they might as well *live* here, get their hands dirty, and have their children learn right next to our children."

"But there's so much loss," Penelope said, and she wondered how much Mrs. Pine knew about her father's store, whether she had ever seen Sprout.

Mrs. Pine held her ground. "The research shows integration has good learning outcomes for our kids, and I agree."

Penelope thought about pointing out that none of the kids who had been forced to move away would benefit from the integration, but she decided she shouldn't upset the principal, and certainly not before her contract was signed.

She had known only one white child during her years at PS 23. Genevieve was a blond girl with unnaturally large eyes that bulged when she cried, which was often. She was a notorious whiner, and the other kids teased her mostly because it was so easy; the girl would stamp her feet, turn crimson, and sob to the teacher. She had a little troupe of friends, but when they went off to play double Dutch or tag with everyone else, Genevieve would stay behind on a bench to pick her hangnails and pout. More than once, Penelope hadn't wanted to play either, so she sat with her during recess. Penelope knew what it was like to be the girl with the mother with red hair. A classmate had once called her white, too. She and Genevieve played hand games and shared fruit snacks, but they weren't friends.

Halfway through fourth grade, after a particularly bad day of crying, Genevieve disappeared from the school. Penelope never saw her around the neighborhood, either. Penelope imagined a class of little Genevieves in the fuzzy sweaters and leggings that were popular when they were girls.

"It's going to be good for the children to have you in the classroom," Principal Pine said. "You're young, you look like them, you were born here. They need visions of success they can relate to. That's getting rarer and rarer around here. You should tell them your story."

Penelope wondered what story she could tell.

Principal Pine stood and said she had to get back to professional development for the full-timers. She handed Penelope a stack of paperwork to return as soon as she could.

"You know I've never met your father," Mrs. Pine said. "But I know he was a friend to the community, and a good man who put his family first." The principal guided Penelope out into the hall, one hand on her shoulder.

"Family is everything." She jabbered on, imparting what Penelope could see she meant to be wisdom. "The toughest part of our job is knowing we can't give our kids the families they deserve; we can't keep them from hurting. You'll see what I mean when you meet our kids."

Penelope shook the woman's hand and staggered out of the school, disoriented. What had Miss Beckett said to make her seem well adjusted, calm, exemplary? Or was the principal too hurried to really look at her? Perhaps the legend of Ralph Grand and his store had protected her and made her seem like someone who could handle early mornings, a regular, formal job.

It was still early, and Penelope had more hours to herself than she expected. The interview had been so short. She would run until the interview was far away from her, and she forgot her distaste for Mrs. Pine, her nerve. She had assumed Penelope needed to meet the kids to see how they hurt, as if she hadn't learned all that when she was a girl.

Penelope finished her run on the sidewalk in front of the house on Greene. The pink cotton of her shirt stuck to her skin, and she felt the ache in her calves, the heaviness of her muscles. Her run had done exactly what she intended it to do: she had lost her self and existed nowhere outside of her body. She was only the throbbing expansion of her chest, the pain in her joints, the sweat coursing down her forehead, the back of her neck, her thighs. Her knees popped as she bounded up the stairs, and she wondered whether she had overdone it, whether she should run a bath with salts, let herself soak in hot water, take an aspirin.

In the attic, Penelope opened a can of soup and sat at the breakfast table with her legs up. The meatballs, noodles, and sallow vegetables bobbed in the salty brown broth. She ate slowly, cooling off in the darkness of the room.

She had a drawing for each day she had been back in Brooklyn—eight—clipped to the back of her easel. Most of the drawings were small, close-ups of objects she could see from her little porthole window: a discarded and deflating basketball, a plant growing in a crushed Café Bustelo can on a nearby stoop, the overstuffed black bags of trash at the curb. She thought of the grad-school sculptor from that night at the Anchor. *More object studies,* he would have said, if he could see these drawings. Penelope could see now that he had been patronizing, the sex blurry and barely adequate. She hadn't slept with anyone since.

Penelope heard rushing up the stairs and then across the fourth floor. She craned her head to listen to the soft footfalls. A little girl shouted out, and she realized it was the landlady's daughter—the one Samantha had mentioned but Penelope had yet to see. Penelope listened as the girl started up some sort of game, dashing back and forth from one end of the hall to another. The little girl's voice floated up to Penelope through the floorboards, and she felt as if she were listening to herself. She too had invented games of her own to pass the afternoons she spent alone. She had run up and down the stairs in her chancletas, hid in the pantry, and waited for someone to find her. She had called out into the empty house and was joined by her echo. When she ran out of games, she turned to the things she had learned in school—drawing pictures, finger painting. She took pictures with her hot-pink Polaroid camera.

"Nope, nope, nope! That's not it!"

The girl threw up the words into the house, and Penelope caught them.

"Try again!"

She wondered what the rules of the game might be, whether she should go downstairs to finally introduce herself. She considered the alternative—another object study, beginning to plan for her new job— and stood to leave. She draped a towel over her shoulder so that a shower could be her excuse for going down to the fourth floor, and if Samantha or her husband showed up, she would duck into the bathroom. She didn't want to field their adult questions about her life, about Pittsburgh, her father, her art.

The little girl's voice grew fuller and clearer as Penelope descended from the attic. She neared the landing and saw a slight girl in lavender pajamas diving for the wall. She hit it with both hands, planting her palms flat on the plaster. Then she pushed off and sprinted across the hall, sliding when she got close to the other end, smacking the wall with both hands again.

"You're fast," Penelope said in a voice that she hoped was friendly. She didn't want to materialize in front of the girl unannounced, startle her, and make her fall.

The child spun around on the balls of her feet, her sheets of red hair whipping around her as she turned to face the stairs.

"I've been practicing," the girl said, and then, "You're all red."

"I'm cooling down from a run." Penelope touched her still-warm cheek.

The little girl took a step forward. Her face was round, and she had golden skin and brown eyes, like her mother. Her lavender blouse and flannel pants were each printed with a pattern of white sheep. She squinted, and the suspicious expression made her seem like a smaller, red-haired replica of her mother.

"My daddy runs," she said. "But not around here."

"I like to run outside."

"On the street?"

Penelope nodded, and the little girl pressed her palms together and tilted her head to the side, as if in disbelief. Penelope went on.

"I've been running in this neighborhood for fifteen years, and it's a lot safer now than it used to be."

"You don't look that old."

"I started when I was thirteen."

"I'm nine."

"That's a nice age."

"It's okay so far. You're Penelope, right? My name is Grace."

They shook hands. Grace's hand was cool and frail in Penelope's damp, brown hand. Penelope inspected the girl and wondered whether Grace would be one of her students at PS 23. Penelope sat on the bottom step and asked the girl whether she went to school nearby. Grace said she went somewhere called the Orchard School in the West Village.

"I used to be able to walk there in the mornings, but now I'm too far." She sat beside Penelope on the bottom step. "But I like this house. If I get another little brother, we'll have lots of space for the both of us."

Grace folded her hands on her lap, as if she were still in school. She was cautious, far more reserved than Penelope imagined she would be when she overheard her shouting and playing alone. Penelope asked her about the game.

"It's called Color Race. One person thinks of a color, and then the other person tries to guess what it is. If someone guesses your color, you're not safe anymore, and you have to run across the hall before they catch you. The wall is base. And if you get caught, it's your turn to think of a color."

"How have you been playing by yourself?"

"A part of me picks a color, and the other part guesses."

Penelope smiled. She had played against herself during many one-girl games of hide-and-seek, Ping-Pong, chess. Grace took her hand and led her to the far wall by the stairs. Penelope would have to guess a color first.

"I should warn you," she said. "I might be very good at this game."

Grace tossed her hair over her shoulder and lifted her chin. "I've been playing Color Race for years. Assume your position."

Penelope bent her knees and shouted. "Green!"

Grace giggled and shook her head. Penelope went on guessing until she finally cried, "Lavender!" and the girl went running for the wall at the other end of the landing. Penelope followed her, taking long but slow strides, so that Grace had smacked the wall and was safe before she could reach her. They went on playing rounds of the game, Grace picking unexpected colors, like teal and maroon and cerulean, so that it took Penelope a while to guess. Penelope chased after her at a half jog, her feet hardly leaving the floor. She didn't have the heart to catch Grace: she was having so much fun slamming into the wall and shrieking that they went on like that, Grace looking over her shoulder each time she reached the other side, the look in her eyes electric.

"Can I play?"

Grace stopped running when she saw her father at the top of the stairs. She skidded across the hall in her socked feet and slid into his arms. He lifted her up and kissed her on the forehead, sweeping back her bangs. They had the same orange-red hair. He tossed Grace up in the air and shook her by the shoulders while she was suspended over his head. She laughed and kicked her feet. He was paler than his daughter. His freckled arms flexed when he caught her. He gave Grace another kiss on the cheek before he set her down. She was out of breath from laughing when she took his hand and led him over to the other set of stairs, where Penelope stood watching.

"Daddy, you have to meet Penelope!" She emphasized the name as if the two girls had known each other for a long time.

"Penelope, it's a pleasure to finally meet you. Call me Marcus."

They shook hands.

"My wife has told me all about you. You studied at RISD?"

"I was only there for a year."

"And are your parents artists, too? Every artist I knew in college was the child of artists."

"It might be that only artists want their children to become artists."

Penelope explained that her father had owned a music store.

"Was it Grand Records? Amazing! I've read about that place—"

"And my mother cleaned houses."

"Houses? Terrific . . ." He trailed off and tried to keep his cool. He planted his hands on his hips.

Penelope had said it to test him. White people had never known how to respond to the fact that Mirella had been a maid. At RISD, her classmates had stammered and then affirmed that cleaning houses was good work to do. Her classmates of color had been no better. They would nod vigorously as she explained, which made Penelope believe they had someone in their families who was a housekeeper, too, but eventually she learned their parents were dentists and college professors who had sent them to art camp and drawing classes when they were younger. They weren't as different from the white kids in their class as Penelope had wanted them to be.

Marcus didn't say anything; he didn't say cleaning houses was important or admirable or even interesting. She could have let him stew in his silence and unease, but she didn't want to embarrass him in front of Grace. It was beautiful the way his daughter had run into his arms. She decided to rescue him.

"I don't know what she does now. They're separated."

Marcus smiled and muttered something about his vinyl collection; he loved the Doors. His posture seemed to slacken, and Penelope could tell he was relieved. She listened to him talk and observed his hair. He had a lot of it—bright, ginger fistfuls. His hair was long, she thought, for a lawyer. It waved from the crown of his head to the nape of his neck. Beyond the hair, he didn't look much like Grace at all. He had a broad forehead and thin lips, sharp and sea-green eyes.

Penelope shifted weight from one leg to another and listened to him talk, aware of how close they were standing. They stared at one another, but there was nothing else for them to look at in the empty hallway.

"What do you mean they're separated? Is that like divorced?" Grace interrupted them, tugging on the hem of her father's shirt.

Marcus seemed to remember his child. "It means they aren't together anymore, sweetheart."

"Litigating?" Grace stared up at her father, her fingers clutching the cloth of his shirt.

"Technically, they're still married, they just don't live together," Penelope said.

"How can they be married and not live together?"

She just left, Penelope thought to say, but she saw the worry in Grace's face, as if a great myth she had believed about mothers and fathers had been cracked open by the facts of Penelope's life.

Marcus petted his daughter's head, but Grace's expression didn't change. Her eyebrows stayed pushed together, an auburn line across her forehead.

"Does she live far away?"

"The Dominican Republic," Penelope said, although she couldn't be sure. Where else would she be?

"I've been trying to convince Samantha we should go visit the DR," Marcus said, leaving Grace to her thoughts and rejoining Penelope. "I miss the ocean. I grew up surfing, and I swam in college, but there are no beaches here, really, nothing to do outside besides run."

"Yeah, I learned how to run real quick," Penelope said, and they both laughed. She wondered right away what the joke meant to him, whether he thought she was admitting how dangerous the neighborhood used to be, or whether he was impressed by her, the idea that it didn't used to be as easy to get by in Brooklyn as it was now.

While he laughed, his eyes swooped over Penelope, from her fluffy ankle socks and lime green sneakers to the black nylon shorts that covered just a third of her thighs. She knew exactly how she must look— her skin orange under the warm overhead lighting, her long legs, dense and bare. Her muscles seemed carved with a blade, her calves smooth, her flesh sharp and lifted away from the bone at her joints. From what she remembered of Samantha, the landlady was more slender and delicate. Penelope wondered what Marcus preferred.

"Daddy, we were playing a game. You interrupted us." Grace yanked her father's shirt hem to get his attention.

"Sorry about that, sweetheart." Marcus kissed the top of her head. "I was just coming up to work." He pointed to a closed door behind Penelope. It must have been his study.

Penelope didn't know any lawyers personally, but once in a while, a group of attorneys would tumble into the bar in Squirrel Hill, all loosened ties and Jack-and-gingers. They would complain about their bosses and their salaries, how low their pay would be if it were calculated by the hour. They were all first-year lawyers at big firms; Penelope had no idea what it was like to be an attorney when you were older, a father, living in Bed-Stuy.

"Preparing for trial?" she asked.

"Not today."

Penelope nodded and uncrossed her arms to show she was interested. He didn't go on, so she searched for something more to say to keep him in the hall. She asked if he ever thought of moving back to California.

"Daddy, I don't want to move again." Grace broke into the conversation they were constructing over her head.

Penelope squatted on her knees until she was eye level with the child.

"I wouldn't want you to move either. We just met."

"I'm glad you're not a ghost," Grace said.

"Ghosts don't sweat," Penelope said and gestured at her arms: hard, actual, and still slick from the run. She picked up her towel from where she had draped it over the banister. "I should leave you two and finally take that shower. I'm disgusting."

"You're fine," Marcus said. He smiled at her.

Penelope waved good-bye to Grace and slipped into the bathroom, closing the door behind her. Grace and Marcus talked on the other side of the door, but Penelope couldn't make out their words. She saw in the mirror that her curls were smashed to one side of her head. She sighed and ran her fingers through the strands, pulling the curls into their rightful halo shape around her head. She peeled off her running shorts and T-shirt and took a good long look at herself. She was pleased at her body and that Marcus had seen her in her ratty little running clothes.

It took a while for the water to heat up, and Penelope let the bathroom fill with steam. Grace was back downstairs, and Marcus must have already settled into his study. She imagined him there now, although she had never seen the room. She could see him hunched over a desk, beginning to type, maybe licking his finger before sifting through the pages of a big law reference book, bound in leather. She saw the nascent lines in his forehead, the slender swimmer's body, his waves and waves of hair. She soaped her body slowly, rinsed with hot water, then cold, then hot again, kneading her muscles. She showered for a long time before enveloping herself in the towel and creeping onto the fourth floor and then up to the attic. She locked her door behind her and wrapped the towel around her head to dry her curls. The house was quiet. Maybe the Harpers were having dinner. She wondered if Samantha cooked for them, or Marcus, or if they made meals together, or ordered in. She had no idea what kind of family they were. All she knew was that the girl seemed lonely, although her father obviously loved her. His love seemed to revolve around her instead of the other way around.

Penelope lay down on her bed and looked up at the canopy of photographs from Pittsburgh: the railroad tracks at Station Square, the lit-up exterior of her bar in Squirrel Hill, the quaint shops along Walnut Street, the truss bridge on Herrs Island where she had gone running past new townhouses that had been built over sawmills and stockyards. She didn't have photographs of any of the other bartenders or the people who worked in the kitchen. None of the men she knew through work and the other bars. She hadn't left anyone behind.

Ralph was expecting her, she knew. He would want to hear about the interview at the school, and order Chinese food from the Emerald, maybe listen to records until it was time for Penelope to walk back to the attic. She had spent every night since her return back on Halsey Street, and she sensed now, for the first time, how much she didn't want to see her father. She would rather stay here, at least for a while, and loom above the Harpers. She could consider their routines, their happiness.

Greene Avenue was dark, and Penelope drifted off without meaning to. The first September drafts blew in through the open window, and she felt the warm air on her skin. She dreamed of black-sand beaches and her mother, sitting on a stone in a sea. The water was a turbulent green, but her mother remained motionless, her back to the shore. Her hair streamed behind her, a flame rippling in the wind.

4

La Copa Rota

Mirella could not rest. It was too quiet in the residence, too far from the road. She heard only the humming of the generator on the first floor of the house, the crickets tuning up their legs. Her lover breathed hard beside her, his hands on the back of his head as he slept facedown. He slept this way every night, and every night Mirella thought he looked ridiculous. Was he under arrest? Was he blocking out the sound of nothing? Of their seclusion here in the residence, where there was no one but other expats, and the watching-man at the gate?

She slid from the bed; Marcello didn't stir. They had been to the beach that day, running through the surf as if they were half their age. They drank limoncello from the porcelain cups Mirella used for coffee, and then stretched out on their stomachs to eat cold pasta. They had made the pasta together that morning, Mirella picking the oregano and basil from her garden in short shorts and her bathing suit top, Marcello complaining in her kitchen that Dominican beef was too tough, and the ragù would never taste the way it was meant to.

He was badly sunburned now, his skin bright red even in the dark. Tomorrow it would be peeling off, and Mirella would cut a spear of aloe from the yard and rub it over his back. They had been lovers for months, and this was their routine: trips to the beach, quiet dinners with cold wine, sex, sunburns, and sleeping in Mirella's bed. Marcello's house was one of the seven in the gated residence, but Mirella refused to sleep in someone else's house now that she finally had one of her own. Even the bed was hers, a four-post frame made of pure caoba, ordered from the best mueblería in the capital.

When she first returned to DR a year ago, Mirella rotated through the apartments of her old schoolmates still living in El Cibao. They had grown up to be teachers and doctors, a few architects, and one wife of a mayor. They seemed to take her in mostly out of curiosity, to discover what sort of life she had lived all those years in New York. They invited her to dinners and encouraged her to look for an apartment there in Santiago, but Mirella declined. She preferred to eat alone, at small restaurants with outdoor tables, and she was sure she didn't want to live in the city. After she found a house near the beach at Cabarete, she rented a truck, packed it with her belongings, and drove it across the island. She didn't leave anything for the women who had housed her; they didn't need her US dollars. She didn't say good-bye.

Mirella walked down the stairs, the tiles cold under her feet. The house was just two floors, but its high ceilings made it seem palatial to Mirella. There were skylights in the foyer, living room, and master bedroom. The eastern wall on the ground floor was all glass. On nights alone, Mirella could watch the moon rise over her garden; during the months that were winter in New York, she watched her skylights smear with rain.

She reached the living room and paused to run her hand over the armoire to check for dust. There was none. She had collected her furniture slowly over the months, just a few big pieces handmade from wood, and the couch. She didn't buy too many things because she wanted the house to feel as airy and as large as it truly was. When she and Marcello spoke in the evenings, their voices reverberated, their echoes unintelligible and hollow. And when she was alone in the house, which was often, it felt like just enough space.

The wall above the armoire was still blank, but it wouldn't be for long. After Mirella and Marcello had returned from the beach that afternoon, a package had arrived. Three paintings packed in a box with foam peanuts and Bubble Wrap. She had chosen the pictures and their frames out of a catalogue. There were two paintings of flowers, tied with ribbon and arranged in vases, on tables in windowless, dark rooms. The last painting was of fruit, the kind Mirella never ate anymore—apples and pears and grapes—also in a bowl in a room with hardly any light. She hadn't known which pictures were the best ones, but these had seemed the most foolproof. They would look fine, maybe even elegant, in their bronze frames. They were the final touches to the house, the last things Mirella needed for the place to be complete. Everything else that she wanted for the house, she already had.

Mirella wandered into the kitchen and poured herself a glass of mabi. She didn't like the fizzy drink, but she had cases of it stored in the pantry. She sat at the counter, underneath her rack of copper pots and pans. All her appliances—the pots, the bamboo cutting board, the plastic Mr. Coffee machine—had been wedding gifts from Ralph's friends. It was as if they had expected her to spend her married life cooking in a stuffy Brooklyn kitchen. They hadn't given her anything else.

She had spent so many years in the United States cooking for other people that when she found herself back in DR, forty-seven, and cooking for just one, she wasn't sure what she liked to make just for herself. She had discovered she liked frying fish and baking bread, assembling salads, and not much else. Dominican food took too long to make, and she only knew how to cook in bulk, a stew big enough to last for days. If Marcello wasn't there, she just had wine and good dark chocolate from the German bakery down the road. She laughed to herself during these dinners and thought that if her mother, Ramona, were alive, she would be horrified at how little she was eating. No chicharrones de pollo, no arroz con gandules, no steaming pot of sancocho—just a little piece of chocolate, like a beggar, and a glass of liquor, like a puta.

Marcello assumed she had grown up in the city like the schoolmates she had mentioned who owned apartments on La Calle del Sol in Santiago. He didn't question why she had chosen to live in the residence instead, where all the other owners were European expats: a few Germans, an Englishman, and another Italian like himself. They had all come to DR for the same reason. Here, they could live like the people they had envied in their own countries. A few of them were retired. Most went home for a few months every year to work, but they always came back. No matter how expensive gasoline or rice became, or how long the electricity was out, in this country, their pounds and euros and dollars stretched far. They had pools and Jeeps, servants, time.

Mirella was the only resident in the estate without a staff. She worked all day in the garden, checked the fuses in the generator, and climbed onto the roof if one of the skylights was leaking. "Why don't you hire someone to clean for you?" Marcello often asked her. Her house was the largest in the residence.

Mirella hadn't told him she spent years cleaning houses in New York: stately brick townhouses, Park Avenue apartments with butter-colored carpets, lower Manhattan lofts with what felt like miles of windows. Marcello knew only that Mirella had been in a bad marriage in New York, and when they finally gave up their business, she left. She told him she knew how to handle the house herself, and he believed her. He left her alone.

The Dominican woman who cleaned for Marcello was a slender Santiaguera named Ariane. Mirella invited her for coffee, but she never accepted. They spoke over the gate around Mirella's house when Ariane passed on her way from Marcello's to the front gate. Mirella cherished their short conversations, the relief of Ariane's husky, melodic voice, from Marcello's flippant Italianate Spanish. Although she had four children, Ariane was not yet thirty; she was Penelope's age.

Mirella took a sip of the mabi, already flat, and thought of her daughter. When she was a girl, Penelope would beg Mirella to buy her the brown soda, and although she didn't approve of sugary drinks, Mirella usually consented. Penelope loved the taste of tree bark and sugar and would be nearly finished with a bottle before Mirella had paid for it.

Mirella reached into one of the cabinets underneath the counter. She felt the rim of an old, chipped cup, and set it on the counter. Inside the cup were a jeweled butterfly hair clip, the broken pieces of the porcelain cup, and a folded-up card.

Mirella held the fragments of the cup in her hand like heavy, cool puzzle pieces. She fingered the fake gems on the wings and thorax of the butterfly. She unfolded the postcard and saw the smudges from all the erasing she had done, her handwriting in the faint gray of pencil lead.

She had bought this postcard on the beach. She went on a walk one morning to explore the town that was now her home. She drank coffee in a Styrofoam cup, cycled through displays of cheap glass jewelry and clay charms, before she found the rack of postcards and thought of writing to her daughter. It was her first time back on the island without Penelope, and she wanted to tell her about the new house.

Mirella had inscribed the card in Spanish first, then erased everything and wrote to her daughter again in English. She worried Penelope wouldn't remember her Spanish. But in English, Mirella was formal and uneasy. There were gaps in her meaning.

They had spoken English all those years in the house in Brooklyn, so that Mirella couldn't remember the sound of Spanish in her daughter's mouth. When she was a child, Ralph would complain he didn't understand what the two of them were always chattering about. He told Penelope to speak English at home, although she was already speaking it at school. Ralph couldn't tolerate feeling left out, even for a few minutes, although Mirella felt that way every day—when someone on the subway asked her for directions and she fumbled her vowels, when the black women at the supermarket stared at her and her light skin as she wandered the aisles, when the white ladies she worked for didn't look up from their hefty magazines to say thank you and good night, when the teachers at Penelope's school referred to her as "Ralph Grand's wife."

Penelope obeyed her father, and soon Spanish was reserved for birthday cards and Mother's Day letters. When Penelope was a teenager, they fought in English, and Mirella always said the wrong thing. She felt Penelope had the upper hand, so she yelled and threw things—the phone, a comb, a plate—to keep up. Maybe that had been their problem. English was for Ralph and Brooklyn and the overly perfumed rich ladies whose houses she had cleaned; she was never meant to raise a daughter in some other tongue.

Mirella raised the postcard to her face and tried to discern the last words she had written before erasing it all and stowing the card away in the cup. *Hija,* she had written, then a few lines, and her signature. Mirella had thought, briefly, that if she wrote to her, maybe her daughter would come, maybe things would be better in this big house in the north than they ever were in Brooklyn or in the mountains where they spent summers when Ramona was still alive, and Ralph was too consumed with the store to miss them.

She was the one who didn't miss him now. She had stopped longing for him, slowly, over the years he left her alone in that dilapidated house in Brooklyn. Penelope was different. You couldn't leave a daughter behind; she was yours no matter where you were. And although she didn't know what they would do if they were ever together again—they weren't the kind to talk or laugh, or even sit beside each other for long— she still craved her girl, as unthinkingly as a seabird longs for the sea.

The house hadn't been ready before. But with the new paintings hung, the custom furniture in place, the curtains clean and fitted to the windows, she finally had something of her own to show her daughter. Penelope probably knew she was here—Ralph would have told her.

After the store closed, and the accident, Ralph needed her again—to pick up his prescriptions, to wash his back with a sponge, to push him down the street in his wheelchair. He could see her again, recognize her presence, but only because he had nothing left. Mirella finally learned to speak the thoughts that had been circling her mind for decades: *This is not why I got married,* and *This is not why I came here.* It took a few weeks for her to pack her things, and all along, Ralph thought that she was bluffing. When she started shipping the boxes, he asked her if she was really willing to abandon him and their life together. Mirella said yes.

While Ralph was asleep one night, she put on a scarf and gloves and her wool coat, and slipped out of the house on Halsey with her suitcase. She knew she could not say good-bye; if she saw Ralph's face, she might lose her nerve. It was better if he were a figment, an idea: the life she had wanted to leave. She walked to Bedford Avenue and hailed a cab to the airport. She left behind her misery and her husband, and all the potted plants there had been no way to ship.

She had thought of Penelope as she rode away from the neighborhood she had moved to as a girl, eighteen and fresh from the red-earth campo, looking for life. *How will my daughter find me?* she had thought as the taxi plunged farther into Brooklyn, although it had been years since Penelope had stopped looking.

Mirella flattened the postcard on the counter and flipped it over. The photograph on the front of the card seemed unchanged by the years: a rope hammock hung between two coconut trees, their leaves and trunks silhouetted against an orange sky. The ocean was bronze and shimmering, a slim beam of light cutting across the water to the shore.

Mirella retrieved a pencil from a jar she kept on the counter. She turned the postcard back to the cloudy blank side and began to write quickly, her words spanning the creases. She could only fit a few lines, but it would be enough, she hoped, for her daughter to detect all that she had left unsaid. When she was finished, she printed the address to her house in DR, no zip code, no apartment number, just the name of the residence, the town, the road, and the number of kilometers to the nearest gas station. It was the best way for her daughter to reach her, if she decided to write back.

Mirella put the clip and the porcelain pieces back inside the cup, put the cup in the cabinet. She left the postcard out on the counter; she would send it in the morning. Mirella finished her glass of mabi, walked back to the living room, and unlatched the gate leading onto the patio.

It was warm in the garden. Mirella felt as if someone had thrown a shawl over her in the dark. The air was damp and clean. She stepped off the breezeway, and the earth gave under her feet. She inhaled the dew on grass. The crickets were louder outside.

The acres behind the house were perfectly pruned and watered. The bean-shaped pool was immaculate, except for two frogs. One squatted on the edge of the pool while the other hopped lazily around the perimeter. She loved her days here in the garden, tending to the banana trees, the herb and vegetable patches, picking the avocado and papaya and lemons that fell in the breeze, uprooting weeds and killing snakes that had slipped through the barbed wire around her land. She loved her birds of paradise: the magenta beak of the buds, the yellow and blue petals like a crown of feathers, the slender green stalks. She could have never grown flowers that bright and intricate in Brooklyn.

You would like it here, hija, she thought. *Penélope.*

5

Intricate and Fragile Things

Penelope entered the classroom a full hour before her students were set to arrive. The fluorescent lights gave the room a green tint, and Penelope lifted the blinds and cranked open the windows to let in the morning light. The garden outside was full of blooming sunflowers, a slowly withering vegetable patch. Over the garden, someone had painted a mural of smiling brown and white children holding hands atop a smudgy blue-green globe. It was embarrassingly bland but better than the old view of the broken-down playground, where a girl had been raped when Penelope was a child, and a boy from her class slashed with a razor by his older brother's friends.

Principal Pine had told her to make the room hers, and so Penelope did. She hung paper lanterns from the ceiling, although she couldn't light them because of the building codes. She liked the shapes of them, white spheres floating over the room. The room was well stocked, even better than the schools in Pittsburgh. A half-dozen tiny easels leaned against the southern windows—the children would have to share—and the back shelves burst with odds and ends: spools of wire, yarn, bundles of shoelaces, old brooches and buttons, tubs of clay. The long tables where the children would sit looked exactly as they had two decades ago:

cheap yellow wood, low to the ground, engraved with initials and curse words, bubble-letter dollar signs and BKs, chubby hearts pierced by two-dimensional arrows. Even the windowsills overflowed with stuff: metal cans filled with paintbrushes, stacks of colored paper, bins of old shirts and aprons for the children to use as smocks. Penelope didn't mind the mess—it was the way a proper studio should look. She washed the board, and when it dried she wrote her name, *Ms. Grand*, in lavender chalk, then she sat with her coffee to wait for the bell to ring.

She wondered whether she should tell the children she had gone to this school; her art had hung from the cork bulletin boards in this room. There would have been no question if her return were a triumphant one, the kind that would have been written up in the black nationalist paper Ralph used to read. She could imagine the headline: *Bed-Stuy Sister Comes Home to Teach Our Youth!* But she'd had no noble reason to return to Brooklyn besides that she didn't want her father to die. In her time away she had conquered nothing. She had merely found a way to be.

When she was a girl, Mirella used to tell her about success stories she had seen on the news—a girl from the Bronx won a citywide science fair, got recruited to MIT, and planned on becoming a chemist; a boy in Queens who finished high school while living in a homeless shelter had returned to his neighborhood to open a clinic and buy his mother a house. Even then, Penelope knew there would be no news story about a girl who decided to paint, who was intent on making even less money than her parents, the orphan and the immigrant who together had built her a good life. Even when the letter arrived from RISD, Mirella had been unimpressed. "Where is that?" she had said. "Massachusetts? Maybe you can transfer."

Her father knew RISD was a good school only from the gloss of the brochures, the faces his Manhattan customers made when he mentioned where Penelope was going to school. Penelope set off, with her paints and her portfolio, ecstatic to finally leave Halsey Street to find her own life.

Not all the students were white, but they all came from places like Santa Barbara, Olympia, and Austin, or the suburbs that surrounded them. Their lives were foreign to Penelope: they talked about nightly dinners with their parents and summers on various shores; they already knew the names of the artists they studied in their foundations class; they'd had such wide lives in their small towns—sports and parties and social clubs and leagues. They spoke French and Japanese; they wore boots made of real leather, tiny nose rings encrusted with gems. Penelope's life in Brooklyn had consisted only of home, school, the store—the neighborhood wasn't safe, and she had no places in it, nowhere to go when she was in high school. And she'd thought herself fortunate, compared to her classmates in Bed-Stuy; for the first time, at RISD, Penelope wondered whether she had been poor. She quickly realized she hadn't been, although her mother had, and her father, when they were children.

The other students dressed the way artists should dress—the girls wore black lacy dresses to galleries on the weekend, the same dresses with cable-knit sweaters over them to work in the studio. They smoked and drank as if they were already defeated, hardened, and long out of art school. Penelope joined them, and these were the best times: when she could sip at cigarettes for the calm, when the taste of gin was enough to dissolve the blocks between her and the rest of them. Once, they all shared a spliff on an empty street corner, and a girl had asked Penelope if she had grown up in the ghetto, if she already knew how to roll a blunt. There was another time, she told someone her neighborhood was called Bed-Stuy, and a boy chimed in, rapping Notorious B.I.G., and Penelope had asked what the fuck was wrong with him and everyone had stared at her until he told her it was a joke and she should chill. It wasn't long before the girls started to keep their distance, and the boys, too, except for a few, who watched her with interest from afar, as if her hoop earrings, thighs, and mass of curls were a statement rather than simply who she was. She slept with a few of them, just to prove that she could, and even after she knew having sex with white boys wasn't the victory she had expected it to be, she kept finding them, fucking them, and turning them away. It felt good, and it was a thing she could control: she could choose someone and have someone and then return to herself, safe.

The only first-year she liked somewhat was her roommate, a nice-enough plump girl named Meg. Meg didn't like to work on large canvases either, and her pieces were tiny—intricate and fragile things on wood, small enough to fit in your palm, made with acrylic and twine and bits of dried flowers she had shipped to her off the Internet. Penelope would often return to the dorm to find Meg's little pieces drying all around their room—on the coffee table, the windowsill, the foot of her bed, beside the radiator. She would stoop down to inspect them and admire how painstakingly Meg had made them with fine-tipped brushes and tweezers and glue. Meg was from Westchester, and they had bonded over New York and the subway, the relative sleepiness of Providence. At first, they went to dinner together every night; then Meg found friends of her own, but she still looked after Penelope when she drank too much. Meg brought her Dixie cups full of water, taught her how to stick two fingers down her throat when she'd had too much.

Penelope hadn't expected to be popular at art school—she never had been—but she had expected her crits to go well. It wasn't long before more than one teacher had told Penelope that she was trying to draw with paint. Her work was clean and literal, too spare. The other painters in her cohort all worked on large canvases, bigger than anything Penelope had ever cared to make. They piled the paint on in big irreverent swaths of color; they used bits of metal and wire, they worked from dozens of photographs, even if they were just painting grass, or a woman. Penelope's scale was smaller, her technique immaculate, and her works soon done. She couldn't make anything as large or as bold as they did. No one had ever shown her how.

One teacher tried to help by telling her that art didn't have to *represent*; it simply had to *be*. Another said that if she wanted to be an illustrator, she'd picked the wrong program. Penelope stayed at the studio late, often working on the weekends, in her party dress, or early in the morning while the other kids slept off their hangovers, but, still, she couldn't stop drawing with paint. She got by in all her classes, but she didn't create anything really beautiful or terrifying. The bad crits, when they came, unmoored her, and Penelope drank and chased boys to regain her ground. Her talent, or the idea of it, was her only permission to be there.

In the spring, when Penelope stopped going to class to draw and drink in their dorm room, Meg was the one who told the dean. The dean didn't issue any threats when she met with Penelope; she was nice-white-lady concerned and offered Penelope mints while she asked about her critiques, whether anything was wrong at home. Penelope said she was fine; she couldn't stop drawing with paint, but, otherwise, everything else was fine. She had already decided privately not to return in the fall.

At the end of the year, she left Meg her fanciest set of oil paints, and when she conferred the tubes, the girl started crying, pressing one of those flimsy dead flowers into Penelope's hand. She gave her a pink Post-it note, too, with her phone number and address in Rye. *If you ever want to talk,* she had said, which had made Penelope want to laugh.

The morning in the classroom went smoothly, even with all of the miniature fiascos Penelope had anticipated. No one flung a box of crayons across the room, and no one slapped anyone else across the face with a ruler. The worst they did was shout and rush to the front of the room to show off their work to their new teacher until Penelope made a rule they had to stay in their seats, and she would come around to see what they were creating. Principal Pine poked in her head at the right time, a few hours into the day, after Penelope had already instituted the rule. The kids were rowdy but working, each of them in a seat. As the day went on, Penelope had to break up a few disputes about which color was whose, and whose turn it was to use the paste. There were two emergency trips to the sink—first, with Jewel, who got glue in her eye, and next with Khalil, who insisted he cut his fingers using the safety scissors. Penelope humored him by holding his hand under the tap in the big aluminum sink at the back of the room.

During the calmer moments, Penelope couldn't help but categorize the motley group of students in her mind: *poor, wealthy, new, not sure.* A quarter of them were white, and they seemed more at ease than poor Genevieve, her old classmate, had ever been. They all seemed to have lived in the neighborhood for a while, and they even talked with half the lilt of their classmates, a little Brooklyn peeking through their speech. The biggest difference she could see between them was that the white children nearly all knew how to use the paints. They squeezed colors into the tiny wells of the plastic palettes, dipped their brushes into water between strokes. Hardly any of the white kids wore the uniform, while the brown children were a mix of cheap bow ties and pleated skirts, sagging play clothes, neutral-colored corduroys and fashionable plaid. She wondered who their parents were, especially for the children who were mixed.

Just before lunch, Penelope called one of the third graders up to her desk. Natalie kept putting her head down on the table even though Penelope had told her four times that she wasn't allowed to sleep in class.

"I can't help it, Miss Grand. My head hurts."

The child wore a hot-pink turtleneck with sleeves that hardly covered her forearms. Her acid-washed jeans had an elastic waistband, like the kind of pants Penelope had worn as a child in the eighties. She held a hand flat against her belly.

"Are you sure it's not your stomach?"

"Yeah, Miss Grand. It's my stomach."

"Are you hungry?"

The girl nodded.

Penelope reached into her purse where she had half a bar of dark chocolate. "Don't let the other kids see," she said, slipping the candy to the girl. "Eat this here, then go take your seat. It's almost lunchtime. You'll be all right."

Natalie popped the chocolate squares into her mouth. She chewed slowly, pensively.

"It tastes funny," she said, but she ate it all. She licked her fingertips, and without thanking Penelope, went back to her seat. Principal Pine had warned her there would be parents who didn't know their kids were eligible for free breakfast, or who didn't wake up in time to bring them in, or who were already at work by the time the kids woke themselves up. She didn't know what category Natalie's mother fell in, but she made a note to herself to tell Mrs. Pine to call.

At the end of the period, the children sprang from their seats and stampeded for the door. She had watched the students do this all morning, rowdy under her watch, and then falling into crooked lines as soon as their teachers arrived to collect them. Penelope had met a few classroom teachers this morning, a few black women who had welcomed her to school and said they remembered her father and the store. There had also been a pair of young white teachers who invited her to lunch. Every day they went out for pizza or Chinese that they ate together in the faculty lounge. "There's a group of us," they said, though they didn't say whom they meant by *us*.

The man who came for the third graders was Mr. Rodemeyer. He was ruddy faced and wore a pink shirt and chinos. He introduced himself as a former North Carolinian and aspiring New Yorker. He welcomed Penelope to the school.

"They driving you nuts yet?" he said, jerking a thumb toward the kids. He had a brazen smile that made Penelope wonder whether he had been a frat boy in college. "Rumor has it you're a real artist—you studied painting?"

"Hm," Penelope said noncommittally. The children fidgeted in line.

Mr. Rodemeyer went on about how his fiancée was getting into drawing. She took a nude-figure drawing class in Gowanus and was looking for a buddy to go with her.

"We've been up here about a year, and she's still trying to make friends. You know, other ladies who share her interests."

"I'll keep an eye out," Penelope said, and she strode away from the door, calling good-bye to the kids.

They waved as they passed. "Later, Miss Grand!" and "Bye-bye, Miss Grand!" For all they knew, she wasn't a substitute. For all they knew, she was a real teacher. Natalie gave her a high five on the way out and smiled brightly at her, a smudge of chocolate under her lip.

Back at her desk, Penelope unpacked her lunch: an egg salad sandwich, a pair of pickles from the bodega, caffeinated soda. It would take only a few minutes to eat, and then she would have the rest of the period to herself. She considered moving to the teachers' lounge. It was her first day, and if she didn't mingle with the other teachers now, when would she ever? The young white teachers seemed to think she was one of them, and so did the older black women. She couldn't imagine camaraderie with either group, so she unwrapped her sandwich and stayed put in the room.

The afternoon light stretched along Greene, the houses on the block shimmering as if they had been dipped in gold. Penelope had worried working the children all day would sap her urge to draw, but she rushed down the block so she could get up to the attic before the light faded. She saw a dozen potential images on the street, and she memorized them as she went: a broken Hula-Hoop, half of its arc peeking from the top of a dumpster, a cluster of yellow leaves on the pavement, a dozen trinkets set out on the curb—ancient dolls, yellowed paperbacks, an outdated video-game console—in a cardboard box marked *FREE*.

Marcus Harper sat on the stoop of the mustard-yellow house, his pants rolled up to his knees, his pale legs burning in the sun. When he saw her, he held up a hand to say hello. He commented on the beauty of the afternoon, the breeze, how much he loved fall on the East Coast. When he was through, Penelope wondered whether she should carry on into the house, whether he merely wanted to be a decent landlord and not a friend. But Marcus waved to the empty spot beside him, so Penelope sat down.

"Grace has been asking about you. Ever since that day in the hall."

"Has she now?"

"You're quite the mystery to her."

"There isn't much to know."

All down the block, children were arriving home from school, parents hustling to the grocery store or the bodega to pick up something for dinner. A pizza-delivery man pulled up a few houses away and honked his horn. A neighbor from across the street cursed him for his rudeness. Penelope and Marcus watched the activity on the block in silence, steeping in the sun. After a while, Marcus asked her about work, and Penelope said it was fine, all fine.

"The only art project Grace brought home last year was a paper turkey. Do you remember those? The ones where you outline your hand on construction paper and cut it out?"

Penelope shook her head. "I can't believe they still do that."

"Are you criticizing the art program at the distinguished Orchard School?"

"I might be."

They smiled at each other, and Marcus asked what she would teach children Grace's age.

"Perspective."

"That sounds pretty advanced for nine-year-olds."

"The kids get it. They know an ant can be larger than a barn, if the barn is in the distance and the ant is close up, that the size of the moon changes depending on your point of observation."

Marcus looked impressed. "Your students are lucky; you have so much to offer them."

Penelope shrugged. "I spent a lot of time sweeping glitter off the floor today."

They went on talking about whether Penelope considered herself more of an artist or a teacher, what she had been working on lately. She explained that she was neither, really; she hadn't painted for more than a decade, not since art school, but lately she had been drawing things she could see from her window. Art could never be her career, but drawing was an impulse, as recurrent, old, and automatic as breathing, except she had chosen to need it. It was as natural as wanting a drink of water, as instinctive as the urge to yawn, to have sex.

"So, for you, drawing is somewhere between a glass of water and sex?"

Penelope had wondered whether to say it aloud, but from the way Marcus looked at her, confused and expectant, she could see she'd made the right choice.

"Exactly," she said.

Marcus lowered his eyes to his lap and blushed, and Penelope looked back onto the street. A tall cinnamon-colored man pushed an icie cart down the street. When he passed the yellow house, Marcus called out to him. He ordered a lemon ice for himself, and then asked Penelope what she wanted. She yelled "Coco!" down to the vendor. Marcus returned with their two paper cups, already wilting from the wet and cold. They focused for a while on the sweet ice.

"Did you have a boyfriend in Pittsburgh?"

Penelope did her best not to seem surprised, but she could feel her cheeks warm. He was working her now, too. When she mentioned sex, she had cracked open the door, but he was nudging it now, ever so slightly. He wouldn't look at her and stared at his icie instead.

"There was nobody there for me."

"I find that difficult to believe."

"It's the truth."

They turned back to the avenue, although Penelope wanted to keep on watching him. She'd never had a thing for gingers, or for white men after RISD. She usually picked men based on how smitten by her they seemed, and the shape of their shoulders, whether they had bodies she wanted to look at, whether she thought they would want her to take command in bed. Occasionally, she was more impressed with herself when she could pull in a white man, if only because she knew they had no predilections to see her or want her. Marcus was very white: the thin bow of his lips, the green of his eyes. But there was much more to him than the question of whether she could win him: he was built beautifully, strong and lean, his skin weathered and freckled, lined more than made sense for a man his age. And he was out here, waiting on the stoop, for his child. He was a man who already knew how to love.

"Does your job let you out early in the afternoons so you can be here when Grace gets home?"

"Actually, I'm not working these days—well, not for money. I've been trying to write. A little late in life, I know. I wish I'd figured it out ten years and a hundred grand ago."

He went on to say he had published a few things in the *Times*, about one piece every six months. It had been nearly two years since he quit his job as an attorney.

"I don't want Grace to think her life needs to be as programmatic as ours have been—wedding, law school, baby. I want her to have adventures, hell, maybe drop out of college if she wants to."

"She should finish school," Penelope said, although a girl like Grace would probably grow up to be the CEO of a Fortune 500 company even if she never finished college.

"Grace is such a limited, cautious child. Don't get me wrong—she's lovely, and bright and sweet—but she's afraid of everything."

"Does she get that from Samantha?" Penelope kept her voice even and light. Marcus probably wouldn't like it if she criticized his wife.

"Absolutely. But you can't blame her. Sam's had a rough go of it."

Penelope looked at Marcus, unbelieving. Nothing about Samantha and her polka dots and car service into the city seemed rough.

"I think moving has only made things worse. Now that we own a house here, she's always worried about bedbugs or asbestos or a break-in, or you know—"

"Getting shot?"

Marcus pursed his lips and looked ashamed.

"Well, she picked one hell of a neighborhood."

The landlady reminded Penelope of her mother. Mirella had been terrified by stories on the news of children slashed in gang initiations, a toddler crushed under a garbage truck that failed to beep as it backed up. For years, she forbade Penelope to go out alone, and she wouldn't accompany her anywhere, not even to the store to meet Ralph. Things happened in the neighborhood, yes, and there were kids she knew who got caught up, but there were others, too, who had taken their bicycles out on the street, or walked by themselves to the playground, and managed to survive.

"If I could do it all over again, I'd stay in the Village," Marcus said. "It's not that we don't like it here, but we're just not a part of anything here. Everything we do is still in the city. We go to dinner there, see our friends there. Our daughter goes to school there. We didn't mean to be such recluses, but now it's probably too late anyway. We've been here so long without reaching out to anyone that everyone on the block has probably already made up their minds about us. They probably think we are the worst kind of white people."

There was a word in Spanish for what Marcus was doing—*desahogarse*—and Penelope didn't want him to stop. Yes, he was *desahogándose*, and he had chosen to do it with her. And yet, it disappointed her that Marcus couldn't see that other people on the block had their own lives, and no one was thinking about him, not really. They might have been thinking about white people in general or the rent or whether one of the neighbors might mistake their son for a burglar and call the police, but they didn't know him, and they likely didn't want to know him. He had the kind of nostalgia for the neighborhood that Ralph had—the vision of Bed-Stuy as a place where there were potlucks and block associations, and the man at the bodega knew your name. The neighborhood had never been anything more to Penelope than where she was from. She'd had no choice in the matter; it was her home.

"If you really wanted to be polite, you wouldn't have moved in at all," Penelope said, and Marcus looked shocked. His eyebrows went up, and Penelope was glad. If they were to go on in this way, she'd have to be able to say what she thought. If she wanted to appease a man, she had her father for that.

"But you're here now," she said. "And you still have time."

"That's kind of you to say."

"Besides, have you seen this block? There are all kinds of white folks out here—I don't think it will be that hard for you to smooth things over."

Marcus laughed, and she did, too, because he had thought her funny.

"Thank you, Penelope," he said and put his hand on her knee.

Penelope didn't move, observing his hand, unmoving, cupped around her knee. They heard the exhale of an engine, a black car slowing in front of the house.

"Daddy!"

Grace bounced out of the car, her school bag slapping against her back as she ran up the stoop. Marcus kissed her, and they rocked in each other's arms, then Grace smiled at Penelope, still exhilarated from seeing her father.

"You're wearing real clothes this time," she said.

"We'd better get inside."

Marcus took his daughter's hand and said something about homework and dinner, their afternoon routines. He was pink behind the ears and jittery, so Penelope waved good-bye and let them go.

Without the Harpers, the block seemed less golden and breezy than it had been a few moments before. She had been left behind on the stoop, along with the wilting paper cups they had used to eat their icies. She remembered that Samantha would soon be home, they were a family, and she was only the woman in the attic.

Penelope pulled out her phone and called her father.

"This is Ralph Grand."

"Are you ready for me?"

"I thought you weren't coming over till later. Didn't you have to run?"

"Well, I want to see you now."

"All right. I'll call the Emerald. You want Chinese?"

"Yes, sir. I'll pick it up on my way."

"You be careful walking over."

"Pop, I'll be fine. I'm not thirteen anymore."

"You just be careful, okay? Some things, they haven't changed."

6

Revitalization

"Rise and shine, Mr. Grand."

A stale smell filled the bedroom, but Penelope tried not to make a face. She shook her father gently. He swept off his covers and frowned at her.

"You've got an appointment this morning with Freddie Elias. Everything is all set, and the car will be here in one hour."

"You already told him we were coming?"

Penelope nodded triumphantly. She was confident that Ralph's pride would get the better of him. He wouldn't fail to show up now and leave himself open to rumor and speculation, least of all from a former friend. Penelope handed Ralph his bathrobe, then left to turn on the water to heat.

When he was dressed, she returned to the bedroom with a tub of Vaseline. Ralph's palms were cracked, and so was the skin on his feet. The appointment had given him at least an occasion to shower. So often when she came to see him, he was still in his pajamas, his teeth unbrushed, and yesterday's dirty dishes still high in the sink.

She started massaging the jelly into the skin of his hands, while Ralph tried with one hand to put on his socks. He had trouble keeping his foot steady on the edge of the bed for long enough to pull on a sock. His foot kept falling off, and his body tipping over, as if he'd fall over if Penelope weren't there.

"Could I have some privacy?"

The car would be arriving soon, but she didn't say that. He didn't need the pressure. She nodded at Ralph, who was focused on his foot. He yanked on a sock as quickly as he could, before his foot fell off the edge of the bed again.

An hour later, Ralph glared at Dr. Elias from the edge of the examining table. The pleasantries between the men had been quick, and Ralph seemed indignant that it was time for his friend to become his doctor. He looked insulted, small and hunched over the table.

"You can take off your shirt now," Dr. Elias said, but Ralph did not budge. "I have to listen to your heart."

Penelope nodded at her father to encourage him, but he ignored her, too.

"I'll give you a few minutes while I find your chart." Freddie Elias made a face at Penelope and stepped out of the room. Penelope rose to help her father undress.

"Does it look to you like my arms don't work, too?"

He turned his glare to her now, as he loosened the top button. His hands moved slowly down his shirt. His flat brown chest came into view, and the soft, small pile of flesh at his stomach. The muscles in his arms were undetectable, the skin loose at the shoulders.

Ralph handed her the shirt roughly, and Penelope folded it carefully. She sat in a chair in the corner of the room to wait. Ralph stared at the floor, his skinny legs dangling off the table. His dress socks drooped at the ankles, revealing the little impressions they left on his skin. Penelope hated the marks, wanted to take off the socks and let his legs breathe, or pull them up so they covered him properly. But Ralph wouldn't have wanted her to touch him. Penelope examined a chart on the wall about how one should properly wash one's hands. It was a while before Dr. Elias returned with Ralph's chart.

"How are you feeling, Ralph?"

"Just fine, just fine." Ralph smiled. His mood had turned. Maybe now he would try honey with his old friend, to see if he could sweet-talk his way out of whatever the doctor would prescribe.

Dr. Elias looked skeptical and hooked the stethoscope into his ears. He and Ralph were about the same age, but he looked at least a decade younger now. They used to be able to pass for relatives with the same dark sepia complexion and misty-light eyes, but Dr. Elias had broader shoulders, and he stood taller now, his back uncurved, the soles of his feet firm on the ground.

He warmed the stethoscope against the hem of his white coat.

"Take a deep one, Ralph."

Ralph was like a balloon that expanded too fast, then deflated and shot away. His shoulders heaved when he inhaled and slumped down immediately after, a theatrical shrug.

"And another."

Dr. Elias moved the stethoscope around different points of Ralph's chest and back. Penelope knew there was a science to what he was doing, but the movements looked random to her. She leaned in as if she could hear Ralph's heartbeats, too.

"Strong heart," Dr. Elias declared. Then he went on to ask if Ralph was still smoking, if he drank, if he ate well, and Ralph smiled and lied about all his good habits, then looked at Penelope, waiting for her to agree. She felt her face begin to burn.

The two men went on, and Penelope heard them through the hammering in her ears. She closed her eyes and tried to push herself away from the examining room, her mind opening just enough for her to slip away. She wasn't gone for long.

"My mood? What do you mean my mood?"

"Beyond the physical. How have you been feeling?"

Ralph cocked an eyebrow and leaned back on the examining table so that he could look Dr. Elias squarely in the face.

"How else could I possibly feel?"

"I don't know, Ralph, that's why I'm asking."

Ralph shrugged. "My daughter's back. So things are looking up."

"You've been through a lot in the last year between the shop and the accident. Mirella."

Dr. Elias said her name *Muh-ray-uh* the way people who couldn't speak Spanish often did. Their tongues tripped over the doble ele of her name. Ralph, who had never learned any Spanish, could seesaw over the vowels in her name, his accent perfect over those three syllables.

"What's Mirella got to do with my spine?"

"I told you after the accident that you needed to keep up with your physical therapy, but you didn't listen."

"If you recall, Freddie, Mirella left me. How was I supposed to get here to my appointments once she was gone?"

"The bus still runs in Bed-Stuy, doesn't it?"

Dr. Elias was smiling, but it was clear he had lost his patience with Ralph.

"If you had come then, right after the accident like I told you to, you might have been able to halt some of the deterioration. But a lot can happen in a year."

"You haven't even examined me yet."

"I don't have to, Ralph. I watched you walk in from the waiting room and get up on the examining table. That was enough."

Penelope willed herself to stay in the room while Dr. Elias said something about disuse and atrophy, Ralph being in a lot more pain than he ever let on. The spine, not being able to point his feet in the right direction. It was all so important. She should have been writing it down.

"What happened to you wasn't your fault, but your life is in your hands now." Dr. Elias edged nearer and put a hand on Ralph's shoulder. "What do you want to do?"

"I'd like to put on my shirt."

Dr. Elias withdrew his hand from Ralph's bare shoulder and pressed his lips together into a line.

"I'll give you the number of a physical therapist in the neighborhood. You decide whether to call. In the meantime, there are some exercises you can do on your own. A few require you get down on the floor. You should do those only if Penny's around to help you get up afterward."

"I can get up just fine by myself."

Dr. Elias removed a packet of papers from his clipboard and offered it to Ralph, but he didn't move to accept them. Penelope stepped between them and took the exercises from Dr. Elias. He took her free hand in his.

"You've grown up so beautifully, Penny. It seems like just the other day you were coming in here with your braces, telling me you had joined the track team." He squeezed her hand again. "Good luck with him."

The men turned to each other to say good-bye. They clapped hands on each other's backs but did not draw any closer. Then Dr. Elias left, swinging his clipboard.

Penelope gathered her father's shoes from the floor and placed them on the paper sheet covering the examining table.

"You ready to go home, Pop?"

"I need to put my shoes on first."

He leaned over, shakily, to draw the shoes onto his lap, and suddenly Penelope needed to leave. He began to loosen the laces, and though Penelope worried he might tip over, he wouldn't forgive her if she offered her help, so it was better just to go. She muttered she had to use the bathroom, and she left him his shirt, loped out of the room and into the hall.

The corridor glistened white and stank of disinfectant. Nurses rushed around her, the phones trilled, the doors to patient rooms opened and closed. Penelope couldn't remember the way back to the bathroom; it had been so long since her last visit to the hospital. She raced past the waiting room and found an empty stretch of hallway where she could pace back and forth between the elevator banks. She stared at the linoleum and tried to catch her breath. She felt a familiar pressure in her chest, one that usually signaled she had run too fast and it was time to slow down, but she had been walking. Penelope lifted her hands to her scalp and gulped in the stale hospital air. She panted and paced, reshaped her curls. Eventually, her heart seemed to echo her footfalls: slower, quiet. She remembered what Dr. Elias had said about a strong heart. She straightened herself, her mind clear again. Penelope checked her reflection in the silver elevator door, then started back to the exam room.

They found a table by the window in a café on Nostrand Avenue. It was a new restaurant with yellow curtains and tiny whitewood tables all cramped together. There was hardly enough room on the table for two cloth napkins, a short vase filled with irises, the ceramic salt and pepper shakers.

"Is this supposed to be a soul food place?"

"Yeah, Pop. I thought it would remind you of that place we used to go to on Utica?"

Ralph lifted the menu to his face with a frown. "That place didn't have flowers on the table. You think they're charging us for the flowers here?"

He was joking, but Penelope couldn't laugh along. She wanted to do something nice for Ralph, to bring him out of the house to someplace

new where he didn't have any memories but where he wouldn't stand
out. It was even harder for him to blend in now because of the way he
walked. He had made a big clatter entering the restaurant; he caught
his foot on the doormat, he had dropped himself too hard into his seat.

Ralph squinted his eyes as he read the menu. Before long, a woman
arrived to take their order. She had shiny shoulder-length locks and a
lace apron tied over her skirt. Her silver bangles rang when she reached
for the pen behind her ear. She must have been about forty, but she was
trim and strong. She wore brick-red lipstick and smelled of rosewater.

"Would you like to hear about our specials?"

"That won't be necessary," Ralph said softly. "I already know what I
want." He smiled up at the waitress until she smiled back, and Penelope
rolled her eyes. He might have resented the restaurant but he would still
flirt. The woman scribbled down their orders.

"And have you got any rum?" Ralph flipped over the hot-pink
cocktail menu, trying to find something he recognized. "How about
rum and Coke? Do you have that?"

"I can mix you one myself."

Ralph thanked her with a wink, and the woman took their menus
and sauntered away. Ralph followed her with his eyes.

"She seems nice," he said. "I hope for her sake this restaurant finds
a way to make it. Otherwise, she'll be out of a job." Ralph shook his
head. "That was one of the worst parts of closing down the store—I
had to let everyone go. I used to worry about whether their kids would
eat or if they'd get kicked out of their apartments. It was a heavy load
over my head."

Ralph swept back the yellow curtain to look out on the street.
The leaves were turning red, the whole block ablaze. Across the street
stood a barbershop that shared a storefront with a black bookstore. Next
door, the hair salon spewed steam onto the street, the fried chicken
spot, a jewelry shop with crucifixes and chains glittering on display,
and the beauty supply store that blasted soca and flashed neon lights

onto the sidewalk. This particular corner didn't have a view of any of the coffee shops that had opened farther east. Those had plush furniture and abstract art on the walls, stainless-steel espresso pumps. They were always crowded with young people in jeans and plaid, typing away on their laptops. There were the bars, too, with a dozen local beers on tap, and short menus that consisted mostly of nuts, pickles, cheese. Penelope could see the changes, of course, but she still recognized the neighborhood—it wasn't like Fort Greene or Williamsburg, which were no longer themselves. Strangers still said hello to her as they lounged on their stoops at sundown. She still had to ignore the whistles from the young men who stood in front of the bodega for so long each day it was clear they were dealing. Church bells rang on the hour and floors thumped with praise for Jesus in the Baptist churches, the one-room Pentecostal churches, the regal AME tabernacles, worship never ceasing in Bed-Stuy. The horizon on Bedford Avenue was just as long, the sirens of the police cars as persistent, the wheeze of the B26 loud enough to wake her up at night.

Ralph let the curtain fall over the window again and shook his head.

"Revitalization. They're revitalizing the neighborhood." He made big swoops with his fingers, quotation marks around the word *revitalize*.

"It's still Brooklyn, Pop."

"Maybe on the surface. But what about inside, hmm?" Ralph gestured over his shoulder at the rest of the restaurant. Most of the other customers were talking over their lunches, nearly all of them white. They weren't the majority outside on Nostrand but they were in here, congregated around the little tables. They were Penelope's age or younger, brightly colored peacoats draped over the backs of their chairs, pashmina scarves wound around their necks. A few of them had babies in strollers who pulled at their socked feet or napped; they didn't fuss, completely at ease in the busy restaurant. An older black couple sat near the back, sharing a slice of pie. The old woman wore a stiff box hat, and the man sat in his frayed wool coat. They ate without speaking, holding hands under the table. Besides the couple, and the servers, she and Ralph were the only brown people in the café.

"It's a shame that making room for white folks mean the rest of us have to go. But it's always been that way, hasn't it?"

She had no reason to disagree with him—the closing of the shop had devastated her, too. The end of Grand Records had been the end of Ralph Grand, and not only because the accident was shortly after. If the store hadn't closed, he would have taken the bus there, he would have used a cane to hobble down the aisles, he would have more to do than play his records and smoke his pipe, drink, and sit around and wait to die.

Ralph had always expected her to listen to him and agree, to let him again be Mr. Grand, expert and legend. He seemed to need it now more than ever. And although Penelope wanted to please her father, she couldn't go back to the girlhood habit of putting away her self. She resolved to push.

"You're not from here, either, Pop."

"I've been here forty-six years."

"You were new to Brooklyn once, too."

"If I'm not from here then I'm not from anywhere. Where should I claim? That boys' home in Harlem? Wherever I lived before then?"

"I didn't mean to mention—"

"I wasn't anybody till I came to Brooklyn."

The waitress returned, carrying their lunches, but Ralph was too upset to manage a smile for her. He started slurping at his rum and soda in the fountain glass even before she had set down their plates. He had decided to ignore her, and so Penelope busied herself with her food. She cherished these big meals, which she only ate when she was with Ralph. If she was on her own, she ate just a little of what she wanted whenever she wanted—a peach, a few pieces of shrimp, a slice of garlic bread, a square or two of dark chocolate. If she wasn't hungry, she ate just to have the energy to run. She had no rituals with food, and it had been her way since she was a girl and neither parent surfaced for dinner, not Mirella from her bedroom, or Ralph from the store. Penelope could have made herself rice, fixed a sandwich from the cold cuts in the fridge, but there was no point in preparing an entire meal to eat alone. She often put herself to bed with her stomach churning, and she had learned to like the feeling of an empty belly, her taut skin. It was a habit she had kept.

When Ralph was done with his food, he looked at Penelope, and pointed his finger up at the ceiling, as if he remembered that she was there.

"What we ought to do is put the house in your name."

"You're going to be fine, Pop. You've just got to do those exercises that Dr. Elias gave you."

"Pfsh!" Ralph waved his hand. "Freddie's always thought he knows everything. I'm trying to tell you about the house. Do you remember Mrs. Jones? Your mother's friend?"

"I don't remember Mami having any friends."

"She sold Mary Kay? And when her husband died we all went to the wake out in New Jersey? Well, she got dementia about a year ago. Real young. Didn't have anybody to look after her. Some big realtor came by the house and convinced her to sell it to him for peanuts. When her niece and nephew came up from Charlotte, it was too late. They had no legal authority, no money for a lawyer, and all they could do was help pack her up. You know where she is now?"

Ralph didn't wait for Penelope to guess.

"A nursing home in the Bronx. They say she's got a tiny room with a view of the highway, and she's only gotten worse since she's been there."

"I didn't know you were such a gossip, Pop."

"It ain't gossip. It's the truth."

Ralph sucked up the last of his Coke and shook his head back and forth.

"These people are cold, Penelope. That's what I'm trying to tell you. They think a neighborhood is only about what you can buy—fancy coffee, flowers on the table, a big old house. It's all just *stuff* to them, stuff they want, stuff they think they deserve because they can afford it. A neighborhood means more than that. It's about *the people*."

Penelope said she wanted to focus on Ralph getting better and not worse. They didn't need to worry about the house. She didn't say she had no desire to inherit the house on Halsey Street. To live there would be to go backward, into a life she hadn't chosen. Without Ralph, she had no reason for Brooklyn; she would rather be off in some other place.

"It's better to have it all written down," Ralph said. "What if I fall again and they find a way to steal the house right out from under us? I already had a man come by the house once. I caught him poking around in the front. When I came out, he said he wanted to take over my mortgage for me so I wouldn't have to worry about debts in my old age, said he was prepared to write me a check right there. And I told him my mortgage had been all paid up for thirteen years and that he had better get the hell off my property."

"You never told me that."

"I never told you a lot of things."

The waitress came back and took away their plates, and Penelope turned to look out the window. A young mother hurried down the block, pulling at the hand of her reluctant daughter, a girl with skin the color of milky tea. Her hair was twisted into thin braids, fastened with a rainbow of plastic barrettes. She was probably no more than three years old; she stamped her way slowly through a mound of leaves. The young mother yanked the little girl's hand, trying to hurry her along, and the child dallied behind, oblivious. She kicked up the leaves in a yellow cloud. Penelope watched as the mother reeled around and smacked the child hard across the face. The girl began to cry, and her mother stooped down to yell into her ear. Penelope turned back to her father.

"Me and your mother, we never had no place," Ralph said. "We don't want that for you."

Penelope knew very well that she would never move back into the house on Halsey Street. She would just as soon go back to having Mirella as her mother, but she didn't want to trouble her father anymore, not when she still had to convince him to get down on the floor at home and try some stretches, not order another rum and Coke.

"I'll think about it, Pop."

The waitress brought them two cups of coffee and a slice of pie to share on the house. It was the sort of gesture businesses made when they were first getting off the ground, when they were courting customers. Eventually, they would stop giving away the free dessert. But for now Penelope and Ralph scraped their spoons along the hand-painted china. The cherry filling was an artificial red; it was gooey and false and delicious.

"This is real nice," Ralph said, and he poured cream into his coffee. "I can't remember the last time I went out—besides that night at Sheckley's. I think it must have been when I went to see you in Pittsburgh for Easter."

Penelope quickly did the math. Her father had stayed inside the house on Halsey Street for over four months.

"Jesus, Pop," she said before she could stop herself. "You didn't leave once?"

Ralph held up a finger and shushed her. "Wait, wait, wait, Penny—do you hear that?" He pointed up at the ceiling. Penelope listened. Coltrane was playing over the speakers.

"'My Favorite Things,'" she said.

"That's right, Penny. First session he recorded for Atlantic with his quartet."

Ralph closed his eyes and began to sway his head to the shifting swells of the piano. The saxophone offered a reply to the bright melody.

They listened to it tremble and moan, and Ralph's fingers played on the air.

"Dah duh dah, dah duh dah . . ."

"Pop, what did you do? What did you do with all that time?"

Ralph shushed her and sang; he swung his head from side to side to the music, as if he hadn't just told her that he went from April to August without leaving the house. She knew he rarely left, but he used to take his cane and go to the bodega at the corner for coffee and bread, at least. She imagined he went a few houses over to visit Una; she imagined he sometimes sat out on the stoop. How did he get his food? How did he buy his liquor? How had he managed for so long without seeing the street or the sun head-on? How hadn't she known? A few times she had called and he wasn't home, and she'd imagined he had run out to the liquor store, or over to see Una, or out to the stoop.

Penelope opened her mouth to speak, but Ralph shushed her again. He listened with his eyes closed, and his mouth twisted into a grimace, as if the music were what had cracked him open.

Back on Greene, the parlor doors were pushed open, the light on in the vestibule. Marcus sat on the polished floor, sifting through the cardboard boxes. She had taken her time along the avenues, after she dropped off Ralph at the house. It had started to rain, and Penelope was wet, everything inside of her sunken. She crossed into the parlor, without an invitation. Marcus and his fistfuls of hair, his bow of a smile, might lift her. She wanted to draw near to the sweetness of his life.

The room was identical to the parlor on Halsey Street but a blinding white. An ivory rug covered most of the floor, creamy linen armchairs faced the fireplace. A map of nineteenth-century Brooklyn hung in a frame above the mantel; a bubble-glass chandelier cast a pure light. Penelope had never seen the room before; usually, the doors were shut.

"Why don't you ever use this room? It's beautiful."

"Samantha is waiting, I think. For our big chance to entertain. None of our friends want to make the trip out to Brooklyn, at least not this far out."

"This isn't very far."

"It is when you live uptown and hardly ever go below Fourteenth Street."

"Yikes," Penelope said, certain that as much as she liked Marcus, she would hate all his friends. He motioned for her to sit down, and she sank onto a fat ottoman. He sat across from her in one of the linen chairs. She could smell Marcus's cologne, something made of citrus fruit and spice. She already felt far from the hospital, the café on Nostrand, her day.

"Were you writing today?" she asked.

"I wish. I've been distracted, fiddling around with these old boxes."

Penelope spotted the rubber nipples of baby bottles, a can of powdered formula, an unopened package of tiny socks. She asked whether he was going through Grace's old things.

"Some of it was hers, yes."

He fidgeted and closed the flaps of a box. "I don't know why I feel the need to keep it a big secret—I don't think it does us any good."

Penelope slid closer to him, across the ottoman. She remembered how he had touched her knee that time on the stoop.

"We were going to have a little boy. That's part of why we bought the house. Samantha didn't want her children to grow up in an apartment. She's still a California girl at heart."

Marcus smiled and sighed. "Needless to say, we lost the baby. But we got the house, and—here we are."

Penelope felt too inept to comfort Marcus. Dead babies and houses and deeds were far from what she knew. So she squeezed his knee, once, the way you should when someone confides in you, she told herself.

"I think it's easier for Sam to be at the office these days than to be here. And I'm hardly helping with the mortgage anymore—God, I shouldn't even be telling you this. I'm sure this is more than you want to know about your old and boring landlords—"

"You're not so old," Penelope said, and this time she kept her hand on his knee.

Marcus laughed, so Penelope went on.

"Maybe you should throw a party in this parlor, so the house doesn't feel so empty anymore. I can already imagine the room filled with guests. It will be the party of the year."

"That's true—none of my Manhattan friends have this much space."

"Or a backyard. Don't forget the backyard."

They laughed together in the living room, and Marcus looked up at her.

"You're a champ for listening, Penelope."

"Of course."

"I don't have many people to talk to these days. Samantha is fantastic, but a wife is too close to be a friend."

What he said seemed true to her. Ralph and Mirella had never appeared to be friends.

"Then that's what we'll be," Penelope said. "Friends."

She took his palm in hers, and Marcus let her. She didn't knit their fingers—that would be too much. She saw a flush rise over Marcus, from beneath the collar of his shirt, up to his temples. The shock of color on his skin made her blush, too.

He didn't speak, but he didn't pull his hand away either, so she traced the lines in his palm, her pressure slight. She ran her finger along each of his fingers. He was motionless, but she felt as if he were touching her, too, a warmth spreading over every inch of her skin.

"Samantha," he said, and Penelope heard the jangle of keys in the door. In unison they sprang apart, and Marcus dropped her hand.

Samantha swept into the foyer, carrying two heavy brown paper bags, her purse dangling from her wrist. Penelope had almost forgotten what she looked like, and although she looked more tired and formal than she had when they met over the summer, Penelope was struck all over again by how lovely she was. She was slender under her trench coat, so short and petite she hardly seemed old enough to be anyone's mother. Her blond hair was wound into a chignon at the nape of her neck, fastened with bronze pins. Gray shadows under her eyes peeked through her yellow concealer, but it didn't diminish any of her prettiness. She had a round face, like her daughter, and the lunar shape of it made you want to look at her again and again.

"Why hello, Penelope," she said, the surprise in her voice obvious as she set the heavy bags down. She unwound the scarf from her neck and hung it on a hook. She entered the parlor, untying the belt of her coat to reveal a red silk pantsuit. The scent of lavender trailed after her. Penelope could tell she was the kind of woman who could work a full day, buy groceries, come home in the rain, and still look and smell exactly as she had in the morning before she left the house.

Marcus stood and kissed his wife swiftly on the lips. "You're home early."

"I could hear the paralegals gossiping all the way in my office. It was amusing, but I couldn't get any work done. I said to myself, *Why didn't they all just go home at five?* And then I realized they had nowhere better to be. But I did. So I called a car and I left."

Marcus kissed Samantha again.

"Grace will be thrilled," he said. "Are you making dinner?" He gestured to her brown bags.

"Yes, but I'll need your help. I'm roasting a chicken."

Marcus nodded dutifully. He hoisted the paper bags onto his hip. Penelope saw the bright green logo stamped on the grocery bags, the tiny seedling curling out of the ground.

Samantha ran a hand through her hair and turned to Penelope, who was still sitting in the parlor, her hands burning, her hair dripping on the ottoman.

"Do you want to join us, Penelope?"

"I have dinner plans with my father," she lied.

"Maybe another time."

Samantha started up the stairs, and Marcus followed with the bags. Penelope trailed behind them.

"What were you doing downstairs?"

"I was looking for my Stanford pennant. I thought it would look nice in Gracie's bedroom. But I couldn't remember which box we put it in."

Samantha laughed. "I told you to label them."

Penelope shrank as she listened to them. It was far better to overhear them from the attic, where their voices were melded and indistinct, no more than murmurs through the floorboards.

"You know, Marcus, when I came in this evening the front door was unlocked."

"That's strange. It locks whenever you close it."

"I mean the deadbolt, love. It wasn't turned. I told you about that burglary over on Gates. One open window was all it took, and the thief left with everything, a trumpet, a keyboard, some speakers. They robbed a pair of musicians."

"I was the last to come in," Penelope said. "I must have forgotten to turn the deadbolt."

Samantha stopped climbing the stairs and turned around to look down at Penelope.

"Could you try to remember next time? I don't mean to be so particular, but I want us all to be careful—for Grace."

"Of course. Sorry."

Penelope instantly wished she hadn't apologized at all. She'd heard about the burglary, too—it wasn't on Gates, but on Stuyvesant Ave, in a building in the projects. No one was going to break into Samantha's renovated brownstone, every door and window locked, a panic button probably nestled behind some bookshelf in her bedroom. Penelope had met white women like her at RISD—women who were certain they were the center of everyone's world. If someone wanted to steal a handbag, it would be her handbag. If someone wanted to pick a lock, it would be her lock. She was no better than the Manhattan friends Marcus complained about. She felt for a moment how much she hated that she was living with them at all, writing them rent checks, promising to deadbolt their front door. But where else could she have gone? Not back to Halsey Street, and their listing had been perfect. An attic was removed enough from the street that she could feel afloat over the block, as if she were at sea, and not tethered once again to the old neighborhood.

They reached the second-floor landing, and Samantha stopped in front of a shut door. Penelope guessed the door led to the pantry and then the kitchen. She had seen a few houses with this design. Samantha put the key in the lock then turned to stare at Penelope.

"Good night," she said, and Penelope realized she had been dismissed. Samantha disappeared through the door.

Marcus stalled and glanced at Penelope penitently, then held up a hand to say good-bye and followed his wife. He closed the door behind him.

Penelope crossed the next flight of stairs, wondering whether Marcus would continue to think of her. Would he feel bad for holding her hand? Would he wish they had been able to hold on for longer? She couldn't predict. But she had wanted more time with him—just to see. She cursed Samantha for interrupting them and felt no guilt. The landlady was a brat, as self-contented and oblivious as the girls at RISD, only she was all grown up, a lawyer, a mother, beyond any kind of reprove.

On the third floor, all the doors were closed and there was no sign of Grace. She heard no games or songs; there was not even a light visible from beneath the doors.

Up in the attic, Penelope sat at her kitchen table. The room was dark and empty, so she wrapped herself in a blanket and lit a cigarette.

She smoked it down to an ace, and then snuffed it out in the ashtray to finish later. She felt calmer with the scent of the smoke in her wet hair and lungs, on her fingertips. She pushed open the window to let in the night.

After she quit RISD, Penelope used to wonder whether she should have stayed around for her BFA. She had been miserable in school but wound up stuck in Brooklyn—it was less miserable only because it was familiar, routine. Pittsburgh had been like another attempt at college, only without the degree, the critiques, the terrible classmates. She had found her morning runs in Frick Park, her nightcaps at the Anchor, how satisfied and unwound she felt when she could bring a man home to fuck in the quiet and privacy of her own home.

The Harpers seemed to have a good life. Dead baby and all, they still had their beautiful house, their weekends in the city. Grace and boxes full of old things, roast chicken dinners. Samantha was a pain, but at least she wasn't alone. Maybe Penelope could have found her life here, too—

But it was late now. The dark lay heavy over the street below. There was no difference between the houses, the remodeled ones and the ones in decay, under the hush of night. Penelope couldn't remember Brooklyn ever being this serene. And yet it was. The percussive fall of rain, the whoosh of rare cars, the blue of the air. She lit another cigarette.

7

The Grands

The guests had started to arrive, but Mirella was still in her bedroom on the second floor. She heard them talking and clinking bottles over a jazz record Ralph had put on. Her hair dripped on the floor from where she sat on the edge of the bed, staring at the wall, bare except for a watercolor painting of the garden that Penelope had tacked up herself. Mirella had returned from work one day and found the painting posted with a yellow tack. The painting was all green and pink and violet swirls, the paper crinkling in the spots where water had pooled. She had known instantly that it was her garden. Penelope had captured the way everything in the backyard was a part of something else—there were no rows or little wooden signs separating the herbs from the vegetables and flowers. The entire yard was a colorful, orderly overgrowth, where Mirella didn't even have to try to lose herself. When she worked on the yard, the traffic on Halsey—the chime of a bicycle bell or the groan of a public bus—was the only proof that she was still in Brooklyn. Mirella had liked the painting so much that she hadn't called Penelope in to yell at her for tacking a painting up in her bedroom without permission and piercing a hole in the wall. It was easy to yell at Penelope for her eight-year-old misadventures: leaving paintbrushes on the floor, forgetting to comb her hair, pressing her ear to Mirella's bedroom door when she had made it clear that she wanted to be left alone.

Ralph's laughter boomed in the parlor, and Mirella drew the thin robe more tightly around herself. This second winter in the house had been especially hard; cold drafts cut through the house on windy days, and even when Mirella sat next to the pipes that heated the house, she couldn't get warm enough. The snow had covered and killed everything she had sown in the past year, and it would be weeks before she could sit out in the yard again. Without her garden to distract her, the days bled into one another. She made oatmeal for Ralph, detangled Penelope's hair, and rode the A train into the city to clean houses for Mrs. Schubert, Mrs. Baxter, Mrs. Engle, Mrs. Farley, whoever had scheduled her for the day.

The work gave her a routine and purpose; she liked the exertion of it, the feel of hot water on her hands, the herbal smell of the purple liquid she used to scrub the floors. She felt alive, deep in her body, when she cleaned. Ralph had wanted her to quit cleaning houses so that she could watch Penelope and give the girl what neither of them had known: a parent alive and devoted to them. But Penelope was old enough to watch herself; she went to school; she was fed; she was clean; she needed nothing else. Mirella was the one who needed things. At least, she didn't have to ask Ralph for an allowance, like a child, and she could see what she had accomplished at work each day, each year, as her little stockpile of savings grew steadily in the bank.

It had been Mrs. Schubert today, her parquet floors and clogged closets, the squadron of little dogs nipping at Mirella's ankles while she tried to sweep. It was a longer day than usual because Mirella had risen early to cook. Ralph had refused to pay for a caterer—he wanted the food to come right from home. So before she left for the city that morning, Mirella had folded dozens of pastelitos, stewed chicken thighs with capers and olives, and filled her largest pot with rice and beans. It was nearly dark when she returned to Brooklyn, and she had no will to help Ralph set up the parlor. She spent longer than she intended in the shower, leaning against the tiles, under the spray of hot water, just standing. It was as if she were asleep with her eyes open. She didn't think anything, and she couldn't hear the party starting up, Ralph moving around furniture and opening the front door when the bell rang. It wasn't until she had finally washed up, shampooed her hair, and returned to the bedroom that she remembered she was supposed to help.

This would be their first party in their new house. They had entertained guests before, always visitors for Ralph. Mirella set out cookies and coffee, sat with them in the living room until she could invent a reason to leave. The women were no better than the men. They hardly looked at her, and Ralph addressed her only to add emphasis to whatever he was saying—"Isn't that right, Mirella?" and "Wouldn't you say, Mirella love?"

She knew his friends didn't take her seriously—they were always commenting on how young she was, asking her questions about Puerto Rico, although she had told them that wasn't the island she was from. They thought she was a beautiful, skinny idiot who cleaned houses and flubbed some of her words in English—*bark* for *buck*, *When-es-day* for *Wednesday*, *minds* instead of *mine*. She didn't admire Ralph's friends any longer for owning businesses or having office jobs in downtown Brooklyn or Manhattan. The bottles of wine they brought over didn't impress her anymore, or the new records they had purchased at Ralph's store. Mirella knew now this was the extent of their lives—stopping into each other's brownstones to drink and play music and talk indifferently about the neighborhood, as if it were some other place, instead of the brutal swatch of the city where they'd chosen to make their homes.

Ever since Ralph and Mirella left their apartment on Marcy Avenue, their house had become a popular stop on the block's gossip circuit. Neighbors stopped in to trade rumors about what had caused that big shoot-out on Myrtle; they complained about the rotting meat left out in the aisle of the A&P, and how long it had taken the police to find the man who had raped two elderly women on their walks home from the train. They shook their heads and remembered the little boy whose face had been cut open in the schoolyard one afternoon while he waited for his father to pick him up. They smoked cigars and listened to the radio, and never tired of the same conversations, the same disasters.

In Aguas Frescas, the neighbors would have formed a search party to find the man who had cut the face of the little boy, a classmate of Penelope's. They would find him and the rapist, beat them both with bats and bars, call them sinvergüenzas, and reprimand them for bringing shame to the barrio. They would reprimand the parents, too, for not keeping their children under better control. The people in her village were poor, but they knew how to defend their homes. Mirella didn't say any of these things aloud; their guests would look at her as if she were an alien, and Ralph's eyes would bulge as if she had gravely betrayed him in front of a crowd he wanted to impress. She kept busy by refilling the coffee and cookies, fluttering back and forth to the kitchen, wondering why no one in this country could be content with just one cookie, just one cup of coffee.

Ralph had risen that morning, humming over the party. Mirella had watched him dress, comb his beard, and put on his tie. "Today's our day, Mirella," he had said. "Fifteen years, can you believe it?" And she had nodded from beneath the covers, shivering. "Big night," was all she said, and Ralph kissed her neck before he left to run errands. He had ordered a banner for the party—"GRAND RECORDS, EST. 1976" printed in black ink on tan fabric. He wanted to hang it in the parlor for the night then string it up in the window at the store to announce their fifteenth anniversary sale. Mirella heard Ralph lock the front door behind him when he left to pick up the banner. She stayed in bed until the alarm rang again and she knew she had to get up or she wouldn't have time to cook before she left for work.

Mirella's skin prickled into gooseflesh, and she wondered how long she could sit upstairs before someone asked where she was.

"Mami," a small voice called from the hall. Penelope poked her head into the bedroom. "Ya empezaron a llegar."

She spoke cautiously, her hands gripping the door for a moment before she finally stepped in the room. Her navy party dress was wrinkled, and her hair was still twisted into that morning's pigtails. She had fastened a jeweled butterfly clip above her ear to flatten the hairs that had come loose at the crown. Mirella had straightened Penelope's hair just a few days ago, but it was already coiling, returning to its unruly shape. The curls were Ralph's fault, the clip the girl's attempt at looking presentable.

"We're all waiting for you, Mami."

Penelope edged closer to her mother, put her hand on her knee.

"How many people are downstairs?"

"Not a lot—maybe nine."

"I hear more than nine voices."

"I counted before I came up."

Mirella crossed her legs and sighed.

"Do you want me to pick out a dress for you, Mami?"

Penelope smiled at her, her back straight and her hands dangling at her side, as if the longer she stood there beaming, the more likely Mirella would be to move.

Se parece igualita a mí, Mirella thought, staring at the tiny double of herself. Penelope had the same squinty, light-filled eyes and slim hands, the bump in her nose, inherited from Ramona. She was browner than Mirella, a little wheat-colored girl who darkened to bronze in the sun. Ralph was the reason she was so dark, the reason her cheeks rounded when she smiled.

"Fine," she said. "Pick something out for me."

Penelope turned triumphantly toward the closet. She sifted through the dresses on their hangers, the dozen silk frocks Mirella hadn't worn in years. She had cleared away the rest, including her favorite: slinky, bright, and emerald green. It had wrapped around her waist, long-sleeved, the neckline low. She had nowhere that justified her wearing such a dress, and so she gave it away. They went to Sheckley's for their wedding anniversary every year, and they hadn't so much as cut a cake for Penelope since her fifth birthday. Ralph never had the time.

Penelope pulled a cobalt dress off the hanger.

"How about this one, Mami? You look so pretty in blue."

Penelope held the dress against her body, the hem brushing the floor. Her eyebrows arched hopefully, as she waited for Mirella to respond. Mirella forced herself to smile at the girl, her frown breaking and dissolving over her face. It was a dress for an old woman, with a collar and fake pearl buttons along the front.

Sometimes it irritated her, the way Penelope saw nothing: how selfish her father was, how much she needed to be left alone. The girl sulked about, carrying a stack of her latest drawings, waiting to be noticed, or marching into the bedroom and interrupting Mirella when she wanted to rest. But other times, the girl looked at her with a shine on her face, the way she sometimes looked at her father, and Mirella wanted to gather her into her arms and squeeze her, to breathe her in. She tapped Penelope on the forehead.

"All right, hija," she said. "For you, it's blue."

Mirella took off the robe and slipped into the dress. The silk clung to her wet skin. Penelope sat cross-legged on the bed and watched her as Mirella dotted on perfume and put on her earrings. She shook her waves of hair behind her. Her hair was no longer burnt red by the mountain sun; it was a dull brown after all her years in Brooklyn, only hints of auburn or gold in certain angles under certain light.

"Se te ves hermosa!" Penelope said.

"Te ves hermosa."

Mirella corrected the child, and Penelope repeated after her and went to the closet to bring out a pair of black pumps. She held them steady while Mirella stepped into them.

She looked at herself in the mirror, the veins in her bare calves, the new freckles on her arms. She had the beginning of a line in her forehead. She might not have been nearly as old as Ralph and his friends, but she wasn't a girl anymore either. A woman on the subway had once mistaken her for Penelope's sister, and a part of her had thought it seemed right; she hadn't lived nearly enough to be someone's mother.

"There's a big sign downstairs," Penelope said. "Everyone is so proud of Pop."

Mirella rolled the stiff fabric between her fingers. The dress gave off a stale smell, like dried flowers in a windowless room.

"Let's get this over with," she said and nudged Penelope toward the door.

Mirella had worn the emerald dress on the night she first met Ralph. An electric sign hung over the door to the nightclub, its red light kissing the curb. Mirella had overheard one of the ladies she worked for talking about the club. She had said the men went there in suits, the women in long hair and long earrings; there were black people, and white people, a few Puerto Ricans. She had called Luisel, from the factory, to go with her because it was safer to ride the train with another woman, and because if she went alone, someone might mistake her for a prostitute. Inside, the people were beautiful, as Mirella had expected. It was the New York she liked to remind herself she lived in. The men wore hats, and the women sparkled in their glittery blouses and melting makeup. They danced by touching themselves: their shoulders, their hair, their hips. They dipped and swung from side to side. The DJ played disco, which Mirella loved. She and Luisel found a table where they drank and shook their shoulders, waiting for someone to ask them to dance. It didn't take long before they were taking turns on the floor, or back at the table, watching their purses and drinks. They sweat until their hair was heavy; they drank until they felt glamorous and as if they belonged;

they whispered to each other in Spanish and felt far from the campo, their half of an island. Ralph found her, fanning herself at the table. He sat down beside her and asked, "Where'd you get all that red hair?"

He was older than her, probably the same age as her terrible aunt, but he was handsome in his unbuttoned shirt and white pants. He had an afro, a big one, and a little mustache. He asked where she was from and where she worked, and he told her about the store. They had to shout over the music, and there were pauses in her speech as she read his lips to understand. Ralph didn't seem to mind. He teased her for saying she was drinking *Esprite*, but he pronounced it that way when the waiter came over, which made her laugh. He bought her one rum and soda, and then another, and another, until they were both out, dancing under the lights. Ralph pointed his index fingers at her while he rocked side to side in a funny American sway. She had imitated him—that she could remember—the rest was blurry and beautiful. When the club closed, Ralph put Luisel in a car—she was angry Mirella had ignored her all night—and then the two of them walked on together, peacefully, toward the train.

He didn't seem frightened at all by where Mirella lived in Brownsville, and he took her right up to the door of her aunt's apartment. She explained that soon she would leave her tía Mercedes and find a place of her own. The old woman had only brought her to this country so that Mirella could cook for her and wash for her and kill the mice in exchange for a corner to sleep and keep her things. Ralph didn't kiss her good night, and when he left, Mirella ran to the kitchen. From the window, she watched him saunter down the block, his hands in his pockets, his head up, until he disappeared around the corner.

The Grand guests swarmed around the parlor, shouting over the Charles Mingus record. They sat in rented folding chairs and on the olive green sofa Ralph and Mirella usually kept upstairs. Ralph must have asked one of his friends to help him carry it downstairs to cover the fireplace, the white marble mouth filled with dusty bricks. A woman rushed across the room to say hello to someone she recognized and knocked over a half-dozen beer bottles. The guests were lining up the empty green and brown bottles in a corner of the parlor, underneath the window.

"I thought there were only nine people here." Mirella pinched Penelope's shoulder. The girl squirmed but didn't cry out.

"There were nine. Dr. Elias and Mrs. Jones weren't here before. I counted."

"You counted wrong."

There were at least twenty guests, most of them other business owners in the neighborhood. A few were old neighbors from the apartment building on Marcy, or new friends from this block. Mirella scanned the room for the Joneses, her favorite neighbors on Halsey Street. Mr. Jones was a bus driver, and Mrs. Jones sold Mary Kay. They lived a few brownstones over and were simple people who never treated Mirella like she didn't belong. They had moved up from one of the Carolinas, and Mirella had been in Brooklyn as long as they had. Mrs. Jones dropped by the house a few times a month just to talk to Mirella. Sometimes, Mirella couldn't get out of bed, so she sent Penelope to the door to say she wasn't feeling well. Other times, she and Mrs. Jones had coffee standing up in the kitchen, as if both of them could spare only a few minutes. They would talk for hours about their gardens or their daughters, nursing small cups of café con leche. Mrs. Jones's daughter was Penelope's age when she died. She got sick with a fever they couldn't lower; her heart gave out at Beth Israel Hospital in Manhattan before the Grands bought the house on Halsey. Mrs. Jones was just as hungry for company as Mirella, and she used her briefcase filled with too-pink blush and gummy lipstick as pretext for visits.

Mrs. Jones stood in front of the sofa, holding a bottle of beer she wasn't drinking. She stared at the drawings Penelope had taped over the fireplace, tilting her head as if she were waiting for the turbulent spirals to announce something to her. Mirella wanted to go speak to her, but she knew Ralph would want her to join him in his circle. Mirella didn't have to call out to her friend; Mrs. Jones looked up from one of Penelope's colored pencil creations and saw her by the stairs. Mrs. Jones smiled weakly and waved before turning back to the drawings.

"Let's go say hello," Mirella said softly, nudging Penelope toward where Ralph stood. She kept her hand on Penelope's back and felt as if she were really pushing herself, and not the girl, into the center of the room.

Ralph was smoking cigars with Dr. Elias and Lionel Sheckley. The men puffed smoke up into the room, and Mirella cringed. The smell would stick to the curtains, which she had just washed that week with bleach. Una Beckett stood among the men, picking at a large plate of potato salad, and listening to Ralph as he spoke. Her plastic fork was stained with lipstick and mayonnaise. Her eyelids were the same garish pink as her dress, cinched at her fat waist with a belt. Miss Beckett and Ralph were the same age, but she already looked much older. Mirella smiled as she approached them, satisfied that even in her dress she looked young enough to be Una's daughter. She undid just the top button of her dress.

"Mirella, aren't you stunning!"

Dr. Elias stepped aside to make room for Mirella in the circle. She smiled at him.

"Hi, Freddie."

She embraced him and then turned to Lionel. Lionel was already drunk, and sweating in a green blazer that didn't quite fit him. He squinted at Mirella through his Coke-bottle glasses, then agreed vigorously with Dr. Elias.

"Lovely as ever, Muh-ray-uh! You're a dream in blue!"

Mirella nodded in thanks. Lionel and Freddie were Ralph's friends, not hers, but she liked them both. Freddie was levelheaded and honest, and Lionel told a lot of corny jokes just to make everyone laugh. They were part of the reason she had fallen for Ralph—they hushed whenever he spoke and listened to him as if he knew more than they ever could. They had all experienced a good amount of success, but Ralph was the only one with no reason to thrive. He had started out not only black and poor, but without even parents or a surname he could be sure was his. They revered him, and Mirella had once, too.

Ralph slipped his arm around her waist.

"Yes, love, you look nice," he said, without looking up from the glowing tip of his cigar. "So these are Cuban, you say?" Ralph held his cigar out to Lionel.

"One hundred percent. I personally know the guy in the Village who sold me these."

"How do we know he didn't just slip these little rings that say 'Havana' on any old cigars?" Dr. Elias inspected the gold band around his cigar.

"He wouldn't do that," Lionel said. "He doesn't have to. These are the real thing."

"Isn't that risky?" Miss Beckett asked in a shaky voice. She looked over her shoulder as if she expected the police to bust into the house at any second, confiscate the cigars, and arrest Ralph.

"Pfsh," Ralph said. "Why would it be risky? No one's ever going to check and see if a shop in the Village is selling Cuban cigars. What does anyone care? Now if that tobacco shop were here on Bedford Avenue—forget about it."

Ralph shook his head, his disapproval enough to complete the thought. The men sucked on their cigars.

Dr. Elias put his hand on Penelope's head, acknowledging the child and flattening her curls.

"Smile for me, Penny," he said.

Penelope beamed at him obediently, revealing her small ivory teeth. She had a gap between her two front teeth, and the bottom two were so crooked they almost faced each other.

"Those aren't straightening out, are they?" Miss Beckett said. She lowered her glasses and leaned in to have a closer look at the girl's teeth.

"My teeth were crooked, too, at that age," Mirella said.

"And they sure straightened out—didn't they?" said Lionel.

"It's nothing braces won't fix," Dr. Elias said. He patted Penelope's head again, and she smiled at him, this time genuinely. "We'll get you some in a pretty color, like pink or blue, if your pop ever finds the time to take you to that dentist."

"I've always got time for my Penny." Ralph winked and pinched his daughter's cheek. Penelope blushed reverently.

Mirella rolled her eyes and squeezed her daughter's shoulder.

"Aren't you hungry, Penélope? Why don't you go fix yourself a plate? I made pastelitos."

"I want to stay here with you all."

"Go and get them while they're still hot."

"Sí, Señora," Penelope said, knowing when she had been ordered away. She wandered over to the table piled high with food, and the conversation returned to cigars.

"Mirella, is it true that you can get Cuban cigars in the Dominican Republic?"

Lionel touched Mirella's arm as he spoke, his voice low as if they shouldn't be overheard.

"Of course, you can," she said. "Cuba is right next door to us, but there's no reason to buy Cuban cigars when you can buy Dominican cigars for much cheaper. Our cigars are just as good, and you don't have any trouble bringing them into the US."

"Now, I disagree there—" Ralph took the cigar out of his mouth and pointed it at the center of the circle. "You can't really compare Dominican and Cuban cigars. The quality of the tobacco is just not the same. Cubans make the best cigars in the world."

Lionel nudged Ralph hard in the arm with a slanted, drunken grin on his face. "Maybe the next time you go to the Dominican Republic, you can smuggle us back some Cubans, eh, Ralph?"

"What next time?" Dr. Elias scoffed. "He's never been."

"Don't tell me that!" Lionel shouted. "Is that true, Ralph Grand? You've never been to the Dominican Republic?"

Ralph puffed a perfect *O*. The smoke ring drifted above the circle before it broke apart.

"No time, old man. You know how things get at the store over the summer."

"I can't believe I forgot you'd never been—" Lionel rubbed the creases in his forehead.

"If you ask me, you're a fool, Ralph," Dr. Elias said. "It's a beautiful country. Kim and I are planning a trip as soon as I can get some days off from the hospital."

"Be careful," Mirella said. "If you go, you'll never want to come back."

"Ralph, if you've never been, who goes with Mirella and Penny every summer?" Lionel asked.

"What do you mean who goes with them? They go with each other," Miss Beckett snapped.

"Penny's always begging me to go," Ralph said, picking at his fro with his fingers. "I'm planning on it—maybe next year if business slows down, but we don't want that to happen, do we?" He held out his fist to Lionel, who tapped it with his own, and the two men chuckled.

Lionel had been Ralph's first friend in the neighborhood. They met doing construction, right out of high school. They took pride now in how much they had done and how busy they were—the long nights spent balancing the books, the hours they put in every day to keep their businesses open. Sheckley's was the most popular and respectable bar on this side of the neighborhood, and Grand Records had become a Bed-Stuy landmark. Ralph was always saying that if Bed-Stuy were included in the guidebooks, Grand Records would be on the first page. He had only recently started selling tapes, too, instead of just vinyl, but the records still sold best. Church ladies came in regularly for gospel albums, but the top sellers were always hip-hop—Run DMC, Eric B. and Rakim,

Fat Boys. Ralph sold Motown, too, and a few rock albums that young people in the neighborhood requested: the Grateful Dead and Pink Floyd. Hipsters from Manhattan took the A train into Brooklyn just to pick up some jazz and blues from *a real* jazz and blues shop. They always asked for Ralph's opinion, and he'd handle their questions as if the answers were obvious and recommend Monk and Miles and Bobby Hutcherson before ringing them up himself.

Ralph still had all that coolness from when he and Mirella first started to see each other. He was starting to gray, but he looked rugged in his brown pants and matching blazer, the neat, shrinking globe of his fro. He laughed now with Lionel, the cigar tucked and motionless in the corner of his mouth, as if he were waiting to be photographed. He was so content Mirella couldn't bear to look at him. She turned away.

She tuned out the men and Miss Beckett, let their voices fade into the cacophony of hard English sounds storming around the room. She watched Penelope. All the food Mirella had cooked that morning was cold on the table.

Penelope peered into every dish before daintily spooning a little bit of rice onto a plate. No one else had touched Mirella's food. The guests were eating the hors d'oeuvres Miss Beckett had brought over instead: soda crackers, pigs in a blanket, milky-white potato salad.

Mirella felt Miss Beckett lean into her. She had stopped listening to the men to watch Penelope, too. The girl had taken a seat by the record player, cradling the plate in her lap, tilting her head to read the label on the album spinning inside.

"I hope she likes the potato salad," Miss Beckett said.

"I think you used too much mayonnaise," Mirella replied dryly.

"I didn't even realize she was standing here with us before. That child is so quiet sometimes I'd swear she was a ghost. I see her in the halls at school in between classes, and I walk right by her half the time before I even notice she's there."

"Well, she is there—every single day. And she's not so quiet."

"I'm not saying I worry about her. She isn't one of those students who sits by herself at lunch. She plays with the other girls during recess. She gets picked for teams because she's so fast. She doesn't ever have problems with anyone—not the teachers, not the kids, but she doesn't really seem to have friends either."

"What are you trying to say, Una?"

"I've told Ralph that it's no good for her to be so solitary. It's obvious that the two of you love her, but that's not enough. She should have friends her own age."

"Penelope is a private girl."

"Wouldn't it be nice if she had been able to invite a friend or two from school to this party? Then she could have someone to talk to while she sat over there. She wouldn't have to pretend to like the music so much, or to be so interested in her food."

"I don't think my daughter's pretending." Mirella raised her voice. "And not everyone needs someone to talk to."

"Now, I disagree with that—" Miss Beckett began, but Lionel interrupted her. He planted a hand on Mirella's shoulder, his meaty fingers on the cap sleeve of her dress.

"Muh-ray-uh, don't be too mad at Ralph for not going with you all to DR."

His breath stank of beer.

"He'll go soon enough to spend time with you and Penny and to meet your mother and all that. I tell you, running a shop is no easy thing. The bar gets the same way every summer, and I'm sure if I were married, my wife would hate me from May to September."

"I know what it takes to run the shop. That's why I used to ask Ralph to let me help."

Miss Beckett's eyebrows went up in horror, as if she could tell Mirella were about to speak ill of Ralph. Lionel didn't seem to notice, he was babbling on about warm weather, how it made people feel like spending all they've got. Ralph wasn't listening either. She went on.

"I wanted to work in the store, to help Ralph, but he never let me do anything but wash the windows and dust."

"That's just how he is," Miss Beckett said, leaning into the little huddle of Lionel and Mirella. Lionel still had his arm around her. "I've offered to help, too, over the years."

"I'm his wife," Mirella said. "You live down the street."

Lionel interrupted the women.

"It's hard work, Muh-ray-uh," he said, almost spitting in her face. "Running a business isn't easy for any of us, but we do it, 'cause it's worth doing. It's worth the headaches to be able to call something your own. Like that shop and this house—they're your little piece of this city, Muh-ray-uh. They belong to Ralph on paper, but they belong to you and Penny as well. They're your *pieces* of this life."

"Yes, Lionel. I'm very fortunate."

"I just sell beers, but what Ralph does—*that's* for real. *That's* important. You hear this music that's playing? This is Charles Mingus. *Mingus.*"

Mirella hoped he was done.

"That's all we've got, you know—our music. Most people in this neighborhood don't have a single thing of their own. Hell, when Ralph and I came here, we didn't even have families. Me without a father, Ralph without either of his parents."

Some of the other guests in the room had gathered around to listen to Lionel's speech. He didn't seem to notice them. He gripped Mirella's shoulder and leaned closer to her. She felt the heat rising from his pink cheeks and heavy hand.

"A drink can help take the edge off the world, that's why I opened my bar. But it's nothing compared to what Ralph does. I'm telling you, Muh-ray-uh, music—"

"It's all we've got. Yes, Lionel. I see what you're saying."

The guests were listening now, nodding along to what he said. Lionel took note of his audience, and went on, addressing the crowd now as much as he had her.

"Do you see how happy everyone is here at this party in your house? It's not the free beer, I'll tell you that. It's because we're all glad to be here celebrating Ralph and you and Penny. We all see what Grand Records has done for this neighborhood. I've seen people walk in that shop and leave *different*, even if they only had enough for one record, even if they didn't even have enough to buy *any* records. It's enough to just walk through the aisles. To see what's there, to see what our people *created*. I've seen young people go into that store and they can't even believe how much good music was made here in Brooklyn, *here*, by their own people. They walk into Ralph's store and they see that black people can do things. They can *create*."

Ralph was quiet, leaning against the wall and listening to his friend's speech. Mirella saw Penelope perk up in her chair, straining to hear.

"Our music reminds us we're all connected. Ella, Billie, Jimi— those are the kind of artists who can change your life. They can *save* it. I'm forty-three years old, and I've been a bachelor all my life, and if I couldn't go home to some Teena Marie or Jean Carne, I don't know how I'd make it through the days."

"Teena Marie is white," Mirella said, but no one seemed to hear.

"Ralph knows what music does—he *knows* it. He's known since he was a kid working in the record store in Harlem across the street from that last boys' home he lived in. And he's dedicated his life to making sure we all know it, too. I'm lucky to call him friend. You're lucky to be his wife, and we're all lucky just to know him."

Lionel thrust his empty beer bottle into the air.

"A toast to Ralph Grand!" he said, and the crowd followed suit, raising their bottles.

"To Grand Records and to Ralph Grand—father, husband, entrepreneur, and friend to the neighborhood."

"Hear, hear," the guests cheered and the parlor rang with the collisions of glass on glass, fevered applause. Foamy beer sloshed out of the bottles and onto the floor. Miss Beckett clapped slowly, letting her palms slide against each other, her eyes fixed on Ralph. Ralph nodded at the cluster of guests, and he smiled, his eyes half closed, almost bashful, as he steeped in the attention.

"Thank you, thank you," he said, nodding in time to his own words. He found Mirella's hand and squeezed it. She wanted to wrench her hand away from his, but she let him hold her hand, swallowing her fingers into his palm. He wanted to share the moment with her, she knew, wanted to say with his hand over her hand, *This is our life*. Mirella waited for the applause to die down, for their guests to turn back to each other and their drinks and the music, the Mingus still playing, too many horns bleating and competing. When they did, she squeezed Ralph's hand so he would release her.

"Excuse me," Mirella murmured as she slipped out of the circle. "I'm going to check on the food," she said, and no one questioned her. Lionel and Ralph were already talking again about summer business, Miss Beckett and Dr. Elias listening in.

She found Mrs. Jones in the same spot she had been at the beginning of the party, staring at Penelope's drawings, three of them in a row, above the fireplace. They looked like a series of squiggly lines to Mirella, the kind of multicolor messes that toddlers make when they first learn how to color. Penelope had explained to Mirella that she was "playing with colors," which Mirella had thought was obvious.

Mrs. Jones looked frail in her black cocktail dress, just brown skin and bones under the lacy sleeves and tulle skirt. She kissed Mirella on the cheek and wrapped her arm around her shoulder. Her face was perfectly dusted with powder, her eyelashes curled, and her lips a deep rose. She could have been a doll, she was so tiny and delicately made-up. She seemed to be shrinking every time she turned up for a visit on the pretense of selling Mirella mascara. Her hands were cold.

"Busy night for your family, hmm?"

"For Ralph."

"You'll have a lot to clean up." Mrs. Jones pointed at the bottles someone had lined up on the mantel.

"Please, I don't want to think about it."

"Well, if you have a parlor this beautiful, you should certainly use it for parties."

"I'd hardly call this a party," Mirella said. "Everyone's just standing and talking, getting drunk. At a party, you laugh and you dance. But you can't move to this music."

"Don't let Lionel hear you. He'll have a heart attack if he hears you say the music is just nice." Mrs. Jones laughed. "He's a nut, isn't he? All that *our music* business. You'd think he was Ralph's wife."

Mirella nodded, but she didn't want to talk about Ralph. She was thankful for this moment away from him and his horde of admirers.

"You haven't eaten anything," she said.

Mrs. Jones smiled sadly. "I don't have much of an appetite these days. Winter is always the hardest for me—but you already knew that."

"Yes, I understand."

Mrs. Jones turned back to the drawings over the fireplace. "Penny's such a talented girl," she said. "These are so beautiful. I can't say why, but there's something more to them than is obvious."

Mirella shrugged. "I don't understand it. I don't mind if she draws, I just wish she'd focus more on school. I tell her that's the only chance she has."

"I used to tell Lily the same thing—to work hard in school so she wouldn't end up selling Mary Kay." Mrs. Jones looked down at her empty hands and then back at Mirella, as if she'd found something there that filled her with regret. "I don't know why I said those things to her. She was just a girl, and I shouldn't have worried her with such grown-up things. Sean and I live a good life."

Mirella shook her head because she couldn't give Penelope that same assurance. She did not have a good life. She did not want such smallness and emptiness for her daughter.

"Drawing isn't a job. Penelope can be anything she wants to be. A lawyer, a doctor, an entrepreneur—" Mirella fumbled over the word. "If I had been born here, I would have been something, too."

"You still can. I'm sure Ralph would support you if you decided to go back to school."

"What would I even go back for?"

"Just for a change."

"I'd never get in anywhere with my English."

"Your English is fine—better than a lot of people's English, I promise you," Mrs. Jones said.

"I don't think Ralph would like it." Mirella felt disgusted with herself as soon as she had said it. "Where's Mr. Jones?"

"Oh, you know how he is. He can't handle crowds anymore, so I left him at home. I should be getting back to him soon. He's probably hungry by now."

Mirella took Mrs. Jones's hands in hers.

"Please take some of the food with you. We'll be eating it for days, and Ralph doesn't even like Dominican food."

"He has no idea what he's missing," Mrs. Jones said, and she winked.

The women hugged, and Mrs. Jones took up as many empty beer bottles as she could in her arms to deposit them in the garbage can by the door. She turned to go and then paused, circling back around to face Mirella.

"Frame those pictures," she said. "Go down to the ninety-nine-cents store and frame those pictures. Put them up like you're proud of her. Make sure she knows."

She nodded at Mirella, once, and then left to throw away the bottles and fix a plate for Mr. Jones. Mirella watched her go, her little body and the load of bottles. She saw Mrs. Jones dump the bottles into the garbage, then place her hand on Penelope's cheek and stoop down to whisper something in the girl's ear that made her shine all over.

Penelope never looked at Mirella with that kind of pleasure. Even though her daughter was gone, Mrs. Jones still had that instinct about her. Mirella hadn't felt any maternal aptitude in years—that ability to soothe and protect. When Penelope was a baby, mothering had been easy. Penelope bit at her breasts, and her arms ached and her back bent from nights spent rocking her, and she panicked whenever she ran a fever or fell, but the girl had been so small, so indisputably hers.

Mirella still marveled at Penelope, sometimes—the way she now expertly shook cereal into her blue breakfast bowl, the adult stance she assumed, hands on her hips, when she gargled in the bathroom, her head tipped back and the water running, how she swirled her fingertips in paint and then tapped at her rice paper in patterns Mirella couldn't discern. The ordinariness of life with Penelope could still astound her; she was Mirella's greatest anchor in this city. But every day, Penelope became less hers. Mirella saw it in the way Penelope sat with one ankle resting on her knee, her leg bent at a ninety-degree angle, a masculine way for a little girl to sit. She had all of Ralph's American habits—feet up on the table, shoes on the couch; she preferred her potato salad white, without capers and without the beets that stained it pink. Even her Spanish—one of the last things just the two of them shared—seemed like a trick she was constantly practicing. She savored her consonants for too long, rounded her vowels, as if she were giving a speech instead of speaking.

Ralph and Penelope were building a language of their own now, too. She had started staying up late to listen to records with him when he came home from the store. For hours, the two of them sat curled up on the olive sofa, singing along to Ralph's favorite albums, until Mirella barged into the living room and lifted the needle off the track, and sent them both to bed.

Mirella could always sense the edges of the girl's cheerfulness, the careful plotting behind everything she ever said: her invitations for Mirella to join her in a game of checkers, her wondering aloud in the hallway where she had left her colored pencils, her traipsing into the bedroom because there was a knot in her hair she couldn't unravel on her own. Mirella knew that she was never the one Penelope was truly seeking; she wanted her father, and Mirella was the one who happened to be around.

With Mrs. Jones gone, Penelope remained where she was, swinging her head in time to the music. The girl was humming to herself, her eyes shut, her shoulders twisting to the music, and Ralph was enclosed behind a wall of guests. Mirella knew no one would miss her, so she weaved through the crowd back to the stairs and walked up to the second floor where she could be alone.

The belching bass notes followed her into the bedroom. She kicked off her heels and lay on the bed in the dark, staring up at the ceiling. She was spending more and more time in this bed, staring at things, letting her mind empty out until she couldn't remember where she was. She wasn't on Halsey, in Brooklyn, or in this country at all. She wasn't back in Aguas Frescas with Ramona either. She wasn't anywhere.

Her wedding dress still hung in the closet; she had seen Penelope's hands pass over it. It was a simple white dress she had bought at A&S the morning they went to city hall. Ralph ordered a Dominican cake with guava filling, and they had fed oversized slices to each other, in one of the booths at Sheckley's, Lionel bringing over rounds and rounds of beer on the house. She had liked that party. Later on, Ralph carried her up the stairs of his building on Marcy Avenue, and they made love in front of an open window, the curtains dancing in the night breeze. It was different than the boy-and-girl love she'd known in the mountains; Ralph was strong, and he could lift her up and move her around beneath him with the simple hook of his arm. They didn't have to hide and sneak behind the schoolhouse or by the river. They were home. Mirella wrapped her legs around Ralph's waist, and she shouted and moaned. Ralph squeezed her close and kissed her ear, a loud smacking sound.

After, he lit his pipe, and put on a song. Mirella listened from where she lay, hot, under the covers, and thought that she wanted a lush life, too, just like the man in the song—more beer and more bars, more of Ralph swinging her around the dance floor, his hands on her waist, and then bringing her back to their little place.

She imagined her father must have been a man like Ralph—of great designs and striving. She hadn't met anyone, in Aguas Frescas or the United States, who was so full of dreams. He had no reason for his boldness, and yet he walked as if he were the tallest man in every room. He didn't talk much about his life in Harlem, but Mirella knew Ralph's childhood had been as mean and lonesome as hers. They both knew what it was to go from no one to one another. Together, she thought, they had a chance to build something of their own: a business, a family, a life.

While Ralph padded around the apartment naked to fix them two glasses of ice water, Mirella called out to him. "I have to call my mother! I have to call her and say, 'Mami! Me casé con un morenito.'" She translated for Ralph and he laughed and said she shouldn't forget to mention she was Mrs. Grand now—the first and only. After he left the boys' home, Ralph had picked his own last name; there had been no Grands before them.

"Mami?"

Penelope was at the door again.

"Qué quieres niña?" Mirella asked. She was exasperated with talking, with English.

"Why did you leave the party, Mami?"

"Porque me quería ir."

"What?"

Mirella sighed. "I was tired, hija."

Penelope crept into the dark room. She lay next to her mother on the bed, the sheets rustling as she crossed her legs at the ankle and tucked her hands behind her head.

"Mami, will you tell me a story about when you were a girl in Aguas Frescas?"

"I told you I was tired."

"Will you tell me about Abuela Ramona?"

Mirella put her fingers to her temples.

"Mami?"

"Shhh."

"I miss her."

"Cállate niña."

Mirella stared at the ceiling, sank into the white plaster, let it fill her eyes, her ears, her nose. She could hardly hear the Mingus, or Ralph, or Penelope fidgeting on the bed beside her. She allowed herself to drift.

"Mami?"

8

ADRIFT

Penelope was working in colors when the snow arrived. It was only November, but the branches drooped under the weight of the clean, glimmering stuff. She had brought out her pastels in an effort to combat the white. Her mind turned toward the mountains, the red dirt of Aguas Frescas, the summers with her grandmother. She clipped a square of cotton paper to the easel. Sweeps of vermilion, brown, and fresh green became the mountains, patches of orange for where the sun warmed the earth. It was not painting, but it was the closest she had come in years. She had needed the color, a smudge of every pink and blue and yellow in her evening sky.

When the phone rang, she lifted it to her ear, one hand still drawing. It was late for Pop to be calling. She said hello.

"Penny girl, have you heard from your father?"

It was Miss Beckett again. Penelope sighed and let the old woman know she had seen her father earlier in the evening and that she was interrupting.

"He won't answer the phone, and I've called at least a dozen times."

"He's probably just asleep."

"Oh God," Miss Beckett said, the *God* was muffled as if the phone had slipped from her mouth and the receiver was pressed against skin.

"I put him to bed before I left, Una. Relax. You're making something out of nothing."

Penelope and Ralph had eaten spaghetti and meatballs from two cans, shared a bottle of root beer. They watched *Men of Boys Town*, and Ralph paused the film over and over to tell her stories about his years in the boys' home in Harlem. He told her about how eagerly he awaited the weekly macaroni night, and the time he had been forced to kneel on rice because the nuns found dirty pictures carved into the pew where he sat every Sunday although he'd had nothing to do with the crude etchings. He seemed worn out from all his remembering by the end of the night, and Penelope had left him in his bed, only his chin visible above the beige sheets.

"Well, he was awake when I went to see him."

"Excuse me?"

"We had plans . . . to play checkers."

Miss Beckett spoke meekly as if she didn't actually want anyone to hear. Penelope asked what had happened.

"I have a key, so I let myself in and I brought up the mail like I always do. You know he can't get down to the box—and when I gave it all to him, he froze up, like a corpse. He got a postcard, you see. From her."

"What did it say?"

"I don't know. But as soon as he was through with it, he asked me to leave."

Miss Beckett began to sob, and Penelope ignored her sniveling.

"I'll find him."

"Will you wait for me? I want to come along."

"Stay where you are," Penelope snapped, and Miss Beckett gasped as if she had been shoved. She resisted the urge to tell the old woman she had done enough harm for one night—why would she ever give Ralph the postcard?

"I'll call you once I've found him."

Penelope felt the panic as soon as she hung up the phone. Her pulse rose loudly into her ears as if her heart were suddenly playing an internal, frantic music. Was this her fault? Had she summoned her mother somehow? She looked at her drawing of the mountains, their mocking swipes of red. She ran out of the attic in a sweater and boots and a pair of gloves, and she didn't bother to close the door behind her.

Out on the street, the cold seeped through the wool of her sweater, the coils of her hair. Penelope ran toward Bedford, her feet landing hard, crushing prints into the snow. *He's fine,* she thought as she sped up the dark street. *He's fine, he's fine. This time I am here. He's fine.* She didn't see anyone else, any signs of life, until she reached Franklin Avenue, all lit up and noisy, weary-looking people surfacing from the subway and slogging through the snow. It was after ten.

A string of lights hung over the entrance to Sheckley's. It looked like a barn in the middle of Bed-Stuy, all unpainted pinewood and shutters over the windows. The same shabby sign hung over the door. Penelope pushed her way inside. The bar was dark and warm, the old radiators hissing heat. The red vinyl booths were still there, and through the glass French doors at the rear Penelope could see that the new management had kept the garden, although everything was frozen over.

Ralph was at the bar. His head hung down on the counter, his fingers curled around a half-empty glass. His cane lay on the floor. Penelope ran past the man at the door who asked to see her ID, the young people sharing pitchers of frosty beer in their booths, swirling French fries in ketchup and mayonnaise. They were all out of the storm, keeping each other warm.

Penelope shook Ralph when she reached him.

"Pop, wake up. It's time to go."

There was a man behind the bar, drying glasses with a frayed white cloth. "He's fine, miss," he said. "Just sleeping it off."

Penelope ignored him, held her fingers under Ralph's nose to make sure he was breathing. His lower lip dangled. She shook her father again.

"Seriously, miss, I'm telling you he's all right."

Penelope finally looked up across the bar. The man cleaning glasses wore a black T-shirt and horn-rimmed glasses, his curly hair pushed off his forehead. He had brown eyes and skin, a tiny stud in each ear.

"Who are you?" Penelope asked.

"I'm Jon."

"Fuck you, Jon. You're a lousy bartender and a shitty human being."

"Excuse me?"

"You had no right serving liquor to my father. But you don't care what happens to him as long as he remembers to tip after every drink, right?"

"Look, lady, how could I turn him away? His picture is on the wall. He just seemed like a nice old man—"

"He's sixty-three," Penelope spat, and she wasn't sure whether she had said his age as proof that he wasn't old, or proof that he was.

She turned back to Ralph and shook him harder now, with her hands on both of his shoulders. Ralph's head jerked up, and he snorted. He opened one eye, tentatively. He said her name.

"Penny, you're five. I mean, you turned five here. You remember that?"

Penelope could see the birthday in flashes: her father's friends raising their glasses of amber and gold ale, Ralph petting her head while everyone sang. Mirella in a bloodred dress, smoking her slender cigarette, nudging a cake toward her.

"That was a nice birthday wasn't it? Your mother made that cake. That was such a nice cake. With yellow sugar flowers? We had such a nice time."

Penelope could see the postcard sticking out of Ralph's pocket. It was a creased and battered card with a white border, but Penelope couldn't make out much else in the dark. Her father reached to pull out the card and show it to her.

"Not here," she said and pulled her father's hand away. She twisted the stool so that he faced her. He began to slump forward, and Penelope separated her legs into a lunge to shoulder his weight. It wasn't very hard to keep him upright—Ralph was all bone and loose skin. The bartender dashed out from behind the bar.

"I don't need your help," Penelope told him, but he stood behind her anyway, his hands raised to catch Ralph if he fell.

Ralph's head hung to the side, his mouth open, and Penelope patted his cheek.

"Jesus Christ, Pop, will you wake up? I need you to stay awake."

"I'm sorry, Penny," he said. "I'm sorry I didn't give you more birthdays . . . more birthdays when I had the chance."

Ralph swayed and the stool spun. The bartender was beside her now, and he asked where they lived.

"Let me help you with your father," he said. "There's no way you can take him that far yourself."

Penelope drew her eyebrows together in the Grand look of disgust.

"You don't know me. You don't know what I can do. And you've done enough."

"Can I call a car for you at least?"

Penelope turned back to her father. His eyes were closed again; his mouth hung open. If she removed the pressure of her hands from his shoulders, he would fall.

"Fine," she said. "Hurry."

The bartender ducked behind the bar and dialed. Penelope leaned against her father to wait, one shoulder against his, the toes of his oxfords scraping the pinewood floor. A few of the customers in their booths had stopped to watch. They stared at Ralph, drunk, his peacoat still on, his eyes shut. They stared at Penelope, too, jacketless, wind-blown hair, holding him up with gloved hands. She stared back at them, unable to read concern or amusement in their faces. They seemed to just be looking. Penelope wished, precipitously, violently, that she was one of them, drinking in a booth with people who knew her name, the drunk man at the bar an interruption to her night and not the center of it.

Ralph opened one eye.

"You can't keep anything in this life, Penny. Not a thing." He started to fumble around for the postcard again, as if he had forgotten where he had put it.

"You want some water, Pop? That will help."

"Not if I pee myself, Penny. What if I pee myself?"

Penelope put her hand in his fro, speckled with drops of melting snow. "Has that happened before, Pop? Have you peed yourself before?"

Ralph started to cry.

"I didn't want you to know."

The bartender announced the taxi was on its way. Penelope told her father, asked him to stand up for her. She promised she would help, make sure he didn't fall.

Ralph placed his feet on the floor and sank into his legs when he slid off the stool. Penelope wrapped his arm around her neck. She gripped him around the waist, and they moved toward the door, Ralph throwing his feet out in front of him. He didn't walk all that differently drunk than he did sober. Penelope had to steer him, and he leaned hard on her, his palm weighing heavy on her shoulder. The bartender picked up Ralph's cane and followed them. He held the door open for them as they left.

Penelope eased Ralph down the steps. It took all of her focus to guide Ralph through the drifts. The sidewalk was all soft snow, powder that unfolded into a path as they inched toward the corner.

"It's cold out here," Ralph said.

"That's 'cause you're not wearing your boots."

"You two, you could never stop fighting. Like you didn't understand what family was for. But I knew. Me and your mother, we had our way. Before I messed it all up over that goddamned store—"

"The store was important, Pop. It brought the people together."

"What neighborhood? What people? All those years . . . I'd have been better off trying to make her happy."

"You can't make anyone else happy, Pop."

Ralph stood tall and still, squinted at Penelope, as if he were suddenly sober.

"Of course you can. Please tell me I at least taught you that."

He waited for her answer, as if any moment she might come to her senses and say, *Yes, yes, that's what you taught me.*

Ralph shook his head. "Here," he said, reaching into his pocket. "It wasn't for me."

He held the postcard faceup, her mother's handwriting visible under the streetlights. Penelope took the card from him, stuffed it into the pocket of her jeans.

The livery car turned the corner, its high beams shining parallel paths into the snow. Penelope helped her father into the car, and then ran over to the other side to let herself in.

"Where to?" the driver asked.

"Halsey Street," she said, and they took off in silence, breaking new ground in the snow.

Penelope didn't finish with her father until after two. She brewed coffee and soaked his feet in hot water, held a bucket for him to vomit, threw away the empty bottles of beer, the handle of rum. When she left, the city trucks hadn't arrived yet to plow, and there was no salt on the sidewalks. The snow was up past her ankles, and it took effort to trudge back to Greene. More than once, she thought about stopping under one of the streetlamps to read the postcard, but the idea made her shake. The postcard felt volatile somehow, as if she could set it off if she weren't careful. If she paused to look, it might explode in her hands. She kept walking east, avoiding the patches of ice, a reel of her father sick and moaning, his ankles swollen, replaying in her head.

At the corner of her new block, Penelope passed two lovers wrestling in the snow. The street was otherwise empty, and they took up the whole sidewalk, pummeling each other with fistfuls of powder. They tugged at each other, pushed each other away, their back-and-forth so quick it seemed synchronized. They were panting through the violence of it, giggling and grunting whenever they got ahold of each other. She didn't see they were white until she had stepped off the curb to avoid their public play. She saw their flushed faces in the light from the streetlamp, the hunger in their eyes as they swung at each other, cold smiles stretching across the width of their faces. Penelope guessed they were a few years younger than she was, recent college grads, fresh to the neighborhood, and far away from their families. They had probably found each other at a house party, or maybe in a café. She wanted their night to be her night, and their life hers.

The lights were off in the yellow house, and Penelope rounded the landings slowly, climbing the four flights of stairs with leaden legs. When she reached the fourth floor, she stepped into a pool of light, shining down from the attic. She remembered that she hadn't closed the door behind her when she went running out to save Ralph. She reached her room and saw Marcus sitting on the floor.

"Penelope," he said and set one of her acrylic-on-wood paintings back in the open trunk. "I came up to say hello, and I saw your door was open."

Penelope took off her boots at the door, her eyes scanning the room, as if she were trying to recognize the place in which she had found herself. Marcus began to stammer.

"I promise I've only been here a few minutes. I wanted to make sure the heat was on up here, given this is the first snow of the year, and I saw the trunk was open, and I couldn't help myself. I didn't mean to snoop, but you said once you'd like for me to take a look—"

It took her a few moments to make sense of all that Marcus had said. He asked if she was all right.

"It's been a bad day," she said. "I'm not all here."

Marcus asked whether he should leave, but he didn't move toward the door.

"Your work is spectacular," he said.

"It's all old."

"I'm no art critic, but really—wow. These paintings are terrific."

Terrific and *spectacular*, Penelope repeated the words to herself. They were large and vacuous, but she gathered them to her anyway.

"Where's Samantha?"

"Stuck in the city."

"I saw people coming out of the station on Nostrand. The trains are still running."

"Ah, yes, well, Samantha doesn't even like taking the subway during the daytime, and it's impossible to get a cab in Manhattan right now."

"I see."

"She'll be very comfortable in her office. She's spent nights there before, if she's preparing something for a client."

Penelope said nothing. The wind outside was shrill. It shook the branches of the trees, the current of air ripped over their heads.

"Are you all right?" Marcus said. "I've never seen you so distracted."

"You hardly know me."

"I thought our plan was to become friends."

He grinned at her, his face plaintive and sweet, and Penelope wondered if this was how he had learned to get his way with women—his propitiating tone, his earnest smile. He was on board already, Penelope could tell, especially since his wife had left him alone in the storm. He wouldn't require very much convincing.

Penelope peeled off her sweater, unraveled the scarf from her neck. She tossed the postcard out of her pants pocket onto the heap of wool and she stepped away. She was back in the tank top she had been wearing before Miss Beckett called, when she was conjuring up the mountain. She wasn't wearing a bra, and she turned to face Marcus, as if she were looking for something in the room. He looked away, back to the trunk, but Penelope knew he had already seen the shape of her breasts under the thin cotton. She was cool and distracted as she pulled an RISD sweatshirt from the top of the hamper. He had already seen what she wanted him to see, and now she could cover herself with this ratty old thing, its sleeves shorn short, the collar ripped out. A large bleach stain covered its left side.

"I'm going to have a drink. Would you like one?"

"Oh God, yes," Marcus said. He was sitting on the bed now, cradling a wood panel on his lap.

Penelope began to cut open a grapefruit. The ceramic bowl on the table was piled with a motley assortment of fruits—grapes, dates, oranges, yellow apples, plums. The ruby pulp spilled onto the tabletop as Penelope quartered the fruit. She squeezed the segments, seed side up, over two glasses. She filled them with as much juice as the fruit would yield. She finished each glass off with several ounces of gin and a few sloshes of bright red bitters. She stirred with her finger, then washed her hands in the china sink and carried the drinks back to the bed.

Marcus accepted his glass and thanked her. He took a large swallow, without wincing, and ran his tongue around the rim to catch the pulp.

"To your art," he said, raising his glass. They clinked.

Together they went through Penelope's work, poring over her sketches, her pen-and-ink drawings. There were fewer paintings, but Marcus claimed to love each that he saw. He commented on her art with the savvy of any humanities major who had sat through one semester's worth of art history lectures, any man who visited the major museums along Fifth Avenue a few times a year. He vaguely complimented her composition, assigned emotions to her colors, and gazed at her as often as he did the art. He appraised her work with light as striking or haunting, once, delicate. She didn't mind his imprecision. She thawed under his attention and with each swill of her gin. *Fuck Mirella,* she thought. Her mother was an ocean away, and yet she was here. *Fuck the postcard.*

She showed Marcus the portrait she had done of Ralph when she was in high school. It was the sort of painting that made you feel as if you knew someone intimately, even if all you could see was his profile, from the shoulders up. It was the piece she believed had gotten her into RISD.

Marcus held Ralph at arm's length. "This is your father? I adore this. It's like the pipe is a part of him."

"He makes that face all the time," Penelope said, smiling at the sternness of her father's expression in the painting. His eyebrows were pushed together and his mouth set in a line as he bit down on the pipe. It was obvious to Penelope that the Ralph in this painting had not yet lived through his accident. His fro was darker and his face rounder, and he seemed freer. His eyes were a clearer gray than the smoke that drifted over the rest of the canvas.

Marcus leaned the painting against the bed and took up another Penelope had pulled from the closet. It was one of the last pieces she had completed at RISD, when she had already made up her mind to leave. She had painted a car crash at the intersection of two Brooklyn thoroughfares. Three lanes of traffic stretched in either direction, and in the foreground stood a gold passenger car, wrecked. It was intact at the ends, but blown open at the center, as if it had been crushed from either side, and then imploded. It was an impossible wreck, the metal warped around a cavity where the passengers should have been. A crowd of people gathered around the accident, the car with the empty center.

"This is so powerful," Marcus said, his cheeks and ears flushed from the gin.

"My professor called it overdetermined. She said it was cold. Too precise. 'Where's the feeling? Where's the feeling?' she said. It's as if she wanted me to confess I'd survived a car crash, and then paint that. Maybe slash open an old scar, and smear some real blood on there. She told me the same thing over and over again, but I could never please her."

The words stuck to the roof of Penelope's mouth—*I could never please her*—and it seemed obvious to her she had been right to leave RISD. If she couldn't give her teachers what they wanted, if they would never accept her, there was no point to sticking around. Why steep in someone else's disappointment? Why linger where you aren't wanted?

Penelope carried the painting back to the closet where she kept the canvases too large for the trunk. She returned to the bed, folded her legs underneath her. The snow hadn't let up since they started looking at her paintings, and Penelope wasn't sure how much time had passed. The sky was pearly lavender, a trick of the light. A steady stream of white flakes fell across the window.

"You are so brave."

Penelope laughed. "Me?"

"Yes, you. Absolutely you."

Penelope took the glass from him and drank.

"You underestimate yourself, Penelope. You go on runs in the *rain* and you teach *children* and you *paint*. You walk around Bed-Stuy at two a. m. during snowstorms like no one could ever touch you! I've never met anyone like you. You are exquisite. You are *epic*."

"Easy there," Penelope said, but she hummed inwardly. She could have Marcus; she would have Marcus. He smiled at her and stole back his glass; he swayed across the room and uncapped the stout bottle of gin. He emptied a few more ounces into his glass, the pulp swirling up into the liquor, tinting the gin a cloudy pink. He was close now.

"It must come from your mother," he said. "Daughters get either their courage or their fear from their mothers."

Marcus made a face after another swig of gin, as if he were shocked by his harshness. "I know being a mother isn't easy—believe me. Samantha's always saying I can't quite grasp how differently you love a child when you've grown one with your own body. The bond—it's carnal."

"Is it? Then where's Samantha now?"

Penelope stood and snatched Marcus's glass from him, took a long, slow drink.

"The snow," he said.

"I never believed any of that stuff—the primal bond, mothers and daughters. It sounds like a convenient excuse, a way for a mother to always defend herself—*But I gave you life.* As if that matters. As if I care."

Marcus stared at her, eyes wide, as if he could finally detect the slow whir of anger in her, louder tonight than usual. She held up the glass to his lips.

"One more sip and then I'm cutting you off," she said, and he was distracted by the drink before him, the way Penelope kept her eyes on his while he drank. She drained what he left. She could feel the liquor now, the way it blurred nearly everything in the room, except for his face. She latched onto it for clarity, to stay grounded while her head swam, the insides of her mouth burned. She was finally ready to win him.

"Do you ever think that maybe Samantha isn't here because she's fucking someone else?"

"Of course not," Marcus said, his expression newly grim. "I might be somewhat of a loser lately, but that isn't Sam. She just didn't want to see me tonight."

"Do you ever think that maybe you could be fucking someone else?"

Marcus looked stunned, as if he hadn't been playing along all night. He stared at her intently, trying to read her, although she had done her best to make it all very plain. She placed her hands on his shoulders and drew nearer to him. They stood close enough that their socked feet touched. Marcus was breathing hard, silent.

"You don't always have to be so careful, Marcus."

She leaned back to look into his face and so that he would have to be the one to pull her closer, the one to begin.

He kissed her with his eyes open. She stared back at him, skated into the sea green. He slid his hands into her hair, pulled the curls back from the crown of her head. She squeezed fistfuls of his hair in her sweating palms. They found the bed and lay down, Marcus lifting the RISD sweatshirt over her head, and then the gray tank top, splattered with paint. She felt the hot skin under his T-shirt, yanked at the drawstring of his flannel pants.

She knew better than to say she loved the way he was with Grace, that the two of them were the best things about being back in Brooklyn, so she muttered that he was beautiful, that she had wanted him since she first saw him. Marcus didn't say anything, but he ran his tongue along her collarbone, squeezed her hip bones hard between his fingers. She pressed herself against him and they both moaned, and it was obvious— for months, they had both been after exactly this.

The wind beat down on the yellow house, and the snow began to cake on the windowpane, whiting out the lavender night. Neither of them thought of the storm, as they sank into each other on the narrow bed. They didn't shut the door and they weren't quiet, as if the whole house was theirs.

9

WINTER

In the morning, Marcus kissed her awake. There was a familiar ring in her ears, and a pressure at her temples, but they dissolved when he reached for her hair, her breasts, and climbed onto her again. Now that they were soberer, the sex was tender, less brusque. They took their time. They slept again for a while until he murmured something about waking Grace. Penelope stayed in bed while he pulled on his pajama pants, his T-shirt. His lips skimmed her nose when he kissed her good-bye. He padded out of the attic softly.

It was still snowing outside, although the light was no longer lavender, but the cold blue of early day. With Marcus gone, the clanging returned to her head. She spread her hand over the side of the bed where he had slept and bundled up his forgotten underwear in her fist.

The phone woke her twice. Once, it was Principal Pine announcing the school would be closed today, which was good news because Penelope was badly hungover, even though she was still thick in the afterglow of sex; her limbs hummed, and the center of her was pudding, silky and sweet. The second call was Miss Beckett admonishing her for not calling the night before. She wanted to know whether Penelope had plans to bring her father breakfast, to shovel the sidewalk before the snow got too high.

"I'd like to come and see him, too, but I can't get there by myself, not with snow halfway to my neck—"

Penelope mumbled that she would go by and collect the woman in a while. She needed to stay in bed for just a while longer, replaying the night, but only the hours after she had returned from Sheckley's. The two of them going over all her canvases, Marcus's praise, the grapefruit rinds, the long pours of gin, then the fucking, Marcus fucking. It was the perfect memory.

Eventually, she smelled waffle batter and chocolaty coffee rising up to the attic. Marcus and Grace were making breakfast together. How she wanted to join them. She couldn't hear Samantha's voice, so the landlady was probably still in the city, held up in the snow. The thought buoyed her: a frozen bridge and a river were keeping her away. Penelope got up and dressed, still damp and aching.

Bread, she thought. *He'll need bread.* She waltzed down the stairs and onto the avenue in search of a bodega still open in the snow. She bought a can of coffee and a loaf of French bread down the block, then forded the large hills of snow across the blocks to Halsey Street.

She spent the day outside shoveling snow, first in front of their mud-brown house, then all along the block. It was better than being stuck inside with Ralph and Miss Beckett. The old woman was fawning over Ralph, serving him cup after cup of coffee, patting down his hair, and nestling closer to him on the couch so that their thighs touched. Ralph didn't reciprocate, but he didn't stop her either. He was back to making speeches, pretending he had not snuck out to the bar and wept in public over Mirella, as if the postcard had never arrived. He used the night before as material for his sermonizing: Watch and see how quickly the city trucks arrive to plow now that Bed-Stuy is full of white people! And not a soul in that bar had been a day over thirty—he hoped the bartender was checking IDs.

It was better to shovel than to fume, to think about how her months in New York hadn't made any difference. She had left Pittsburgh, and he was no better—still living on the second floor, still drinking. He hadn't phoned a physical therapist, or started to do the exercises Dr. Elias had given to him. When her back ached and she couldn't stand it anymore, she brought the shovel inside, washed out the coffeepot, and turned out all the lights. Miss Beckett and Ralph had fallen asleep on the couch. She left to find the snow was already deeper. She let herself into the yellow house, cold and emptied out. Marcus was waiting for her again in the attic.

They started earlier this time, so they had several hours, between when Grace was put to bed and when they expected Samantha to arrive. She had phoned about spending a second night in the city—the weather was bad, she had so much work. They fucked two times, three times, Penelope lost count, long pours of gin in between. They sat up in bed, naked, the door to the attic open so they could hear Grace if she woke, but they didn't expect her to. They talked, Penelope prostrate between his legs, Marcus's hands on her shoulders.

It had hardly been twenty-four hours, but it felt like much longer, as if they had been holed up in the attic for days. It was quiet and dark enough in the house that it felt to Penelope that they were very far away, in a cabin of their own. The snow had started to slow. This would likely be the last night they could share this easily. It would be harder when the landlady returned. They would have to plan around her, shut the door. Penelope said so.

"Let's not think about that," Marcus said. "Not when I have you here." He kissed her ear. "And to think it all started with your art and ended up with—" He made a nasty joke, and Penelope laughed, tossing her hair. She was certain that she looked gorgeous—she could tell by the way he looked at her. Penelope asked about his writing.

He had wanted to be a travel journalist, but a serious one, who wrote about history and culture, current events, like a pop anthropologist, but not as dry. But since they had Grace, it made sense to stay local and write whatever he could get paid to write, usually reviews and profiles. He had written a few things about Brooklyn—essays about its renaissance were in high demand.

"I want to read something of yours," Penelope said. "I want to be walking around and see your name on the cover of some magazine—*Marcus Middle Name Harper*."

"Anthony. My middle name is Anthony." He laughed and that was all they needed to start up again. Penelope sat atop him and began to turn her hips. He covered her eyes with his hands and tilted her head back. He slipped his finger in her mouth, his lips on her throat. For all of those minutes, she didn't hate where she was. She thought of nothing but Marcus, and she murmured his name, until he covered her mouth, gently.

Penelope woke to the sound of a tiny gasp, a whimper. She sat up in the bed and strained to hear. It was Grace. She was calling for her father.

Penelope slipped from the bed and surveyed the mess in the attic. Clothes were flung everywhere—on the back of the chair at the breakfast table, over the windowsill, underneath the bed. Her drawing of the mountains was still clipped to the easel, the floor littered with the mugs they had used to drink when she ran out of glasses. The odor of sex and sweat. Penelope opened the window to let in the night and dissipate the evidence of what they had done. Marcus was dead asleep, and she didn't want to wake him. She liked the sight of him, naked in her bed, his arms tucked close to his chest as if he were trying to rock himself. Was this what marriage was like? Night after night, the same man, his bare ass up, his drool on your pillow?

When they were together, it didn't matter that he was white or that she had accomplished nothing with her life. Their lives were far, but they wanted each other. It was enough.

Penelope dressed quickly, her body still aching and damp. She followed the sound of crying down to Grace's door and knocked once before pushing it open. Grace was upright in her bed, her back unnaturally straight, knees clutched to her chest. She was making a great effort to keep quiet, her breaths ragged, snot spilling onto her pajamas. Her red hair, woven into a bedtime braid, was coming undone around her shoulders.

"Did you hear it, Penelope? The crash? Something happened outside."

Penelope hadn't heard anything, and she said so. She doubted it could have been a gunshot—not in this weather. Everyone was inside.

"It was terrible," Grace said. "Like bones breaking."

"It was probably just the storm."

She asked whether Grace wanted to look out the window to see what had made the sound, but the girl shook her head.

"Please, could you just sit with me?"

Penelope sat on the edge of the bed while the little girl sobbed. She wiped her cheeks with a handkerchief on the nightstand.

"My little brother died in this house. Did you know that? He died inside my mother in the middle of the night, but we didn't know it. We all had to go out onto the street to try and flag down a cab, but we couldn't find one for a long time. It was snowing then, too." Grace shuddered. "You don't believe in ghosts, do you, Penelope?"

"I don't know," Penelope said. The only person she had loved who had died was her grandmother, but she liked the idea of Ramona haunting her, disembodied, but somehow still close.

"If your little brother is a ghost, I don't think he'd haunt you. He'd probably just want to be near you. Keep you safe." Perhaps that would comfort her. She petted the girl's head.

"That's impossible," Grace said, sniffing. "I know there's no such thing as ghosts—I'm just being superstitious because of the sound I heard. That's why I was calling Daddy, but he didn't come. And he forgot to leave the light on for me in the hall."

Penelope felt a flash of guilt that the girl had been left alone. She smoothed the hair back from Grace's forehead, gathering up the loose strands in her hand. She unwound the braid and began to twist the hair again, more tightly this time.

"Did you play in the snow today?"

Grace shook her head.

"Maybe tomorrow. You can meet some other kids on the block, make some friends. It's not good to stay inside all the time."

"I already have friends, Penelope. I just live too far away now to have any playdates." She started to explain the cliques in her elementary school, the way they had formed in kindergarten, based on neighborhood. "There's the Gramercy girls, and the West End girls, the Prospect Park girls . . . I used to be a Hudson Street girl."

Penelope wasn't sure how to comfort her. There likely wouldn't be any Orchard School playdates in Bed-Stuy at least for a while longer. Grace blew her nose in the handkerchief.

"It could be worse," she said. "One girl in my grade just moved to Queens. No one's *ever* going to visit her."

Penelope couldn't help but laugh. Grace looked at her, puzzled, and then she smiled too, although it was obvious she wasn't quite sure what she had done to amuse Penelope.

Grace switched on the light and lifted a mealy paperback off the nightstand. On the cover, a white child in a long dress sat on a bench on a platform of a railroad station. She carried a large carpetbag on her lap and wore ribbons in her hair.

"It's about a girl with no place to go," Grace said, and she asked whether she could read to Penelope. It was what she did with her father, sometimes with her mother, to help her fall asleep. Penelope agreed.

They read until the girl drifted off, and Penelope covered her with blankets, swept aside the curtains to peer out onto the street. The girl was right. The storm had brought down a tree, a massive London plane. It had snapped cleanly in two: the trunk along the edge of the sidewalk, the branches spreading like arms into the street. Penelope returned to Marcus. She would tell him about the tree in the morning, point it out to him from her window.

Samantha arrived before the sun. They were naked under Penelope's sheets when they heard the front door unlock, the landlady making her way up the stairs. Marcus cursed and flew out of the bed, rummaging for his pants. He ran shirtless out of the attic, and Penelope opened her eyes to the sight of him fleeing. Soon, she heard their voices on one of the landings below, husband and wife greeting each other. It took all her strength to stand and close the door. She tried to return to sleep as the house stirred to life below her. She heard gurgling in the coffeepot, Grace's voice joining her parents, the three of them resuming their routine.

The phone rang and Principal Pine announced Penelope would be needed that morning at PS 23. One day off for snow was more than enough, the principal said, as if she were the one who had decided the public schools would open today. Penelope dragged herself from the bed and started to brush her teeth at the china sink.

A crowd had gathered below, the block congregating around the little disaster, marked off with orange caution tape. There were a few black couples, younger than Ralph but not by much, outside in snow boots and coats, shaking their heads and glancing up and down the street, as if assessing the sturdiness of the trees in front of their homes. There were a few yuppies, too, shivering in robes and pajama pants. Nearly everyone was a couple: the units of life on their block. There were other streets with more single people, four or five hipsters to a floor of a house, but this stretch of Greene wasn't one of them. Penelope spotted Samantha outside in a parka and riding boots, running her fingers through her pale hair, crumpled like crepe paper. Marcus stood beside her, holding a silver thermos that steamed in the cold. He had his other arm wrapped firmly around her shoulders.

The children at PS 23 were wild after the day out of school. At the start of every period, they stormed into the art room, chattering and whining, and all the noise made it harder for Penelope to tolerate their usual accidents: spilled paint, a student falling out of a chair, glitter in the eye. The things she liked about teaching—the boundaries, control, their need for her help and approval—were all gone, as if the blizzard had swept it all away.

She didn't want to be an art teacher today. She wanted to be back in the attic with Marcus. She made her rounds among the children, but she was replaying their twenty-four hours in her mind. She conjured up his lavender skin in the storm light, the quickness of his breath, the way he had laughed when they sat up talking, halfway sober.

"Miss Grand, Miss Grand! Hello, Miss Grand!"

A child was shouting at her, a mixed girl named Camille. She had bushy hair and a tea-and-milk complexion, a handkerchief tied around her head, little plastic skulls for earrings. Her parents were both artists; her mother was some kind of designer, and her father built mobiles. They had asked Penelope more than once about their daughter's prospects as an artist. Camille had all the accessories of a miniature artist—her beaded bracelets stacked nearly to her elbows—and none of the talent or focus.

She waved her little hand violently over her head, let out a big sigh when Penelope reached her table.

"Miss Grand, I'm done." She dropped her hand on the table as if she had been holding it up for hours. "I *been* done."

Out of ideas, Penelope had given the third graders a break from their long-term projects so they could work on pieces inspired by their snow day, and they were allowed to work in any medium they had already learned. Giving them so much freedom had been a mistake—she could see that now. For every kid working with colored pencils, there was a kid making a snowball out of papier-mâché or constructing a shoe-box diorama of a street covered in cotton-ball snow. They were running out of time. They were using all the supplies. They were making a mess.

Camille held up an expressionless snowman taking up half of the sheet of construction paper. He had a stub of carrot for a nose, a pipe rammed into his face, a dimensionless hat flat across his round head.

"Do you think this is finished?"

"Yup, Miss Grand. It's definitely finished, and I don't know what to do now, can I be excused?"

"Did you make a snowman yesterday?"

"Nah, but I did make snow angels with my mom, and me and my brother went sliding down a hill with the blow-up raft we take to the pool in the summer, and he fell off and busted his nose."

"Why didn't you draw any of that?"

"'Cause I'm bored, Miss Grand. This class is boring."

Penelope felt her eyes water, and she was surprised. She was not a crier, and a snotty eight-year-old was not going to bring her to tears.

"Boring or not, you're here, so you better fix it."

Camille looked at her aghast.

"Do you get to skip out on your other classes? No—so, stop trying to take the easy way out."

"Maybe you should make some smoke come out of his pipe," said a boy named Benny. "And fix his hat. It looks like it's about to fall off."

Benny was a pale Dominican kid with hazel eyes and protruding ears, a diligent though unskilled artist. He was one of those kids who volunteered to hand out supplies and stay behind to wash the board.

He usually hugged Penelope when he came in, although he was on the verge of being too old for such displays.

"How's a snowman gonna *smoke* a pipe, Benny? He's not real." Camille sucked her teeth.

"It's *art*, Camille. It doesn't have to be real."

Penelope shushed them both, and Benny turned back sullenly to his drawing. Penelope pretended to survey the work of the other kids at the table, circled the room once, and then went back to her desk. She would stay here and drink her coffee until the end of the period, forget that she was at school at all. She heard a few students call for her, but she pretended not to hear. It wasn't long before she noticed someone standing at her desk.

"I'm hungry, Miss Grand."

It was Natalie again. The girl's face looked pinched, the skin around her eyes ashen. She looked slimmer, too, as if her pants would slide right off if she moved too quickly. Was it possible for a child to lose weight over just a single snow day? Penelope asked whether the girl's mother had brought her in for free breakfast this morning.

"We got here too late, Miss Grand. Mommy overslept."

Penelope wanted to bang her fist on the table. She had forgotten to pack her own lunch, between Marcus and the tree, and she had nothing to give the girl. She scratched out a hall pass and told the girl to go to the nurse's office and stay there until lunch.

"She'll have something for you," Penelope said, although it was likely the nurse wouldn't have much more than peppermints.

Natalie took the note, lifted up the backpack larger than her whole torso, and shuffled out of the room.

"Fucking hell," Penelope said to herself, and she slurped her coffee. Who were these mothers who didn't rise early enough to feed their girls? Who left their children alone during snowstorms, then returned and assumed their place?

She hadn't met Natalie's mother, but Penelope was sure she would hate her. She'd meet her soon enough at the next parent-teacher conference, if she was one of the few parents who bothered making time to talk to the art substitute. If she came, Penelope would tell her exactly what she thought of her. And who could blame her, if she was speaking the truth? Why did women have children they would someday hate?

Penelope ran harder than usual after school that evening. The streets were clear again—no more fallen tree, and the snow had been pushed into hills at every curb. It was easy to find paths to run. Still, she found herself cursing as she recounted the day. They were children, and she shouldn't begrudge them, but she did. The students had been distracted all day, and it seemed to be proof of her incompetence. She had been meticulous over the years about sticking only to what she had mastered—drinks, sex, runs, *object studies*—so that she wouldn't have to face her own inadequacy. But her students had managed to make those dreaded feelings return. She had failed. She was nothing.

Penelope thought of the postcard from her mother, still in her jeans, on the floor, next to the pipe that heated the attic. She didn't want to throw it away, and she didn't want to know what it said either. She fantasized about checking her pockets and finding it gone.

She pushed herself to go faster, and sweat exploded over her body, even in the cold. She felt a click in her knees, and she turned in her thighs to stabilize her joints. She looked down at her feet to check her alignment, her lime green sneakers a blur. She focused on the pain.

The light was on in the vestibule of the yellow house when Penelope was done, and she ran up the stairs. She wanted to see Marcus. He would be a bright spot in her day.

When Penelope reached the fourth-floor landing, Grace dashed out of her father's study and into the hall. She flung herself into Penelope's arms. The child had never hugged her before. Penelope squeezed her back. Her face was open and radiant.

"Daddy and I are reading the same book you were reading to me last night," she said. "*Anne of Green Gables.*"

On cue, Marcus emerged from the office, scooping up the book from the floor. Grace had let it drop when she ran out of the room. He smiled at Penelope in his usual reckless way, and she beamed back at him. It was the exact face she had hoped to see.

"Hi, there," she said, and he leaned against the doorway and nodded at her, a hand on his hip. It was as seductive a posture as he could muster in front of his daughter. He didn't look the same to her, not now that she had seen him with his clothes off. She knew the other side of him, behind this meekness, his deference.

"Come in and read with us," Grace said.

Marcus slipped his hand under the hair at the nape of his daughter's neck, while Penelope still had her hand on the girl's shoulder. They were both touching her.

"Where's your mother? Is she around?"

Penelope wanted to see inside Marcus's study. She imagined a desk and a straight-backed chair, an antique typewriter that he kept just for show. She could picture the three of them on the floor, paging through the book.

Marcus stepped out of the doorway into the hall, and Penelope saw him in fuller light. The skin under his eyes was a faint blue from staying up those nights with her. He held the paperback loosely in his hand.

"Gracie, would you give me a minute to talk to Penelope?"

Grace nodded and stood on her tiptoes to kiss Penelope on the cheek before turning on her heels and slipping back into the office. How quickly children give up their allegiance. Marcus shut the door once Grace was inside.

"I've been wanting to see you all day," Penelope said.

Marcus nodded, and Penelope went to kiss him. He held up a hand to stop her.

"Penelope, these last two nights—"

And suddenly Penelope felt edgeless because she knew what would follow. He was going to erase her with his words. She cut him off.

"They were nice," Penelope said.

"More than nice. You were amazing, and it was everything I've been wanting—" He stopped himself, a high red flush around his ears.

Penelope switched her feet to feel her joints click again, to bring herself back into the hallway, into this moment with Marcus.

"Samantha came home and admitted she spent those nights away because she was avoiding me. We've been avoiding each other. But we talked and we decided that we're going to try and get back on track."

We, we, we. Penelope waited and shifted her feet again.

"But that doesn't change that our time together was very special. To me. Suffice it to say that you mean a great deal to me. And it was the best time I've had in what feels like forever. I just wanted you to know."

"Is that all?"

"I'd better get back to Grace. I promised her we'd finish the chapter before bedtime."

"Don't let me stand in your way—I know you're a man of such solid commitments."

"Penelope, I lost my head."

"You came up to see me."

"Please try to understand—"

"You know it's not easy for me to be here. I have no one."

"You didn't have anyone in Pittsburgh either."

Marcus's words startled her. She felt as if she had been holding some shroud around herself and Marcus snatched it away. He must have seen on her face that he had hurt her.

"I know you're lonely," he said, mildly, but it was too late. She could see that he was through playing sweet and smitten with her. She had hoped they would have more time to test out what was between them—it wouldn't have been hard with him working from home and Samantha so often in the city. She had only wanted to have him close, to be close to him. But he was already turning away from her, back to his real family, and Penelope wasn't one to be left behind.

She stepped around him and knocked on the office door, just once, before she pushed it open. Grace sat on a plush leather loveseat with her hands folded on her lap. She was sifting through a pile of old *New Yorkers* Marcus had stacked on a side table beneath a brass lamp with a green shade. As Penelope had guessed, there was a desk of dark wood and a matching straight-backed chair.

"Come in, Penelope. I found a funny cartoon."

Penelope crossed into the office, kneeled beside the loveseat, and put her arms around Grace. The child let the magazines slip from her lap. The weight of her arms was a brief comfort; Penelope felt tangible again, flesh and bone, here.

"Good night, Gracie," she said. "Only sweet dreams tonight, okay?"

"You aren't going to read with us?"

Penelope left without a word to Marcus, and he didn't stop her. She climbed the last flight of stairs up to the attic, her calves in knots, her knees pulsing, and there was another disconnected pressure in her chest, as if someone had crushed all the air out of her.

Penelope retrieved one of the bottles of gin from the floor, where it had grown cold over the course of the day. She lay down on her bed and rolled up her leggings to her thighs. She held the bottle of gin to her left knee, then her right. She rested the bottle on her chest and let the cold seep into her.

The house was quiet again, and Penelope felt her body begin to shake. She didn't recognize, at first, that she was crying, but there was no other way to explain the tremors in her limbs, the compression in her chest, her wet face. She twisted off the cap and let just a little drop into her throat: the sweet taste of juniper, the clean burn. She tipped the bottle back and drank more. It eased the aching in her knees. She drank until the room went black.

Penelope dreamed of Coney Island. She was riding the Gravitron alone, feeling the whoosh of air as she spun. Ralph started climbing into the ride while it was in motion, and Penelope screamed for him to stop. She woke with a sense of inward velocity, her head awhirl. She felt a familiar slosh in her stomach, and she catapulted down the stairs. *I'm going to fall,* she thought. *I'm going to die in the Harpers' house, and they will find me in the morning.*

She made it to the fourth floor, burst into the bathroom, and gagged quietly into the bowl. She hadn't eaten dinner, hadn't done anything but drink and weep after Marcus had told her he didn't want her, so it was all bile. The hot and bitter liquid scorched her throat as she heaved. When she was done, she flushed the toilet and rested her head on the cool, clean seat. There was thunder, a brief illumination of lightning through the window. It was fitting, she thought. Another storm, but this time without any magic, no lavender light, no dancing snow. She found her way back to the attic.

Penelope went straight for the little pile of clothes she had left on the floor by the pipe. The postcard was dry and cold. On its face, a sun set over a honey-colored beach. An empty rope hammock hung low between two trees. Penelope flipped the card over. It was postmarked several days ago, from a post office in a province where Penelope had never been. The mail between countries could take so long. She stared at the inky postal signature—*La República Dominicana.*

The card was gray from too many erasures, as if her mother had spent several minutes trying to find the words, writing things down, and striking them out. Perhaps she had even spent hours. The message was just a few lines, in pale pencil lead, her mother's slender, slanting hand. Penelope decided to read. What more did she have to lose? What else could be taken away? *Nothing,* she reminded herself. *Nothing.*

It was only a few lines.

Hija—

No, she would not break. She braced herself and started again.

Hija—
I am here. I have another life. I bought a house. I am
not the same. Come see me. Write to me. Call me. Knock
on my door. I am ready now for you. We could try again.
   —Mami

10

THE MOUNTAIN

The red clay from the road caked under Mirella's nails; it settled in a powdery film on the lenses of her sunglasses. The red earth was the consistency of mud more than dust, and yet it rose and covered the back of the truck where Mirella sat in the midst of all her luggage. She had packed enough clothing and soap to last two months in the mountains. Penelope sat on her knees, clutching the edge of the truck and peering down into the valley, where they had started their journey nearly two hours before. She stared at the green plain, probably searching for burning weeds on the face of the cliff. Every summer, Penelope behaved as if it were her first and last time in Aguas Frescas, as if she had to ingest the mountains and the sunlight right away, or it would all vanish.

The truck lurched and Mirella groaned. "Fernando, por favor, despacito," she called.

She lowered the brim of her straw hat, already feeling her skin begin to crisp. There was no shelter from the sun while they were on the road, nothing Mirella could do but squirm and burn. The truck skipped and sank on the rocky path; the incline nauseated her. When she was a girl, she had watched a dairy truck fall off this road. The tanks of milk had burst open on the rocks, and the truck had teetered for what seemed like whole minutes before it rolled onto its side and skidded down the slope of the mountain. The driver and his two sons went over with the truck; they must have screamed, but all Mirella heard was the screech of metal against earth.

"Ya no aguantas el paseo," Fernando observed, calling to Mirella from the cab of the truck. "Lavaste la tierra de tus manos!" he laughed and stuck a thumbs-up out the window to show he was just teasing. Every year he mocked Mirella, kindly, for how much of a newyorkina she had become. She and Penelope had spent the night before in a hotel near the airport, and she had passed easily as a woman who had lived in cities her whole life. Her gargantuan leather purse, her slick unparted hair, the exacting stare she directed at almost everyone, concealed that she had only ever lived in one city—Brooklyn—and her DR, like Fernando's, was the red-earth campo, a village with one colmado, one chapel, one school, and many rivers.

The truck slowed down.

"En Nueva York no se ve ni una montaña," Penelope called above the racket of the truck. Her accent was flawless, the cadences perfectly Dominican. Mirella was impressed by how well Penelope had learned to imitate the lurching up-and-down lilt of her own speech. She could be mistaken for a girl born on this mountain.

Mirella's head throbbed from the dust and their shouting. She buried her face in her hands. When Fernando asked Penelope whether the only mountains in New York were piles of trash and shit, Penelope giggled and agreed, "Ay sí, pura basura y mierda."

Mirella turned her head sharply in Penelope's direction. She didn't scold her aloud, but Penelope stopped laughing at once and turned back to the valley. Fernando kept driving. After a while, she spoke again, tentatively, as if to make amends.

"Mami, is it all right with you if I draw?"

She had been doing this—asking for permission—since they left for JFK the day before.

Mami, can I call Pop from the pay phone to say good-bye? Mami, can I buy some gum to chew on the plane? Mami, can I lift the window shade to see the clouds?

She was thirteen and acting as if she were helpless. Maybe it was Penelope's way of showing she was still a good and obedient daughter. Maybe she wanted to have something to say, just so that the two of them were talking. Either way, it irritated Mirella how the girl suddenly needed her, now that they had left Ralph and Brooklyn.

Ralph hadn't accompanied them to the airport this year because the flight was in the evening when he had to close the shop, and he refused to leave the front girls to lock up. Sure, they could work the register and sort the records, but *could they run a business?* Ralph had explained it all to Mirella the morning he kissed her good-bye. She hadn't said a word to him, not as he dressed or waved to her from the door. She didn't get up until it was time to leave for the airport. She was exhausted and sore from spending the day in bed, sweating and doing nothing as the sun emptied itself on Halsey. In the living room, Ralph had left a wad of twenty-dollar bills and a scrap of legal paper on which he had written *TAXI*. Not *Ralph*, not *Be safe*, not *Te amo*, which they still said to each other the times they made love, and Ralph stroked the backs of her legs and played the keys of her spine, and she would kiss his ears and fleetingly think that at fifty, he was still a handsome man, and it may not have all been perfect, but it was theirs, *this* home, and *this* life.

Ralph had left Penelope twenty dollars of her own for the trip and a hot-pink Polaroid camera. He wanted her to take pictures of the mountains that he had never seen. He'd written her note on a scrap of paper from the same yellow legal pad: *Penny, Pop loves you. Come home safe.*

Penelope asked again whether she could draw.

"If you open that bag, the dust will cover everything in it. Is that what you want? Dust on your sketchbook? Dust on the new camera?"

Mirella sucked her teeth, and Penelope set down the book bag, looking stunned and deflated. Her hair crinkled in the humidity. The blowout, which Mirella had paid for at a Bedford Avenue salon, was already being overtaken by a ripple that started at her crown and wound into a full curl at her waist. Her kinks had grown more persistent, but after a good wash and rolos, her hair still resembled Mirella's, long and thick, but coarser and without any hint of auburn at all.

Penelope was becoming quite beautiful, already more of a woman than a child. Her hips had widened since she started her period, and her breasts were nearly the size of Mirella's. Her sad, small eyes hadn't changed, and the round apples of her cheeks were still pure Ralph.

Mirella looked away so she wouldn't have to watch Penelope sulk. She withdrew a Kleenex from her purse and blew her nose. Specks of red covered the tissue. She sighed. The dust was already filling her nostrils and the back of her throat.

"Fernando, cuánto nos falta?" she yelled, and then added, more gently, "I'm not sure how much more I can take."

She didn't want Fernando to think she blamed him for her carsickness and vertigo, the dust. Although they had never been friends, they had grown up together in Aguas Frescas. Fernando was thirty-five, like her, but he had been married and a father by the time she left DR at eighteen. Mirella had known Fernando's father, a pious and alcoholic widower who worked in the valley as a farmer, moving from crop to crop and terreno to terreno, depending on who was hiring for the day. Fernando had never met her father, although he knew the legend of Eleazar and Ramona's love, which was popular on the mountain long before Mirella was born. When she moved to Aguas Frescas as a girl, everyone seemed to know that her father had been fair-skinned and plump, descended from a long line of Spaniards, and that he had walked with a limp and smoked cigars.

They all knew he was dead and had left Mirella nothing except her red hair.

Eleazar Jiménez had owned an American-style diner in Santiago, not far from La Plaza Valerio, where the rich of the city built their homes. They served hamburgers and French fries at a red-and-white tile counter; the jukebox played tangos and boleros, no Dominican music at all, and certainly not the American rock 'n' roll that would have matched the décor. Ramona was thirteen when she first visited La Billonera and sat at the counter for a soda. She had come down from Aguas Frescas to help her father sell beans, still whole and green in their pods, packed in sacks that weighed as much as she did. Ramona and her father ate American hamburgers for the first time in their lives, the brownest customers in the restaurant, dirt under their nails and in their hair.

Mirella had heard her father boast that he loved Ramona as soon as he saw her, a stunning woman-child with eyes, lips, hair, and skin all the same caramel color. Eleazar gave them their Coca-Colas and burgers for free, and so they returned to La Billonera every time they were in Santiago selling beans. Eleazar plied Ramona with ice cream and soda and pickles until she was too full to go outside and help her father unload the truck. They stayed inside and talked. Ramona's father had no sons, and she had been helping him her whole life, plucking beans and lugging them, bargaining in the market, counting pesos, making change. When Ramona turned fifteen, Eleazar asked her father if he could marry her. The poor bean farmer didn't object.

Wealthy Santiagueros were horrified by the match, not because the brown-gold girl from the mountains was so young—it wasn't so strange for a man of Eleazar's wealth and position to marry a girl who could be mistaken for his daughter—but because she was so simple, so dark, such an absolute campesina. She was nothing like the high-society Santiago daughters who might have hoped to marry Eleazar. These girls spent their days sitting in the shade and scrubbing their elbows and knees with halved lemons. These girls played the piano and flipped their hair with a kind of precision that could make even the most righteous and long-married man sick with desire. There was nothing coy or pretty about Ramona, nothing gentle about her calloused hands and her skin the color of tamarindo. Still, they were married in La Catedral on La Calle del Sol, and Ramona moved down the mountain into Eleazar's white house near La Plaza Valerio. She was pregnant within a few months, and Mirella was born with her father's red hair and Ramona's stringy body. Mirella had a room of her own, as well as a nurse, a maid, and a professional photographer who came from la capital from time to time to document every milestone of her early life.

Eleazar spoiled Ramona and Mirella both, buying them dolls and dresses that came from as far as New York and Canada. When she arrived in Aguas Frescas, the other children asked Mirella if it was true that Eleazar had held her on one knee, and Ramona on the other, and watched them play for hours. Mirella hated the rumors about her father; she remembered him as doting and generous, and, to her, there was nothing scandalous about the way she and her father had loved each other. She remembered La Billonera, too, the tall fountain glasses filled with chocolate syrup and soda, the click and whir of the jukebox as it switched records. Mirella had only one family portrait of the three of them, which she had taken with her to New York. The sepia photograph shows a fat white man in a suit, Mirella in a starchy pale dress, and Ramona, a dark teenager with matted hair and the muscular body of an Olympian.

When Eleazar died—of sunstroke or a heart attack, no one was ever sure—the government took the house on La Plaza Valerio and La Billonera. Eleazar hadn't left his estate in order, and his business partners argued they were the rightful inheritors to all he owned. Whether Ramona hadn't cared to dispute their claims because she missed the mountain, or whether she had tried to stand against these Santiago sophisticates and failed, Mirella didn't know. She was newly seven. She watched strange men pack up everything they owned; she said good-bye to the photographer, nurse, and maid, who returned to their pueblos or went to work in the neighboring houses. Ramona's father came to Santiago to take them back to Aguas Frescas, and Mirella learned to live on the mountain.

At first, she cried for her own bed and a toilet that flushed, her porcelain muñequitas, her dresses, her nurse. Ramona went back to harvesting beans and diving in the river for crabs. She smoked tobacco in the evenings and visited her childhood friends, who had all become mothers as well, with boys from the village. When her father died, the house was Ramona's, and she planted a lime tree in the yard. Mirella would sit under the tree and cry for the city and her father, who had given her the red hair that burned even brighter in the mountain sun.

"This trip never ends." Mirella sighed and fanned herself with her straw hat. "I don't know why I keep coming back if this trip is so long."

"We're almost there, can't you see?" Fernando called back. "Or have you really been away so long?"

"I can't see anything, I'm so dizzy."

"Ya casi, hermanita. Ya casi."

The earth flattened as the truck lumbered into Aguas Frescas. The women opened their windows and the children came out to the road when they heard the rattle of the truck. Penelope waved, and, for the most part, they recognized her. "Penélope, bienvenida," a few called out, and Penelope beamed back at them, sitting up on her knees on the flatbed like a proud returning beauty queen.

"What's the matter with you?" Mirella yanked the collar of Penelope's T-shirt. "You'll fall—sit back down."

Penelope kept leaning over the side, pumping her hand back and forth, with no restraint at all, not a shred of dignity. For all anyone knew, she was Queen of the Campesinas under her Levi's and Yankees cap, her green track-team T-shirt.

Some of the smaller kids trailed after the truck, calling Penelope's name, and kicking up the dirt. They passed the chapel, the colmado, the schoolhouse, and turned the bend in the road.

Ramona's house was the color of sea glass, a shack with a zinc roof and white shutters. Three plastic chairs were stationed on the strip of concrete that ran around the house; a dirt path cut from the road to the front door. Ramona's old mutt, Lulú, was barking and circling the front of the house. The truck hadn't come to a full stop when Penelope leaped over the side of the flatbed and landed running toward the house. The truck stuttered over the rocks and mud, and Penelope could run faster than Fernando could drive.

"Penélope!" Mirella whipped her sunglasses off and started to scream. "Maldita niña! Qué haces? Come back!"

Penelope sprinted up the road, and Lulú bounded to meet her.

Mirella cursed and slapped her own leg, hard. "Maldita niña," she repeated.

Fernando laughed, and Mirella muttered to herself, "She's crazy." She watched as her daughter launched herself into Ramona's arms.

Her mother stood in front of the house in a turquoise dress stained bluer by her sweat. Her dark hair, which was not yet gray, was piled on the top of her head in a moño. She was only a few years older than Ralph, but Mirella hardly remembered how close they were in age. Her mother's skin was leathery from a life in the sun, her fingers and knees knobby from years of stooping and picking. And yet, she was still a striking woman, even from afar. Her gums and teeth and nails gleamed pink and white against the dark gold of her skin. Her alien, Amazonian loveliness hadn't faded with age.

Ramona and Penelope were covering each other with kisses while Mirella started to unload the luggage. Fernando helped her. They listened to the old woman and the girl proclaim their love for one another.

"Abuela!" Penelope bleated.

"Mi reina," answered Ramona. "Look at you! You're even more beautiful than your mami."

"I love you, Abuela."

"I've missed you, mi cielito. Once a year isn't enough!"

Mirella rolled her eyes.

"Así son los niños y los abuelos," Fernando said indulgently, as if every girl in the world would greet her grandmother with such fanfare and melodrama.

"Ella no es tan niña," Mirella replied, dragging her suitcase onto the dust.

They unpacked the truck quietly, while Ramona and Penelope raved. When they were done, Fernando stared at her, probably waiting to be invited inside. If Ramona had seen, she would have called him in, but Mirella was tired from the journey and irritated at how amused he was by the reunion of her mother and her daughter, how swiftly they had left her out. So she thanked him for the ride, pressed a bundle of American dollars into his hand.

Dusk in Aguas Frescas was warm and breezy, the sky deep lavender. The mosquitoes were beginning to circle the women as they stood in the yard. Penelope chopped onions while Ramona fried plantains and eggplants in strips. Mirella made the rice, pouring water from an empty can of tomato paste into the dented aluminum pot. The scent of oregano and garlic dissolved in the night air. The wooden house was peaceful aside from the sound of sizzling and water sloshing and the unsteady chop of the knife. Even Lulú was quiet, dozing on her mat beneath the lime tree.

The stone kitchen was the part of the house Mirella hated most. It was hardly a room: just a stone sink, stove, and two gas tanks on a square of cement in the backyard. Mirella had spent years outside in this kitchen, following Ramona's orders to stew crabs and wash rice, or beat the laundry dry, while she went to visit the neighbors. The wind would scatter the cilantro she had chopped and sweep her hair into her eyes, and Mirella would curse how high in the mountains they were, how far from La Plaza Valerio.

"You're cutting the onions too small," Mirella said, jabbing Penelope on the shoulder. "You'll never finish chopping if you keep doing it that way."

"How else am I supposed to do it?" Penelope said, holding the blade in one hand and using the other to brush sweat from her forehead. She looked even more disheveled than she had when they arrived. The heat from the stove had curled her hair; her hands and face were almost as dark as Ramona's. She looked misplaced in the stone kitchen in her American sneakers and jeans, chopping the onions delicately while the oil began to smoke. Penelope knew nothing of how to cook and serve others. Penelope's life in Brooklyn was too comfortable. They had spoiled her.

"If you didn't spend all your time locked in your room and drawing, you'd be able to do simple things like chop an onion. When I was half your age I already knew how to cook for myself."

"You never taught me," Penelope said plainly, setting the knife down on the wooden board.

"Do you ever ask to learn? Do you ever say, 'Mami, teach me'? No, you stay in your room and draw. You don't cook for me."

"You don't cook for me anymore either."

Before Mirella could yell, Ramona stepped between them, taking the knife from Penelope.

"Tranquila," she said. "The both of you. I'll show Penelope how to do it."

She made three slits lengthwise on the top half of an onion, and then three crosswise into the side. When she sliced through the top, horizontally, the bulb broke apart in dozens of identical purple and white squares.

"If you do it this way, the pieces will already be small. You won't have to keep cutting and cutting."

Penelope cut another half an onion in this way, carefully, her eyes clouding as she sliced. When she was finished, Ramona brushed the hair back from her forehead and kissed her.

"Muy bien," she said. "Muy bien, mi reina."

They finished preparing the meal just before dark. Mirella planted the wooden spoon in the center of the pot of rice to be sure it was ready. When the spoon stood upright, she knew the proportions of water and grains were right; the moro would be moist but not too wet. They carried the food inside the house and sat at the round table in the living room. Ramona brought in three yellow bananas, unpeeled them, and set one whole on each of their plates. Ramona prayed for the food, and Penelope shut her eyes. Mirella watched the two of them cross themselves.

"Amen," they intoned and began to eat.

Ramona chewed with her mouth open, picking apart the oily strips of eggplant with her fingers. She licked the salt and grease from her palms, and Penelope did the same.

"Did Fernando tell you he had another son?" Ramona filled the silence with her sharp, sweet voice.

"He doesn't know when to stop, eh? How many is that now? Four? Five?"

"Six. He and Angelina are happy. They want a big family."

"For what? So they can starve together?"

"No hables así Mirella. Someone will hear you. For all you know, Fernando's at our door right now."

"I only said the truth. I'm sure he already knows he can't afford to feed another child."

"It's wise to have a lot of children," Ramona went on. "What better gift can you give your child than a brother or a sister? Someone to be with them when you're gone?"

Mirella laughed. "Is that why I have so many brothers and sisters, Mami?"

"Ay, Mirella, don't start with me. I couldn't give you a brother or a sister, not with my husband dead and in the ground—God rest his soul."

Mirella looked away as her mother crossed herself anew. Ramona was as theatrically emotional as everyone else in this village. When someone died in Aguas Frescas, relatives hurled themselves to the ground during the funeral, clawing at their chests while their neighbors held them up and stuffed sedatives into their mouths. When a wife discovered her husband had been unfaithful, she locked him out of the house, and he spent the night, drunk, trying to climb in the windows, maybe even crooning a song, a contrite bachata, to convince her to forgive him. It was the stuff of novelas, melodrama no one even endeavored to keep private in a town of three hundred.

Mirella knew Ramona had loved the mountain more than she had loved Eleazar. Back in Aguas Frescas, when she was finished picking beans, she was free to swim in the river in her housedress or smoke a pipe, pour herself a traguito on the porch of a neighbor. In the morning, she could watch the sun rise over the valley, listen to the radio, and drink her café con leche privately, stirring in milk from a can. Mirella was the one who had grieved for Eleazar and their old life; Ramona was happier as a widow, young and untethered, with a house of her own.

"How's el morenito?" Ramona asked without looking up from her plate.

"Ralph's fine. Making money at the store. He says hello."

"Tell him I say hello, too."

They went back to their rice and gossip about the neighbors.

Penelope drank from a bottle of mabi and listened to the women. She looked strange to Mirella, with her elbows on the table, grease smeared across her lips, beads of sweat creeping out from the puffy halo of her hair. They had stopped eating meals together in New York, and Mirella wondered how they would learn to be together here, over the next two months in this house.

Penelope hadn't grown any quieter in the past year, but she seemed to love her solitude now, rather than fight against it. She still asked for permission to go to school dances and art shows, but when Mirella forbade her, she hardly flinched, and returned, unperturbed, to her room to draw. She didn't come into Mirella's bedroom anymore to say good night, which must have been normal for a girl of thirteen, but she didn't hug her anymore either, didn't rise onto her tiptoes to kiss the air next to her cheek. Sometimes, when Mirella found Penelope on the floor of her bedroom, bent over a sketch pad, or staring out her window onto Halsey Street, she felt a swift sinking, the conviction, for just a moment, that she had ruined the child somehow.

It would be better for her here, Mirella thought, in Aguas Frescas. She would spend her days wandering through the hills and hiking to the waterfalls with the other children. She would swim in the river and eat sancocho at the neighbors' houses, play soccer in the road, the only child wearing shoes when she kicked the ball of rolled-up socks. She was a different girl in the mountains, her legs covered in mud, her face burned pink and brown. She returned to Ramona's house every evening, insatiable and ecstatic, armed with stories about the day. Mirella wondered how many years Penelope had left before she began to see Aguas Frescas for the small, dull campo that it was.

When Penelope finished her first bottle of mabi, she got up for another. She used the metal opener to uncap the bottle, and when she raised it to her lips, she didn't look like a little girl at all, her lower lip swallowing the mouth of the bottle, the dark liquid dribbling down her chin.

"You're going to get full on soda."

"It's not soda, Mami."

"Just because it doesn't say *Coca-Cola* on the bottle—"

"Oh, déjala quieta," Ramona said. "I bought them for her. Now, tell me about school."

"Her grades are nothing special," Mirella said. "She's lucky she got into this middle school—there was a lottery. She needs to work harder if she wants to go to a good college one day. They won't care if she has As in art."

"Maybe that's all she needs. Maybe she'll be an artist one day."

"Who do you know who left this pueblito, went to New York, and came back an artist?"

"Penelope isn't from this pueblito. She was born in New York."

"You think that matters, Ma? It's not easy over there. Dominicans in New York work hard."

"How would you know what Dominicans do? Your only friends are morenos."

"I don't have time for friends, Ma. I work. And if Penélope doesn't work hard now, she'll be working hard for the rest of her life, too. If I had been born in New York, I would have studied. I would know better than to spend all my time drawing."

"Why would you spend your time drawing? You were never any good at it."

"My art teacher says my art could help me get into college," Penelope said. "I could get a—" She turned to Mirella and spoke in English. "Mami, how do you say 'scholarship'?"

"Beca," Mirella said begrudgingly.

"I could get a beca, Abuela. For college."

"You'd be the first one in our family to go," Ramona said.

"She wouldn't be the first Jiménez. Papi went to college. In la capital."

"Well, she'd be the first Santos."

"Mami, can I go get my paintings to show Abuela?"

Mirella waved her hand indifferently, and Penelope went to the bedroom, where they had left their luggage. The bedroom had no furniture besides a bed, a dresser, and a footstool where Ramona kept a shrine to la Virgen de la Altagracia. She had covered the footstool with tall votive candles, a dried branch of red framboyan, and a broken teacup that held coins and a gold chain. Penelope would sleep in the bedroom with her grandmother, and Mirella would find them in the morning, wrestling for blankets, their arms and legs intertwined, as if they were a pair of little girls.

"You shouldn't encourage her," Mirella said. "Filling her head with tonterías. I'm the one who has to make sure she is prepared for life."

"Being an artist doesn't seem to be the problem in Penelope's life."

"Y eso?" Mirella leaned across the table and pointed her finger in Ramona's face. "What are you trying to say?"

"Nothing, except I know how you all live over there. Without neighbors, without friends. At least, Penelope has something she loves."

"It's not the campo, Ma. You can't leave your door open at night and yell at anyone who passes, 'Oigan! Que vengan para 'ca. Hice un sancocho y me quedó bien rico!'"

Ramona ignored Mirella's parody of her.

"Penelope's my granddaughter. If she wants to draw, I want to see her drawings. If she decides to be a fisherman, I want to see her fish."

"Don't try to teach me how to raise a child. I raised myself, didn't I?"

"I was young. I didn't know how to be a mother. We lived in the same house, and I thought that was the same thing as raising you. Now, I'm old, and I see things."

"I was thinking of Penélope before she was even born. I left this little campo because I knew I'd never raise a child here."

"I thought you left because you were ashamed to be a campesina like me."

Mirella watched her mother pick up a grain of rice from the edge of her plate and lick her finger.

"It doesn't matter," Ramona said. "We all make choices to chase our own happiness. You made yours."

"And I am happy."

"Good."

Mirella looked around the little shack, its mint green walls.

"But listen to me—you better make things right with that girl. She won't keep waiting for you."

"What do you mean 'waiting'? I am already her mother."

"You'll see."

A bang on the door ended their disagreement. Mirella should have known visitors would arrive. It was their first night back, and everyone in Aguas Frescas had seen them arrive that afternoon.

"Ramona!"

Angelina's voice rang clear and high from the road, just as Fernando pushed open the door. He, Angelina, and their six children poured into the house. There were hugs and kisses, as if they didn't all live within the same square mile and see each other every day. Angelina gave Mirella a kiss on the cheek; the children gave her limp hugs. Penelope bounded back into the room with a stack of her watercolors, and the other children charged at her. She lifted her hands high so they wouldn't crush her work. She hugged them back and gave them kisses, the three young boys, the eldest girl, and the girl who was her age.

"I'll get the drinks," Ramona said, heading for the cabinet stocked with rum, malta, and mabi. Penelope set her paintings down on the table and went to help her grandmother carry the bottles. Fernando, Angelina, and their children arranged themselves on the sofa and started asking Mirella questions rapid-fire. How did she manage to look so much younger than both of them; was the water in New York softer on your skin? How old was her morenito now, and was he treating her well? Penelope was becoming so beautiful; did she know how she was going to keep those New York tigueres away?

Ramona returned with the rum and the radio. Penelope sat on the arm of the couch to trade secrets with the eldest girl, who Mirella could see had been changed by the past year as well. She was tall and willowy in the pink leggings and dirty striped tank top she wore without a bra. Even her feet looked like the feet of a woman, the nails filed and clipped, neat, although her flip-flops were caked with mud. She and Penelope began to whisper to each other, the other daughter craning her ear to hear what they were talking about. The adults began singing along to a ballad that had become popular in the years since Mirella had been away. She didn't know the words.

They opened the bottles and turned up the radio, the bachata and laughter filling where there had been silence. Mirella began to let herself drift, out of the house, beyond the stone kitchen, the mountain, the red dirt road.

Mirella woke up on a mattress on the living room floor, her nightgown clinging to her skin. She had forgotten to open the windows, and no mountain breeze cut through the house to soothe her. Her ears rang from the rum, the dark syrupy taste still on her tongue.

Mirella fumbled in the dark for the cup of water she had set beside her. She took a sip and watched a mango-green lizard spring onto the wall and crawl up to the ceiling.

The water tasted like tin. *At least it's clean,* Mirella thought. She had bought Ramona a water filter years ago after hearing a news report about parasites. Mirella had told her mother she could do whatever she wanted with the filter during the year, but to make sure she installed it every summer before she and Penelope came to visit.

Mirella listened for the sound of Penelope breathing in the bedroom. She heard nothing. The mountain was quiet, only the wind and the sound of fruit dropping from the trees until sunrise when the roosters started to crow. Aguas Frescas was the sort of place where married couples clamped their hands over each other's mouths while they made love, where teenagers snuck off to las cascadas to do the same.

Mirella had taken only one boy, Dionysus, down to the waterfalls. The other boys were too afraid of her; she was untouchable with her red hair and golden skin. She spent evenings sitting in a plastic chair in front of her house, wearing short shorts and a translucent T-shirt without a bra, because it pleased her to catch them watching, lingering on the road, but never venturing to her door to say hello or to gossip. She kept her schoolbooks open as they passed, satisfied to see how they slowed to watch her watch them.

Mirella kissed Dionysus one day at the river. She was fourteen and still attending the youth hour at the chapel every Friday. The kids went swimming after the service, disappearing into the trees or behind the waterfall at dusk. Mirella and Dionysus stayed by the riverbank, dipping their legs in the current, marveling at the tiny fish that circled their feet and pecked at their toes. These fish ate the dead skin off their heels, and it tickled, as they slowly cleared the old flesh away. Dionysus was midlaugh, pointing at their feet in the sand, when Mirella tipped his head back and kissed him, just to see what it was like.

Mirella finished her water, crept toward the bedroom, and eased open the door. The bed was empty. Ramona's mud-encrusted chancletas were under the bed beside the Adidas sandals Penelope used as house slippers. Had they gone out barefoot? Mirella took the grainy bedsheets into her hands; they were still damp.

Back in the living room, Mirella searched for a flashlight. Her fingers brushed plastic plates and tin cups in the cupboard, the sticky edges of a cobweb. She cursed. The lights were out, and there was no generator to power the little house. She knew Ramona had to keep a flashlight somewhere for the blackouts that came to Aguas Frescas daily.

Mirella found only Ramona's collection of candles, each for a different saint. She picked a candle with a sticker-portrait of a brown-skinned woman with no hair, just an emerald-green mantilla flowing from her scalp. She was more sensual than holy, with lips as pink as the undersides of river fish. Mirella struck a match and lit the wick and carried it with her out of the house.

The candle cast just enough light for Mirella to follow her feet on the road. The darkness closed in around her, and the quiet seemed to fill her ears and crush. She passed the tiny houses, all wooden planks and zinc roofs, a few plastic chairs in every yard.

Mirella spotted Lulú, sleeping just off the side of the road in front of a small stucco house with a slanted roof. She couldn't remember who lived there, and it bothered her to see the old mutt with her chin in the dirt, sleeping anywhere in the pueblo that she pleased. *Maldita perra,* Mirella thought, and she considered kicking Lulú in the side to wake her and send her back to Ramona's house.

The dog had never been a part of Mirella's life in Aguas Frescas. She and Penelope returned one summer to find her pissing under the lime tree, a scruffy pup that yapped at night and hunted rats, dragging their carcasses into the yard to show off to Ramona. Mirella had liked Lulú only briefly, during the summer when Penelope was four and chased the dog up and down the road, squealing, and grabbing at her grubby fur.

Mirella decided not to wake the dog and turned the bend in the road. The moon loomed low over the trees, and an uncountable number of stars stretched across the sky, but they were too small and distant to emit much light. It was the moon that kept Mirella on the road and off the rocks. She didn't need the candle anymore, but she let it burn, the waxy smell familiar and comforting.

The framboyan-red shack at the top of the road that led to las cascadas was the schoolhouse. Mirella circled the shack looking for her daughter. Were they sitting on the stones watching for shooting stars? They weren't.

Feathery curtains hung over the schoolhouse windows; discarded coils of wire and deflated balls lay dead in the yard. Mirella had spent years in the schoolhouse, listening to the illustrious biographies of dead Dominican presidents, and singing rhymes the teacher taught them to fill the time. She made her way back to the road, the old couplets returning to her.

Los zapatitos me aprietan, las medias me dan calor
Y el anillito que yo tengo, me lo regaló mi amor.

Mirella had been spared attending secondary school in the red shack by one of the teachers, Señorita Chelsea, a nun who had come to Aguas Frescas on mission. She was an American woman with ice-blue eyes, and she suffered constant sunburn from her years on the mountain. She recommended Mirella for a secondary school in Santiago, and with Ramona's permission, Mirella found a man with daily business in Santiago, who was willing to drive her and two other girls down to a Catholic school in the city, where they could continue their lessons. The girls rode down in the truck every day, unless the rain was too heavy and there was a chance the road would dissolve to mud.

Mirella had loved being back in Santiago, winding through the maze of narrow, cobbled streets. She paraded down the avenues and sat reading in El Parque Valerio, watching the fountain spout water, until it was time for her to meet the truck to take her back up the mountain. At school, she took an English class, and she learned how to sew and make dresses. She practiced her English vocabulary, words like *Eucharist* and *ascension* and *Holy Ghost*, while the truck lurched back to Aguas Frescas in the afternoon. She had hoped her schoolmates in Santiago would have heard of her father and La Billonera, that her skin and hair would be proof she had been one of them. Instead the girls laughed at the red stains on her calves, how dusty and nauseated and disheveled all the Aguas Frescas girls were when they arrived in the morning.

When Mirella was seventeen, her tía Mercedes called from New York. Mercedes wasn't really her aunt; she was an elderly vecina who had left Aguas Frescas several years ago and never returned. She knew a clothing factory that was hiring—did Mirella want to come to New York to work? She needed someone to help take care of her, and in exchange, Mirella could live with her for free.

Mirella said yes, although she had never dreamed of living in the United States. She had planned on finding a job in Santiago after she graduated, but she would still have to live in the mountains with Ramona. In New York, no one would know she was from the campo. She could work in the factory and make dresses, save enough money and then leave her tía to find an apartment of her own. In Santiago, girls her age didn't live apart from their families; in New York, they might, either on their own, or with an American boyfriend.

Dionysus had asked her not to go. He had grown into a handsome man, lithe and dark, with hands that were blistered from swinging a machete and pulling weeds from the ground. He had quit school after sixth grade to help his father, who grew coffee. Mirella never admitted they were novios, but she met him every night, after she finished proofreading her homework in the front yard and tormenting the other local boys. They kissed for hours and for years, at the river, in Ramona's stone kitchen, behind the colmado. Dionysus groped her flat chest, and Mirella massaged him over the fly of his jeans. When they started making love, she charted her periods, and wouldn't let him near her for half of the month. The other times, she ordered him to come in his hand or on the wall of the schoolhouse, in the sand at the riverbank, and he listened, chuckling every time, the same throaty laugh he had at fourteen, when they went swimming after church and let the fish peck at their feet.

Dionysus knew to love Mirella was to obey her, to worship her, to expect to be remembered but only after whatever else she was chasing—English, Santiago, the Mother Superior's list of prized students. He consented to adore her in secret, never inviting her for dinner at his mother's house, or visiting her when she was studying or practicing her sewing. He didn't ask her to drink and roam the mountain with the other young people who were all out of school and free every evening. But when she said she was leaving for the US, he told her to stay. He would marry her and let her work in Santiago if she wanted; he would wait until she wanted to have children. He kept pleading during the months it took her to raise the money for her ticket and receive her visa, but for Mirella, there was no question about whether to leave. On her last night in Aguas Frescas, she waited for Dionysus behind the school, but he never came to meet her.

The bats swooped overhead as Mirella neared the center of town. They flew up from the caves in the valley and were gone as suddenly as they had appeared.

The shacks at the center of the town were all dark; the gate to the colmado was pulled shut and locked. Could they have gone to the river? Ramona was crazy enough to do it—to hike to the waterfall at midnight, convince Penelope to dive for crabs and collect stones. If they were there, Mirella would find a way to punish her mother. For taking Penelope downhill in the dark, for bringing her home wet and cold.

She kept walking toward the edge of the town, where the houses stopped, and the chapel stood, and the narrow Aguas Frescas road joined with the main road leading back down the mountain. Mirella couldn't make out the steeple in the dark, but she knew the way, and kept on.

She had been living in New York for six months when Ramona mentioned in passing that Dionysus had been killed. It was a routine piece of Aguas Frescas gossip, mentioned just after Ramona finished detailing who was newly pregnant, who had miscarried, who had failed to show up to Sunday mass. He had moved north to Puerto Plata—just a few days after Mirella had left, incidentally—and found a job in a resort. He rented chairs on the beach to the tourists and delivered piña coladas to the topless European women who spent hours in the sand, roasting themselves. He was headed to the beach one morning, riding on the back of the motorcycle, when the driver stopped abruptly and he was thrown off the back. The crash hadn't killed him, and he was taken to a public hospital nearby. During surgery, one of the doctors sliced open an artery in his thigh, and he bled to death in the operating room. He was buried by his relatives in Los Chocos, in the ground for days before word got across the island and reached his mother. She was wild with grief, collapsing in the road and sobbing nearly every day. Ramona had taken her a sancocho; wasn't it a shame—such a young boy?

Mirella had mourned him in private, crying in the bathroom at the factory, or when she was cooking for her tía Mercedes. She knew better than to cry on the subway, or to Ramona, who hadn't known Dionysus was her first love and her friend, the only one in Aguas Frescas who ever came to know her as more than the red-haired girl who did her lessons outside each afternoon, on a plastic chair in the shadow of her little shack. She mourned that he'd stayed behind, although she'd never fantasized about him coming to New York with her. This is what it meant to be Dominican—to be bound for life one moment, and the next, left for dead on the road.

The wind extinguished Mirella's candle just as the chapel came into view. The road rose, and Mirella climbed. The church stood on a small hill, the only building in the whole village made of so much concrete. The lights were off inside, the rainbow colors of the stained-glass windows undetectable in the dark. The front door was ajar, and Mirella pressed her hands into the whitewashed block and peered into the sanctuary.

It was a spare room, dozens of metal folding chairs, gold vessels for swinging incense, and stacks of battered Nueva Reina Valera Bibles. All the Aguas Frescas services were held in this single room: prayers, baptisms, funerals, and weddings. It was where Mirella first received the Eucharist; it was where Ramona's body would rest before she was buried. It was impeccably kempt, white shiny tile, large potted palm fronds, and a large baptismal font in the center of the room. The font was more of a pit, a cavity three feet deep, in the shape of a boxy cross. Mirella had seen many baptisms here, on Sundays when a priest came up to Aguas Frescas for mass and confession. The townspeople would line up to be immersed in the pit, the red earth drifting off their skin and settling on the white tile while they were blessed. The font was dry now, and sitting inside the pit were Penelope and Ramona, their bodies tucked into the broad, hollow head of the cross.

They spoke in low voices, and Mirella strained to listen. She pressed her ear to the crack in the door.

"I can see him in the way you smile," Ramona said. "In your cheeks, and the way you like to listen to the radio with me in the morning. In your pelo crespo. I know you don't get those things from your mami. I know they must come from him."

"Maybe next year he'll come and you can meet him. It's the store, Abuela. He can't leave it. It's the reason we have our house. And it has to stay open for the neighborhood—the neighborhood needs its music."

Mirella rolled her eyes as Penelope quoted Ralph. *The People need their music, Mirella. It's not just me—it's all for The People.* Ralph and Lionel's speeches about blackness and Brooklyn, entrepreneurship, all centered on The People, the community that needed their businesses. The People thrived when they thrived. After all her years in Brooklyn, Mirella had come to know buildings and strangers, her daughter, the neighbors, the men who worked at the drugstore, Ralph and his friends. She had yet to meet The People.

"My father gave me a camera so I could take pictures of the mountain and of you. He wants to come here, but I don't think Mami wants him to. She likes to get away."

"Your mother has hot feet. She can't stay in one place for too long."

"She doesn't like Brooklyn."

"She doesn't like it here either."

"We come back for you, Abuela."

Ramona laughed. "No, niña. Your mami doesn't make the trip for me."

"I wish I lived here."

Mirella cursed the girl's stupidity silently and waited for Ramona to correct her. The old woman raked her nails over Penelope's scalp.

"You'd get bored here, mamita. You're like your mother that way. This town wouldn't be enough for you."

"Abuela, will you ever come to New York?"

"Maybe one day. But you know, Penelope, no one lives forever."

Penelope was quiet.

"You know, this pueblo will always be here for you, mi reina, even when I'm gone. My house, and the mountain—they're for you."

"I know, Abuela."

Penelope tucked herself in closer to her grandmother. They sat in the font in the silence.

Mirella pushed the door loudly, it squeaked as it scraped across the floor. She stepped into the sanctuary.

"Waiting on the presence of the Lord?" she said.

Ramona and Penelope squinted at the doorway but neither of them stirred. They stayed put, wrapped up in each other, low in the pit.

"Yes, hija," Ramona finally called. "We are waiting. Waiting, always waiting." She gestured to the other end of the font. "Te quieres meter?"

Mirella ignored her mother's question and stared at Penelope. She leaned her head to the side and put one hand on her hip, and Penelope revealed her first signs of guilt. She looked down at her hands and clicked on a flashlight she had in her lap. She pointed the beam up at the ceiling.

"I came all the way here with nothing but a candle," Mirella said.

"You were asleep, Mami. We didn't think you'd notice we were gone. I didn't mean to worry you."

"I wasn't worried."

Penelope stood and climbed out of the cross. She helped Ramona up, both of them leaving red footprints on the tile. Mirella stared at the girl's bare feet and shook her head.

"*Súper,*" she said. "Súper Ma, qué bien. You take her out of the house in the middle of the night and you don't even put on her chancletas. Next time, take her out naked, eh?"

"She didn't want to wear them."

"Oh, and at thirteen Penélope's already la que manda? She can do whatever she wants?"

"Calm down, Mirella. La tierra no mata. She's fine."

"She's not like you, Ma. She's not used to walking barefoot."

"Mami, I'm fine."

"Ni pensaste Ma, eh? Ni pensaste!"

"Calm down, Mirella," Ramona repeated.

Mirella glared at the two of them, standing in the dark chapel, only Penelope penitent, but it still wasn't enough. She stomped out of the chapel, slammed the door behind her, walked quickly along the black road. Penelope caught up to her quickly, her flashlight shining in the dark. She ran in front of Mirella and lit the way.

Ramona caught up, too, and tried to get Mirella to calm down, but Mirella couldn't hear her. She saw her mother, folding her arms across herself in the cold, the wind sifting through the hairs that had sprung free of her moño. She tried to take the candle from Mirella to relight it with a book of matches she kept in the pocket of her housedress, but Mirella shook her head and snatched the candle away.

"Cálmate, hija," Ramona whispered, reminding Mirella that everyone in the pueblo was sleeping. They hadn't meant to upset her, it was just a night walk, no harm had been done, la niña was fine.

"It's not about la niña!" Mirella screamed. "Ni pensaste en mi, Ma," she said. "Ni pensaste en mi. If I hadn't come looking for you, you would have left me there alone."

11

PARLOR GAMES

December fell on Brooklyn as rain, and the water swept the old dirty-white islands of snow into the gutters. The days were wet, but Penelope ran every day for longer than she was used to. She didn't want to be in the house on Greene. When she ran into Marcus on the stairs, he was cordial and shamefaced, but it sickened her to think of how much of her she had let him see. She had learned to time her arrivals and departures to avoid the landlady. Halsey Street was no better. Ralph was still smoking his pipe and playing records, waxing on about the state of the neighborhood instead of his own. She was growing sick of moving between the two houses. She needed some other place.

Sheckley's was mostly empty when Penelope pushed open the door one blue and frozen afternoon. Punk music grumbled softly over the sound system. A pair of young women sat in the booth by the window, draining pints of lager and laughing, peering out at the cold street. One of the girls wore a floral patterned scarf wound haphazardly around her neck; the other wore brown plastic spectacles so large they seemed to swallow her face. Penelope recognized those glasses as the sort of hideous frames the poorest kids at PS 23 were forced to wear; they were now the vogue among Bed-Stuy hipsters, it seemed. Would this really become her bar? Penelope passed the girls, and they carried on talking in hushed voices, gripping the large pints with their skinny, manicured hands.

A man in his thirties sat alone watching a rerun of *The Wonder Years* and finishing off a basket of fries. Sometimes he glanced at the girls by the window and rubbed his blond beard with interest. The only other customer was a woman in an argyle sweater, sitting at the bar with her legs crossed. A leather bag hung from one of her knees, and she stirred the clear liquid in her martini glass with a toothpick, stripped of olives. Penelope had served many women like her at the bar in Squirrel Hill. They would come in with their hair in perfect waves or a neat chignon, wearing tailored pants, and a skimpy, silky shirt under a conservative blazer. They drank martinis or top-shelf whiskey in silence, surveying the bar in between sips. When they finished one, they ordered another, and then pulled out a hardcover or their phone. They tapped away at their screens or idly flipped the pages of their books, smiled at Penelope whenever she caught them staring at her. She felt that she was one of them: less elegant but still a woman who drank alone at bars around town. They fascinated her and filled her with an unexpected sadness— their quiet drinking and pretty hair. They rarely offered their names, but she felt kindred to them, and they seemed to watch her back, as she wiped glasses or cleaned the ice bin, dropped a new pellet of soap in the sanitizing solution and scrubbed down the bar. They were often good tippers, as if they were also paying for Penelope's company, her work as a guardian of their solitude.

The bartender spotted Penelope before she reached him, and he raised his eyebrows high and comically at her approach. It was the same man she had cursed at the night she rescued Ralph. She would have to make amends with him if this was to be her bar. She forced a smile and waved, and he lifted his hands in a mock surrender.

"Don't shoot," he said.

"I'm unarmed." Penelope lifted up her hands. "See?"

The bartender spread his legs in a wide and confident stride, his arms crossed.

"You strike me as the sort of woman who's always carrying something."

Penelope sat at the bar, and he slid the happy hour menu across the counter. Penelope flipped over the single glossy sheet, a list of cocktails on one side, standard bar fare on the other. There were asterisked notes about where the ingredients and the spirits had been sourced. When she was a girl, the only things she ever ate at Sheckley's were onion soup and fried pickles. Lionel had been raised in the Carolinas and he had served Southern fare. He told Penelope stories about riding in the back of a truck, filled with cotton he had picked to make pocket money. Penelope thought of Grace and her fear of ghosts. If there were such things, then Sheckley's was certainly haunted—dead Lionel, her father's friends who had moved away and lost touch, a fitter, younger version of Ralph.

Penelope pushed the menu back across the counter. "I came to apologize," she said.

The woman in the argyle sweater looked up from her martini, suddenly intrigued. She closed her book. She wanted to watch.

"The other night."

"Go on. I'd like to hear this."

"You had no right to serve my father the way you did. It was shitty and irresponsible, and you endangered his life, but you didn't know that."

The bartender whistled, a shrill, sinking sound. "Some apology," he said and started to walk away from her.

"Look, I know what it's like to have to deal with other people's shit when you're on the job. And for that I am sorry."

"For the record, I didn't even serve your father. He came in drunk. I just let him sit here and talk."

Penelope apologized again. The bartender leaned against the mirror behind the counter and unfolded his arms, as if he were considering what she had said. Penelope could see now that he was boyishly slender in his black T-shirt and black jeans. His long curls were pushed off his face with a thin black band, the diamond studs in his ears glinted in the light of the bar. He looked amused, and Penelope wondered if this was his only expression. He offered his hand over the bar.

"We're good," he said.

His palms were damp from the soapy water, sticky and puckering. His skin was the color of walnuts, or strong tea with a dash of milk. Or her own hand after a summer in Aguas Frescas.

The woman in argyle was staring at them plainly now, her chin cupped in her hand.

"I owe you thanks, too. For helping me get my father out of here and for calling the cab for us. That was decent."

"I am a decent man when I'm not being shitty and—what was it you said? Inconsiderate?"

"I'm Penelope by the way."

"Jon."

They shook hands again.

The music in the bar switched to a mellower tune, the kind of melodic and melancholy rock that had played at the bar in Squirrel Hill. The CMU kids loved that soft, strange music; they sang along as they flashed Penelope their IDs, and ordered whiskey sours with an extra cherry. She had liked the music herself, and the weird, beautiful band names—Smashing Pumpkins, Soundgarden, Radiohead. She had grown up with jazz but was nothing like it; this music sounded like she felt—slow, dark, solemn—much more than her father's jazz, which was chaotic, complex, emphatic.

The woman in argyle swayed to the music. She closed her eyes and combed her hands through the airy layers of her butter-yellow hair. Penelope marveled at the woman and at how they were both enjoying the same song. They were patrons at the same bar, and for all Penelope knew, this stranger could have lived on Greene.

"Do you have time for a drink?" Jon said. "Or are you making the rounds and apologizing to all the bartenders you've insulted lately?"

"I'll stay," Penelope said. She ordered a gin and tonic with double the gin. She recited the three brands of gin she would drink and in what order. Jon laughed.

"Where do you think you are, girl? Manhattan? Let me make you something."

Penelope agreed, and the woman in argyle dropped a few dollars on the counter, then picked up her purse and her book and went over to one of the booths by the window.

"I guess we bored her," Penelope said.

"Day drinkers," Jon agreed, and they shared a knowing look. No one who drank this early in the afternoon was ever really fine. All you could do, as the bartender, was sling their drinks and then tell them to go home when they had had enough.

Jon set to work making Penelope a drink. He was fast and clean, wasting nothing, shaking up bourbon, apricot liqueur, fresh lime juice, and muddled blueberries that he sank to the bottom of the glass with a straw. Penelope leaned in to smell.

"Mmm," she hummed. She let the bourbon wash over her teeth, her tongue, to the back of her throat.

"It's perfect," she said. "Why aren't you working at some place in the West Village that charges fifteen bucks a cocktail?"

"The owner lets me keep my bike in the back," Jon said, and he left to tend a couple that had appeared at the other end of the bar. Penelope laughed at his answer and shook off her coat.

Jon sent the couple away with two mugs of beer, came back and noticed the paint on Penelope's shirt. A portly first grader named Rodney had planted his hand firmly on her arm to get her attention during third period. She had been wearing a smock, but he managed to find the fabric of her shirt anyway, his fingers covered in bright white. She'd wanted to yell at the child, for his clumsiness, for his need, for the way he grabbed at her, but she sent him to the sink to wash his hands in as even a tone as she could manage. She had been on the verge of erupting ever since Marcus, her mother's scheming request—*We could try again.*

She told Jon about her job, and that, no, teaching art at PS 23 did not feel like coming full circle, at least not in a good way. He was from the South Side of Chicago but had arrived in Brooklyn just after Penelope left. He had been living off Broadway and Myrtle for five years. He called Pittsburgh a grim town, and Penelope thought, *They're all grim towns,* but she didn't say so.

They traded bartending stories. Once, a drunk accountant gave Penelope a forty-dollar tip for being "ridiculously fucking beautiful." Another time, she'd made a gang of bitchy bridesmaids appletinis without any vodka, and they hadn't noticed. Jon had served two famous comedians at Sheckley's who came in one afternoon, ordered wine, and talked shit about the director of the hit TV show they were both on. Another time, a customer complained the glasses weren't sufficiently chilled, so Jon shoveled a scoopful of ice into his pint of beer and said he was a bartender not a magician. They had a lot of stories in common, but Jon had a few that were distinctly new Brooklyn: he'd seen women breast-feed their babies in the front booths while their boyfriends or husbands downed pints; he'd seen more than one overintellectualized breakup occur, one lover insisting on the transience of everything, how natural it was for love to reach an end, while the other lover ordered rounds of beer that couldn't come fast enough. Penelope liked the way Jon scissored his hands when he talked. She couldn't quite keep up with him, never speaking more than a few sentences a time, but she still felt caught up in an exchange. It took her a while to finish her drink.

"God, I needed that," Penelope said. She pointed to her empty glass, but she meant all of it—his stories, the mod music, the familiar interior of Sheckley's. "I've needed to get away."

"From your old man?"

"I didn't say that."

"Looking after him must be exhausting."

Penelope felt a line being drawn between herself and the bartender.

"I don't mean to offend, seriously, I don't. I just relate. My father has the same problem."

"Your father's disabled?"

"Alcoholic."

"My father isn't—he's had a hard three years."

"I used to have to do the same thing with my old man. Chase him down in bars when he didn't show up for dinner, or my mom's birthday, or when my grandparents were in town. Christmas. Every time, I'd give him a big talk and throw out his bottles, hide his keys. Once, I even let the air out of his tires, and he just called a friend to come get him. I got older, and I didn't want to help him anymore. I wanted to smash his face in. So I moved here, and he joined AA 'cause there wasn't anyone left to pick up the pieces for him anymore. He needed me to leave."

"Pop and I aren't like that."

"You're lucky then."

The word hardly seemed right, but Penelope didn't object.

"There's a picture of your dad hanging in the back. Have you seen it?"

Penelope remembered the old coatroom, its wood paneling. If it got too loud, Lionel would let Penelope sit back there, atop the mountain of wool coats, and draw while the grown-ups drank at the bar. A few times her mother had retreated into the back room, too, and once, she even brought her a Coke. Penelope had been so moved that she was still thanking her mother for the soda an hour later, and it had become a big joke among the grown-ups, how gracious of a little girl she was. The memory now made Penelope sick—how pathetic she had been, how full of need.

Jon asked what had been troubling her lately, if it wasn't her old man. Penelope said she was having trouble with her landlord.

"Can you afford to move?"

It would be hard to find anywhere she could be on her own for so cheap, and she couldn't imagine having roommates, not after five years of being on her own. And if she moved, where would she go? If she left again, she might only find herself back in a few years, Ralph even worse off than he was now. Besides, where would she go? Here, she had at least her father, a job. There was nothing and no one else to follow. The thought uncorked a sadness in her, and she rose to leave.

Jon asked her to stay for another round.

"Wish I could," Penelope said, and she was half-sincere. She liked the bartender. He had a sweet and hospitable way about him, and she didn't have to worry about what she sounded like to him, or what he was deciding about her based on the things she said, the words she used. She felt less alert than she did with Marcus, loose and calm, although she'd had only one drink. Jon was familiar to her. He could have been a boy she knew from PS 23, who left the city, grew out his hair, pierced his ears, and came back a man.

"Come on, it's going to be slow in here for at least another hour. Make my shift go by faster. Stay."

"You're not as bad as I thought you'd be," Penelope said. "As a bartender, I mean. Although I'd have chosen honey and lemon over blueberries and lime. Given the weather."

"Next time."

Penelope waved good-bye, wrapped herself up in her coat and her scarf, and made her way to the exit. The music swelling from the ceiling PA was a buzzy, sweet melody, all synthesizer and tambourine. It was the score to her exit, and Penelope couldn't help but smile. She had found her bar. She turned east toward Greene and the house where she at least had the traces of a life.

Penelope entered the house on Greene and saw the parlor doors were pushed open. Marcus had a guest, another white man in a plaid shirt and blue jeans. They were sitting on the ottomans drinking beer. Penelope squinted at them, the parlor a blinding white, the bubble chandelier pumping too much light into the room. A clanging guitar echoed out of a portable record player.

"Hello," Penelope said, although neither man had addressed her.

She saw panic flit across Marcus's face. He placed one hand underneath his bottle, and gripped the neck with the other, as if he expected, suddenly, to drop it. It hurt her to see him look at her that way—as if she couldn't be trusted, as if she were no good.

The man in plaid stood. He must have been in his midthirties, his dark brown hair already receding, revealing a ridge of bone across the width of his forehead. He had a dozen keys on a ring in the belt loop of his jeans, a pair of glasses in the breast pocket of his shirt.

"You must be Penelope. I'm Marty. Marcus and I grew up together."

"Another California boy," she said, deciding to flirt. "You must have been a swimmer, too?" She inspected his torso, the span of his shoulders. If Marcus was going to be afraid of her, she would give him a reason.

"I was even better than this guy." Marty jerked a thumb toward Marcus, then offered Penelope a beer. She sat next to him on the ottoman, sucked the cold beer out with her tongue. She proclaimed it a good saison and easy to drink, and Marty seemed impressed. She kept playing along, tossing her hair from one side to the other, while she drank. She felt dark in the bright room, cold beside their warm, pale bodies.

Marty announced that he was thinking of moving to the neighborhood. He had been looking at a house over on Macon Street. Marcus spoke for the first time since Penelope arrived.

"I thought you'd never leave the Lower East Side, man. I'm still in shock."

I'm still in shock, Penelope repeated to herself. She drank more of her beer. She tried to enunciate each word perfectly, although the sentence threatened to roll in on itself in her head.

"Why are you leaving the Lower?" she asked.

"I love my place now, really, I've got everything you could ask for—wine chiller, washer, dryer, all new kitchen in granite and stainless steel. I can see the Williamsburg Bridge from my balcony. But one of these days, I'm going to want what Marcus has—hot wife, sweet kid, plans for another. And my one bedroom is not going to cut it. No matter how killer the view."

"Right," Penelope nodded. *Another.* She swallowed down more of the beer. She pointed to the keys dangling from his belt loop. "So are you buying a whole block?"

"No, no—the real estate agent, he forgot them. Handed them to me with the paperwork and forgot to take them back. Can you believe that? Must be a rookie." He slurped from his bottle. "Black kid. Says he grew up in the neighborhood. He told me what I already knew—now's the time to buy before rates go up in a couple of years. But I wish I had done what Marcus did, honestly. He got this place for dirt cheap, really, when you think about it. It's a hassle being out here, sure, but he and Sam are making a fortune on this place just by living in it."

"Well, it's a historic house—" Marcus began, but Marty didn't let him finish.

"And all the things they hate about this neighborhood—they just have to wait it out, and in a few years, it'll be better. Totally different. Worth the wait."

"Marty, we don't hate it."

Marcus flushed behind his ears, but Marty didn't stop. He lowered his voice, flung his arm around Penelope's shoulders, as if he were about to let her in on some tremendous secret. He was close enough that Penelope could feel his breath, smell the appalling mixture of ale and salmon. She lifted up her bottle of beer between them.

"Take Williamsburg."

"Take it how?"

"Twenty years ago, that place was all Puerto Ricans and Hasidic Jews and empty warehouses and crime. Now? Galleries. Condos. Decent bars. And it didn't happen overnight like people think. It took time. It's going to take time here. But this neighborhood will turn around soon. I don't have to tell you that—you knew enough to move here."

"Actually, this is where I'm from."

"Marcus said you were a painter? From Pittsburgh?"

"I was born here."

"Right here? In this parlor?" Marty laughed at his own joke. "Come on, Penelope, you know what I mean—you may have been born here, but you're still a part of the new Brooklyn. You've got a college degree, right? You're an artist, you're a part of the creative class. Don't tell me you haven't taken advantage of all the new places around here—that brick-oven pizza place, the whiskey bar, the sherry bar, Sprout—"

"Is that why you're moving here? For the sherry bar?"

"Marty, you sound like a cad," Marcus said, frowning. "There's a lot more to this neighborhood. Didn't you see all those murals on your walk over here? And it's not just art—there's history."

"Yeah, no kidding. Of course there's history." Penelope glared at Marcus. He seemed lamer than he ever had to her.

"Marcus, I'm not talking about some mural to ODB—I saw that one on my walk over here—and I'm not talking about *history*. I'm talking about the future. I'm talking about *possibility. Potential.* There's no telling what this neighborhood could become—a new Chelsea, an East Village, an Upper West Side. Right now, *anything* is possible. This neighborhood is a blank canvas."

Penelope felt a charge in her fingertips, her cheeks. "Is that what you see?"

"Penelope, I get it, people have all kinds of romantic attachments to where they grew up, but that's life in this city. You lose everything you love here."

"What have you lost? What has Marcus?"

"At least, the three of us in this room can all benefit from the changes—"

"Don't you dare compare me to the two of you—"

"Safer streets, better schools, more amenities. Tell me you don't like good coffee. Tell me you didn't like that beer. And why not? Why not enjoy good things? Would you prefer if I complained about it? Would you prefer if I were miserable? Playing the martyr never did anybody any good—"

Marty still seemed so calm, although his voice was raised, as if it were all a game. Penelope stood so he could see that she didn't want to play. Marcus stood, too.

"There are people here, real people, who already have *potential*. Just because we're not white and didn't go to Stanford—"

"Let's take it easy," Marcus said, and he put up his hand, a few inches from Penelope's chest.

"You can keep your condo and your fucking wine chiller, fucking Sprout. You entitled little shit—"

"Penelope, that's enough." Marcus folded her hand into his and marched her out of the room. As he pulled her out of the parlor, she turned around and called Marty an asshole, and he stood there, stunned, red-faced. He crossed his arms and muttered, "Wow!" to himself, as if he were the one on the higher ground. So Penelope yelled back that he wasn't just any asshole—he was a racist asshole—and she let Marcus take her away.

He took her into a small side room. There was nothing inside but empty shelves, a bare lightbulb hanging from the ceiling, and a chain to turn it on. Marcus pulled the chain and closed the door.

"A racist? Jesus Christ, Penelope. Marty's been my friend for over twenty years."

"He wants to make money off black people being cheated and pushed out! And to say you're making a fortune just by sitting in this house? That's 'cause you're white, and you know it!"

"It's a historic house, Penelope."

"It's always been a historic house, but it hasn't always been worth a million, two million, whatever you and Samantha Harper, Esquire, paid for it. Do you even know who used to live here?"

"What are you doing, Penelope?"

"I am right. You know I am right."

"God, Penelope, don't pretend you're all worked up like this over gentrification—"

"He's talking about things that ruined my father's life. He lost his store, and then he had an accident, and nothing has ever been the same—"

Marcus looked at her gravely. He pressed his fingers to his temples and sighed.

"Marty's an idiot. He's a good friend to me, but he's an idiot. Still, you have no right to make a scene like that. This is my house."

"I live here, too, don't I?"

Marcus didn't answer.

"Don't I?"

He shushed her and put a finger to her lips. "Penelope, you're drunk. And you're embarrassing me."

"I'm sure you'll both have a laugh about it as soon as I go upstairs— *Crazy lady in the attic, ha ha! Ignore her, Marty, ha ha*—"

"Penelope, when will you stop punishing me? My whole life can't change because we had a few nights together. I have a family. You know them."

"I don't know Samantha. She's never here."

"They're my life, Penelope."

"And what about me? Don't you have any ties to me?"

"I've said it before: I think you're beautiful, and you're brilliant, but—"

"You used me. You wanted to get away from your sad marriage, and I was your break. I was your sabbatical. Your tropical vacation—"

"Penelope, stop. Don't talk like that."

"I'll talk about you however I like! You're not my husband. You're not my father. You're nothing to me."

"And what do you think you are to me? You're just an easy fuck who lives upstairs."

Marcus's fists were balled at his sides. His eyes shone darkly. Penelope stepped away, and Marcus seemed to come to his senses. He hung his head in his hands.

"God, I'm sorry. I really can't understand what's come over me since I met you."

"Maybe this is just who you are."

Penelope brushed past him and opened the door. "Consider this my thirty days," she said. "I'm moving out."

The next day Penelope went for a run to scout out where else in the neighborhood she could live. She crossed north past the Y, and the plantless lots, the liquor stores that had hung up wreaths for the holidays, the fried chicken spot on DeKalb, the twinkling lights in the windows of the projects on Myrtle. She ran the industrial stretch of Flushing—*a blank canvas*—then back along the residential streets. She was in Williamsburg now. The houses here were shorter and less stately than in Bed-Stuy, but they were filled with white people. Here the takeover seemed nearly complete: there were the rare Puerto Rican families that had managed to hold out, the blocks that belonged to the Hasidim along the fringes.

Penelope half expected to see an old classmate from RISD while she ran. Her old roommate, Meg, probably lived here now. She might have been a curator, or an assistant to a famous foreign artist, or maybe she was still just painting, living off her parents' money. And here was Penelope, too, with her broken-down life: motherless, her drinking father, a trunk full of *object studies*.

She turned onto Kent with the goal of reaching the water. She was close. A pack of young people were halfway down the block, slowly making their way toward her, their bodies taking over the entire width of the street. The girls wore sheer tights and pleated skirts, the men knee-length coats, unkempt beards.

When they didn't move aside to let her through, she yelled at them. It felt good to raise her voice, to see their startled faces. They muttered after her as she passed, but she couldn't make out what they had said, and she didn't care.

She was rounding the corner when she hit a patch of black ice and slid. She landed hard on her hip, skinned her hand on the curb. The shock of the fall made Penelope dizzy, and she lay flat and waited for the sky to stop revolving. She felt she couldn't move, and she wondered whether she had hit her head and she was dying. She couldn't remember. When she sat up, she saw she had slit her running pants, and she was bleeding where she'd scraped her thigh. She had ripped a hole, too, at the elbow of her insulated shirt. She looked around for anyone to help her up, but the hipsters were gone, disappeared into one of the warehouses.

Penelope hobbled toward the pier, a current of pain transmitted from her heel to her hip with every step. She wondered whether this pain was what Ralph felt when he tried to move around.

The East River was choppier than usual, chunks of ice afloat in the waves. Manhattan was an apparition behind a screen of mist. Penelope found the Empire State Building, the needle glowing a ghostly holiday blue. She would have liked to live here, near the water, if she could afford it. More likely, she would wind up in Flatbush or Crown Heights, maybe farther—Ridgewood. She had thirty days to decide.

Penelope couldn't run back to Bed-Stuy, so she walked, limping as she went. It took her an hour. When she reached the house on Greene, the light was on in the vestibule. She heard a woman singing. Penelope took off her sneakers and held them in her hand so that she could move more quietly.

The door to Samantha's study was open, and her back was to the hall. The room was colored tawny and cream, the long desk fashioned out of what looked like driftwood and metal. A potted orchid sat in the window overlooking the empty backyard. All she could see of Samantha were her feet up on the desk: golden, short nails painted crimson, a silver charm dangling from an anklet.

There was a white ceramic carafe on the desk, a stemless wineglass, and a matching ceramic coaster. The music played from somewhere overhead, another woman's sad, shrill voice.

Penelope tiptoed in her socks, careful not to step on the floorboards that creaked. The chair swung around.

"In a rush?"

Samantha looked like a tiny egg, skinny and white, nestled in the center of the plush desk chair. She wore a chocolate-brown cashmere sweater and red silk pants. Her heels were kicked off to the side, and she had rubbed her face clean of makeup. She looked tired. Penelope decided to say hello, to ask how she was doing.

Samantha shrugged, gesturing toward the air with her glass, giving a toast to no one.

"I'm enjoying the quiet. I can't remember the last time I had the house all to myself." The landlady went on about how Grace was at a playdate in the city, and Marcus was working on a story he had booked. "I'm off for the night!" She made the exclamation without any joy and took a sip of her wine.

"I won't disturb you," Penelope said and turned back to the stairs.

"Don't be ridiculous," Samantha said flatly. "Actually, I've been hoping to catch you. Come in, won't you?"

Penelope sat on the beige loveseat and crossed her legs. She saw Samantha eye the rip in her leggings, but she said nothing. The landlady sat and watched her and drank, as if she were trying to discern something by studying Penelope's face, her mannerisms. Penelope kept cool. She let the music fill the room, the woman's voice quivering out of the overhead speakers.

"*Little Earthquakes.* Do you know it?"

Penelope shook her head.

"I used to listen to this album all the time when I was pregnant with Grace. Marcus hates it. He hates most of my music, actually, says it's all just women complaining about their lovers, but that's not true at all." She smiled. "Marcus and I have been together long enough that we know the things we can share and the things that we can't. Marriage is like that."

The women stared at each other, neither of them moving.

"Where are my manners? Would you like a glass?"

"I'm not much of a wine drinker."

"Hm, neither is Marcus. He's a whiskey man. But he's not always so particular. He'll drink other things, if they're around."

Penelope scanned Samantha's face.

"You must know each other so well after all these years together."

"We've been through a lot. School, and marriage, and then more school. Quitting jobs and finding jobs. Grace. This house. Both of our mothers dying the year before we moved to New York."

"I'm sorry to hear that."

"You're not close to your mother, are you? What a shame. Parents don't live forever, you know."

"I'm aware."

"You'll feel differently when you have children of your own. It's obvious you're very good with them. Grace adores you. Lately, whenever I tuck her in for bed, she's all *Penelope this and Penelope that*. She seems less lonely with you around."

Samantha swirled the wine in her glass, inhaled the bouquet.

"When I was your age, Grace was already four. I had her in my second year of law school, and our parents thought we were nuts. That was the hardest part, the beginning. But you never regret starting a family. You can create the life you want. It's a beautiful thing."

Penelope didn't believe her.

"But I remember the years before—when I wasn't committed to anyone, anything. I hope you're taking advantage. You must be seeing someone?"

Penelope could see through the landlady now. All this talk had been a preamble, and she was finally closing in on what she really wanted to say.

"Come on now," Samantha said, her smile growing even more strained and gorgeous. "I'll keep your secret." Her teeth were violet from the wine.

"There isn't anything to tell."

"I don't believe you. Someone like you must have many options—you're so athletic, exotic. I'm skinny, yes, but you have all these muscles and curves. I'm just straight up and down. You're far more striking than someone like me. And your hair—there's so much of it. And it looks so *messy*, but in a good way. That's the whole beauty of it, isn't it?"

Penelope slid onto the edge of her chair, not as if she were ready to leave but to show the landlady she wouldn't be intimidated. "Is there a point you're getting at?"

"All I'm saying is there has to be someone. There's no way that teaching a bunch of kids how to finger-paint and running a couple of laps around the block is enough for a woman like you. I remember what it's like to be single. To date and flirt and fuck around. Have pity on me, Penelope. I don't have that freedom anymore, and I don't have any single girlfriends to tell me their war stories. So *dish*. Tell me. I promise I won't tell Marcus."

"Samantha, is there something you want to say to me?"

"Why would there be? Is there something you want to say to me?"

"Look, I used to be a bartender, so I can tell when people are drinking because they're actually feeling good and trying to celebrate something—like having the house to themselves—or if they're just drinking to work up the nerve to do something they could never do sober."

"And which kind of drinker are you?"

"Excuse me?"

"You're not just a former bartender, are you, Penelope? You're quite the connoisseur yourself. Of very expensive, very chic gin."

"Were you in my room?"

"Of course not. That would violate our agreement, wouldn't it? I've seen the bottles. Marcus might be the man of the house, but I'm the one who takes down the recycling."

"Do you have a problem with my drinking?"

"Your drinking is your concern, not mine."

"Well then what did you want to talk to me about?"

"Marcus tells me you might be moving."

"I've already given him my notice. I'll be gone by the new year."

"He said you didn't give a reason for wanting to leave."

"The lease doesn't require that I do."

Samantha frowned. "You've put me in quite a pickle."

"How is that?"

"Someone has to pay the mortgage while Marcus goes off and becomes a writer, and I'm not around nearly enough. Grace is often alone, and it helps her, I know, to have someone in the house. I never meant for that to be you, but Grace has grown very fond . . . The last thing I want is for her to lose someone again. Even if it's just the idea of someone."

Penelope didn't say anything.

"Please don't rush this decision. It would crush Grace. We can talk about it after the holidays when we get back from California. Deal?"

Samantha smiled, as if there was a lever inside of her that she had pulled, but Penelope could see that her lips were shaking. She murmured about the room being too hot, fanned her face, and lifted the carafe to pour more wine into her glass. Penelope saw her hand slip. The landlady knocked over the glass and the carafe, the dark wine began to seep into the pale wood.

"Damn," she said, and instinctively Penelope rose to help her. Samantha was fishing tissues out of a box on the shelf, the flimsy Kleenex coming apart as she tried to sop up the mess. The wine dripped onto the beige carpet. It leaked onto the suede chair.

Penelope took a few blank pages out of the printer and spread them over the desk. They absorbed the liquid but not the stain. Penelope could feel the warmth of Samantha's little body beside her; their elbows brushed as they tried to stop the spill. "Damn," Samantha muttered again. "Damn, damn."

She stopped and clenched the desk, tilted her head up to the ceiling with her eyes closed.

"I think you should go," she said.

"I have some paint thinner upstairs. It might help with the stains."

"You've done enough, Penelope. I want you here for Grace—not for me."

"Is that everything then?"

"It is."

Penelope had hardly stepped into the hall when Samantha slammed the door.

12

Nobody Wants to See

The Harpers left on Christmas Eve. They weren't careful about making noise, although the sun wasn't up yet, and Penelope could have been asleep for all they knew. She was at her window, listening to Samantha and Marcus shout back and forth to one another from different floors of the house. Had he remembered to pack the rubbing alcohol in case somebody had a fall? Flashlights and extra sweaters for walks on the beach?

Just before the car arrived, Samantha dashed around the house, sealing all the rooms shut. Penelope strained to listen in case Grace called out to say good-bye or to wish her a merry Christmas, but she heard nothing. A black town car drove them away, and Penelope watched, her cup of cold, murky tea balanced on her knee. She hated to admit to herself that she still envied them—Marcus may have fucked the tenant, and they may have lost a baby—whether the boy had been the size of a thimble or a peach or a softball when he died, Penelope didn't know—but they were still indisputably one. She had heard it all morning: the evidence that they were all moving parts of the same thing, yelling and carrying, packing and leaving together.

The house felt emptier, as if Penelope could sense all the closed doors. She didn't like the feeling of being left behind. Penelope lit a cigarette and pushed open the porthole window. She promised herself she wouldn't fantasize about the Harper family Christmas on the beach, not when she had a family and a holiday of her own. Tonight would be her first Christmas in New York with Ralph, without Mirella.

She wasn't due at Halsey Street until evening, so she let the radio play and read from a library book of poems by Gwendolyn Brooks. She drank from a small bottle of gin as she read, until she fell asleep facedown in the winter sun, the lines of a poem orbiting in her head: something about burrowing away from the light, finding comfort in the haze. It was dark when she woke. Somehow she had lost the whole day to poems and gin and sleep. She took a shower to sober up under the cold spray.

She put on the best of everything she had to prepare for the night: coconut oil in her hair, burgundy lipstick, her leather skirt, a cashmere sweater a customer had left one night in the bar in Squirrel Hill and never returned to reclaim. She inspected her reflection in the mirror above the china sink, and decided she looked beautiful. She wanted someone to tell her so. She took a photograph of herself, half her face in the shadow of her camera.

She left to pick up the beef pastelitos she had ordered from the Dominican spot on Fulton Street. The girl who rang her up wore blue eye shadow and door-knocker earrings, and she spoke to Penelope in curt English, although she'd been chatting with the woman behind the counter in lazy, beautiful, sprawling Spanish. Could she tell Penelope was Dominican? Penelope wanted to say something to let the cashier know, but what was there to say? *Dos fundas plásticas? Feliz Navidad? My mother is alive. She lives across the ocean. She sent me a postcard. I threw it away.*

Penelope settled for "Gracias," which anyone could have said, and she headed for Halsey Street, even lower than she had been when she first heard the Harpers leave.

Miss Beckett opened the door, and Penelope shouldn't have been surprised but she was. Ralph hadn't mentioned inviting the old bird. She wore a festive, sparkling green dress, and led Penelope up the stairs, as if she were the one hosting a party and it was her house. Ralph was upstairs on the old sofa, elegant in an evergreen sweater, wool pants, his battered oxfords. He smelled clean, like detergent and sweet tobacco. Miss Beckett must have done the laundry. Penelope kissed her father, and he didn't look up from the television. He was watching reruns of different shows from the seventies, flipping between channels.

Penelope occupied herself, arranging her spread on the coffee table, iced cookies and bottled eggnog, the pastelitos. Miss Beckett had outdone her with a Christmas ham, a tureen of string beans, biscuits, and a bowl of her infamous potato salad, nearly all celery and mayonnaise. The women served food onto plastic plates and settled down to watch TV with Ralph, who offered commentary on each of the sitcoms. They drank cup after cup of the eggnog, which Penelope had allowed herself to spike. It was Christmas, after all.

"This is nice," Penelope said, raising her voice above the commercial. She looked around the living room and regretted not putting up decorations. A few blinking lights around Mirella's empty flowerpots, a tinsel wreath over the mantel. Dollar-store old-fashioned Christmas cards dangling from twine. Just a little would have spruced up the room.

"Isn't this nice?" she said again.

"I've got to pee," Ralph answered, and Miss Beckett was over him in an instant, offering the crook of her elbow. Ralph lumbered to his feet, and they crept slowly to the hall. Penelope sat on the couch obsoletely and waited for them to return.

"Well, I think it's time for presents, don't the two of you?" Miss Beckett stood in the middle of the room and put her hands on her hips, as if she were some kind of talk-show host.

"We wait until midnight," Penelope said. "It's tradition."

Miss Beckett gave Ralph a questioning look, and he explained.

"That's how they do it in DR. They wait until twelve o'clock and then open up everything. That's how we've always done it."

"I don't know if I can wait that long. I'm afraid to have too much punch."

Neither Ralph nor Penelope offered a solution.

Miss Beckett bowed her head and muttered something about a headache, how she should probably just leave Penelope and Ralph to themselves—she didn't want to intrude on tradition. Penelope didn't stop her when she shuffled out of the room to retrieve her gifts, and Ralph didn't look up from the TV. Penelope wondered whether her father could even tell the old woman had left the room; did he even know Penelope was there beside him? Had he noticed her fix his drink and lay out the iced cookies he liked?

Miss Beckett gave Penelope a powder-pink turtleneck, fuzzier than anything she could ever imagine wearing, and an enamel teapot. No one had given her a gift in years, and she found herself thanking the woman sincerely and offering to walk her home. She lied and said she had left the old woman's gift at home, and Miss Beckett shook her head and said, "Never you mind, never you mind about me. As long as you like your things! You do like your things?" Penelope assured her that she did, and she felt an unexpected pity for the woman. They were just alike, pining for Ralph's affections, hunting for family.

Ralph's gift was a tambourine that he immediately started to whack. The jingles rang, and Ralph put on a soulful face to amuse the women, and they all laughed. Penelope wrapped her arm around his shoulders although she felt the beginnings of heat in her face, tension behind her ribs. She gave him a kiss. He didn't have a present for Miss Beckett either.

When they were through thanking her, Miss Beckett clapped her hands and sat between them.

"This truly is the Lord's day! What joy! Last year I was by myself on Christmas Eve, just wondering about how the two of you were doing in Pittsburgh. But it finally feels like Christmas this year. It truly does."

Ralph reached for Miss Beckett's hand and squeezed, and Penelope decided to wait downstairs while they said their good-byes. In the foyer, Penelope wondered when exactly things between her father and Una had shifted. Maybe it had been after Sheckley's, and the postcard that announced Mirella wasn't alive somewhere thinking of Ralph. Maybe it had gone on for a long time. Either way, Penelope couldn't begrudge the old woman. She knew how it felt to have Ralph finally turn his attention to you, to squeeze your hand, and look at you, before he returned to his record or himself. If Ralph was an island, Miss Beckett was another woman rowing her boat, waiting for the tide to turn and bring her closer to shore.

When they were outside, Miss Beckett reached for Penelope so they could tread over the ice together. They linked arms, Penelope without her jacket, Miss Beckett in her bright pink peacoat. The old woman thanked Penelope for seeing her home.

"Least I could do."

"You never do the least, young lady. I see that about you now. I never understood why you left—and why you stayed away even after your father was alone, and, you know, disabled. I used to say to him, *Why hasn't she come back!* And your father, he'd say, *Penny has to find her own way.* And I had my doubts about you, Penelope—the kind of woman you'd become, whether you could see how lucky you were to have a father like Ralph."

Penelope nodded, although she hardly felt lucky. She worked hard to keep her feet steady over the ice, and she felt acutely how cold she was, her numb fingers, her dry throat. She had been thirsty all day, she realized, ever since she woke up that afternoon in the attic, but all she'd had to drink for hours was eggnog and rum. She'd drained cup after cup, although it was too sweet and it blurred her sight, and it had sated nothing. She coughed into her hand.

"You lucky girl," Miss Beckett said and patted Penelope's hand before she unlocked her door and disappeared into her little hovel of an apartment.

Penelope returned to the house to the sound of vinyl scratching. Ralph hadn't been able to stand to start the record over again. She lifted the needle and set it on the outer edge; she thought, briefly, of unplugging the whole apparatus, tearing out the cords, and smashing it all underfoot.

The strings started up again, and the horns joined in. Ralph shook his tambourine.

"You should have told me Una was coming so I could buy her a gift."

Ralph slapped the tambourine gently in his own time, fracturing the melody.

"Una doesn't care about that kind of thing—she's a simple woman."

"I'm sure she'd have liked a necklace or another sweater."

"Pfsh," Ralph said. "I'm sure our company was enough."

"Did you even get anything for me?"

"Of course I did," Ralph said. "You go get it." He sent her off to the bedroom with instructions to look for a black garbage bag inside the closet.

She found the bag on the floor. Something flat and angular threatened to pierce through from the inside, and Penelope carried it carefully out of the bedroom. On her way out, she passed the little bulletin board where she had tacked up the exercises from Dr. Elias. The tiny, robust ink men reached for their ankles and pointed their toes; they touched a palm to one knee.

She left the bag on the side of the couch and went into the kitchen to wash dishes. She didn't want to sit next to Ralph. She squeezed detergent on the dishes and scrubbed them, turned the water on hot and held her hands underneath, let her skin redden and pucker.

He wasn't any better than when she had arrived in the fall, and it was plain that her life wasn't any better either—she'd wasted months looking after the Harpers and wanting their life. When the dishes were clean, she decided to go home. She went back into the living room, and Ralph was shaking the tambourine.

"Merry Christmas, Penny! It's midnight. You come here and open your gift."

Penelope didn't want to stay, but her father smiled at her so broadly, she consented and sat next to him. He watched her tear open the garbage bag and extract a wooden frame. The molding was ashen white and grainy to the touch.

"The lady at the store said any serious artist would appreciate one of these. I found the number in one of your old catalogues—we still get them in the mail. Maybe you can paint me something. I'll hang it up over the fireplace."

"I don't paint anymore, Pop."

"Since when?"

"Since ten years ago."

"Pfsh. You never told me."

"I did."

She knew she should thank her father, so as not to upset him, but she couldn't bring herself to do it. She leaned the frame against the couch and handed him his gift instead. Ralph ripped it open with the sad, expectant smile of a man who never had a proper Christmas as a boy. He looked at the gift, then tucked one hand into the crook of his arm, as if that was where he had his heart.

In the photograph, he was forty-three, his afro not yet gray, and his skin like tinted glass, honey brown and smooth. He had a cigar tucked between his fingers, and his mouth half-open, as if he were advising the cameraman on angle, or about to laugh. Lionel Sheckley and Freddie Elias stood on either side of him, their arms around his shoulders. Dr. Elias looked slender and sophisticated, Sheckley satisfied and plump in a tilted fedora. Ralph was clearly the leader of the bunch, charismatic, handsome, leaning forward in his pants and blazer, a skinny dark tie flying away from his shirt. The bar behind them didn't look like a bar at all. With the unpainted wood and shutters, it could have been a cabin in some woods, if not for the pavement they stood on, the cement steps up to the door that gave the scene away as Brooklyn. The back of the photograph read *Franklin Ave, 1987* in blue pen.

Ralph drew the photograph closer to him, bowing his head to examine the younger men. He tapped their faces through the glass of the frame.

"This is from another life."

Watching her father smile, Penelope softened. "Would you believe it's been hanging in the back of Sheckley's all this time?"

"Look at Lionel! That suit is really something. And Freddie—goddamn, he looks the same."

Ralph didn't say anything about himself in the photograph. His black loafers, his pants hitched up to show off just a bit of his argyle socks. His feet pointed straight ahead.

"Put it up on the mantel for me, will you?"

Penelope obeyed and placed the frame on the center of the mantelpiece. When she sat down again, Ralph hugged her, the wiry hair on his cheek scraping her skin. She felt lifted for a moment by the sense she had done something right. Ralph's grief had a density and a taste; like a gas, it could fill a room. Penelope hoped that every time her father looked at the picture, it would open a window and let in some light.

Ralph kissed Penelope on the cheek, and she almost forgave him for the frame.

"Do you think it will snow this year? For Christmas?" Ralph said. "Your mother always loved the snow."

Penelope wondered whether Ralph was teetering on the edge of some reminiscence about Mirella. She tried to steer him away.

"It's probably better if it doesn't—if it snows, the ceiling on the fourth floor will leak."

"I can fix that."

"Don't you go climbing up no ladder by yourself."

"You know, it snowed the Christmas your mother was pregnant with you. It was probably the busiest December we'd ever had at the store. It was really something, Penny."

"I bet," Penelope said, and she stirred to leave, but Ralph stopped her, locking his fingers around her wrist.

"We had so many orders I had to bring some of them home with me after the store closed. Me and your mother gift wrapped everything in this shiny blue paper—we must have wrapped a record for every living person in Bed-Stuy that year. We killed a lot of trees.

"And when I couldn't come home, your mother, she'd bring me dinner—a pastrami sandwich and a pickle every night. She'd walk over, and it would take her almost half an hour, through all that snow, and I'd take a break so we could eat together in the stockroom. It was never more than a few minutes, but it was the best part of every day.

"She couldn't stay, because I'd be at the shop until two most nights. I had to record every sale in my book and clean up for the next day. It took a while. The streets would be empty on my walk back, except for teenagers, jitterbugging up and down the block. And I'd see a few ladies, too, sitting on the stoops, mad as hell, waiting for their men to come home.

"But on Christmas Eve, everybody was out. Heading home *from* parties, heading out *to* parties, drinking, carrying on, carrying big bags of presents, sliding on the ice. I said hello to everyone I passed, even if I didn't know their names, and most of them, they knew me. 'Happy,

happy, Mr. Grand,' they said, and 'What's happening, Mr. Grand? Merry Christmas!'

"You know, no one ever believes old men when we say how good our lives were then. But they believe us when we say how bad our lives are now."

Things were better before you fell down the stairs. Things were better before you drank rum like water.

"Anyway, so it's Christmas Eve, and when I got home to Marcy that night, Mirella was waiting up for me. She was in the kitchen with her big belly in a red dress and heels. She was eating rice pudding right out of the pot with a spoon. *Arroz con leche* with raisins and a whole lot of cinnamon. That was all she wanted in those last few months.

"We sat at the table and we talked and we ate that pudding, and even if we'd been married for a while, it felt like a date. We were still getting to know each other. All we really knew then was that we liked each other and our life and that we wanted you.

"We stayed up all night, listening to music and talking, then we went out for a walk before sunrise. Your mother—she was still in love with this city, everything in it was new to her, even the snow—I think it was her second winter. She kept kicking up snow and touching her stomach, and she was happy. She knew we'd have the whole day to our-selves 'cause the shop was closed. A rare thing. I don't even know what we did after that walk. But it doesn't matter, because it was perfect. Yes, Penelope, it was perfect."

"Sounds like a fairy tale," Penelope said and dropped her head in her hands.

"What's the matter with you? You drunk?"

"I don't want to talk about Mirella. You think she's in DR reminisc-ing about us?"

"I don't know what she's doing. She didn't write to me—"

"Jesus," Penelope said, and she stood, irritated, although she knew Ralph was bound to ask sooner or later.

"Did you ever write back to her?"

"Pop, it's Christmas."

"She's our family."

"I don't know that woman from your story, Pop. My mother wasn't some big-bellied saint. My mother never even wanted me."

Penelope had never said it aloud before, so plainly, but the truth of it struck her, palpably, like a palm to the chest.

"Now that's a lie, Penny. All we ever wanted was to give you a family."

"And we have one," Penelope said, and she took her father's hand and laid it against her neck, as if he could feel her pulse and remember that she, too, was a person. That she was here beside him. "We don't need her," she said.

"You don't see, Penelope. Nobody wants to see. My life is the way it is because she's gone. You think I care that I can't walk? Sure, but not nearly as much as I care that she's gone. It's not my legs that are killing me, Penelope. It's not my spine. *It's her.*"

"But what about me, Pop? What about me?"

"What about you?" Ralph said, and he flung her hand away.

Penelope couldn't help but remember Marcus and how he had spoken to her in the room just behind the parlor, while Marty drank his beer on the other side—*And what do you think you are to me?* She had been as foolish to run to her father as she had been to turn to Marcus.

Her mother was right—she had never been more to Ralph than a thing, like the house, the store, some proof he'd made a good life and left the orphanage for good. And still she had devoted herself to him because he was willing to offer her something, no matter how partial, how meager. Penelope stood and started to assemble her things.

"What are you doing?"

She was already back in her coat, and she lifted on her gloves, her hat, the scarf, revolving around her neck.

"Why am I here? If you don't want me here, then why am I here?"

193

"Penny, calm down. Take off your jacket and calm down."

"I've tried with you, Pop," she said. "I've really tried. But you don't see me. I'm not even here."

Ralph called after her, but she ran down the stairs away from him. If she didn't move fast enough, she was afraid she would change her mind, so she charged out of the house, heavy-footed in her boots.

She ran in the gray and snowless dark, unthinking, quick. Her throat was closed with thirst, her eyes blending together the trees, the stone fronts of the unlit houses. But she went on, Halsey Street sliding off her soles. She didn't have to stay if she didn't want to; there was another place for her to go, another way to be.

She reached the avenue and came out from under the cover of trees onto the curb where the sky shone an imperial blue. She looked up into the night and saw nothing but color. No clouds, no stars, without rupture—clear.

13

Despegando

It was the last day that Mirella would ever have to clean a white woman's house. Mrs. Spillers needed her just for a few hours, to dust, to clean the floors, the bathroom. The stooping and scrubbing in the bathroom hurt her back, so she worked quickly. She would miss cleaning—the exertion of it, the smell of hot soap and bleach, the feeling she could transform a ruined thing. But it was time. She was forty-four, the age her father had been when he died, and who knew how much time she had left? When she was done, she let Mrs. Spillers know. She was reading a magazine on the velvet couch, the tiny dog with his head on her feet. She rose and shook Mirella's hand, thanked her for all the years, wondered how she'd ever find someone as good. She handed her the last fat white envelope, and Mirella pulled on her jacket and rang for the elevator. It was then that Mrs. Spillers asked her what she would do now. She could have asked at any point that morning instead of flipping through one magazine after another, waiting for the hours to pass. Now she expected Mirella to fit her whole life into the moments it would take for the elevator to reach the apartment door. She said something about spending more time in her own house, with her husband and her daughter, although it wasn't true—she hadn't quit her jobs for that.

Mrs. Spillers said, "Your daughter still lives at home?" and when Mirella nodded, the white lady deemed it lovely. Then she wished Mirella well and the elevator arrived. On the train back to Brooklyn, Mirella fretted over Mrs. Spiller's question, her surprised expression. She had pointed out with her question how little Penelope had progressed since she was a girl. Mrs. Spillers's children had framed diplomas on her wall, photographs of them in faraway places, safaris, bridges in cities that looked like Europe. She had nothing to show for her daughter, and her daughter nothing to show for herself. Penelope was stuck, and Mirella had known it for a long time—apparently, so did Mrs. Spillers.

When she got off the A, Mirella went to the new drugstore on Fulton Street. It was one of the nicer pharmacy chains, but there had never been one in the neighborhood before. She found a thirty-dollar face cream, pale green in a little apothecary jar. It was her reward for her retirement, a reward for her new life. She thought of buying something for Penelope—one of those purple lipsticks that she liked, a lotion to calm that hair—but the girl didn't deserve it. She had earned nothing, returned nothing, after all that Mirella had given, so she walked on in the midday cool, feeling free. No more white women's houses.

At her vanity, Mirella traced the planes of her face. Her fingers slipped into the shallow cavity beneath her eyes, glided across the steep angle of her cheekbones. She rubbed the cream along her jaw, her hairline. So far, her only wrinkles were the fan of lines at the corners of her eyes, the faint parentheses that enclosed her lips even when she wasn't smiling. She would have to be careful. Her mother dead, she wasn't sure exactly how she would age.

Mirella dabbed on more of the cream. This would be one of her routines, part of her retirement. She didn't know what to do next, but she imagined finally living a life somewhat more akin to the lives of the women she had admired when she was a girl living near La Plaza Valerio. These women never worked; they oversaw their households and raised children, bought fabric for new curtains, sat in rocking chairs on the patios with their husbands to listen to the evening radio. They were in the business of being beautiful, and although Mirella wouldn't be busy with friends, her daughter, her husband, or the household, she remembered these women when she sat at her vanity, rubbing the cream into her neck. They had been married to her father's friends and would visit on the nights Eleazar hosted parties. They would crowd into Ramona's room, standing around the vanity table Eleazar had bought for her and which she never used. They gossiped about their husbands, the stench of their cigars, the bellies they were growing from sitting around and drinking rum while they argued about politics as if talk were all it would take to arreglar el país. The women weren't bitter; they seemed to love their husbands, or, at the very least, find them amusing. They laughed as they sprayed their hair and dusted their noses. They ground the points of their dark pencils into their cheeks and shoulders to create false beauty marks that would make other men wonder where else they had marks hidden on their bodies. They addressed Ramona while they groomed themselves, asking about La Billonera and the maids and whether Ramona was going to put any makeup on, but Ramona wasn't made for their dizzying, chaotic talk. She was Mirella's quiet, dark mother, and after a while, she would leave to help the workers in the kitchen although she wasn't needed there. Mirella would stay behind, perched on the mahogany bed her parents shared, trying to discern the meaning behind their female chatter, their ideas about Balaguer and boleros, their figures and each other's, the best scrub to use on hot days to smell like flowers and not sweat down there, the news they had heard about the men they had loved before their husbands, who fled to San Juan during the Trujillato, married Puerto Rican girls, and never returned. Mirella basked in the mystery of their gossip and perfume, until one of the women called her over and began sweeping powder on her freckled nose. The makeup smelled of chalk dust and hibiscus, and it seemed to hold the power to make Mirella one of them.

She wouldn't spend all her money on creams and makeup, no—not her twenty years' worth of fat white envelopes. And she wouldn't spend it on the house either, which had started to decay, although neither Ralph nor Penelope seemed to notice. The paint on the front of the house was peeling, the rich chocolate of the stones giving way to patches the color of mud. The ceiling on the fourth floor swelled with craters of water damage, and still Ralph refused to call the repairman. He would climb onto the roof with his toolbox, and experiment with duct tape and plaster and spackling and boards of wood, while the rain blew bubbles into the fourth-floor ceiling. Mirella had tried to reason with him—if the leak were in the shop he would just give in and call a professional—but Ralph didn't concede, coming down from the roof every time, shivering and smiling, certain that *this time* he had finally done it. To spend her savings on the house would be a waste.

Mirella wanted to travel. She could start in Latin America, visit cities where she spoke the language. Sit in cafés, drink wine, be anonymous. See things. She had considered Europe, too, maybe Canada, or Florida, there were beaches in this country, too. She would go anywhere just to let in a bit more life. Her entire world had been Aguas Frescas and then Halsey Street. It was too grim to think about—but she had her savings, and now she had her time. All she had to do was work on Ralph, manage to lure him away from the store so that he could go with her. And she had to fix Penelope, too, before she went away.

Mirella knew that Penelope would never listen to her advice. She had lost that power over the girl a long time ago. She had seen the uselessness of intervening when Penelope dropped out of RISD and moved home. She had said nothing when Penelope finished at the public college and took her job shelving books at the library. It was different for Mirella—she was old and married, had never been to college, faltered in English. She knew nothing. But Penelope—she didn't have to live her whole life out in Brooklyn, drawing, running, wasting years. She could do anything.

It's only been a few months, Ralph said when Mirella asked if he intended on having Penelope live with them forever. *She's my daughter,* he added, as if she didn't know. *I'm not in any rush for her to leave.*

Penelope's days were predictable. She arrived late from her nights in the city, where Mirella had gathered she must have had a boyfriend. She took the steps three at a time, quick and quiet in the running shoes she wore with everything—her leather jacket and pleated skirts, the dark blue jeans so tight they seemed to be spray-painted on. She went straight to the kitchen to wash the dishes Ralph had left in the sink, then she poured herself a glass of water, then another, and another, before returning to her room. In the mornings, she would come out to start the coffee in the kettle, so Ralph could have a cup before he left for the store. She would pour herself a mug then go back into her room to sleep until it was time for her shift at the library. She came home, she ran, she went out again. Was this all that women with degrees in art history could do? Couldn't they work in museums? Teach in schools? Go back to school and get a degree at a higher level?

Mirella stood from the vanity, her skin saturated and new, and herself more disheartened than she thought she would be on her last day of work. She considered lying down. *My garden,* she thought, and it was the only thing that kept her from turning in to the bed and drawing the blinds.

The sun was still bright, the branches of a large maple tree bending in the wind. She put on her work boots, sun hat, and gloves, and left for the garden, counting the hours until sunset, until Ralph and Penelope returned.

Everything in the yard was familiar: the water hose, the bags of mulch, the fertilizer and packets of seeds, the trowel and scoop and shovel and rake, the watering can, and her knife. She took up the tools in her hand. They had waited for her in the shed, faithfully. This work would fill her days now.

Mirella pruned her rosebush first, watered the flowers, and pinched the vegetables to see if they were ripe. It was fall, and in a few weeks she could pick the squash and the lettuces. Mirella sweat in her jeans and paisley blouse; she swatted away the bugs drawn by the scent of her new face cream. She smoked a cigarette while the sun set, catching the crumbling ash of her Parliament in an ashtray. She sat underneath the dirty neon umbrella at the round glass table they had set outside for entertaining but hardly ever used. They had gotten life all wrong, she and Ralph.

Mirella could point to the moment she had lost what little claim she had on her daughter. It was during her first winter home from RISD. Penelope was the one who answered the phone, then she fell onto her knees and screamed, *Abuela's dead.* She was doubled over and crying, *Por qué pero por qué que pasó,* so Mirella took the phone and handled the rest of the news. Ramona had been sick for three weeks, vomiting and headaches. The neighbors had brought her soup. That morning they went to check on her and she was dead, across her bed, Lulú's head on her lap.

Mirella called Ralph at the store and told him to come home. It was snowing outside, and it took him a long time to reach them. When he arrived, Penelope was still sitting on the floor, beating her thighs, making animal sounds while she cried.

Ramona's neighbors called again, and Ralph took Penelope into the living room to listen to a record he said might calm her down, while Mirella handled the logistics. She wired money for the burial and decided against paying for a doctor to come up from the valley for an autopsy. It didn't matter whether it had been cancer or an aneurysm or a parasite she had caught from neglecting to use the water filter—Ramona was dead.

Mirella could hardly think about the fact that her mother was dead. It was too terrible watching Penelope, wild and inconsolable. Penelope's face turned red, she struggled to breathe, and she clutched at her chest, as if something burned there, and Mirella imagined that Penelope might die, right there in front of her, screaming. How did hearts work? Could someone die from grief? Mirella wasn't sure. Her father had died mysteriously, and then, her mother. Maybe it was something in their genes—death by too much feeling. She tried to help Ralph, who sat beside Penelope while she moaned, and patted her hand every few minutes. "Calm down, Penelope," she said, but the girl didn't listen, and Mirella left the room, her mother's death revolving in her mind. She had never been attached to Ramona, and she wouldn't miss her. She felt sad not that she had lost something but rather that her mother had—Ramona had loved her life, her pipe and her blue casita and her mountain. Mirella was sorry the old woman wouldn't live any more of the days she had loved so much. She was sorry for Penelope, too, afraid she would be unable to stop crying, the way Mirella had been after her father died. She had cried every day for a year, and then only once in a while, abruptly and for no reason at all, at times that seemed to have nothing to do with her father. And then Mirella learned to put away her sadness, to store it in her body, somewhere out of the way, higher than her stomach, below her throat.

Ralph bought Penelope's ticket to DR, and he had offered to buy one for Mirella as well. *What's the use?* she had said. *She's in the ground. Penelope shouldn't be going either.* Mirella had asked Ralph to tell Penelope not to go—her second semester at RISD was starting up soon—but he said Penelope was eighteen and old enough to travel on her own. On the morning of her flight, Penelope was still crying, shuddering at the table and neglecting the toast Ralph had burned for her. "I can't believe you're not coming," Penelope had said, and Mirella had answered her, "Why are you? She's dead. She won't be able to tell who's there and who isn't." Penelope had gone on crying.

Penelope didn't call when she landed, and Mirella spent the days wondering whether the plane had crashed, whether there had been an accident while Fernando drove her up the mountain. She wondered whether Penelope collapsed onto the floor of the chapel during the funeral service, whether she made those same low moans, so terrible and primitive. Aguas Frescas was colder in the winter, wetter, and the sky converted to an eerie, foggy blue. Penelope had never been there during the wet season, and Mirella dreamed of her daughter in the empty casita, brewing coffee in Ramona's cafetera, combing her hair with Ramona's comb, going for walks to las cascadas in the rain with Lulú, both of them whimpering.

When Penelope returned from DR, she cut off all her hair and glared at Mirella when she saw her in the hall. She was home for only a few days before returning to RISD, but she hardly spoke. She didn't call Mirella anything, not Mami, Ma, or even her name. Mirella asked her once about the funeral, and Penelope said something about communion and a lot of yellow candles, a big sancocho and habichuelas con dulce afterward at Angelina's house. Lulú ran off that night, after they buried Ramona. No one found her before Penelope had to leave the mountain for her flight. Mirella wanted to say to her, *Your father didn't go with you either,* but she couldn't bring herself to say the words, to step into the ever-deepening gulf between them. Penelope hadn't brought Mirella anything from the casita where she had grown up; for herself, she had taken Ramona's collection of candles, her old radio, and favorite blue housedress. Before she left for Providence, Mirella overheard her listening to that old radio; she smelled the candles burning in her room.

One more semester, and Penelope would return. Mirella had never wanted her to go to art school, but she hadn't wanted her to quit either. She started at the college, and they began to skirt around each other as best they could, although it wasn't easy. Penelope almost a woman now, the two of them living on the same floor of the house. Mirella would walk into the bathroom to wash her face just as Penelope was rinsing charcoal from under her fingernails at the sink; she would wander into the kitchen to make toast to find Penelope at the counter, waiting for her crust to brown; she would wash her underwear by hand and then hang it to dry only to find Penelope's bright, stringy panties already dangling from the showerhead. The most they said to one another was, "Where is your father?" or "Where's Pop?" unless they found a reason to fight—a misplaced sponge, a failure to hand over the mail—then they could yell at each other for a good long while.

The dark came, and insects materialized in the garden. They circled her, but still she didn't move, except to bring the cigarette to her mouth, to tap off the ash.

Habla con ella. A voice rose in Mirella as if transmitted from the dead. *Mothers don't live forever. Talk to her.*

Mirella put out her cigarette, the bugs finally enough of a nuisance for her to leave. She opened the shed and put away her tools, walked out of the garden into the basement and back up into the house, taking nothing with her.

Inside, she heard running water and dishes. A faint light spilled onto the second-floor landing. Mirella made her way up the stairs by that light. The first novela in her nightly lineup was starting in a few minutes, but she didn't turn into her bedroom. The hardwood floors gave way to peachy tile, and Mirella stepped into the narrow kitchen.

Penelope didn't look up from the sink. She cleaned the dishes roughly, a few swipes with a sponge, and a short rinse. Suds pooled in the dish rack. She was in shorts and a tank top, her hair pinned in a messy bun of curls at the top of her head. Mirella marveled at her daughter's hairless limbs, their smooth amber glow. How did she get her skin to gleam? Penelope was all muscle and skin, but she was broader than Mirella, too broad, her shoulders solid, thighs dense.

Penelope lowered a dish into the rack; it clanged against another, as if both were made of metal. She didn't look up from her scrubbing.

Mirella opened the refrigerator and pretended to search for something inside. It was empty aside from bottles of ketchup and old cartons of Chinese food. She inched past Penelope toward the sink to fill a glass of water instead. A pot of water simmered on the stove. They skimmed elbows, and finally she spoke.

"Are you cooking something?"

"Mhm." Penelope dried her hands and reached under the sink. She swung a bag of groceries onto the counter: onions, still whole in their orange-gold skins, and the starchy scent of rice filled the kitchen. They blotted out the smell of the garden, of dirt and flowers and smoke.

Mirella drank her water and watched Penelope arrange spices on the counter. Oregano, thyme, and garlic: all dry. Mirella thought to offer some of the fresh herbs from the yard, although she wasn't sure Penelope would know how to use them. She hardly cooked, and now she seemed determined to make a full meal. She unpacked ears of corn and cans of pink beans, bone-in pork chops glistening in their Styrofoam-and-Saran-Wrap packages. *¿Qué te dió ganas de cocinar?* Mirella would have asked, but she couldn't think of an adequate translation in English.

She refilled her glass.

Penelope began chopping onions on a board, nearly catching her fingers with the end of the knife. She cut vertically into the onion, then lengthwise, then sideways across the top. She remembered the way Ramona had taught her.

"Did your father tell you I quit my jobs?"

"I overheard," Penelope said, the sound of the blade striking wood. "Is it all right with you if we eat in the garden? Pop's having another slow day at the store."

"Of course," Mirella said, and she wondered who *we* were, whether she was invited to dinner in her own yard.

"I think it will cheer him up," Penelope said, scraping onions into a clean bowl.

Sales had been down since the summer, although Ralph had felt untouchable for years because Grand Records stayed open through the boom of the Internet, all the closing of the corporate CD stores. He didn't know what was causing the slump now, but he'd been coming home each day, defeated. Penelope had never cooked for her on one of her bad days. Mirella decided not to surrender to her envy. She offered Penelope a little advice.

"Make sure you rinse the rice first. There might be bugs in that bag."

"There aren't bugs in the bag."

"Sometimes they're so tiny you can't see them with just your eyes. You're supposed to wash rice—"

Penelope cast down her knife on the counter.

"Don't insult me. I know how to make rice. Abuela Ramona taught me. Remember her?"

"It was a simple suggestion," Mirella said. She picked up her empty glass and started for the hall. She had tried to reach her, and now she was through.

Penelope began to yell. "Don't assume because you didn't teach me, I didn't learn! I learned all kinds of things without you!"

Mirella turned back into the kitchen. "What do you want, Penélope—a prize? For me to say 'CONGRATULATIONS!' because you're twenty-two and you know how to boil water all by yourself?"

"I don't want anything from you," Penelope said. "Why don't you just go back to your room?"

"So you're la que manda now? You think you can send me to my room if you don't want to hear what I have to say? This is *my* house. I'll go wherever I want to go. I'll do whatever I want to do."

Penelope laughed once—a stiff, phony laugh.

"All you ever do is what you want to do. You don't care about anyone."

She dropped the words as if they were stones, and then turned back to her cooking. She turned down the heat and put on the lid; the water inside roiled.

"Am I supposed to still take care of you! Am I supposed to take care of you and your father until I'm dead!"

"I said you don't *care* for anyone, not that you don't *take care* of anyone."

Penelope spoke with an overstated precision she reserved for correcting Mirella's English. These were the small spots in their arguments when it was clear Penelope was winning—that, in a way, she had already won.

"Nobody took care of me! Who are you to talk! I was more of a woman at ten years old than you'll ever be! You've never had to take care of another person. Your father gives you everything. You can't even take care of yourself! You're a spoiled, sad little girl," Mirella said. "Imprudente. Comparona. Consentida! You can't see how much you have, how much you've thrown away. Is this what artists do? Live in their parents' house? Make eight dollars an hour? Is this what you went to art school for? I made more money cleaning!"

"At least I have a job," Penelope spat. "You never contributed anything to this house—not even your money."

"I don't have to contribute anything! It says MIRELLA JIMÉNEZ SANTOS on the deed. This is my house."

"Oh, please, Mami," Penelope said. "You and I both know you didn't pay ni un centavo for this house."

"Was I supposed to pay? What else am I supposed to give? You took my whole life."

"I didn't take anything from you."

"Everything you have you took from me."

"Pop gave me things. Pop and Abuela Ramona."

Mirella smacked the stove with her open hand, and the pot of boiling water shifted on the burner. "I gave birth to you. I fed you. I washed your clothes. I took you to the Dominican Republic to see your grandmother. What did 'Pop' do, eh? Play you a few records and call you 'Penny'? Por favor, Penélope, that's not love. That's your father doing his best not to feel like an orphan anymore. No seas tan boba."

"How many names are you going to call me tonight, Ma?"

"You think your father loves you more than I do? He just wants to keep you here! That's not love!"

"Don't talk about Pop that way."

"Oh, right, *Pop*. El Rey, His Majesty, El Único y Precioso *Pop!*"

Penelope slit her eyes so that she looked even more like Mirella than usual. It was as if Mirella were looking into the mirror at a darker, more muscular version of herself: a self with tiny eyes and wild hair, a younger, more beautiful self that hated her.

"I don't give a damn about you," she said.

"I'm your mother."

Penelope shook her head, a false smile washing over her face.

"You're just the cunt my father married."

Mirella hit her with the heels of her hands. The skin on skin made a low, dense sound. Penelope didn't flinch, and Mirella hit her again, the same thump in the center of her daughter's chest. A third shove, and Penelope staggered back toward the window. Mirella raised her hand to strike again, but Penelope caught her. She twisted Mirella's wrist hard and flung her hand away.

"Touch me again and I'll break your fucking arm."

Mirella clapped her hand over her wrist and shut her eyes. Her skin burned where Penelope had held her, but she would not cry in front of her. She should have hit her more when she was a girl, like the other Dominican mothers at the salon who compared stories of triumph over their children—power struggles they had won with telephone receivers, wire hangers, chancletas, hairbrushes, the broom. But Mirella had never needed to beat Penelope to teach her respect. She had been an obedient girl.

This Penelope was wild. And when Mirella tried to rein her in and remind her who was the mother and who was the daughter, Penelope had embarrassed her. She wouldn't survive if Penelope followed through on her threat, if she twisted her own arm behind her back until the bones came out of place. Was she capable? The thought of Penelope hitting her made her dizzy. Mirella realized she was panting. She felt the moisture under her arms and between her legs, above her lips.

"Do you hear me? Don't you ever fucking touch me again."

Mirella opened her eyes. "Get out," she said. "If you're so determined to ruin your life, then leave."

Penelope didn't speak.

Mirella screamed. "Lárgate!"

Penelope turned off the fire and pushed the handle of the pot hard. The pot skittered across the stove, hot water sloshing on the floor.

"Fine," she said. "Fine. Hallelujah. Thank God."

Penelope left the kitchen, twisting past Mirella so gracefully they didn't brush fingers or shoulders. They didn't touch at all, but Mirella felt her go.

"Penélope, wait." Mirella followed the girl into her bedroom. She already had her suitcase up on the bed, the leather one Ralph had bought for her to take to RISD. She was stacking her jeans and fancy underwear, her boxes of charcoal and pastels.

If she left this way, Ralph would never forgive her. Mirella said so. "He doesn't even know you're leaving. You'll break his heart."

"I won't leave tonight," Penelope said. "I'll talk to him when he gets home."

Penelope dragged a heavy chest out from her closet. She undid the lock and the chest yawned with drawings, some loose and crinkling, others stuffed officially in manila sleeves.

"Besides, it's not a real good-bye for me and Pop. He'll always be a part of my life."

Mirella rubbed her wrist and sighed, sat down on Penelope's bed. She felt color seeping from the room, the bedspread dark, the Polaroids taped around the room faded, the skin of her own hand blanched.

"Don't pretend to be devastated," Penelope said softly. "You're getting what you always wanted. You don't have to be my mother anymore."

They heard keys downstairs. The front door swung open and banged the coat stand against the wall. It clattered to the floor and was set upright again. Mirella was suddenly out of time.

"Anybody home?" Ralph's voice soared up the stairs. "Smells good in here!"

"At least think about where you're going. What will you do there?" Penelope didn't answer her.

"Think about your life. Don't go anywhere just to get away."

"Just be good to Pop, will you?" Penelope said. "We're all he's got. Try to think of him, and not just yourself."

Mirella felt so exposed and misunderstood that she wanted to yell at Penelope again, but she watched her pile socks into the suitcase and then zip it shut. These might be her final moments with her daughter. Like her, Penelope knew how to hold a grudge.

"I know you won't do anything for me," Penelope said. "But do it for him. He deserves more than us."

Mirella could hear Ralph's heavy footfalls on the stairs. He panted a little with the effort.

"I bought some bean pie, Penny!

"Hello, hello? Where are my girls? Penelope?"

He was nearer now, almost at the landing.

"You were never really mine," Mirella said, and she turned away from Penelope's room and walked down the hall, without feeling her feet touch the floor.

"What's going on?" she heard Ralph say, but she shut the door to her bedroom as soon as she was inside. She sat down at the vanity and didn't hear the rest.

14

The Bridge

The Harpers returned a week into the new year. They arrived without much commotion, like a machine quietly whirring back to life. They didn't come knocking to wish Penelope Happy New Year or to invite her to dinner, but still she witnessed every bit of their first evening back—the doorbell ringing when the pizza arrived, the smell of the mozzarella and olive oil as they opened up the box, the scrape of chairs on the floor, the rush for napkins when one of them knocked over a can of soda. Samantha might have wanted her to stay, but no one came to say hello.

I just live here, Penelope reminded herself. There was no reason for them to say anything to her. She lay down and took a few swigs from a bottle of good bourbon Jon had given her during her last visit to Sheckley's. Along with the bottle, he had also given her a tiny card that said *Don't go breaking this over someone's head. —Jon.*

She had been to the bar nearly every day since her fight with Ralph. It was the only place left for her to go. If she spent too long in the empty yellow house, she began to feel unreal, as if she were haunting the Harpers in their absence. Jon always made her something good, and they talked about how different Brooklyn seemed with all the transplants gone home for the holidays. Jon said these nights were better for him and his friends to go out and tag deserted buildings in the dark. He had invited Penelope to join them, but she had never agreed to go. He had touched her once, a bar napkin between his fingers and her cheek, where snow had stuck to her skin. It seemed that he was after camaraderie more than anything else because he seemed content to talk and listen to her, and nothing else. She liked the look of him: the strange elastic band he used to keep his hair off his forehead, the perfect minuscule circles gouged out of his earlobes by the gauge piercings he had gotten when he was sixteen and had to live with now. If she were still a painter, she would have painted him, mixing a half-dozen shades of brown to capture the light in his hair, the color in his cheeks, the scruff on his chin.

She thought of Jon to help her sleep, to knock out the sounds of the Harpers back down below. She had lost her own family and now had the theater of another instead. She couldn't bring herself to make up with Ralph, to go seeking the love of yet another parent who didn't want her. She and Miss Beckett, they were the same to Ralph. He was no different than Mirella, only willing to make as much room for her as he wanted, when and if he wanted.

On her first day back at PS 23, the students were bursting with stories from the holidays. Penelope passed out paintbrushes and markers, and listened to the children recount long drives south, flights home to Grenada or PR or Barbados for the holidays. They told her about the new video games and other electronic gadgets they had found underneath their polyvinyl trees, and Penelope felt old. Some of them received sneakers, but they were all for show: the kids wouldn't be able to run more than a few blocks in their clunky, name-brand, candy-colored kicks. Penelope indulged the ones she could tell were lying when they said they'd received everything they wanted on Christmas. She was no better. At lunch, she lied in the same way when the other young teachers cornered her in the faculty lounge while she heated up her soup. They told stories of snorkeling with their fiancés, skiing with their fit and able parents. So, Penelope said something about eggnog and jazz, wishing for snow. Wasn't that what they wanted to hear—that her life was sunny and beautiful, too?

She felt drained and remote by the time she returned to Greene in the afternoon, the sky already dark. In the attic, she brewed tea and counted out her aspirin, ordered her usual from the Emerald. The food arrived quickly, and Penelope felt her way down the stairs in the dark. The light in the vestibule was off, and she didn't bother to turn it on when she opened the door to pay the delivery boy. He handed her the food, grease and soy sauce seeping through the brown paper bag.

"Shit," she said, trying to catch the liquid in her hands. "Shit, shit."

"Hello, Penelope."

Penelope switched on the light and found Grace in the parlor, curled into one of the linen armchairs by the fireplace. Her slippered feet dangled over the floor, and her hair fell pin-straight around her, scorched a rusty blond by the sun.

"What are you doing sitting alone in the dark?"

"It wasn't dark in here a few minutes ago. I was reading and then the sun went down."

Penelope sat on the ottoman across from Grace. She popped open the can of soda that had been free with her order. The girl was still in her school uniform: a green plaid jumper, a white blouse with a scalloped collar, a navy sweater buttoned over her shoulders. She glanced at the bag of Chinese food at Penelope's feet.

"Mommy left me soup upstairs. I'm supposed to warm it up at six."

"Where's your father?"

"He's covering a story."

"Want some company?"

They went upstairs to the kitchen, which Penelope had never seen. Samantha had left the door unlocked. The room was shabbier than the rest of the house. Penelope had expected espresso-stained cabinets, a sparkling glass table, stainless steel appliances, and maybe a bad, photorealist painting on the wall. Instead the refrigerator was short and white with a large dent in the door; the cabinets were made of the same splintering wood as the cabinets in the house on Halsey. The acrylic countertop was black and gray, patterned in a way meant to evoke marble, and it was coming loose at the edges. Only the floor had been replaced—it was the same reclaimed pine that was in the parlor: unscratched, lustrous, the color of sand. A felt magnet from Sprout hung on the fridge.

They sat at the small kitchen table, Grace with her carrot soup, Penelope her noodles. Grace swung her feet below the table absentmindedly, and Penelope asked about her days in California.

"It was cold. Too cold to swim. But we went for walks on the shore every day. And at night we made fires and had popcorn and took out my grandpa's dogs. He has two of them. Hermes and Venus. They're old dogs now, but they used to be guard dogs. They still bark whenever someone comes to the door, even the mailman. We played fetch on the beach.

"And on Christmas, we made fried chicken and watched an old video of Mommy dancing in *The Nutcracker*. She was Clara."

The ballet explained Samantha's frailty, the thin limbs, her constant chignon.

Grace pushed aside her soup and poured a whole packet of soy sauce on a single dumpling Penelope had offered. She chewed with her mouth open.

"Mommy and Daddy were happy, too. They gave each other the same book on Christmas. Isn't that funny? And I got all the books I asked for. And these." Grace lifted her hair off her shoulders, and

Penelope saw the pearl studs in her ears. They were nested in gold petals. Lucky girl.

"I'm sorry I didn't get you anything." Grace looked at her seriously, her lips pursed, and Penelope assured her it was fine.

"It just doesn't feel right not to get you something—you live with us."

"Well, I didn't get you anything either. So we're even."

Grace gave a magnanimous nod of her head and looked relieved.

They each took a dumpling onto their plate, the last of the food, besides the soup Grace had abandoned. They finished eating and licked the soy sauce and scallions off the ends of their chopsticks.

"Best Chinese in Brooklyn," Penelope said, and she reminded herself of Ralph.

Grace took up the plastic bag and stared at the logo, the name of the restaurant in boldface, a glittering green gem in the place of the *A*.

"Have you ever been there? To the Emerald?"

"Of course. I pick up food there all the time on my way to Halsey Street."

"Is that a long walk?"

"You don't know where Halsey Street is?"

"I've probably seen it, but I don't know which one it is. You can't see the street signs in a car. You're going too fast."

Penelope looked over Grace's head at the old-fashioned clock hanging above the stove. It was hardly past five.

"Would you like to go? To the Emerald? I'll buy you dessert."

"What about my mother? She'll be expecting me here. She's coming home at nine."

Penelope tried hard not to frown. Samantha balked at an unlocked door, but she was willing to leave her child alone. She condescended to Penelope but expected her to look after the child.

"We'll be back long before she is," Penelope said, and she ordered Grace to go put on her snow boots. She used the same voice she used to tell kids to rinse out their brushes at the sink, to start clearing up their tables and lining up for their next class. Grace looked skeptical, but after a nod from Penelope, she ran out of the room, her slippers thwacking as she raced up the stairs. It would do them good to get out, Penelope thought. The last thing either of them needed was another night alone in the yellow house.

Grace held on to Penelope by the crook of her arm as they made their way along Nostrand Avenue over the ice. The girl's face was waxy from the Vaseline Penelope had spread beneath her eyes and around her ears like a shield. "So you don't become a popsicle," she had said.

Pedestrians broke out from underground and onto the avenue. They clogged the sidewalk as they rushed more slowly than usual, through slush and puddles, careful not to slip. Nearly everyone was brown—pale as wheat, deep as coffee grounds, the endless palette of shades in between. These neighbors wore bubble coats and steel-toe Timberlands, toothpaste-white sneakers and hooded peacoats. The white people making their way home from the train were all young. They wore bright scarves and jackets that seemed too thin to be warm. They carried grocery bags from supermarkets in the city; they flicked their unfinished cigarettes into the dirty piles of snow; they laughed into their cell phones.

Grace seemed more interested in the stores than the people, perhaps because she passed the same ones every day without ever looking inside. She peered into the one-room Pentecostal church next door to the beauty salon, the steam from the hair dryers blowing onto the street. The quivering old voices in the church swelled up in a Spanish hymn. She brushed past a quartet of children, probably siblings, stalled on the street and fighting over a white paper bag. They dug their hands inside to rip out pillowy hot chunks of coco bread. She poked into the bodegas, sized up their identical yellow interiors, the way their racks overflowed with bags of chips and corn nuts and expired rainbow candies.

At the corner, they passed the old woman who danced nightly on that curb to the music playing inside the beauty supply store. She boogied by herself there, for hours, under the flash of the mirror ball revolving inside the beauty shop. Each time Penelope saw her, she wore a knee-length coat, unbuttoned over a wrinkled black housedress, white tights drooping at her ankles. She didn't seem high, or insane, not even when her moves slipped from the steady and old school to the vulgar and newly invented. She was a neighborhood fixture now, it was clear, but Penelope wasn't sure how long she had been. Had she been dancing on this corner only since the summer when Penelope returned and first saw her? Or had this corner been hers for years? Did she ever go on hiatus?

Grace watched the old woman spin around twice on the balls of her feet, stomp in place to the soca like a soldier, swing her hips, and sink down to the pavement, her bottom nearly touching the street, before she wound back up, twisting her fists, as if they were attached by a hinge at her wrists. The old woman caught Grace staring at her, and she winked and wriggled her fingers at her: *Come over here.*

Grace paused, as if considering it. Penelope tugged her along, and they kept winding through the banks of people.

She wondered what the two of them looked like together, there in the cold. If Samantha, Grace, and Marcus ever walked the avenue together, it would be clear to anyone they were a family. When Penelope was a girl, and Mirella and Ralph took her out, it was clear she belonged to each of them. Could anyone mistake her and Grace for family? Who did they think Penelope might be?

At the Emerald, the smell of French fries and noodles met them at the door. Penelope joined the line while Grace took a seat in one of the stiff white booths.

"Let me get two red bean rolls. And two teas. To go."

The red-faced woman behind the counter jammed the rolls into a Styrofoam tray, stapled shut the top, and slid two hot teas across the counter, the amber liquid sloshing out.

Penelope joined Grace in the booth, where it was still cold from the door opening and closing as customers entered the Emerald. A few potted bamboo plants flanked the door, a green neon light shone from the ceiling. Penelope put sugar in her tea, and Grace sipped at hers without any, grimacing a little before she said, "This is very good. Thank you."

The red bean rolls were flaky, and bits of pastry stuck to their coats. The sweet bean paste reminded Penelope of habichuelas con dulce, which Ramona had made for her whenever she asked, with evaporated milk and cinnamon, whole cloves and a cut-up sweet potato.

"That's a funny calendar," Grace said, pointing at the wall.

It was the Emerald yearly calendar: a glossy stock photograph of a New York City landmark featured for each month. The Statue of Liberty, Times Square, the arch in Washington Square Park, Bethesda Fountain in Central Park, Canal Street in Chinatown. The calendar hung year-round in the kitchen on Halsey Street. It had for as long as Penelope could remember. She wondered whether Ralph already had this new calendar, just a few days into the year. January was the Brooklyn Bridge.

The tea was too hot for either of them to drink very much, but they warmed their hands over the coverless cups. They finished the rolls, wiping the sticky near-black paste from the corners of their lips. A customer near them spoke loudly on his phone while eating fried chicken wings from a wax paper bag; a couple divided an order of beef with broccoli between three Styrofoam plates that three small children kept trading between them. For all Samantha's sheltering, Grace didn't seem wary of anything. She didn't even panic when a man came into the restaurant, waving around his bag of takeout and shouting that he had asked for no eggs in his moo shu pork, and there were eggs in his moo shu pork, and he was allergic, and were they trying to kill him?

Grace giggled a bit when the man left with a fresh order, and Penelope felt guilt for the first time that she had fucked this girl's father. The freckles on her nose were the same as his; he twisted his lips when he smiled, too.

"I'm sorry, Grace."

"For what?" She collected fallen sesame seeds on a plastic spoon and licked them off.

"For not taking you out sooner. I should've shown you around the neighborhood before."

"You're so nice to me, Penelope."

"There's still a lot for you to see. The library on Franklin. The little garden behind PS 23."

Grace offered her a spoonful of sesame seeds, and Penelope shook her head.

"What I'm trying to say is, even after I don't live in the house anymore, I'll still be around. If it's all right with your parents."

"But it's only January. Aren't most leases for a year?"

"I'm not going to live with your family forever, Grace."

"But you'll stay close by, won't you? 'Cause of your dad?"

Penelope said nothing, and Grace looked devastated, the black sesame seeds stuck to her upper lip. She offered Penelope the rest of her tea, and although she didn't want it, Penelope accepted the cup and drank.

"At least you're not leaving today."

Penelope looked back at the calendar on the wall, the bridge silhouetted in the dark. Fireworks burst in the sky above.

"Come on," she said. "We still have a few hours before your mother gets home."

The girls emerged from the A train at High Street, just at the mouth of the bridge. Here, in downtown Brooklyn, the sidewalk wasn't as icy. It already felt more like Manhattan, the high-rises in Brooklyn Heights and the new condominiums in Fort Greene harpooning the sky.

Grace kept a good pace, matching each of Penelope's strides with one of her own. Her arms swung at her sides while she walked, the way Marcus's did, and she angled her chin upwards to take in the city as it came into view. The Manhattan skyline was already lit orange and white, the needle of the Empire State Building blazed violet. The sky was a steady cobalt, cool despite all the electricity. They eased their way up the incline of the bridge.

Winter never seemed to relieve the bridge adequately of crowds, but tonight the pathways were more serene than Penelope had expected. Pedestrians crossed the bridge in both directions, neglecting the bike lane as they wandered from one side of the bridge to the other to snap photographs. The bikers, only one every few minutes now, skirted the absentminded tourists easily. They didn't even bother slapping their bells; they simply sped by, shaking their helmeted heads and muttering.

The cement underfoot gave way to the bridge's wooden planks; beneath the bridge, the paved streets gave way to dark water.

"Is that where the World Trade Center used to be?"

Grace pointed down by the seaport, at the pier empty in the dark.

"Close to there."

She didn't have to do the math to realize Grace hadn't been in New York City when the towers fell. She had been an infant, if she was even born yet. Penelope had been in Brooklyn the day of the attacks. She was waiting for class to start in a grubby classroom at her new college, but she left and went straight to the store. Ralph hadn't closed the shop, but people weren't buying anything. Penelope sat in the back room among the boxes of unsorted records and watched the news on an old antenna television set. The same video of smoke and debris blasting through downtown looped onscreen. A middle-aged anchorman gave a disarmingly calm narration of the disaster. Penelope didn't look away from the screen until the shop was closed, and Ralph came in the back to get her.

"Do you think anything like that could ever happen again?"

"I hope not," Penelope said. "I think we'll all be fine."

The Q train rose across the Manhattan Bridge to the east, and they passed through the high stone arches, nearly halfway across now.

"These cables are *gargantuan*," Grace said, and she stopped to grab hold of one of the thick silver cables on either side of the bridge. They were the metallic ligaments keeping the whole thing up. The girl yanked one, as if she expected it to move, and her little body jerked. She yanked again, this time with both hands, leveraging all of her weight.

"Pretty steady," she said and kept walking.

"Are you worried we'll fall down?"

"I know it's silly," Grace said. "Millions of people cross this bridge every day. But, it still doesn't make sense. These cables are the only thing keeping us up here."

"It's mathematics," Penelope said, vaguely remembering something about catenary curves from a class she took at RISD.

Grace looked up at Penelope, the golden moon of her face calculating. "Cool," she said.

They were on the other side, the bridge beginning to slope ever so slightly downward. It was only about a mile across, Penelope knew from her runs. They'd be finished even sooner than she expected.

"Here." Penelope took Grace's hands in hers. "I'm going to show you something. It's spectacular but a little scary. You'll have to be brave."

Penelope told Grace that she'd have to look down and run. No matter how frightened she felt or how fast they went, she had to keep her eyes down. Grace agreed, and Penelope began to lengthen her strides, almost skipping, and Grace followed. The girl lagged behind at first, and Penelope tugged her hand, until they were side by side, Grace taking three strides for each of Penelope's.

They ran as the bridge sloped downward, catching glimpses of what lay beneath the bridge through the gaps between the wooden planks. They saw water and darkness, the reflection of office building lights on the waves. The faster they ran, the less they saw of the wooden bridge; the gaps between the planks began to blur together, the way the images in a picture book blur into a cartoon if the pages flip fast enough. They picked up speed until there didn't seem to be any bridge at all, the wooden planks fell away, and they were just running over blue-black air, the water moving below.

Grace laughed—not the hesitant giggles Penelope had grown accustomed to, but shrieks and roars. She was equal parts fear and delight.

"Keep looking down," Penelope said, but she was laughing, too, the adrenaline rising in her like a sweet whir as they sped toward the city. She remained watchful, looking up every few seconds to make sure they didn't smash into anything, anyone, and she felt the same magic she had the first time she discovered this trick about the bridge—that she could come here and run and feel she was bound to nothing, that she was racing over sky.

The bell of the AME church was clanging when Grace and Penelope turned onto Greene; it was eight o'clock, and they were back, heels sore, still giddy from the bridge, their night away. Grace had found Penelope's hand again when they got off the A train, and she remembered the way back to the house easily. The old woman was still in front of the beauty supply store, winding her hips and winking at the passersby. Grace's face was pink but unchapped, and one of her hands was bare. She had lost a mitten on the bridge.

Penelope didn't notice the lights in the vestibule, and she searched for her keys to the house. Grace began to tell her about the running club at her school, a group of girls who arrived an hour early to run along the Hudson River, but you had to be in fifth grade to join.

Penelope hadn't turned the lock when the door opened from the inside. Samantha stood before them, the stains of old mascara dried beneath her eyes, wisps of her hair unpinned and floating around her ears. She wore an angora sweater and hugged herself, as if she weren't all one piece.

"Jesus Christ." She pulled Grace into her arms. "Jesus Christ."

"Hi, Mommy."

"You're freezing."

"I'm okay."

Samantha drew the girl into the house; she didn't look at Penelope until they were in the parlor. Marcus sat in one of the linen armchairs, his elbows on his knees.

"Where were you?" Samantha kneeled to level with her daughter.

"We went out for a walk, Mommy. To the Emerald and then across the Brooklyn Bridge. Have you ever done that, Mommy? Not in a car—have you ever walked across the bridge?"

Samantha looked up at Marcus. Her eyes filled with tears.

"Go say hello to your father."

Marcus hugged his daughter, burying his face in her hair. He was blonder, too, from their days on the beach.

"What the hell were you thinking?"

Penelope was watching Marcus comb his daughter's hair back from her face with his fingers, and she didn't realize right away that Samantha was talking to her.

"Answer me, Penelope. Answer me, goddammit."

"We went for a walk, exactly like Grace said. We didn't think you'd be home until nine."

"I got here at seven. And I nearly broke my fist knocking on the door to the attic, trying to find out where the two of you were."

"We're fine. Grace is fine."

"Mommy, it's okay," Grace said, untangling herself from Marcus, who stood now, in a cornflower blue shirt, a tan belt over his trousers. He was sunburned, his skin a pink-gold behind the ears and on his brow. He put his hands on his wife's shoulders.

"Yes, Sam, everything is all right now. No need to get up in arms about it."

"No need?" Samantha repeated. "I was here for over an hour, and I didn't know where my daughter was. I didn't even know if she was alive."

"Mommy, I was safe the whole time. Penelope took care of me."

Samantha bit her lip again, this time for so long, Penelope waited for her to draw blood.

"Go to your room, Grace. Your father and I will be up soon."

"Mommy, you're not understanding—"

"Grace Harper, I will not repeat myself."

"But Mommy—"

"Do you still consider me your mother or not? Then listen to me. Upstairs."

Grace folded her arms in front of her chest and crossed to the stairs. She kept her eyes on her feet as she went up the stairs, but Penelope could hear her begin to sob.

"What right do you have to remove my child from my home?"

"I found her sitting by herself in the dark. I thought it would be good for her to get out of the house."

"It doesn't matter what you think is good for her. She isn't your child."

"You left her here."

"You didn't have my permission. You aren't her guardian. We hardly know you—"

"But you still left her here, expecting I'd watch after her, expecting I'd be here if she needed anything. So, you expect me to watch her but not talk to her? Make sure she's safe but keep away from her? I'm not the help, Samantha, and you were the one who told me I was good for Grace—"

"I would never say that!"

"Let's all calm down." Marcus spoke from his stance between the women. "Sam, Penelope didn't mean any harm. She adores Grace."

"My nine-year-old was roaming the street! Who knows where she took her? Just because *she* thinks it's safe—"

"It is safe. As safe as anywhere else. As unsafe."

"Are you speaking to me in goddamned riddles now?" Samantha cocked her head to the side and stepped toward Penelope, and her movements were so close to the ones Penelope had seen in catfights, those high-pitched, hair-pulling brawls that went down outside night-clubs on Flatbush, that Penelope began to laugh.

"Penelope, I'm talking to you. This is no laughing matter."

"So I see."

"This is unbelievable. She's a child herself."

"Why did you move here? Why did you all move here if you're so afraid of everyone who lives here?"

"Don't you dare make assumptions about me and my family."

"No one here wants to hurt your little girl. Or your family. No one gives a shit about you."

"Don't talk down to me like this! Like I'm just some oblivious white lady."

"Samantha." Marcus put his hands on her shoulders. Penelope could see that she was shaking. "Sam," he said again, and he spoke to her in such a low voice Penelope couldn't make out the words, as if she were back up in the attic, a silent witness to their troubles. He massaged her shoulder, and there was nothing erotic in the way he touched her. Penelope was certain no one had ever touched her that way.

Samantha took a deep breath to calm herself, her thin belly inflating. She exhaled and wiped her eyes, the rings on her fingers glinting in the parlor light.

"Penelope, you cannot stay here. I'm going to write up the termination to your tenancy, and you're going to sign it and leave. That's how this is going to end."

Penelope watched Marcus standing behind his wife, squeezing her shoulder. He didn't say anything, and he wouldn't meet her eyes, and Penelope could see that was as it should be.

"Put the letter under my door," she said. "I'll sign it right away."

She left, unsure of how she was climbing to the attic, how she was making it through the house, step by step, the staircase gone from beneath her, no railing, no landings.

In the attic, she took stock of her room, the unwashed teacups, the jars she filled with cold soapstones and gin, the empty fruit bowl on the kitchen table, the toothbrush and hand soap balanced on the china sink, the Pittsburgh photographs on the sloped ceiling above her bed, the scarves draped over the walls, the unmade bed, the trunk peeking from beneath the eyelet sheets.

Penelope crossed to the porthole window. All her drawings were still clipped to the back of the easel, one for every day she had been in Brooklyn, so many at this point that the mass of drawings bulged, the clip straining to keep them all together. The clip bit into the top of the paper, leaving its imprint on each one. Penelope gathered up the clip in her hand, the pages rustling. She rolled up the drawings, her object studies, into a fat scroll, and threw them into the trash can beneath the sink. Then she returned to her easel, felt for the knobs on either side, and snapped it closed.

15

Putnam

Penelope came for her boxes one Sunday afternoon in the rain. Sheckley's was nearly full, the neighborhood's young professionals getting trashed because they didn't have to go into work on Monday—Martin Luther King Jr. Day. Al Green was playing in the bar when Penelope arrived, "Love and Happiness" slinking out of the speakers, while the customers slapped their tables and laughed, draining mugs of beer. Jon complained about not having control over the stereo system because the owner liked him to play only Motown on Sunday afternoons, but Penelope caught him shrugging his skinny shoulders as he went to the back room. There were a dozen boxes, flattened and wrapped with twine.

"So, when is move-out day?" Jon asked. "You're cutting it close, aren't you?"

"It only takes a week or so to find a place."

"You better get looking."

Penelope waved her hand, and Jon looked worried. He had mentioned a few options to her. A friend was looking for a roommate in a place above the laundromat and beneath the M train tracks, another was renting out a floor of a house on Pulaski Street, and Penelope was uninterested in them all. He made her a drink—a tall shot of something top-shelf, mashed-up slices of green melon, vodka, and soda—then he left to tend to the other customers. Penelope watched him smile indulgently at the ones who were already slurring their words. One woman requested whatever Penelope was drinking, and he told her simply, "Sorry, that one's not available," which made Penelope relish each sip more. She admired him in profile: the slant of his nose, the stubble creeping from his chin up his cheeks, his too-large earlobes.

When he returned, he slapped a newspaper on the counter in front of her. The pages were inky enough to stain her hands, and the front page read *New Horizons: A Bed-Stuy Gazette.*

"They dropped off about fifty this morning," Jon said, and Penelope stared at a photograph on the front page of a new community garden. It was strung with lights, and a multiracial group of people, young and old, stood in front of it, cutting a burlap ribbon with an oversized pair of scissors.

"Gross," Penelope said and flipped through the paper, scanning the headlines.

Sashimi Rolls onto Putnam
Utica Gallery Showcases Emerging Bklyn
Photographers
Lewis Ave Boutique Welcomes Eco-Handbags from
Local Designer
Outdoor Patio to Open This Spring at Macon Street's
Best Spirits Bar

Jon turned to the cover story about the new community garden and pointed to the byline.

"Isn't that your landlord?"

Penelope took back the paper. *Marcus A. Harper,* there he was, a four-page spread. She skimmed the article, a quick history of how the garden had been forgotten, then reclaimed, named after a local hero who had passed away the year before. It had all the buzzwords she would have predicted Marcus would use: *green space, community, leadership,* and *crossings.* She read aloud from the end of the article: "'The garden is a decisive step toward a new Bed-Stuy that is fair and equitable, and knows how to keeps its roots.' What a terrible pun."

Penelope flipped to the staff pictures at the back of the paper. A bunch of tattooed kids in their late twenties with college backgrounds in journalism and graphic design, and Marcus in an overly glamorous head shot, and a two-line bio about environmentalism, classic rock, and being a Brooklyn dad.

"They named the garden after an old organizer who did housing rights back in the day. Isn't that ironic as shit? The rent on that block is going to shoot right up."

"At least she'll get a plaque," Penelope said and tossed the paper away. Jon opened it back up and pointed to an ad for the new sushi place around the corner.

"We should go there," he said, and Penelope laughed.

Jon tried to explain that he was serious—he hated sake but he loved sake bombing, the mess and the shouting and the pounding on the table. They could eat tuna rolls and chug Japanese beer until they were both sick, and they wouldn't have to worry about commuting back from the city. Penelope wondered if he was asking her on a date.

"We can't go there. If we do, then how are we any different than they are?" Penelope flipped back to the staff photographs and pointed directly at Marcus.

"We just are," Jon said.

He was swept back into his work, and she watched him as he shook up a martini and hauled out drafts. She stared at the sleeve of tattoos on his left arm, the startlingly feminine blue foxgloves, the tall violet weeds, the spotted green serpent slashed in half, bleeding into the grass of his forearm. Who did others see when they looked at him? A hipster? A black man? And when they saw Penelope with him?

She left him a big tip before she went, waving good-bye in her usual awkward way, as if her hand were cleaning an invisible pane of glass between them. It was raining outside, and the boxes were wet by the time she returned to the attic, the smell of cardboard filling the room. It wasn't long before nearly everything was sealed in boxes that advertised midshelf vodka brands, nothing Penelope would ever drink. There hadn't been much to put away: just books and clothes. She left her bed and trunk and breakfast table where they were, since she still had two weeks before she had to go. She would miss her porthole window, the view of the street from this high up.

She was taking her afternoon aspirin and tea when the phone rang. It was Jon. He and his friends were going tagging that night, and did she want to come along? She surveyed the room, all tucked into boxes. She'd spent enough nights as a castaway in the Harpers' house, and she was certain that Grace was no longer permitted to speak to her. There was no Ralph to see—he didn't even know she was moving away, whether out of Bed-Stuy or New York altogether she hadn't decided. What else did she have to do?

"All right, why not?" she said and felt covered in guilt as soon as she got off the phone. What would Ralph be doing this evening while she was walking about and free, no longer mourning whatever had broken between them? She lay on her bed and vacated her mind, the room, until it was dark and time to go.

They met under the elevated train on Myrtle. Jon's friends were men at the end of their twenties, wearing backward caps and white T-shirts under their jackets, as if they were still all living in the nineties. They said their names in such a flurry—Javier, Darnell, Vincent, Tomás—Penelope couldn't match them each to the right man. One was a department store security guard, another a bike mechanic, one a barista, the other in graphic design. They worked their day jobs and lived for the nights when they went out tagging. They all had their trademarks: one did superheroes, another did mash-ups of quotes from his favorite philosophers, one liked painting doorways on the sides of buildings, some open and some closed, and the bike mechanic liked to do flowers and grass, rising up from the street onto pipes and brick. Jon did circles, big multicolored, overlaid shapes, swelling like bubbles across the sides of buildings, bright and emphatic.

There was no agreement that they'd all meet up at the end, or even that they had to stick together. They kept an eye out for cops and the security cameras in front of the lit-up condos, but they came together and drifted apart for a while, until Jon and Penelope went off on their own.

He had three colors in his backpack, and they sprayed the wood boards closing off an abandoned lot beneath the JMZ line. The train rattled overhead while they worked in the dark. They shook up the cans and made little arcs, his green on her blue, her orange enclosing his green. It didn't feel like painting; she was following his moves, but she felt exhilarated and calm, cold, and deep inside herself. She had been longing for color.

It was after two in the morning when they finished. They found a bodega on Havemeyer Street, bought two cups of coffee, Juicy Fruit, and a pack of menthols. The coffee was bitter but it warmed them through; Penelope's neck and face stung from the cold, and Jon lent her his scarf, a scratchy wool thing he circled around her shoulders and ears.

They walked to the Williamsburg Bridge, and as they strolled across, Penelope thought about how this was her first night with Jon anywhere but Sheckley's. They reached the Lower East Side, then turned around and walked back. Jon pointed out the old Domino sugar factory to her, as if she had never seen it before, as if they hadn't just passed it on their way across. He slipped his arm around her as he pointed, wrapped his hand around her shoulder.

It was a slick move, a classic high-school-date trick that no one had ever tried on her before. Jon talked about cycling over the bridge, the collisions he'd seen, the time he crashed into another biker and had to pay out of pocket for six stitches on his chin at the hospital on Wyckoff. Penelope listened and wondered what was happening between them. She could have him tonight, if she wanted. She was sure of that. But she wasn't sure what Jon was after; she wanted to see what he would choose.

Off the bridge, they found a place to squat on the curb and smoke. The coffee was gone, and they piled the ash into the little cups.

"I've got a feeling," Jon said. "That maybe you're going to leave New York."

"What makes you say that?"

"You don't seem to be really searching for a place. And there's nothing keeping you here but your pops, and playing caretaker gets old real fast. I know." He snuffed out his cigarette on the ground, dropped the butt into the cup.

"Well, at least we've left our mark on the city tonight." She laughed and held out her orange-stained hands. Jon slid closer to her, across the curb.

"I'd like to kiss you," he said. "Just in case you're going away."

His face was chapped and cold, framed by the globe of his curls. Penelope nodded, and he kissed her, cupping her throat in his hands. It was unnerving to have someone touch her there, but she let him, and he held her loosely, his fingers brushing her chin. After, he kissed her ear, her cheek, and her lips again. He helped her stand, and then they hailed a cab. Jon told the driver they'd be making two stops, then he turned to Penelope for her address, although they were closer to his place. They didn't talk on the ride, but Jon kept his arm around her, his chin in her hair. When the livery car stopped in front of the yellow house, Jon kissed her again, and Penelope tripped out of the car, cloudy-headed and unsure whether it had all really happened. She was sober, but it had been so sudden and so quiet, and now it was over.

Jon stuck his head out the window before the cab reeled away. "Goodnight, Miss Grand," he said, and his hair blew around his bare neck. He had left his scarf with her. Penelope pulled it up around her face, and it smelled of chewing gum, whatever cheap cologne he wore behind his ears, and the perfume of their Brooklyn night—wind and cold, cement, the steel bridge, cigarettes, and the zinc-aerosol stench of spray paint.

Penelope woke the next day, as ecstatic and dopey as if she had spent the whole night with Jon. Her body was warm and light; her legs like overcooked spaghetti. When she stood to stretch and look around the attic, she almost expected to find him there, his limbs peeking from under the covers, his clothes scattered on the floor: black underpants, wool socks, a T-shirt worn soft. She put on his scarf and pulled at the fibers, pinching them between her fingers, while she made her toast and tea. She hummed as the water boiled, the scent of browning bread in the room, the chamomile flowers waiting in her cup.

The phone rang, but she didn't answer it. If it was Jon, she wanted to enjoy this—the remembering, the replaying—for as long as she could. It rang again as she pulled on her running shoes and a pair of gloves, and strode through the door.

The cold washed over Penelope like a clean drug, and she set out for Bedford, running against the wind. It was a bright day for January, and she made it to Fort Greene Park, twice around, and then back. She beat the B26 bus on its way down Fulton, sprinting through the crosswalks, the sweat dripping off her brow into her eyes.

She reached that sweet spot where she'd been running for long enough that her movements had become automatic, and inertia drove her body, so she did not feel as if she were working at all. It took a while for the pain to blossom in her joints, and her body beckoned her to stop. She eased into a jog when she turned down Putnam. She felt wide awake and strong.

Penelope passed the mural of ODB, a string of abandoned houses, and Liquid Love: A Sophisticated Meeting Place, a lounge for middle-aged folks to drink and dance. It was early in the day, but the liquor stores were already open, the workers passing bottles through the revolving doors of bulletproof glass.

Penelope crossed onto a block of dilapidated brownstones. The houses shimmered blue in the winter light, and some looked even worse off than the house on Halsey Street. At the corner stood the new sushi restaurant mentioned in the gazette. It was all glass and dark wood, long communal tables and exposed lightbulbs hanging from the ceiling. The open kitchen was filled with steam, the chef chopping something Penelope couldn't see with a large knife. Everything inside looked new.

Past the sushi spot was another blighted block, an empty lot, the slumping houses, and then a blockade in the middle of the street: a pack of men standing around, smoking and leaning on metal dollies. As Penelope got closer, she saw the men were movers. A black van was parked in the street, its back wheels up on the curb. Inside, upturned furniture and rolled-up rugs, stacks of brown boxes sealed with silver duct tape. At the top of the stoop of a run-down brownstone, a girl sat among more boxes, a blue handball at her side. She must have been about Grace's age, but Penelope didn't recognize her from PS 23. She wore jeans and a sweater in the cold, no mittens or hat. Her hair was splayed around her face, unbrushed and afloat in the currents of wind. She watched the men smoke, took up the blue ball and tossed it between her hands.

Penelope stepped off the sidewalk to avoid the men, but one of them whistled after her anyway. A woman came out of the house, carrying two old suitcases, a leather purse slung over her shoulder. She had a slender copper face, her hair perfectly pressed, curled at the ends. She handed one of the suitcases to the girl, who struggled to bring it down the steps, one hand on the rail. A man followed them out of the house. He was much older, lean and muscular with a graying beard, his hair cut into a neat fade. He carried down a box filled with frying pans and pots, the handles sticking out of the open top. The three of them approached the van, dropped their things into the back. It was then that Penelope recognized the woman.

"Denise?"

"Penny, is that you?"

The women smiled at each other and hugged, the little girl with the suitcase looking on suspiciously.

"Look at you! I haven't seen you since you were a little girl."

"You were practically a girl then, too," Penelope said, and the woman looked bashful. Denise had been one of the front girls at Grand Records, a teenager whom Ralph trained to run the register and not chew gum while helping the customers. Now she must have been nearly forty. She introduced the man beside her, the little girl.

"And then there's these gentlemen," she said, sweeping her hand out at the movers. "Who are still enjoying their break."

The men pretended not to notice the edge in her voice. They tapped on their phones, shifted feet, took longer drags on their cigarettes. Penelope offered to help, and Denise thanked her.

She and the man went back into the house, and the little girl took a moment to size up Penelope, then she tucked the ball into the back pocket of her jeans and started shoving the suitcases toward the back of the van. Penelope joined her. When they were done, they leaned against the bumper of the van to wait for the next batch.

"He's not my father," the girl said. "He just lives with us." She slapped the ball down on the concrete.

The couple returned with another set of boxes, one filled with cloth dolls and old toys that Denise must have passed on to her daughter, the other with dresses on hangers in demure colors like peach and beige and cream. Had Denise—with the candy-colored plastic shoes and long braids and high-waist, tight-ass jeans—turned into an old church lady? Penelope asked where they were moving.

"East New York. My sister is letting us stay with her for a while."

"The hood," her boyfriend said.

Denise swatted at him. "Please, that what's people used to say about Bed-Stuy."

"It's the truth," he said, folding closed the flaps of the boxes. "We moving to the hood."

"You sold the house?" Penelope asked.

"We never owned it. We just lived on the first floor."

"For seventeen years. She's been here for seventeen years. And the landlord's been trying to get her out for five," said the man.

Denise smiled and shrugged her shoulders. "It might be nice," she said. "Having family close for a change."

"Yeah, real close." Her boyfriend went back into the house.

"How's Mr. Grand?" Denise asked, and Penelope made up some lie about how he was doing great, just great. Enjoying his retirement ever since the store closed. She followed Denise back into the house to help with the remaining boxes, and Penelope thought of telling her that she was moving, too, but she knew they couldn't find any real camaraderie there. What reason would she give? *I had a fight with Pop. I had sex with my white landlord. I never liked it here anyway.* It was true she couldn't afford to live on her own in Bed-Stuy, but she could have moved in with Ralph, if she wanted. She didn't have to leave.

Up on the first floor of the brownstone, the rooms were all empty. There were balls of hair in the unswept corners, nails in the plaster where things had hung, traces of old crayon scribbles on the walls. Denise pointed to a tangle of chaotic blue lines by the door.

"I thought about painting it over," she said. "But the landlord hasn't painted once the last ten years, and I figure, if he's kicking us out, he can paint the damn place."

There was the Denise she remembered, the strength and sass that would emerge when a customer was rude, or one of the other front girls reordered a display she had toiled over. They carried down another set of boxes, and then the man clapped his hands together and shouted at the movers, "All right, I think y'all's break is over," and the men muttered and started shuffling around.

"I think we'll be fine from here," Denise said, and she gave Penelope a little hug. "You tell Mr. Grand I said hello, all right? I miss him."

Penelope wished them luck and walked down Putnam to the fading sound of the little girl beating the pavement with her handball. A pair of white men passed her on the sidewalk, carrying takeout from the sushi place, the plastic bags between them, as they sped through the cold. Penelope watched them go happily, right past Denise and her moving van. Penelope spat a glob of mucus onto the sidewalk. There was a shine on the street from all the rain and snow, the melting and re-forming that had gone on for weeks.

She saw the police car when she turned onto Greene. The sirens were off and the red lights weren't revolving. Penelope felt her heart quicken, as it did whenever she saw the police, their guns. Something was wrong. Had there been a shooting? Had she broken the law and they were waiting for her? They were parked across the street from the Harpers' brownstone, in front of the plot where the London plane tree had been, the one that had snapped in half during the storm.

Miss Beckett sat on the stoop of the yellow house in a bright pink peacoat, her handbag flat on her lap. She stood when she saw Penelope. Samantha and Marcus were standing in the doorway, in their bathrobes, their arms around each other, looking at her. The police car doors opened, and two officers began crossing the street. In her peripheral vision, she saw them look both ways; one was short, the other a woman, but she couldn't make out their faces.

"Oh, Penny!" Miss Beckett called out. She started to cry, and Penelope ran to her.

Her hands found the old woman's shoulders.

"What is it? Talk to me, Una. What happened?"

Miss Beckett's mouth twisted shut, and she opened her eyes, the heavy lashes sticking to each other, dripping black mascara.

"He fixed the leak," Miss Beckett said. "The one on the fourth floor. He fixed it, and then he climbed down the ladder and he fell—"

"Where is he?"

"I tried to call you—"

"Where is he?" Penelope said again, feeling her fingers dig past the wool of Miss Beckett's coat, to her fat, her muscle, the joint. The shape of her shoulder in Penelope's hand.

"Where is he?"

Miss Beckett moaned and closed her eyes.

"Jesus Christ, Una, where is he?"

"Excuse me, Miss Grand."

One of the officers, and then the other.

"Miss Grand, we need to speak with you."

Penelope didn't turn to look at them, the beating in her ears overtaking everything, the street receding, the bare trees, the porthole window up in the attic. Nothing anchored her there to the block but Miss Beckett, weeping, the bones in her fleshy shoulders, the hideous pink of her coat.

16

Mujeres

Marcello arrived for dinner, swinging open the door hard, and calling her name.

"Mirella! Mirella! Tu hija!" he said. "Cuanto te parece."

Mirella heard the mention of her daughter and ran to the foyer from the living room where she had been watching a novela and filing her nails. Marcello was drinking from a bottle of Chilean red, and brandishing a photograph of Penelope.

"Increíble!" he said, pointing at Penelope's face. He shouted in his lurching staccato Spanish, going on about how alike they looked, but Mirella could only watch the Penelope in miniature waving in his hand. She had received the postcard. She had written back. Mirella snatched the photograph from him, and the envelope, already open, and rushed to her bedroom on the second floor to read.

The photograph was a blurry Polaroid, Penelope a brown-skinned smudge of a woman in a navy dress, surrounded by white borders. She was skinnier than she had ever been, her breastbones visible above the deep V neck of the dress, her arms slender and bent, tucked behind her waist. She leaned against the side of a building with shuttered windows—was it Sheckley's? The old bar? With a fresh coat of paint? She wore snow boots but no coat, her hair shorn into a fuzzy halo. The short cut made her seem somehow naked in her dress, her long neck and her ears exposed, the curve of her hips obvious from the way she propped one leg up on the wall behind her.

Penelope had the same athleticism and darkness as Ramona, but the look in her eyes was all Ralph—superior, unflinching, but obviously wounded.

Penelope hadn't sent a picture of him, but she explained the accident. She wrote in Spanish, her grammar native, although Mirella suspected she must have thought every word in English first. He had been fixing the leak on the fourth floor. He plastered the ceiling himself, managed to get up on the ladder and down. It was after he finished and bent down to pick up the can of plaster that he slipped on the rag he had used to sop up the leak. Mirella imagined him on the floor, and it made her sick to see Ralph that way, even if only in her mind. She saw him bleeding from his knuckles, his hands limp. The sight of him was a memory and a premonition. She felt herself begin to gag, so she shut her eyes and waited for the impulse to pass.

In the letter, Penelope explained how she had received Mirella's postcard and thrown it away without reading it. But she had looked at the address and remembered it, thankfully. She knew the name of the nearest gas station, the number of kilometers down the main road to the residence. She had gotten only the house number wrong, which was why the letter had gone to Marcello and not to her. Mirella decided not to concentrate on the fact that her daughter had destroyed her postcard. At least she had written to explain about Ralph and to say that she wanted to see her. Her daughter wanted to see her.

Penelope had mentioned a date in February when she intended to fly over a long weekend. She wanted Mirella to call and let her know if the date was all right. Her phone number began with 718 but it wasn't the landline at Halsey Street.

How long had she been back in Brooklyn? Had she returned before what happened with Ralph? Was she living in the house again?

Marcello was still downstairs, playing an opera, and singing as he worked in the kitchen. She took the phone with her into the bathroom and sat on the edge of the tub.

Penelope was unsurprised to hear her mother's voice on the line. Mirella told her daughter, yes, the date was fine, and the address was right, except for the house number. She lived in Casa Número Cinco, not Número Seis. Penelope said she would fly into Puerto Plata, and that Mirella didn't have to worry about sending a car. She would rent a car and drive herself. When had Penelope learned to drive? She didn't call her Mami or Madre or Mom or anything at all, and Mirella didn't mention Ralph, or the accident Penelope had described in the letter.

It must have been Penelope who had found him. She saw Penelope finding her father unconscious, and she felt the room grow cold. She thought of saying something to comfort her—*I'm sorry*, or *How are you doing?*—but anything she said would have made Penelope harden against her, unconvinced by her empathy. So, instead, they carried on with the logistics. When they were through, Mirella said, "Nos vemos," matter-of-factly, not noticing she had slipped into Spanish, until Penelope answered her, "Hasta pronto." The word rang in Mirella's head long after they got off the phone. *Soon.*

Penelope closed the porthole window against the early-morning snow. There was no end to this winter in Brooklyn, and Penelope couldn't help but look forward to the warmth, the feeling of sun in her bones. Her mother's new town wouldn't be Aguas Frescas, but it was still DR.

She locked the attic door and carried her suitcase down the stairs as quietly as she could, her boots in her hands. She sat down on the steps in the foyer and had started to pull on her shoes when she heard Marcus clear his throat. He was standing in the parlor, the doors barely ajar.

"So, you're on your way already."

Marcus was in his pajamas: a flannel robe to match the flannel pants she remembered pulling off him that first time up in the attic, a white T-shirt, and a pair of silver-rimmed glasses. They made his green eyes swim in front of his face. Penelope hadn't known he wore glasses.

"Can I help you at all?" he said.

"I'll be all right."

"I could walk you to the train if you want. It's still dark out. I just need to change my shoes."

"I have a ride."

"Of course." Marcus pushed up his glasses with his index finger. The red wave of his hair was undisturbed by sleep, tucked neatly behind his ears.

"I thought of bringing down Grace to say good-bye, but she's still in bed."

Penelope didn't look at him. She wound the laces of her boots around her ankles.

"She's scared, you know. She thinks she'll never see you again."

"We'll say our good-byes when I get back. All my stuff is still upstairs. Thanks again for the extra time."

Marcus muttered something about the circumstances, and no trouble at all. He sat down beside Penelope, and when she looked at him, he frowned, as if he were in some kind of mild pain, like from being stuck with needles, or a cramp. As if he were the one to whom comfort was owed.

"How did this all happen, Penelope? Between the two of us, and your father—I can only imagine how hard this time back in Brooklyn has been for you. I feel terrible for my part in everything. I'm deeply sorry."

"I know you are. You're always sorry."

Penelope stood and Marcus stayed seated, beneath her. He pressed his lips together.

"I can understand your hatred of me. You told me you could use a friend, and I—I deserve your hate."

"Jesus Christ, Marcus. I don't hate you."

He stood up suddenly, and Penelope worried he might kiss her.

"Of all the things I've been feeling these last few days, hate for you hasn't quite registered," she said.

Marcus nodded and laid his hand on her shoulder. Even now, it was easy to let him touch her. His fingers cupped the nape of her neck. He smiled. "At least, we'll still be neighbors."

The doorbell rang, and Penelope stepped away to unlock the door. Jon strode into the house, blowing on his gloveless hands, his black sweatshirt dusted with snow.

"It's cold as shit out there," he said and kissed Penelope on the cheek. "How you doing?" He turned to Marcus, and Penelope watched the two men shake hands, Jon in his black skullcap, curls fanning around his pierced ears, and Marcus, dazed in his robe, his bare feet.

"Nice to meet you, M," Jon said, and he took up Penelope's suitcase.

"Let's go," she said.

Jon hooked his arm with hers as they made their way down the stoop, already covered in an inch of snow. She didn't need his help, but she let him hold on to her. He opened the car door for her and loaded her suitcase into the trunk. Penelope watched him in the rearview mirror. She didn't have to look back to the mustard-yellow house to know Marcus was out on the stoop, watching him, too.

The morning Penelope was scheduled to arrive, Mirella woke next to Marcello. His skin was its usual tomato red, and he didn't seem to be breathing, facedown on her pillow, his hands pinned to the back of his head. A snore erupted from him every few minutes, a sign he was alive and still drunk from the night before. They had finished two bottles of wine, Mirella too nervous to eat any of the risotto Marcello had made.

When he was done eating, he had crawled into her lap and started to apply his tongue to her neck, the underside of her chin. The weight of him crushed her legs. She had stood and led him by the hand upstairs, where she put him to bed and shut off the light. When he was unconscious, she slid beside him and slept.

The night had passed too slowly, and now Mirella rose and sat at her vanity table, unpinned her hair from the tubi she wrapped it into each night before bed, and brushed it carefully to the ends. She put on a white dress that reached her ankles. It was backless and fell straight over the planes of her body. She chose turquoise earrings from her jewelry box, spread her day cream under her eyes, colored her lips a deep rose, and penciled the usual mole onto her chin. She inspected herself in the mirror, and when she was finished, she shook Marcello awake.

"You have to go," she said. "My daughter's coming. I don't want you here."

Marcello flipped over and opened his eyes, rubbed the dark hair on his belly.

"Buenos días," he yawned.

"Make the bed," Mirella said and left to call the taxista Emanuel. Marcello had offered to take her to the airport in his black SUV to pick up Penelope, but Mirella didn't want him there when she met her daughter. She would introduce him later, as a neighbor from the residence.

After he was gone, Mirella sat in the garden to wait. The sun was warming the cement and stone; the morning baked her skin. She sank her feet into the pool and thought about her daughter.

Penelope had called Ralph every day after the accident. The phone in the living room rang and rang. Mirella knew not to answer the phone, but sometimes she carried it into the bedroom where Ralph was laid up, all bandages and bruises, dozing off while his records scratched.

"How's my Penny?" he would say, waking and lifting the receiver to his ear, and Mirella would leave the room. There was plenty for her to do while Ralph and Penelope talked. She dusted and swept and washed the dishes, deep in old labors and new ones. She counted out pain pills for Ralph, changed the gauze around his hand, and mopped the bathroom floor after he sloshed water from the sink or missed the toilet when he urinated. They were routines she had never expected.

Ralph laughed when Penelope called, asked her about Pittsburgh, and promised her he was "fine, just fine." For all her concern, she hadn't visited, and Ralph still indulged her, holding up the phone to the speakers in the bedroom so Penelope could hear whatever record he was playing.

Even though they didn't speak, Mirella knew Penelope blamed her for Ralph's accident, the way he spent whole days in bed now, and needed to be pushed around in a wheelchair if he chose to go outside. He would need the wheelchair for only a few weeks, while he healed, but Mirella knew that even once he could walk again, Penelope would never forgive her. Any chance she and Penelope might have had at becoming mother and daughter again was obliterated the day Ralph fell.

But now she was coming. She might have torn up the postcard, but it had worked, her words had reached her daughter and had some influence on her for the first time. With her postcard, she had stirred up her old affections, her purest, oldest instincts as a daughter. Because of her words, Penelope was finding her way back.

The airport was already filled with other people, carrying cheap balloons and handmade signs, whole families sweating in ironed jeans and pastel polo shirts. Many of the women hadn't unwound their hair from their morning tubis; a few still wore a hairnet and rollers. Infants cried from the heat, unappreciative of the slow breeze that filtered through the plaza every few minutes, rustling the palm trees and carrying the scent of everyone. Pigeons swooped overhead, releasing shit all over the airport. Emanuel gave Mirella his baseball cap to wear, and she took it.

She bought pan tostado for the both of them and two cafés con leche. They sat in the waiting area to eat and watch the birds, watching for Penelope's flight number to appear above the gate.

"When was the last time your daughter came to visit you? I don't think I've ever met her."

Emanuel squinted at Mirella, rearranging his hair to cover the bald spots in his scalp, exposed without the baseball cap. He was a sweet man, nearly seventy, soft-spoken, but strong. When he didn't drive his taxi, he worked in the gardens of other houses in the residence. He sat with her on the breezeway during his breaks, and they ate lunch together, complaining about the mosquitoes, the government, the Englishmen in the residence.

"I haven't seen her in five years."

Emanuel whistled. "Horible, no? Este mundo? What kind of world is this that parents can't see their children?" He shook his head, as if God might be watching, take note of his disapproval, and be moved. He patted Mirella's shoulder. "I know what it's like, Doña. I haven't seen my Lourdes in ten."

He unearthed his wallet from the pocket of his jeans and handed two photographs to Mirella. The first was of a woman who shared his freckled complexion and light eyes, the other of two toothless children, smiling in navy school uniforms, their arms wrapped around each other. "Mis nietos," he explained. "And my Lourdes. She fell in love with a gringo. That's why the children are so blond. They live in Florida."

"They're beautiful. Is she ever going to bring them to see you?"

"No papers," he said, slipping the photographs back into the slim and battered brown leather. "Their father won't bring them. He owns an auto shop in Orlando that he can't ever leave."

"Are they married?"

Emanuel shook his head. "But he loves the kids. They're crazy about him. Call him Papi and everything. He doesn't speak a word of Spanish, but they do. They call me every Sunday. On my neighbor's phone. To ask for my blessing, tell me about school. The girl—she's bright. Una lámpara."

"Make sure they keep their Spanish. It's the sort of thing you lose in that country."

Emanuel laughed. "Qué no se pierde para allá?"

And Mirella laughed, too, although it was hard to make the sound.

They announced the flight around ten, after Emanuel and Mirella had been waiting for two hours. Mirella bought Emanuel a magazine he couldn't read, but he flipped through the pictures of Punta Cana and Samaná, the famed white-sand beaches on the other coast of the island that all the tourists came to visit but that he had never seen. Mirella had another café and soon she could feel her heart thumping in her ears. She smoked a cigarette, collecting the ash in her empty cup, but she only felt sicker, sweating through the thin linen of her white dress.

The passengers poured out of the gate, lugging overstuffed suitcases sealed shut with silver duct tape and plastic wrap. During the holidays and the summer, the tourists flocked to this airport, pasty and carting designer luggage. They usually went straight from the gate onto charter buses that shuttled them to the resorts along the shore. But it was a Friday in February, and everyone on this flight from JFK was Dominican. They were absolute New Yorkers in fitted caps and tailored jeans; the men in blindingly white T-shirts, and the women raking their hands through immaculately straightened silky hair.

Mirella and Emanuel pressed through the crowd forming at the gate. They were surrounded by cheering and sobbing, mothers dropping their carry-ons to lift gangly children into their arms, lovers kissing mouths and cheeks and hands, men slapping each other on the back and jeering, *Qué lo qué cabrón?*

Mirella wiped the sweat from her upper lip and forehead, felt her hair beginning to inflate just a bit at the roots. It was humid in the airport, and Mirella hoped for rain. The day would cool off after the shower, and her roses needed the water. If it rained, they would stay inside; Penelope would admire the house and talk to her.

She began to fan herself and pant, rising onto her tiptoes. She searched for a blurry woman in a navy dress, but she found herself distracted by a teenage girl with toffee skin and small eyes. She carried a sketchbook, a graphite pencil tucked behind one ear. Her hair was only kinky at her roots, the rest of it waving cleanly to her waist. She was slight in Spandex jeans and an "I Heart NY" T-shirt she had sliced open at the neckline and sleeves.

Sometimes, Mirella believed in race—that there were things in her DNA that bound her to other Dominicans. She felt it when she was in the airport, at the beach on a Sunday, in the market in Puerto Plata, when Ariane told a joke she had heard herself twenty years before on the other side of the island. She would remember, for a moment, that her little gated residence wasn't all of the island, and she was in a place where there were thousands of people who looked as if they could be related to her—a long-lost tía, a neighbor who had left Aguas Frescas for the north, her American daughter.

An old man and woman, both weeping, swallowed the teenage girl in their arms. She wrapped one arm around each of them and they rocked together. Mirella watched as the old couple stole the girl away through the crowd.

Mirella turned back to the gate and discovered Penelope a few yards away from her. Her hair was tied in a knot on top of her head, the curls pushing their way out of the elastic, falling around her face. She was as thin and as muscular as Mirella expected from the photograph, but up close there was nothing of girlhood left in her face. She looked her age, almost thirty, and although her skin was still taut and fresh, she was no longer young. She wore gray pants and an oversized collared shirt with the sleeves rolled up—Ralph's, but not one of the ones Mirella used to wear to work in the backyard.

Mirella waved, although Penelope had already seen her. Penelope nodded back at her and cut through the crowd confidently, carrying only her black leather suitcase, the one she had taken with her first when she went to RISD, and then when she finally left Halsey Street for good.

Mirella felt herself shaking, her fingertips and her wrists, then her cheeks and the corners of her lips. Her teeth knocked against each other. Her sweat turned cold.

"Tranquila," Emanuel whispered, placing his hand on her shoulder. "Ya casi."

He took a step behind her, leaving room for Penelope. Mirella saw the pigeons nesting in the corners of the airport ceiling. There were small ledges where they had piled sticks to make their homes.

Penelope stood taller than Mirella in her leather boots splattered with paint. The stale scent of the airplane cabin had stuck to her skin; beneath that, she was Vaseline and coconut oil, and something bitter.

"It was snowing in New York," she said. "That's why the flight was late."

"We weren't waiting long."

Mirella shook and stood silently, waiting.

"I told you not to come," Penelope said. "This suitcase is the only luggage I brought. I'd have been fine on my own."

"It's no trouble," Mirella said. "I wanted to come."

Penelope sighed and let the bag drop. It clattered softly to the ground. She stretched, her hands reaching for the ceiling. There was silver in her daughter's hair, just a strand or two, spun into her moño.

Mirella stepped forward, wondering whether to touch her.

"Here," she said, lifting the suitcase from the ground. "I'll take this."

Mirella raised her free hand and placed it on Penelope's shoulder. They didn't have to draw near to one another, they could preserve the space between them, but Mirella was still touching her. She closed her cold fingers around her daughter's shoulder.

Penelope slid out from underneath her mother's grasp and walked past her to Emanuel.

"Hola, Señor, mucho gusto. Yo soy Penélope Grand."

Penelope clapped both her hands around Emanuel's, then kissed him on the cheek. Her face swiping against his, her arm patting him on the back. She asked him where he had parked and set off, ahead of them, walking in the direction of the car. She left Mirella with the suitcase.

On the ride to the airport, Penelope and Jon had inched along Atlantic Avenue, over the ice, listening to some early-eighties radio show. The station played rock ballads that all seemed to revolve around the word *heaven*.

Penelope stared out the window at the undersides of the Long Island Rail Road tracks. The early risers were out in their oversized coats. The older folks trotted slowly enough to seem still, and packs of kids dashed and slid across the ice, leaving their parents at the other end of the block. Not one of them seemed to be in any danger, despite the ice, the wind, the blur of snow. They were fine, cold but fine, and it seemed terrible to Penelope that a day like this could seem so pretty and benign as to trick you into believing this was a good place to live, that every instant, someone in this city wasn't losing something, that bad news couldn't come anytime anywhere, that every day might be the worst day.

They stopped at a red light, and Penelope turned up the radio.

"Either you're really into the music or not in the mood to talk."

"I'm just thinking."

"How are you feeling?"

"I said I was thinking, not feeling."

Jon stared at her sideways across the front seat, and Penelope reached for her coffee so that she could look away. He seemed to accept her silence, and kept driving, the tiny paperboard scented tree swinging above the dashboard. The car belonged to a friend, one of the guys they had gone spray-painting with that night under the JMZ.

"It's beginning to irritate me," Penelope said, "the way you're always so optimistic. And calm. You do realize why I'm going to the airport right now? You do understand what's happened in my life these past few weeks?"

"I'm fully aware," Jon said. "I'm also aware that what's happened in your life the past few weeks isn't my fault. So, I'm not sure why you're turning on me."

He indicted her so plainly it was worse than if he'd used melodrama, yelled, or thrown a plate or a brush. He had simply pointed out how badly she was behaving, and now she had to sit beside him in the car, unmasked and with nowhere to escape.

Penelope looked out the window at the slush and ice. "Why are you so nice to me?" she said.

"You'll get used to it."

"I should be terrified, but I just feel like I'm going to see my mother. It seems normal. Like something I could have been doing all along."

"You've been holding up real good, Penny. You're gonna do just fine."

Penelope looked back out the window, a butter roll untouched in her lap. When they stopped at the next red light, she handed him his cup, and he sipped his coffee with one hand on the wheel. The car vibrated beneath them.

"So, I can't help but ask," he said. "Is Marcus the real reason the landlady asked you to move out?"

"How could you tell?"

"He was looking at you as if it physically hurt him to see you go."

Jon turned on the windshield wipers, and they cleared away the snow.

"What did you like about him anyway? He seems like a square."

Penelope shrugged. "He liked me."

"There must have been something more. For both of you to risk what you did."

He was kind to me. I was lonely. He's a good father. It was something to do. She could have said any of these things, but she didn't want Jon to know them yet.

"I should have never been there in the first place. My father needed me in his house—"

"And you needed to be elsewhere. So it goes with parents and their children."

The windshield wipers squeaked in time to a jingle for laundry detergent.

"Well, whatever you and Marcus had, I don't care, as long as it's over. I'm jealous, yeah, but he has nothing to do with you and me. You're moving out when you get back, and we have our own thing."

Our own thing, Penelope thought, and for a moment, all the sorrow she'd been carrying around thinned. Jon's jealousy had shrunken it down.

"Will you be all right driving back from the airport? Over all this ice?"

"Chicago boy, remember?"

He smiled at her, and it seemed like the opposite of a smile from Marcus: uncoded, clean.

A synthesizer hummed on the radio, the muted pulse of a bass. Jon beat out the percussion on the steering wheel. At the next light, he opened the glove compartment, fished out a white envelope, and handed it to her.

Penelope felt along the sealed edge of the envelope. He'd scribbled her name across the front of it, the letters pressed together, angled forward, as if they might tip over.

"What is it?"

"Pictures," he said. "So you remember to come back."

The house was more elegant than Penelope expected. It was white and cavernous, so much space between the ceiling and the floor, between the walls. Mirella's footsteps echoed as she gave her the tour, pointed out the skylight, the wood and wicker furniture she had ordered from the capital.

Her mother's house didn't have the of-the-moment sophistication of the Harpers' home, nor was it as old-fashioned as the house on Halsey Street. It was clean, and bright, and empty, a marble kitchen counter, a glass wall, the white columns on the breezeway. It was someone else's vision of a good life. Even the oil paintings Mirella had framed in the living room were forgettable still lifes of flowers in vases, fruits spilling onto a sunlit table.

Mirella lingered in front of the paintings to give Penelope enough time to inspect them. Penelope's eyes flashed over them, disinterestedly, and she said, "You started collecting, I see," and Mirella wasn't sure whether she was making fun of her. She had wanted the paintings to touch Penelope, to show her she could appreciate art. Maybe the garden would impress her. Mirella led the way.

Penelope had to be careful not to give away how beautiful it was. Here was her mother, this green overgrowth, surging with flowers and trees. Short papaya trees and birds of paradise and bushes of hot peppers and tomatoes filled the first quarter acre; small palms lined the perimeter, and rosebushes close to the edges of the house, alongside white eruptions of velo de novia, the flowers as delicate as tissue paper. Farther back in the garden the banana trees grew, and more plants, so thick and green and near to each other Penelope couldn't see where the property ended, how far back the garden reached.

Mirella waited for Penelope to say something, to notice the rosemary plants, like she'd grown back in Brooklyn, or the care she'd taken in circling her herb garden with blue-gray pebbles she'd collected from along the side of the road. The sun bored through the clouds, and Penelope squinted toward the back of the garden.

"How much land do you have?"

"Two acres. Not counting the house."

Penelope said nothing.

"Do you want to go swimming?"

"I'd like to run."

Penelope asked to see where she'd be staying so she could change, and Mirella led her back into the house. She felt as though her tour had been interrupted, but there wasn't anything more to show Penelope, unless she wanted to go upstairs to see her master bedroom, her walk-in tub, the cedar wood closet she'd had built to keep mosquitoes away from her clothes.

The guest room was at the front of the house. Mirella had washed a set of sheets for the bed, opened the window to let in the perfume of the rosebush planted nearby. It was furnished only with a dresser and a ceiling fan, a four-post bed of pure caoba. Now that Penelope was here it would finally contain more—clothes and books, shoes, her daughter.

Penelope swung her suitcase onto the bed and began rummaging through, without taking in the sheer white curtains, the pale blue of the walls.

"I can make us some lunch," Mirella said.

"If you want."

Penelope kicked off her boots and began to unbutton her shirt.

"I think it's going to rain," Mirella said, and when Penelope didn't turn to look at her, she backed out of the room and left her daughter undressing.

From the kitchen, Mirella saw her run out of the residence, past the watching-man and Ariane, who was mopping the steps in front of Marcello's house, her long hair pulled back, her shirt already damp with sweat although she was just starting the day's work. She and Penelope couldn't look more different, although they were nearly the same age. Ariane was dark from the sun with slender limbs but a soft stomach, the layers of flesh a woman gains after childbirth. Her clothes would have been in style in the US a decade ago, but they were in as good condition as she could manage to keep them in, the collars ironed, the buttons secured with extra thread. Her shoes were made of plastic. And there was Penelope in lime green running sneakers, smeared in dirt but surely no more than a year old, skimpy shorts, a faded T-shirt. Her hair flopped loose behind her, pushed off her brow with a black elastic band that fit around her ears. Her body was the kind that you shape for yourself, not the kind that is the sum of all your accidents, labor, appetites, and genes.

Ariane saw Mirella standing in the kitchen and waved to her. Mirella waved back and then returned to the guest room, where Penelope had left her suitcase open on the bed. Mirella was careful not to unfold anything as she sifted through, wiping the sweat from her hands on her dress. She found the same lacy panties Penelope had always worn, the matching brassieres, and fluffy athletic socks. She had packed enough clothes for a few days—she hadn't told Mirella yet when she planned on flying back. Inside the sleeve of one of Ralph's shirts, Mirella found a flask. It was cool steel with a black cap; full. Penelope had packed one book, a slim hardcover without the jacket. Between the pages, there was an envelope with her daughter's name across the front. Inside were Polaroids, one of a brick wall covered in green and orange circles of spray paint, another of two glasses of beer on a wooden counter, several of sunny, cold Brooklyn streets. She found a Polaroid of a man sitting on the front steps to a brick building. He held a cigarette in his hand, his whole body caving in on itself as he laughed. Mirella could tell he was young, despite the smile lines, the creases in his forehead and around his eyes. He wore his dark hair long, and he almost looked like Penelope, his curls swept off his face with a band like the one she had put on before her run. He was darker than Penelope, but not as dark as Ralph. There was snow on the stoop, and he wore a sweatshirt instead of a coat, but nothing about him seemed cold. Mirella examined his face, then put everything back in the suitcase, and returned to the kitchen to wait.

She filled two plates with the food Marcello had made the night before: pork shoulder and risotto with herbs from her garden. She sat at the kitchen counter and fumbled in the cupboard below, searching for the broken cup, like the one Ramona had kept at her shrine in her bedroom in Aguas Frescas. With the postcard gone, all that was left in Mirella's cup was the butterfly clip Penelope had worn as a girl.

She had left the clip behind when she moved to Pittsburgh. While she was gone, Mirella and Ralph had kept the door to her bedroom closed, but Ralph went inside sometimes. Mirella heard Penelope's bed creak under his weight; she heard him pick things off her desk and then set them back down, open her drawers and close them. Mirella entered the bedroom when she was finally packing up to leave herself. Penelope had abandoned her collection of mood rings and charm bracelets, tiny gold hoop earrings and glow-in-the-dark wristbands, an array of purple and pink lipsticks she hadn't worn after high school. The clip reminded Mirella the most of when Penelope had been a girl, still unable to handle her hair by herself. She had resorted to bobby pins and the butterfly clip to bite into her curls, keep them fast to her crown.

Mirella felt the sharp, fragmented edges of the cup, the crease in the postcard, the fake jewels adorning the butterfly wings.

"Nice road."

Penelope startled Mirella, loping into the kitchen from behind her. Mirella shut the cupboard.

"If this were Aguas Frescas, I'd be up to my knees in dirt. But the road here is nice."

"It's paved. It makes a difference. You know how Dominicans drive—" Mirella held up her hand and made it lurch from side to side, as if she were slicing up a road of air.

"I can see why you decided to live here."

Mirella kept her eyebrows from going up in shock. It was the closest thing to a compliment she'd heard from Penelope in years. She seemed to be in a good mood, red-faced, nearly all of her skin blushing and exposed. Maybe someone had said something to her while she was on the road, leaned out of a pickup truck to call her beautiful, honked at her to say she shouldn't go so fast, slow down, they wanted to watch. Whatever had happened, Mirella hoped the mood would last.

"I made some food," Mirella said, pulling a plate from the microwave. "And there's mabi in the refrigerator." She didn't mention the cases and cases she had saved in the pantry for the day her daughter finally came to visit.

"I'll take water," Penelope said, and she sprang onto a stool and yanked the elastic from her hair. With her curls around her ears, she looked, for a moment, like a girl again.

Mirella filled a glass for her from a bottle and explained to her the tap water wasn't filtered, and she shouldn't drink from the tap anywhere in the house.

Penelope gulped down the water quickly. "I never worried about the water here. I left that to you."

"I had to worry. You were my child."

"That I was," Penelope said and raised her glass. She looked Mirella squarely in the eyes for what felt like the first time since she had arrived that morning. "Salud." She drained the glass.

They sat and didn't speak, Penelope chuckling darkly to herself and shaking her head while she pushed the food around her plate. Mirella watched, waiting for her to blast. She poured her first glass of wine for the day, without offering any to Penelope, and abandoned the food for her drink. She no longer had an appetite either.

"Are you even going to ask about him?"

Penelope glared at Mirella, fork and knife in her hands, her eyes filled with fire.

There.

"I was waiting for you," Mirella said.

Penelope laughed and shook her head. "No, you weren't."

"How is he?"

"He's alive," Penelope placed both her hands flat on the counter. "He's the only man under sixty-five in the home we found for him, which is depressing, but a lot of people there are still in their right mind, so at least he has regular company now. And he has a room of his own, and an aide to take him out on walks in the evenings. Well, the aide walks, and Pop—"

Penelope swallowed hard.

"I'm negotiating with the management to get a rack put in the wall, so he can keep more of his records with him. We're waiting for their approval, but it doesn't matter what they say—I'll go in there with a drill and put in the rack myself if I have to."

"Yes, you're right. The records will make him happy."

"The home isn't far," Penelope went on, as if she had been waiting all morning to tell Mirella precisely this, and now that she was finally telling her, she could relent and be calm. She didn't grip the counter quite as hard, her voice was even and low. "It's just over the BQE. You can see the Clock Tower from his window. I go see him a few times a week, and so does Miss Beckett."

Mirella cringed. "Una? She's still alive?"

"She's the one who found him. She saved his life."

Mirella didn't say anything. They sat across the counter from each other, and Mirella could see Penelope was already starting to brown. She was the color of dark honey.

"So who else lives here? Or do you live alone?"

"It's just me."

"Big house for one person."

"It's not a problem for me."

"Of course not. You're not the one who fell down the stairs—"

"I'm not sorry I left."

257

"You think I came all the way here for an apology?"

"I don't know why you're here."

"This is where I'm from," Penelope said. "It's a part of me, too."

Penelope stood and carried her plate to the garbage. She scraped the untouched risotto and pork into the can, refilled her glass at the tap.

"Besides, it's been a long time."

I wanted to see you, too, hija.

"I thought about calling him," Mirella said. "After I got your letter."

"What would you have said?" Penelope stood with one hand on her hip.

"I would have said, 'Hi, Ralph, how are you?'"

"My father has to fracture his spine and nearly die to get you to call him? When is the next time you'll call? The funeral?"

"We're separated."

"So he's nothing to you? Is that how you treat someone you spent half of your life with? Do you even know what it means to be part of a family?"

"Watch yourself," Mirella said. "You left Brooklyn before I did."

Mirella didn't want to explode now. It wasn't like before, when they lived just a few rooms away from each other. She wanted clarity and slowness, this control over her words. Penelope was finally in her house. Her daughter was here.

Penelope smiled and sipped from her glass, the tap water clear and cold.

"Ah, you see, Mami, there's a big difference," she said. "You're nothing to me. As far as I'm concerned, you're already dead."

It grew dark while Penelope lay on the bed in the guest room. She put the Polaroid of Jon on her chest and gulped from the flask. She hadn't brought any cigarettes with her, but she imagined the smoke curling out of her hand, floating to the teal ceiling. After all these years, she still couldn't control her tongue around her mother. It was Mirella who had first taught her to say whatever would wound most after she herself had been wounded. After she left Brooklyn, she never had someone draw close enough to trade cuts, but it was an instinct she hadn't lost. This was all her mother had given her—sharpened edges.

Penelope wasn't surprised that her mother was living among expats; she had never wanted to belong to the mountains. The house was beautiful, and the garden more so, Mirella still elegant. It was obvious that her new life suited her. Penelope had sent a photograph with her letter to make it plain that she was no longer a girl, to say somehow, *Take this so that you will recognize me—it's been five years, and I am not the same.* But Penelope was, and it was her mother who had become different. She felt envious and, also, devastated that her mother's life had bloomed only after she disentangled herself from the trouble of loving Ralph, of being a mother.

Penelope thought of her grandmother and drank again from the flask. She closed her eyes and conjured up the old woman, held her close. She was dead and yet she was nearer to Penelope than Mirella had ever been. She couldn't say whether she had once loved her mother, only that she had once pined for her mother's love. She reminded herself that she had not come to pine again—she would get what she came for and then leave. It was simple. It was easy. She braced herself with a few long swills.

She could hear Mirella out in the garden with her shears, clipping the plants, turning the hose on and off. They would be old women, she and Mirella, carrying on in just this way—they would bicker, and leave each other, then come back together again. Penelope closed her eyes and listened to her mother, watering things, snipping them apart.

After the garden, Mirella went upstairs to be alone. She didn't want to be on the same floor as her daughter, so she chain-smoked in bed and watched novelas, catching the ash in a marble ashtray, some of it still finding its way onto the sheets. She turned over Penelope's words in her mind, and wanted to stomp down to the guest room and throw her out of the house. Send her out onto the road in the dark, let her walk—or better, *run*—to the airport. Go back to her precious Ralph, who was still *alive*. Mirella was more alive than any of them. She had left so that she could live.

It was night when Marcello rang the doorbell, and to Mirella's surprise, when she went downstairs, Penelope had already let him in. He had brought a fig tart and a bottle of perfectly chilled pinot grigio. He and Penelope were chatting easily, moving between Spanish and English, according to the words and phrases that Marcello knew in each language. Penelope was elegant in a strappy navy dress and a small moño held up by gold bobby pins, revealing the rippled undersides of her hair. Mirella noticed a sway in Penelope's walk as they made their way to the living room. She caught a whiff of the alcohol and discerned instantly how her daughter had spent the afternoon.

The three of them sat on Mirella's beige couch, leaving the tart untouched between them. They were all on their second glasses before long, and Marcello prattled on and on about the residence and how life in DR wasn't as cheap as he had hoped. There was the gardener to pay, and Ariane, the watching-man, and the teenage boy who cleaned the pool. Dog food was more expensive here, imported from the US, and he had *three dogs* to feed. He sighed and huffed and poured them all more wine, and declared, in his strange Dominicanized Spanish, *La vida no es fácil,* and Penelope swirled the wine in her glass and agreed, *No, no, la vida es dura.*

When the bottle was finished, Marcello left, kissing Penelope on the cheek. Mirella blushed when he kissed hers. He said he wanted to leave mother and daughter time to themselves, to keep enjoying the day together as they had. He left without protest from either woman, stumbling in the dark, down the walkway, in roughly the direction of his house.

"Nice neighbor," Penelope said, and Mirella nodded.

"Yes, he's a nice man. Habla mucho, but he's nice."

They didn't mention the afternoon. Penelope pulled down another bottle of wine from the cabinet in the kitchen, uncorked it expertly, and poured two glasses without spilling a drop. They had a pizza delivered from an Italian restaurant in Sosúa. Mirella divided the slices onto heavy china plates, and they carried the box and the wine, the crystal glasses, out onto the breezeway. They ate overlooking the pool, a citronella candle burning between them.

"This is different from Aguas Frescas," Penelope said, pinching an artichoke heart between her fingers. "No stone kitchen."

"Thank God." Mirella rolled her eyes at the mention of the mountain. She crossed one thin leg over the other. She spun the merlot in her glass.

"Well, haven't you arrived?" Penelope said smugly, but Mirella wasn't sure what she meant.

"Arrived where?"

"Never mind."

They picked apart the pizza slices with their hands, the flour and oil sticking to their fingers. Penelope avoided the carrots; Mirella relished the olives. The pool hummed and a pair of frogs appeared, unafraid to be seen indulging in their nightly dip.

"So, Marcello's just your friend?"

"Mhm."

"Is he your friend who you fuck?"

Mirella set down her glass.

"Penélope, I may be dead to you, but I'm still your mother. Even when I'm dead, I'll still be your mother. So watch how you speak to me. What kind of words you use."

Penelope shrugged. "Somos mujeres," she said. "We can talk about these things." She almost seemed sincere in her drunkenness. She poured herself another glass.

"And what about your friend? The one in the photograph in your maleta?"

Penelope sat up straight in her chair, as if prepared to lash out at Mirella for snooping, and then she slumped back into the seat.

"He's a friend."

"A good friend who you fuck?"

Penelope cringed. "Mami, please—"

"Is he?"

"It's a bit late for you to begin worrying about who I fuck. That would have been useful earlier in life."

The women sat in silence, nursing their drinks.

"He's a good friend," Penelope said finally.

"Lo que tú digas," Mirella said, although she couldn't remember Penelope ever having any friends, good or otherwise.

"Mami?"

"Hm?"

"I want the house."

Mirella set the wine down before she dropped the glass. "So that's why you're here."

"I brought the deed. All you have to do is sign the rights over to me."

"Does your father know about this?"

"Pop agreed it's best if the house is in my name, and my name only. He already signed his rights over to me."

Mirella laughed. "Of course he did. Now that he can't live in the house, why shouldn't you, his precious little Penny, get it all to yourself?" She began to feel the anger she had been staving off all day. It was like a sickness in her blood, recirculating, reclaiming every limb.

Penelope was the calm one now, sitting with her elbows on her knees, a businesswoman making a pitch.

"I don't want the house for myself. I just don't want us to lose it, like we lost the store. It will be like Pop never built anything, he never had anything at all—"

"That house was mine, too."

"You haven't lived in Brooklyn in years. You have your own house now. The only reason for you to hold on to the brownstone is so that if Pop dies, you can sell it and get your half."

"How dare you! How dare you accuse me of thinking like that! Of just waiting for your father to die!"

"You've taken his money before—I know how you paid for this house."

"I worked for this house, Penelope. I saved for over twenty years! How little you know! You know nothing! Sinvergüenza! Babosa! Malcriada!" Mirella spat the insults at her daughter, leaning forward in her chair, but she didn't stand up. "Who do you think you are? Coming into my house and telling me I don't care about the man I married."

"Yo no nací ayer Mami," Penelope said. "Whatever money you had when you came here isn't going to last forever. You're going to need more eventually if you want to keep up with Marcello and the rest of your neighbors."

"I didn't take anything from your father! And I'll find another way!"

"I don't care what way you find. I just want the house. It's easiest if you just sign the papers."

Penelope reached into her purse, withdrew a creased square of papers. She unfolded them onto the table.

"You just sign at the bottom, twice, and write your initials, and it's done. You'll see Pop has already signed."

"And what if I don't sign?"

"Then the house still belongs to the two of you. His disability checks and insurance are paying for the nursing home, but he can't afford to pay the taxes on the house, too. It'll fall to you. And since I'm—What was your word? Useless? An artist?—I can't help with the payments. It will fall to you."

"Maybe I'll sell the house."

"You can't without my permission, and I am going to honor Pop's wishes. He wants the house to stay in the family, even if that includes you."

"You're doing this to hurt me." Mirella strained her neck to keep her head upright; there was the haze of the wine over everything: her daughter, the pool, the palms swaying in the night breeze. Penelope seemed alarmingly sober, eyes alert, hands on her knees, sitting on the edge of her plastic chair.

"Mirella, I didn't come here to hurt you. And I'm not interested in taking away any of your pain either. I came here for the house. It's all I want. Sign the papers."

How had Mirella missed the papers? Her hands must have passed right over them. The hardcover book, the short shorts, Ralph's shirts, the panties, the Polaroid, not the pages, the contract, the deed. Was it the same one they had signed in 1992? Ralph wore a gingham shirt and jeans, the pen they had used tucked in his breast pocket. Mirella couldn't remember what she was wearing, or even if Penelope was there, although she must have been, all dressed up, as Ralph would have insisted. Ralph had signed first, and then she had, *Mirella Constanza Isabel Jiménez Santos de Grand*, the comically long Dominican name Ralph had mocked her for—first name, middle, confirmation, and the two last names she had carried before becoming his wife. Her name had spilled over the line, but she had written it all, and it was done, the house was theirs. They were still in Brooklyn, but they had four floors, and a backyard. Ralph had turned to her and asked if she was ready to plant a garden, bring a bit of the island to the Republic of Brooklyn.

Penelope stood and straightened her dress, smoothing the easy fabric with her brown fingers. She was an elegant, terrible stranger, her neck long and her hair wound up.

"I'm leaving them here," Penelope said, striking the folded square of papers once with her knuckles, as if Mirella could forget where they were. "After all you've done, it's the least you could do."

Penelope turned and left, Mirella's head spinning as she went. She didn't hear the back door open and close, didn't hear Penelope at all, just the crickets, screeching, and the hum of the lightless pool.

Mirella watched the tops of the palm trees shift in the wind; they blew away from each other then sprang back together. They made a scratchy rustling sound over her head. The crickets played their nightly symphony, a few dogs somewhere down the road howled at each other, back and forth, from wherever they were fenced in. A tiny red spider made its way across the breezeway, crossing beneath the round table. Mirella let it crawl, didn't smash it with her chancleta. She had been wrong about the postcard—her words hadn't changed a thing.

She tried to picture Ralph in a nursing home. She was certain she would recognize him anywhere, in any state, but she couldn't imagine him in a wheelchair, not permanently. The days she had seen him hobbling around the apartment on Halsey, wincing when he tried to rise from the bed or bend down to tie his shoe, were so few compared to the years she had spent watching him circulate proudly among the aisles at Grand Records, march up the stairs from work, his jacket slung over his shoulder, carrying a bottle of rum and a bouquet of wildflowers on a day sales were particularly good and he was feeling romantic, the nights before Penelope when they would go dancing in the Village and Ralph would point his index fingers at her, and rock his hips from side to side, bobbing and dancing in his funny American way, and the mornings after when he would dash around the kitchen on Marcy Avenue, smoking his pipe and burning eggs, humming along to whatever record he was playing, tapping his foot sometimes for emphasis, as if it were a horn he could blow. What sort of Ralph was he now?

Mirella left the pizza box, wine bottle, and glasses outside, even if she knew the leftovers would attract animals in the dark. She took the creased square of papers with her into the house and locked the door behind her. She stopped in the kitchen to wash off the scent of garlic and olive oil from her hands. She scrubbed her rubbery, golden, ringless hands together. Mirella dried her hands before she took up the papers again.

If she ever went back to New York, it wouldn't be to Brooklyn. She would go back as the tourist she never got to be. She would finally visit the Metropolitan Museum of Art, just to say that she had been there. She had been to Central Park and Times Square and the waterfront on the West Side of Manhattan, but it would be different if she went back now. She wouldn't be stealing time on her way to work or on her way back home from cleaning—she would be there just to watch, just to stand, just to be. She would stay in a hotel with fat bathrobes and tiny bottles of shampoo she could take back with her to DR. She wouldn't need the house. That life was over.

As she climbed the stairs, Mirella felt an unexpected relief that Penelope had wanted something from her—as long as she had the papers, as long as they were unsigned, the girl would have a reason to stay. Her daughter might not love her, but she was here, in her house. The deed was gold. Maybe she'd take Penelope to the beach tomorrow, to stretch what time they had. Hours at the beach often felt like days, and even if the girl hated her, wished she were dead, maybe she'd consent to go, if she thought it might convince her to sign. Mirella would take time, if Penelope wouldn't offer anything else.

The store closed on a Thursday. Mirella and Ralph emptied out the shop themselves, stacking the records that hadn't sold into dozens of boxes. Ralph wasn't sure where to put them all, and Mirella suggested the shed, which he agreed was a good idea. She swept the floors, and Ralph took the shelves out in the back, broke them apart with a long-handled hammer, then put the wood in the dumpster. The new shop owners were willing to buy the shelves, in case they would use them, but Ralph refused. They didn't need them in the house, and they probably could have donated them somewhere—to a church or the Salvation Army on Quincy Street, but Ralph smashed them instead.

Ralph drove the boxes of records back to the house on Halsey in shifts. Mirella waited for him to pick up the last load and her as dusk came over Lewis Avenue. She sat on the front steps and smoked her Parliaments, thinking about the store, and the stiff, empty look Ralph had worn all day, sweating and packing, climbing up ladders to take down framed posters, uprooting nails from inside the walls.

Just one link in a chain of bad news, Ralph had said. Sheckley's was already gone; the bar still had the same name, the same wooden shutters, but Lionel was gone, and the regulars—the ones who hadn't moved away—didn't care for the new craft beers, didn't like being the only patrons who were old and local and black. Every block in Bed-Stuy was its own universe, the changes coming at a distinct pace on every street, but Ralph didn't see the difference. *Everyone* was leaving. *Everyone* was gone. *Nothing* was the same. For him, if the shop was over, the neighborhood was, too.

The rent for the store had been increasing steadily for the past seven years, but Ralph kept paying, finding a way not to dip into the red. Grand Records had been one of the first stores to open on this dreary strip in the seventies, leading the way for more and more shops to shoot up. Ralph hardly made a profit anymore, but the brownstone was all paid for, except the taxes, and he and Mirella didn't need much. Penelope supported herself. And they kept the store because they could and they had to, Ralph said. *The neighborhood needs its music.*

They were all right until someone offered the landlord double what Ralph was paying. A young couple from Seattle was looking to open a health food store. Ralph crunched numbers for weeks, tried to find a way to pay the new rent. He could lease out the other floors in the house on Halsey to make up the money they would lose, but Mirella didn't want strangers living in their house. And even with tenants they would need sales to go up to cover the new rent.

When the couple from Seattle offered double and a half, Ralph caved. He and Mirella were offered a large check to end their lease early so the Seattle couple could get in and renovate. Ralph and Mirella had witnessed an elderly Puerto Rican lady lose her bodega across the street. She had been priced out, no money to show for the years she had given, or the thousands spent out of her own pocket to fix the floors, the pipes, the leaky ceiling. They had replaced her store with a wine bar, taken down the "La Nueva Victoria" sign, and never put up another. This wine bar was unmarked, but the new clientele all knew how to find it. They could tell it by its tinted windows, the absence of a building number. Mirella encouraged Ralph to take the money so they wouldn't end up like the old Puerto Rican woman from across the street. They agreed to the payout and lost the shop, a full five months before their lease was up again.

Penelope sent flowers and a card, as if someone had died, and a mix CD. She put all her and Ralph's songs on one disc, which wasn't how he liked to listen to music, but he played it anyway on the stereo. It was an odd mash-up of Ralph's tastes and favorite artists: Bill Withers and Herbie Hancock, Earth, Wind and Fire, Nina Simone, Public Enemy, Wu-Tang, Chuck Berry, Leadbelly, Billie Holiday and Ethel Waters, Duke Ellington, Louis Armstrong. It was playing in the rented car when Ralph pulled up, his pipe in his teeth, the clouds of tobacco smoke drifting out the window onto the street.

Do you have the keys? he'd said, and Mirella reached into her jeans, unjoined the store keys from the ring they shared with the house keys. Ralph got out of the car and slipped the keys into an envelope. He walked to the front door of the shop, tried the knob to make sure it was locked, and then slipped the envelope under a green mat the new owners had dropped off for the front entrance. WELCOME.

Idiots, Ralph said, letting himself back into the car, where Mirella sat waiting. *Fucking idiots.* All it took was for one person to look under the mat, find the keys, and take the store apart, but they had wanted the keys under the mat. They would be by in the morning to pick them up. *Idiots, fucking idiots,* Ralph sang, driving to the gas station where they would return the car. It was all the way under the train tracks. They would make the long walk back to Halsey; Mirella hated the bus.

In the days that followed, they didn't talk about the future, although the check arrived. Ralph referred to it as "the blood money." He looked over the check, made a note of the amount in one of his money books, and then left the tiny slip of paper on the nightstand. Mirella waited a week and then went to their bank downtown, the old Dime Savings Bank with the white pillars and dome ceiling. She made copies of the check and the invoice, left them in their safe-deposit box in the basement vault, then stopped by Junior's to buy a whole cheesecake, two burgers with steak fries and pickles. The meat was cold by the time she got off the A train, but she and Ralph still ate the burgers together, sitting on the olive sofa in the living room. They listened to the mix Penelope had made. Ralph set the CD to loop.

The days were indistinguishable from each other, and Ralph and Mirella slipped into a new routine easily. She was unaccustomed to the company, but it was nice when she turned over in bed and Ralph was still there, the covers rising and falling with his breath. She got up and made them coffee, went out across Nostrand to Delight, a bakery that had opened just a few months ago. It was the sort of place Mirella had always wanted to live across the street from, a café with black-and-white photographs on the wall, a glass display of fresh pastries every morning, and bright yellow paper cups filled with hardly any coffee, mostly foam. She bought hefty slices of cake, and Ralph rose when he heard her return. They ate the cake in bed, Mirella placing the cafetera on a cloth on the nightstand to cool, so they didn't have to go into the kitchen for a refill. Ralph squeezed Mirella's hand once in a while, and she squeezed back, and the crumbs gathered on their bedsheets, and in his beard. Mirella cleaned up and they watched the news, and then a game show, the shopping network, the news again. Eventually, they made their way out of the bedroom. They showered and ate again and made more coffee. Mirella worked in the garden, and when she came back to the house, she found Ralph poring over his money books, as if he would find something new there, or he would be listening to records or Penelope's mix. In the evening, Mirella watched her novelas and Ralph sat with her, reading the paper. She translated the most dramatic moments for him, and he seemed to listen, his eyebrows perking up, as he followed her plotlines. *This is the preacher, and here is his lover, she turns eighteen next week, and this is the girl's fiancé, the mayor's son, and her fiancé's sister, who is a widow and the most beautiful woman in town and very devout, but she's in love with the preacher who, remember, is the secret lover of her future sister-in-law.*

The days passed and no one called besides Penelope. Lionel was dead, and Ralph had stopped talking to Freddie when he left Bed-Stuy for a tiny condo at the edge of the borough, down between the two bridges. Freddie had never boasted as much about the neighborhood as Lionel and Ralph. He thought it wasn't safe enough or beautiful enough to go on living there, so he and Kim left for somewhere with a view. It wasn't Freddie's fault Ralph felt so alone, but Freddie was the only one he could blame—Freddie wasn't his daughter, and he wasn't dead.

After a week, Ralph finally left the house. He went to Sheckley's and got drunk. Mirella didn't begrudge him drinking. He was mourning, and sometimes you needed to drink until the world blurred, and your eyes slipped shut, and you had succeeded, in a way, in obliterating everything that hurt. But the world was stubborn and kept coming back—you could count on its return. So Mirella let him drink.

She joined him one night, and they sat in a booth. Mirella wore heels. She admired the new menu and ordered a martini—her first.

Ralph plowed through his beers sullenly. They paid the bill without leaving a tip and walked home, crushing the leaves underfoot. In the bedroom, he kissed her and thanked her. He didn't say for what.

As they were undressing for bed, Mirella felt an unexpected exhilaration, her heart beating in her ears. She could feel her blood warming her face. It wasn't the anticipation of making love. Ralph was too depressed, and it had been so long, she no longer relied on him to satisfy her. But she could feel a shift between them. With the shop gone, all they did was in sync. Rise, eat, sleep, rise again. They could do this for the rest of their lives; they had the time, and nothing to worry about, now, besides each other. With the shop gone, they could do anything. They could take a trip to California, or rent a car and drive south. Mirella had never been to Washington, DC. They could visit all fifty states. She could take him to DR. Ralph could apply for his passport and take her to Spain. They could sell the house and move to Manhattan. They could start over.

When they got down under the covers, Mirella's heart was still knocking sweetly in her chest, and Ralph asked her if she was all right, did she drink too much? Did she need some water from the tap? Ralph got up and brought her a glass of water, put his hand on her thigh and said, "There now. Drink up, you'll be fine." He clicked off the light.

Mirella reached for Ralph in her sleep, but she didn't find him. She woke up, her throat dry and vision bleary. He was gone. The bedroom door was shut; the house was quiet. No cars on Halsey Street; it was too late even for the neighborhood goons to be roaming outside. It was the hour that hangs between the end of one day and the beginning of the next. The sun wouldn't rise for a while; it smelled like empty street corners, burning paper and herb, Brooklyn slumber.

"Ralph," Mirella whispered, although she knew he wasn't near enough to hear her. She said his name again and smiled, thinking, wherever he was, he was in this house, and he would return to bed, and they would sleep, and then wake again to another day. And they'd live day after day like that, for a long time.

She rose from the bed, found her chancletas, her robe. She slipped into the dark hallway, running her hand along the flat banister, following the light into the kitchen. She heard the familiar whistle of the cafetera. Ralph was boiling water. Coffee at four a.m.? For their hangovers, she thought.

Ralph stood at the stove in a white undershirt and the long pants he wore to sleep. In silhouette, he didn't look too different than he had when they had first met. There was the pouch of his belly, and the circumference of his fro shrunken, but he was still Ralph, his pelvis pushed up against the stove, his muscles still detectable under the loosened skin on his arms.

He was yawning into his hand, his face dark, as the gas burned violet-blue under the aluminum kettle. The cafetera was dented, but they still used it; it made the best coffee, the darkest and sweetest taste.

Mirella smiled at him, chin resting in his cupped hand as he groggily made their coffee for the day. She stepped over the threshold into the kitchen, and he looked up at her, startled. His eyes glittered in the dark, wet streaks on his cheeks, the catch of a breath in his throat.

"Ralph, what's wrong?" she said and put her arms on his shoulders. "Are you crying?" she asked, although she could see he was. "Why are you crying?" She was no good at this.

"Mirella, go back to bed," Ralph babbled. "I'm fine, everything is fine. I just couldn't sleep."

"Ralph, talk to me. I'm your wife, talk to me."

Ralph shook his head, rubbing his eyes with one hand. The whistling grew louder, and he turned off the flame. Steam rushed out of the mouth of the cafetera. Mirella felt it heat the kitchen, all the windows closed.

"Ralph, what's wrong?"

He kept shaking his head, his fingers covering his eyes. He was crying without caution now, heaving and sighing like a child, and Mirella wrapped an arm around his shoulder. He took her hand and gently unwound himself from her.

"You shouldn't have to see me like this. It's not right."

"It's fine," Mirella said. Were there other words she could say? Would another word have been better? It's "normal"? It's "natural"? It's "fine with me"?

"It's fine," she repeated.

"Jesus," Ralph gasped, and his shoulders shook. He loped out of the kitchen, his hands still over his eyes.

"Ralph! Stop right there," Mirella called after him.

"I don't want the coffee anymore, Mirella. And I don't want to talk."

"Is it Penélope?" Mirella said. "I miss her, too."

She wanted to walk out to the hallway, to hold him where he'd stalled by the stairs, but she didn't want him to move her hands again, to step away from her and say he didn't want her to see him like this. *This* is what she had wanted—for Ralph to falter and lean on her, to need something from her again. Here was the opening, and she stood alone in it, waiting.

"Ralph, you can tell me. She's our daughter."

"God, it's not Penelope," Ralph said. "If I let myself feel this way every time I missed Penelope, I wouldn't have made it past the first month she was gone."

"Is it us?" She had never asked before, but now she could. Their marriage had devastated her, too. She had wanted more, too. Now they could speak about all that was wrong, without it crushing them.

"We're getting better, Ralph," she said. "I can feel it. You too, yes? You can feel it?"

Ralph's face broke again, his lips skewing to one side. His eyes sealed, his body trembled. He put a hand on the banister to steady himself.

"Ralph, I'm here. Look at me, Ralph, I'm here."

Ralph muttered into his hand, but Mirella couldn't hear what he said. He moaned, "God, oh God, oh God."

"Ralph!" she screamed.

"My store! It's gone—my store."

Ralph's voice rose to the pitch he used only when he was laughing—not his perfunctory laugh for when someone gave him a compliment, or amused him or he was biding his time thinking about how to pick apart an argument he disagreed with. It was the pitch of the high throaty laugh he used for Penelope when she was a girl and had gotten paint on her face, or had accidentally said something ruder than she realized, or when Mirella mixed up her words in English and invented new ones like *watching-machine*. But he was weeping now in that high terrible pitch.

"My store, my store," he said. He hiccupped between sobs.

"Is that what you're crying about?"

Ralph uncovered his face and opened his eyes, sheepishly, but he didn't say anything.

"Ralph, come here. Let's talk about this." Mirella tried to make her voice easy and light. He needed comfort; she would comfort him, although she felt that she was losing herself. She could no longer see in colors, and her mind turned toward instinct: a set of impulses she couldn't explain, none of them mercy, patience.

"Everything is going to be fine," she said.

"Mirella, can't you see? I have nothing left. It's all gone."

"I'm here, Ralph. Look at me."

He began to shake his head.

"Ralph, look at me."

He blubbered and lowered his face. He was only a few yards away, but he seemed much farther, just the outline of a man.

"Coño, Ralph! Look at me!"

She banged her hand on the kitchen counter. The cafetera rattled on the stove.

Ralph didn't turn to her. "Nothing, nothing. I have nothing."

"Look at me!"

Mirella's fingers found the handle of the cafetera, and she hurled it at Ralph, where he stood at the top of the stairs, just beyond the border of the tiled kitchen. The lid of the cafetera stuttered open, and hot coffee flew onto the wall, Mirella's hands, Ralph's undershirt. Ralph lifted his hands to cover his face; he twisted his body away from the spray of the kettle. He stepped back onto the top step, and his ankle turned. He pitched sideways down the stairs. Mirella ran after him, but he was already off the landing, tumbling down to the first floor, and he wasn't Ralph anymore, but a blur in the dark, a tall thing doubled in on itself, thumping out a terrible rhythm, as if his body hit each step, as if he didn't miss a single one.

In the morning, Mirella knocked on her daughter's door. The girl was already awake, sitting on the floor in shorts the length of panties and a T-shirt, a book open on her lap, a cup of coffee on the floor. She might have been awake for hours.

"I'm going to the bakery," Mirella said. "You can come with me if you want." She thought she'd start small—*Hija, will you cross the road with me? If you want the deed, you will.*

Penelope yawned, looked down at her book, then slapped it shut.

"Fine. I'll put on my sneakers," she said, and Mirella went to wait for her in the hall.

When they were out of the house, walking along the paved sidewalks of the residence, Mirella couldn't tell if Penelope was any angrier than usual—had she expected her to just sign over the house right away? To break the silence, she asked her when she planned to return to Brooklyn.

"Tomorrow," Penelope said. "I have to get back to work."

Mirella shouldn't have been surprised Penelope had a job—of course she did, she was a woman now, but she hadn't mentioned anything about it. Was she still at the library? Had she found a job to do with her art? What if Penelope had become famous, and Mirella never knew? She wondered, but didn't ask. She said she would call Emanuel so he could drive her to the airport, and she decided silently that she'd ride along to say good-bye.

At the gates to the residence, a Dominican watching-man sat with a rifle in his lap. He wore a khaki cap, and he tipped it to them as they climbed out to the road.

The cars sped by in two main thoroughfares, one running east and the other west. There were no marked lanes, but the cars clung to either side of the road. A few drivers lurched across the road into oncoming traffic, to pursue a gap and pick up speed. Cars often came within a few yards of colliding, until one swerved away, back to its proper side of the road.

Penelope watched the dizzying pattern of the cars, the density of bodies and machines on the road. The concho vans were stuffed with people, men and women stood on the backs of pickup trucks, their hair and T-shirts flapping in the wind. Even the motoconchos were crammed, three, four, five riders on a single motorcycle seat. Penelope had run along this road, but she hadn't tried to cross it. She realized she didn't know how.

Mirella took her daughter's hand. "Come on," she said, and she led her daughter through an opening in the cars. On the other side, they let go of each other, and Mirella proceeded to the bakery, which was down a grassy slope, through a grove of tamarind trees. They left the whir of the traffic behind them.

The German bakery was a squat stucco building with a black clay roof. When they entered, the baker greeted Mirella and guessed immediately that Penelope was her daughter.

"Yes, yes," Mirella said in English. "She is my daughter."

Penelope noticed how genuinely Mirella smiled, as if she were truly thrilled the baker could tell they were related. Her lips spread apart, wide and crooked—her unaffected smile—and her whole face shone from beneath her sun hat, even with her bug-eye sunglasses low on her nose. Looking at her, Penelope couldn't believe this was the woman who had ruined her father, who had thrown a coffeepot at him, who had made him tumble down the stairs, and then left him. She looked so harmless, beautiful, while she talked to the baker and squeezed the loaves with a leaf of parchment paper. She asked which rounds were which: she wanted one with cinnamon, clove.

Back in the house, Mirella made breakfast. It must have been fifteen years, no, longer, since Mirella had last cooked for her—Penelope was determined not to count. They each had a single scrambled egg, a salad made from lettuce, lemon, and herbs from the garden, a whole avocado, sweet bread from the bakery, and cold glasses of white wine. They were halfway through the bottle by the time they switched to coffee, Mirella offering her fragments of dark chocolate.

Penelope watched her mother drink. She would pick up a finger of chocolate, bite off the end, then take a sip of coffee, and return the chocolate to the cup, so it would continue to melt. How long had her mother been doing this? When did she discover it? Penelope did the same with her coffee, imitating her mother. Mirella gave her a spoon for the dregs and chocolate that stuck to the bottom.

Penelope was nearly done with her coffee when Mirella announced, "I'm going to the beach." Penelope licked her spoon clean and said nothing. If she didn't move quickly, her daughter might disappear into her room and stay there until her flight the next day.

"Get your things. I'll call a car," she said, and Penelope laughed.

"Sí, Señora," she said, saluted her, and then left to change.

Mirella tried not to let Penelope's smugness needle at her. Wasn't it natural for a mother to give orders? To tell a daughter what she should and shouldn't do? Ramona hadn't done that much for her—she'd had no words about whether Mirella should move to New York, or marry so young, no instructions for how to get ahead in school, how to hang clothes on a line. Penelope couldn't see that through all her meddling, Mirella had never left her alone.

The beach was empty when they arrived, the afternoon sunless and warm. A skinny man ran out from one of the shacks set back from the shore to bring them two vinyl lawn chairs and ask if they wanted drinks. The women agreed piña coladas served in hollowed-out pineapple halves would be too sweet, and they weren't tourists after all. They ordered Presidentes, a bucket full of them.

They drank in silence, dropping their empty bottles in the sand when they were through. Neither of them wanted to leave the purses unattended on the shore, so they took turns swimming. When they weren't in the water, they slept to the sound of waves and wind, the rare bird.

Mirella couldn't believe that time was passing and they weren't arguing. Penelope was controlling herself, and so was she. Maybe they were both playing nice, trying to each get what they wanted with the deed. They chewed on chips of ice and gulped their beers. By the end of the day, they were both sunburned and drunk, and they decided their purses would be fine hidden underneath the chairs. They went into the water together.

Mirella paddled around, unable to swim very far on her own, and Penelope swam away from the land, although the waves were growing choppier and taller in the dusk. She swam out to a bench of coral, where she hauled herself up and sat, although the surface was rough and caught on the fabric of her bathing suit. She watched her mother, swimming in little circles on her own, pausing sometimes to gather her hair in her hands to wring out the seawater. Then she would twist it back up into a moño that unwound as soon as she dove back into the water.

The beach was beautiful. Short coconut trees stood guard along the sand, and farther uphill, framboyan trees grew, scattering their feathery red fronds along the cobbled paths. It wasn't the mountain, but it was DR, and Penelope was with her mother again. They didn't turn to look at each other, but Penelope felt they must have been thinking the same thing.

Penelope watched her mother climb out of the water and onto the dunes. She lifted up the lawn chair to be sure their leather purses were still there. She dried herself with a towel and began collecting the bottles they had buried. She stamped her feet on a rock to shake off the sand, her body bony and smooth, her hair swinging behind her like she was still the twenty-year-old she had been when Penelope was a girl. The wind and tide swelled, and soon they would have to return to Mirella's house.

Her mother had no reason not to sign the deed—she was fine here in DR, perhaps better than she had ever been. Life was so unequal, Penelope thought. She had ruined Ralph's happiness and found her own. To keep the house would be spiteful, unless she wanted to hold on to some scrap of her life before, the last evidence that she'd ever been a Grand. The thought that her mother would want to keep some final stake in Brooklyn, their family, shook Penelope. The force of the idea— *She wants us*—made her tremble. Penelope stood on the coral bench and dove headfirst into the silver bay, and let the water enclose her. She swam for as long as she could without coming up for air.

Back in the residence, Mirella and Penelope showered and ordered pizza again, then went into their separate rooms for the night. Penelope left her room only once to fetch a glass of water from the bathroom sink. She found Mirella on the sofa, watching a soap opera with the volume turned low, clipping the split ends of her red hair with a pair of nail scissors.

Mirella watched novela after novela, the hours draining away from her. She didn't want the night to end. *My daughter is here; my daughter is asleep*—she thought of Penelope through the theme song, commercials, the credits. It was dark but nearly morning when she turned off the television and went up to her room.

She sat at her vanity to read the deed, but the words were too technical for her to understand. It would be easier if someone could speak it aloud to her. She gave up after the third page and flipped to the end, where she found Ralph's signature—the careful, small letters, the ink smudged from where he pressed too hard on the pen. Beneath, Penelope's—three big loops for her first name, then a *G* and a flourish for *Grand*. Her name looked like a drawing, some beautiful code.

Mirella tiptoed down to the guest room, the deed in hand. Penelope was asleep on her side, her curls gathered like a spray of flowers on the top of her head. In the starlight, Mirella thought she saw streaks on Penelope's face. Had she been crying about the house? Leaving DR? Her? Mirella moved closer and realized it had been a trick of the light. Penelope hadn't been crying and wouldn't. Neither of them would. It wasn't a part of their Santos blood.

Mirella sat on the edge of the bed and looked around at the things her daughter had scattered on the floor: neon sneakers and mesh shorts, the still-wet yellow bikini she'd worn at the beach, a fine-tipped black pen with a point so sharp it looked as if it would cut right through paper. Mirella scooped the pen from the ground, twirled it between her fingers. She unfolded the square of papers in her lap, signed along the two blank lines Penelope had marked with *X*s. She initialed next to another *X*, folded up the deed, and tucked it next to Penelope's head.

Penelope went on sleeping, unaware of what Mirella had done. She would find out soon enough, in the morning, before the airport. If she could have written more things she would have: how we do things we do not mean; we do evil things; if we see an open door, we will dart through it, before we lose our guts, no matter who is left behind, we will move at the chance to be free.

Mirella could hear the crickets outside, the sound of a lone motorcycle chugging down the road. She thought of going out to her garden, but she didn't want to leave the girl yet. The cool night breeze poured into the room the scent of grapefruit-tree leaves, her roses, and gasoline. Mirella considered placing her hand on Penelope's cheek to feel the globe of her round face, or wrapping her finger around a strand of her coiled hair to give it a new shape, but she did neither. It was not their way. Mirella drew the sheets up around her daughter's shoulders. They still had, at least, tomorrow.

17

Seams

"Poor Penelope Grand."

Jon stood at the corner, far off enough that Penelope could hardly see him through the dark. The street didn't have many lampposts, and the only light came from windows high in the apartment buildings. She was doubled over the gutter, waiting to vomit, and she hadn't wanted Jon to see her in pain. He was making jokes from the end of the block, but she couldn't answer him. She waited, felt her gut shrink and knot. The sour vapor taste filled her mouth.

Jon came back to her, leaned against a puny city tree, and helped her straighten up.

"You should just go on without me," she said and drew out the bottle of pills from her bag. "Fucking antibiotics. They should have worked by now."

"Takes a while to kill a parasite," Jon said. He watched her swallow down a pale green pill.

"My mother would laugh if she could see me now. She told me not to drink out of the tap."

Penelope knew instantly that she had blundered. If she brought up her mother, she gave Jon a window to ask whether she had heard from

Mirella yet, whether Penelope had decided she would be the first one to call. But Jon didn't say anything and offered her his arm. He seemed to be learning when to keep himself away, when to circle her perimeter until there was a sign to come back in.

He was the one who had met her at the airport. She had called him after she left the little plane bathroom foul with the smell of her own bile. She had vomited up all that water her mother had warned her not to drink. Jon took her back to Greene and, over the next few days, helped her move her few belongings to Halsey Street. She decided she would live on the first floor, going up the stairs only for the kitchen. He had helped her repaint the walls of the little room she had made her bedroom, a tiny room that was meant to be a large pantry, with a window that faced the backyard. He had gone with her to the thrift store to buy a loveseat for the barren living room, helped her carry it back on the bus. She went to see him at the bar, and sometimes he came by before his shift, and they would eat and talk until they were through talking, then they would wrap themselves in each other and kiss until Penelope decided it was time for him to leave. She liked his unselfconscious humming and the sight of him walking barefoot through the rooms of the house. She liked to watch him rearrange the few inches of his hair. They had found their own rhythm, and he made her feel that the house was somewhat hers. The only nuisance was when he brought up Mirella and asked about the trip, and what Penelope planned to do now that her mother was in her life. He had stopped prodding after Penelope told him, without blinking, "Why don't you ask me about my father? He's the one in a fucking nursing home, you know." She didn't know how long he would remain patient with her, or how long she had before he realized her bad moods were her.

For now, they carried on toward the avenue, their arms linked. Penelope felt her nausea begin to pass. There was no one else on the street. They had turned the corner of winter into March, but there was no one else on the street, the night too cold. Chunks of ice dissolved in the gutter, and the city trees were still without their buds. Jon had dressed up for the show in a leather jacket and striped T-shirt, too-short jeans, his skinny ankles exposed to the cold. He had pulled back his hair into a small nub on the top of his head, which Penelope loved because she could admire his face more easily: his protruding brow, the large almonds of his eyes, the gaping holes in his ears, the crow's feet he was too young to have. She didn't want to go to the gallery, but if it meant something to Jon, she had to at least make an appearance. He clasped their hands together as they strode down the block.

"I'm glad you're feeling better," he said, and she realized he meant her nausea. "I don't think I could get in without you—Darnell put your name on the list. I'm just 'Guest.'"

He winked at her and kissed her knuckles, and Penelope felt both bewildered and charmed. How did Jon survive this way, with so much ease and brightness? Had he always counted on smiles and his good humor to get him through?

She steered him toward the side of a building, leaned him back against the cold wall. She kissed him, slow and diligent in the use of her tongue. He slipped his hands under her shirt and around her waist; she sunk her fingers into the waistband of his jeans. Neither of them moved any further: this was their dance. Penelope usually cut them off before it got too far, but Jon hadn't pressed either. They kissed for a long time until Jon pulled away and started laughing.

"Hot damn, Miss Grand," he said. "You're going to make me miss my friend's show." He kissed her cheek and pulled her in the direction of the avenue, toward its foot traffic and lampposts, away from the shadows and quiet of the block.

The gallery was no more than a storefront, the brick inside painted white. The paintings were displayed inside large glass boxes mounted on the wall, as if they were images on a television screen. Penelope saw all the manicured women with multicolor tattoos, the men with waxed mustaches sipping from cheap green cans of beer.

"I can't," she said and pretended to feel sick again. "Give me your key." She volunteered to wait for him in his studio, which was less than a mile away.

He told her to give the pill some time to kick in. She'd feel better after some water and if she found a place to sit.

"Don't you want to see Darnell's show? He told me he can't wait to hear what you think."

Penelope didn't say anything to Jon but pushed past him into the gallery, the room too bright and loud. She went straight for the bar and asked for a double with diet tonic. By the time Jon reached her, she had already made eyes at the bartender. Jon put his arm on her shoulder and she shook him off. He had been her ally on the street, and he was an irritant now. He left her there at the bar, and she stood, drinking, trying to coax herself to return to him, to make nice. After a few minutes, she found him looking at the sequence of Darnell's works, near the back of the show. He tried to put his arm around her again, and, this time, she let him. They didn't speak but waited for the rift between them to close.

Darnell had three paintings in the show, all of them glossy and erupting with color. They weren't bad at all, considering he had a day job in graphic design and no formal training as a painter. The first piece was a deconstructed face in pinks and blues. Only the mouth, agape, was in place; the eyes and nose and coils of hair were disarrayed on the rest of the canvas. The subject's organs were rendered in miniature, little anatomical drawings in ink, stark lines underneath big washes of color. When they went out tagging, Darnell sprayed big streaks of color onto the walls, then hand-painted lines from philosophy and rap, all mixed up together, to make new aphorisms he wanted people in the neighborhood to see. Penelope had found it calculated and strange; he had carried a little notebook with him, the lines he wanted to stitch together already written inside. The other two paintings were also acrylic, ink, and enamel. They were violent, bright, and precise, overloaded with detail. Penelope read the little plaque underneath the last piece. It had

Darnell's full name and his place of birth (*Fayetteville, North Carolina*), and it listed his preoccupations (*mythology, cosmology, the body, the street*) and his influences (*Basquiat, Ernst, Lawrence,* and *Watts*)—no surprises there.

Jon leaned in to whisper in her ear.

"I'm out of my league," he said.

She didn't agree with him aloud. The show was familiar to her, even if she'd only tasted the game at RISD. She could have written the copy for Darnell's paintings; she could have helped someone else understand it; what she couldn't do was create any of it—not anymore. Maybe if she'd spent the last ten years differently, but she hadn't.

When Darnell came over, she didn't want to hug him. She didn't feel any happiness for him. He wore a T-shirt with suspenders, a pair of red-rimmed spectacles she was certain he didn't need. He had cut his hair into a fade, his twists long on top. He wore shell sneakers and wool slacks, his outfit a mash-up of things his crowd would either recognize or wonder at.

"It's a costume, Penny," he said, when he noticed her staring. "It's surreal, man. All these white people with nice things to say."

Jon wrapped an arm around Darnell and squeezed him close.

"I'm proud of you," he said, and the two men started talking about the pieces. Penelope had a few moments to step out of the gallery and into herself. She wondered what it would be like to be Darnell, to hang her worth on the wall and put names on the list, to drink white wine and have an entire night devoted, at least in part, to her.

It wasn't long before a little convoy of Darnell's colleagues from the graphic design firm came over. They all congratulated Darnell and chugged from their free beers. They were all formally trained—painters—but they had all landed in the same place as Darnell in their careers. Some were a bit ahead, a few behind, but Penelope could see the jealousy in their teeth when they complimented him on the show. She didn't want to be like them. She had started to drift away when Darnell reached for her hand and pulled her into the circle. She hoped he wouldn't mention RISD or that she was from Brooklyn or that she was Jon's girlfriend—it all made her sound like she was more than she was. She was grateful that Darnell introduced her only by saying that Penelope was a part of their tagging crew now.

A woman named Margot with fuchsia-painted lips nodded at Penelope. "How nice," she said, before turning back to Darnell. She asked whether he planned on finally finding an agent.

"I might," he said. "It's hard without the art school cred. I'm not like you all." Darnell pointed at his colleagues and then Penelope, and, within an instant, she had been found out. The convoy turned their eyes on her.

"I draw a little," Penelope said.

"So you're an illustrator?"

Penelope said no, and Margot shook her head and said, "Thank God. I've got a friend who's an illustrator, and you wouldn't believe the kinds of kitsch she churns out—tote bags and little coasters with dogs on them, and wedding invitations, even a few book covers. She gets paid more than any of us could ever hope to make."

Another woman chimed in. "Thanks for nothing, SVA."

They all laughed and started to circulate the names of the schools where they had earned their degrees: Pratt, Cooper Union, Parsons, MIT. They went on about debt but good times, and soon they had forgotten that Penelope and Jon were there. Somehow they had even forgotten Darnell, too, who sipped from his beer, and adjusted his glasses and tried to laugh along as they commiserated. Penelope was the first to leave, while Jon and Darnell held out, their faces dazed and grave as if they were at a funeral and not an art show.

There was a woman who had art up in the show. Her works were on slender, long cuts of handmade paper, all of them watercolor and ink. The watercolor figures were edgeless, the ink all edges and knots. The one she liked best was all orange and gold, except for the black ink; like a knife, it slashed through the layers of color. *Here is something I would like to create,* Penelope thought.

It had been nearly a month since she returned from DR, and she had started to feel the impulse to paint. It might have been the nights spent tagging with Jon, the feel of a paint can in her hand had activated her muscle memory. Or maybe it was being on Halsey Street, a desire to put things on the wall to make the house hers. Or it might have been her mother. She had seen Mirella, talked with her, swam with her, and convinced her to sign the deed—maybe the things she thought were impossible were no longer so. Maybe her mother would call her. Maybe she would visit her in the summer. Maybe they would see each other again. Maybe she would paint. Maybe. It was a game Jon liked to play, but she could only wonder about her mother by herself. To nurse these possibilities on her own was terrifying enough.

Penelope closed her eyes. Although the gallery was clogged with people and bottles and light, she managed to conjure up her mother. She remembered her at the airport gate, how cold her mother's skin had felt in the open-air heat, as if every pore had been closed by a cream or a serum, a dab of scented oil. It was then, as they were saying good-bye, that Penelope felt that she wanted to paint her—not to capture the slope of her nose or the shape of her eyes, or even the anomaly of her red hair. She wanted to capture this sensation of skinny arms and chilled skin, the collusion of herbal lotion and floral perfume, coffee, morning wine, and how close the two of them could be—at least, their bodies— her mother tipping onto her toes to align her hips with Penelope's, to press their cheeks together, as if they could cradle something between the two of them if they stood near enough.

How could she paint such a thing? She imagined it might be orange and gold, open, blurred, but with edges, pointed and clean.

Jon handed her a glass of water. She didn't know how long he had been standing next to her. She didn't take the water from him, in case it was his way of suggesting she was drunk. She wasn't, and he ought to be able to tell. He put an arm around her and spoke into her ear.

"I should have known this would be hard for you. But I wasn't sure—you haven't told me much about RISD, and I can only assume."

"Is that a habit of yours? Assuming? Maybe you're no better than they are."

"Easy," Jon said. "We're in public."

It was his first indication to Penelope that he cared what other people thought. He didn't want her to raise her voice; he didn't want a scene. Penelope wanted more than ever to give him one. She wanted to scream and yank the beautiful scrolls off the wall; she wanted to smash a bottle. She could imagine the shards of glass, ramming one into her cheek.

"I hate these people," she said.

"I don't think you do," Jon said, without even waiting for her to clarify whether she meant artists or smug artists or rich people or rich white people.

"Excuse me?"

"I don't think it's them you hate."

Penelope took a step away from him and raised her voice. "Are you an expert now in Penelope Grand?"

"Maybe I am. I'm as close as anyone has ever been. I've been watching you for a while now, Penelope. You don't make things; you don't talk to your mother. Just work, run, see your pop. Work, run, see me. And gin. So much gin. You go on like the world is happening to you, like you're not here. But you're here, girl. *You're here.*"

Another woman might have taken his hand; another woman might have said she needed to step outside and would he come along? Another woman might have told him what he got right and what he got wrong; she might have been surprised by Jon, by how much he could already see her. This other woman was long-haired and pretty; she had different parents, a different life. Penelope could see this other woman, but she wasn't her.

"You cocky motherfucker," she said. "If I wanted a shrink, I would see one."

"Maybe you should."

"I'm going home."

She tried to slide past him, but he put his hands on her shoulders.

"I'm serious, Penelope. How long had it been since you'd seen your mother? Five years? It's like you two came back from the dead to each other. And your father—"

He was closing in on her, and Penelope felt in herself the urge to cry. She couldn't dispute the physicality of it, the need as sharp and particular as the need to vomit or to drink a glass of water or lie down. It was a stinging in her eyes, and heat in her face, but it was also a line she could feel running along the front of her, from between her toes, up to her forehead: a seam that if pressed against would force her to come apart.

She shook off his hands and headed for the door. Jon followed her, and Penelope saw Darnell and his coworkers notice them. They had another reason to dismiss her now, to look down at her: she was no one, a nobody. She was nearly outside when Jon caught her arm.

"Why are you touching me? I told you I was leaving."

"Fine. I'll come then."

"Is this a sex thing? Are you finally tired of waiting to fuck me?"

A few heads turned toward the door, and Jon looked down, embarrassed. A gaggle of new couples arrived, and Penelope and Jon had to step out of the doorway to let them into the gallery. They were all silk and denim, laughter, silver and gold.

"Will you just stay with me?" he said. "We have to talk about this."

Penelope could see herself saying yes. She could see Jon folding her back into the party. They would spend another miserable hour there and then go home to his studio, its eggplant-colored walls. He would unfold the futon so it was wide enough for them both, and they would share a quilt and fall asleep to the faraway rattle of the M train. Perhaps he noticed her soften.

"I don't want the night to end," he said.

"Things end, Jon."

"Jesus Christ, Penelope, what's wrong with you?" He spoke through his teeth, and Penelope could see he was finally angry at her. It was the first time he had looked at her this way: his eyes wide, his hands on his hips. They had never fought before, and here they were. She had been waiting for this. He had finally reached his limit, and soon they'd be done.

"It's not my fault," Penelope said, "if you don't know whether you want to fuck me or leave me alone."

"I don't know yet," Jon said. "I'm having trouble deciding whether to fuck somebody who occasionally treats me like dirt."

His voice was low, but Penelope had a terrible feeling that everyone had heard, everyone knew what he had said to her. She leaned in and gritted her teeth before she spoke.

"No wonder your father drank."

Penelope left before she could see his reaction. She made it three blocks, and then she stopped to lift a lid off a trash can and hurl it into the gap between two buildings. Then she kicked the aluminum can over and over until she had dented it, then she threw the trash can into the alley as well.

"Holy shit, girl. You mad or something?"

She hadn't noticed two men at the corner, shivering and smoking. They had seen her rage, and now they were laughing at her. She flipped them off and cursed them and marched down the block. She was breathless before long and had to sit down on the curb. She waited for her eyes to focus, the colorlessness in her brain to clear. Fucking antibiotics.

It took a few minutes for her to stand, but when she did, she could breathe again, her head emptied out. It would take her an hour to walk back to Halsey Street, and she didn't think she could make it on her own. She was frightened, suddenly, sure that something awful might happen to her soon—she would be murdered on the way home, she would trip over her own feet and fall into the path of a moving car, she would get another call about her father, this time to say he had fallen out of his wheelchair.

She stopped in a bodega to calm down. She needed the light inside, the voices of other people. She wandered the aisles. She wanted a cigarette—something to hold in her hands, something to breathe in. They had Parliaments behind the bulletproof glass, and a thrill ripped through Penelope when she saw the rare blue pack. It was her mother's brand: the scent of her hair, of the burning air she would leave behind her in a room, the ash that fell between the rows of vegetables in the yard. By the time she reached Halsey Street, Penelope had demolished five cigarettes, her head full of fog.

Penelope half expected to find Jon waiting for her on the stoop. Perhaps he had gone home to get his bicycle, maybe he had rushed here to catch her to make up. She reached the gate and there was no one inside, and Penelope thought, *Fine.* She blew a gorgeous gray puff of smoke above her head into the starless, clear night.

It would mean nothing to lose Jon, to never sit in his studio again, to never have him over to sit in the parlor, on the navy loveseat they had found together. Life without him would be no different than this: night walks with herself, the ease of darkness, silence, the street.

Inside the house, in her new bedroom, Penelope went through the humble pile of mail she had left on top of her trunk. It was a stack of catalogues, supermarket circulars, and health insurance bills she hadn't delivered yet to Ralph, and her letter from Mirella. It had arrived nearly a week after she had returned to Brooklyn, but Penelope hadn't told anyone, not her father and certainly not Jon. She had read it, many times, measuring what she could say, whether it was safe to say anything at all.

The envelope was crinkled and stamped with an inky seal—*La República Dominicana.* Penelope slid out the letter and her chest began to expand so quickly she had to remind herself she wasn't dying. It was her body's response to her mother, to Mirella extending a hand to her across the ocean. The letter ended without a signature, the date printed in the upper right corner. Mirella had written to Penelope the day she left DR, but it had taken days for the letter to reach her. The mail took so long between countries.

Penelope switched on a light and sat on the floor. She read the letter over and over again.

Hija—

You are gone, and the house is not the same. I have learned that to be a mother is to be left behind. I did it to Ramona; you have done it to me. When you were a girl, you used to follow me around, and I did not like it. I was not fit to be followed.

Sometimes, I dream of you, here, in this house. You are a girl, and I am different. Your room is the one that faces the garden. I know you loved the mountains, and my mother's little shack, but I was never from that village, and you didn't belong in all that dirt.

Did you ever hear the story that my father swallowed pills so that he would die? They say he had debts; they say that's why we lost everything when he was gone. I do not believe it. I know my father loved me.

But I do wonder if he wanted to die. I have often wanted to die. Maybe there is something in our blood. Something ancient and ugly that my father gave to me. Sometimes, I think maybe that is why I hated Brooklyn, and, eventually, your father, being a wife. But then I think, no—anyone would have hated that.

The day you left us, I was happy for you. I was sad for me, and I was happy for you. You needed to go and find your life. Have you found it?

18

NOTICIAS

It was April when the phone rang, a Saturday and warm. Penelope was reading on a pillow beneath the window in her new room, only a few minutes of light left in the day. A cup of tea cooled on the floor. She had her brushes splayed out beneath her, and a new roll of paper on the easel, as if she might paint. She had been working up the nerve and losing it for days. She had thought often of what Jon had said to her—*You live like the world is happening to you*—and it made her put down her brush every time she picked it up. If he had been trying to motivate her, he hadn't done a very good job.

She thought it might be Jon calling until she realized it was the landline ringing upstairs in her parents' room. And then it was obvious who it might be—Mirella. Anyone else would have called her on her phone. Penelope bounded up the stairs, rushing to answer before her mother hung up.

She found the phone on the nightstand next to Ralph's empty bed. She sat down and lifted it to her ear. She was shaking, happy, desperate to hear her mother's voice. She had never found the nerve to write back to her, but it didn't matter. Here was her mother, chasing after her, reaching out her hand again.

"Mami?"

"Buenas." It was a man on the other end, and Penelope asked who it was.

"Marcello. Remember me? I am your mother's friend."

"Buenas," she said and waited for him to explain why he had called.

"Ay, Penélope," he said. "Something very grave has happened."

"What's wrong?"

"Penélope, I am so sorry. Penélope, Penélope, I am so sorry."

"What happened? Is this about Mami's letter? I'm going to write back to her soon."

"She's dead, Penélope. Your mother, she died."

Penelope felt as if someone had turned over a load of gravel into her throat.

"What happened?"

"She was crossing the road. To go to the German bakery. You know, the one she took you to when you were here? She was hit by a motoconcho."

"But how?"

"I don't know. I wasn't there. I was at home. I was in the shower. The watching-man came and found me."

Penelope felt the gravel again. It seemed to fill both lungs. "I don't understand, Marcello."

Mirella had been crossing roads since she was a girl, in Santiago, in Aguas Frescas, then in Bed-Stuy, and Manhattan. She was the one who had led Penelope across to the bakery. How could she have forgotten to look both ways? How could she have been blind to the motoconcho?

"A baby was killed, too. It was riding on the motoconcho with its mother. You know how these Dominicans are—three, four, five people on the back of a motorcycle just so they don't have to pay as high a price. Everyone else survived. Except the baby and your mother."

Penelope shut her eyes as the room began to seesaw beneath her.

Marcello explained that he had been trying to reach her for days. Mirella didn't have a number for her written down anywhere—she must have known it by heart. And the day of the accident, they lost power in the town for days. As soon as it came back this morning, he went straight to the Internet café and found this number.

"How long has it been?"

"Three days. We burned her last night."

Penelope wondered if she was really speaking to the same Marcello who had appeared in the foyer of her mother's house, red-faced and carrying a bottle of wine, a little pastry box tied with string. The same man who had fetched her mother dessert plates, topped off her glass without her asking, and looked at her as if she were all shine. For a moment, she considered asking him, "Is this the same Marcello I met?" But what other Marcello could there be? What other Penelope was there with a mother named Mirella? What other daughter on Halsey Street had a mother who had lived by the sea? She was a daughter with a dead mother. *My mother is dead.*

"I have her ashes."

"Ashes?"

"Yes. In a little urn. I don't know if that's what you wanted—for her to be burned—but I had to make a decision."

Penelope shut her eyes.

"My sister is coming in from Assisi soon, and I will leave with her in a few days. I don't think I can stay here—"

"I see," Penelope said. "I don't know what to do."

She couldn't imagine her mother in an urn in a box being flown across the sea. What if something happened to the urn? What if her ashes were lost? She wouldn't fly to DR—what would be the point? She should have flown to see her when she was alive. She should have written back to her while she was alive. She had waited too long.

"I know it's not easy, Penélope," Marcello said. "You'll have to talk to your father to make a decision about the remains."

Penelope was hit doubly by Marcello's words: first, *remains*, and then, *your father*. Her mother no longer had a body; she had left only dust behind. And how would she ever tell Ralph? He would be destroyed, crushed even more by Mirella in death than in life.

"Fuck," she said.

"Oh, I am so sorry, Penélope. Your mother—she loved you so much. I know she wanted for the two of you to spend more time together in this house. The morning you left, she went into the guest room where you stayed and she just sat on the bed with the lights off for a long time, and I went to check on her, and she said, 'Marcello, déjame en paz, por favor,' and so I left her, and I thought to myself—"

Marcello blew his nose and started up his crying again.

"I thought, 'Oh! She's waiting! She's waiting for her daughter to come back. For the flight to be delayed, for Penélope to change her mind. Maybe she thinks if she doesn't make the bed, if she doesn't turn on the lights, she can keep her . . . She can keep her here with her.' Oh, she loved you Penélope, she—"

Penelope hung up. She yanked the cord from the wall so that Marcello couldn't call back. She lay back on the bed and stared at the ceiling, the web of thin lines crawling through the plaster.

"Jesus Christ."

Penelope heard her own voice and sat upright. "Jesus Christ," she said again, and she realized she didn't know how to arrange herself: Should she stay on the bed, or sit, or stand, shift to her side? Should she close her eyes and let the silence of the old house fill her ears with its liquid weight? Should she wrap herself in these sheets—her parents' beige and fraying sheets? Penelope got up and ran down the stairs, out into the yard, to the garden. Her mother was dead.

It was newly dusk, the night coming on blue and calm. Penelope sat on one of the old dusty lawn chairs, gathering dust from the seat onto her fingertips. It rolled apart as if she were shearing wool. She opened the neon orange umbrella overhead, and then she didn't know what to do. She lit a Parliament from her back pocket and smoked it fast, scattering ash over her lap.

"Fuck," Penelope said, and she waited for someone to answer. A voice to shush or reprimand her. "Fuck!" she said again, testing the air, the night, as if she might find someone there to speak to her. "Holy fucking shit," she shouted, but again no one answered.

A fat orange tabby cat appeared from behind the shed. He stared at her, his fur fanned out in a mane around his square head, his white paws drawn close together. Penelope made a weak kissing sound, hoping he would come to her, but instead he leaped to the top of the shed and out of the yard. It was then that she started to cry. She shook out a second cigarette, lit it, and dragged hard. The smoke caught in her throat and she coughed; she snuffed out the glowing end on her wrist. It hurt as much as she expected, enough to make her pound her foot on the ground. She pressed the hot end again onto the inside of her arm, and the burns were the worst thing happening to her. She counted: three, four, five, and then she waited for the pain to pass, the flash points of heat on her flesh. When the pain didn't lessen, she ran inside, defeated, to hold her arm under the tap. She had failed, unable to sit out in the garden and bear the pain until her skin blistered.

Even under the cold water, she felt her skin burning. It made her cry harder, how pathetic she was—her plan hadn't worked, and now she would have the scars. When she could stand to pull her arm out of the water, she went to find her phone, tracking water through the house. She found it on the floor of her room, near her easel, the unused brushes, her cold cup of tea.

It took Jon a while to answer.

"I didn't think you were ever going to call again."

"Hello."

"So you've changed your mind about me then?" His voice was cold, distrustful.

"My mother's dead."

"What?"

"Mirella, my mami, she died."

"What happened?"

When Penelope didn't answer, he asked if she was home. She answered yes, and Jon said, "Twenty minutes."

She lay down on the floor to wait for him, facedown. She splayed out her arms so that her sores could rest on the cold floor. When she heard Jon knock, she stood and crossed to the door, unsure of how she went. Her body moved itself forward, and she rolled down her sleeves to cover the burns.

"What happened?" Jon said, as he charged into the parlor.

"She died."

"Fuck, Penelope." He laid his hands on her shoulders, and they felt heavier than hands. They fixed her to the ground where she stood. He was talking to her, but she didn't understand. He said her name, "Penny," and then he stared at her, as if he expected some part of her to come bursting through.

"What?" she said. "What do you want from me? What is there to say?"

He shushed her, like in the movies, although she wasn't crying. He hugged her, too, although she wasn't there with him in the parlor anymore.

She was overtaken by the accident, and she felt that she was there, at the precise instant, the precise spot where her mother was hit. She saw the motorcycle knock Mirella off her feet, the other cars spinning to avoid the crash. Penelope didn't see the child who had died; she didn't care about the child. She saw the woven basket in her mother's hand bursting, her white dress ruined by gasoline. Blood on the road.

And then, she was off the road and with her mother, in the airport, on the morning she left DR. She had the signed deed in her purse, and her mother was there, in front of her, in her ridiculously oversized shades. The air glided through the palm trees, the clamor of passengers, rude honks and shouts, the call of birds.

Without warning, Mirella had pressed her cheek to Penelope's cheek, roped their bodies together with her skinny arms. Her perfume and cold skin, the clang of her metal bracelets.

"I want you to come back, hija," she had said and kissed her, as if they had always said good-bye this way. "Come this summer. You can bring that boy from the photograph."

And Penelope had said only good-bye. It was all she could muster then.

* * *

Mirella's curtains flapped in the breeze. They skimmed the floors, and rose, then fell against the window once more, like sails, although the room and her house weren't floating toward anywhere. She watched the curtains inflate and drift. She contemplated the invisible strength of the wind.

Soon the midday sun would be overhead and scorch everything in her garden, and Mirella would have to go out to meet it with her hose. Who else would make sure her plants were watered? That they were safe in the dirt? But she stayed where she was, on the edge of the bed. The guest room was dark, except for a small pool of light beneath the window. It stretched toward her and shrank away as the curtains fluttered.

Mirella breathed in the roses, their faint sweetness. They grew outside, just below the window. The blooms were impressive, like pink miniature cabbages. She left on the thorns in case anyone should try to steal a bunch.

It was quiet in the residence, and the day already seemed much longer to Mirella than any other she had faced. So many hours lay before her, hours without her daughter. How would she fill them now that she was gone?

Penélope, Penélope, Penélope, flying in an iron bird over the ocean. *Penélope, Penélope, Penélope,* crossing leagues of water, back to the city that was still her home.

The crow of a rooster somewhere in the residence. The yapping of the Englishman's dogs. The curtains dancing in the air, the roses rustling outside.

Maybe she should write to her. Yes, she would write to her.

For now, Mirella cherished the vibrations inside of her, the chord still resounding in her body. *Penélope, Penélope, Penélope.* It was her only music.

19

Acknowledgment

The next day Penelope rode the train to Willow Lake to tell Ralph the news. She brought a sweet potato pie and a bunch of poppies with her, as if it were any other Sunday visit. In the home, she greeted the orderlies, drifted through the halls. The olive carpet in the hallways was freshly cleaned, and soft, bland music played over the PA system, not quite loudly enough to cover up the drone of the nearby BQE.

Ralph was in his suite, in the green armchair by the window. One of the nurses must have helped him transfer from the bed to his wheelchair to the armchair this morning. Maybe it was Faye, the young one with the triple-pierced ears who liked to flirt with her father. She knew he liked the view of Brooklyn from the window. At night, he could make out the Williamsburgh Savings Bank Tower, the orange hands on the clock the size of matches from his room.

Her father smiled at her when she came in. She set the flowers and pie on the windowsill, squeezed into the chair beside him. He smelled of tobacco and whatever aftershave they used here. His wheelchair lay on the floor, beside the wooden transfer board he was learning to use. He had less function than ever before—that's what the doctors called it: *function*—but he seemed stronger to Penelope. His skin was brighter, his body fleshier, his hair more carefully combed. He got three hot meals a day, and snacks, vitamins, and shortbread cookies after dinner, no more than a cup of beer in the afternoon. Penelope had worked out a deal with the staff—she bought the six-packs, and Faye kept them in the orderlies' refrigerator, rationed out the drinks. He was safer here, too. No more holding on to the wall, no foot catching on the edge of a rug. Miss Beckett came to visit, and so did she. He was all right, perhaps even better than he'd been on Halsey Street. And Penelope was here to ruin it all.

"What's wrong, Penny girl?" Ralph looked at her more tenderly than usual. She leaned in closer to her father, took his hands in hers, and said it all as quickly as she could. In an instant, Ralph sprang into his grief. His sobs were high and quivering, as if he were singing, and she didn't shush him. She patted the soft fluff of his hair and let him moan.

He asked her questions as he cried. Who was this man who'd called with the news? Why didn't he try harder to contact them before? Consult them? Ashes? What right did he have? What did he know? Her wishes—what about her wishes? How could this happen? How?

Penelope answered what questions she could. She said the word—*cremated*—because it was the best she could think of. It was technical and neutral, not like the others. *Incinerated, burned, embers, ash*—they made her feel woozy, and she had to keep steady for Ralph.

He cried for a long time, wiping his eyes with his knuckles. He stared out the window, and Penelope couldn't believe she was living this moment: Ralph mourned a dead Mirella instead of a living one, and she was finally motherless, after all her years of claiming motherlessness.

"Oh God. Oh God, God."

Ralph blew into his handkerchief and seemed to put away his grief a little, tucking it back so that it wasn't visible all at once.

"So, what are we going to do about a funeral?" he said.

"There's nothing to do, Pop. She's already gone."

"You're just going to leave her in an urn in an empty house in the Dominican Republic?"

"I'm not going to bring her here. She didn't like this country, remember?"

"All right, then we'll go there. Give her a proper funeral."

Penelope hung her head. She should have counted on her father making this all worse than it had to be. Mirella was already dead, and Ralph wanted theatrics—ceremonies and speeches, honor and praise for his saintly wife. He wanted them to worship an urn, the idea of a woman Mirella had never been.

"You want to go be in that house? See where she lived after she left you? After she pushed you down the stairs?"

"She did not push me. You know that."

"And what about the ashes? You think you can handle that? Why do you want to torture yourself?"

"It's not about want, Penelope. She's the mother of my child. My wife. I'm not going to leave her alone, like she had no family, like she wasn't loved."

"She's already dead. She won't know what we did or didn't do, and she doesn't deserve any different."

Ralph looked at Penelope, horrified.

"I'm not saying she deserved to die. But I don't want to pretend she was someone I loved."

"Penny girl, I'm heartbroken for you if you have to pretend."

Ralph looked away from her, out the window. He was quiet and somber, as if he had reached a lower rung of sorrow that didn't allow for tears.

"We can find another way, Pop. Some way to honor her and say good-bye from here."

"Like what? Put on a record and eat this here pie? Sit together and say, *What a shame, what a shame?*"

"You can't even get to DR the way you are! We'd have to get you to the airport, on a plane. And what about once we land? You think they have wheelchair ramps and elevators in the campo?"

Ralph looked at her, his eyes watering.

"I guess you don't think any more highly of me than you do your mother."

"Pop—"

"I'm no vegetable."

"I don't want you to get hurt."

"What else could happen to me? What could happen that hasn't already happened?"

"I won't go with you. I won't have any part in it."

Ralph folded his hands in his lap like some monarch, raised his chin. "You're a grown woman, Penelope. You live your own way. I'll live mine."

Penelope tried to dissuade him, but Ralph held up his hand to silence her.

"That's enough now. I'm going to see my wife."

He leaned over and picked up the wheelchair. He unfolded it and placed the wooden transfer board on the edge of the seat. Penelope went to help him, but he shook his head at her. She watched as he slid himself into the wheelchair.

"Now, you'll excuse me," he said, "but I've got to go down to the main desk and see the head nurse. I have travel arrangements to make."

He wheeled away from her, out the door.

Penelope rode home in a daze. Once the train got to Broadway and Union, a trio of dancers entered the car. They were all black and young, not a single one of them seemed over sixteen. They carried a stereo that discharged muffled beats and static.

They started their clapping and stomping to hype each other up, and the two boys went first. Their bodies stretched and snapped like rubber bands; they dangled upside down from the pole at the center of the car. They grabbed for the rails overhead and somersaulted like underground, underage aerialists. The girl was the least acrobatic and the most electrifying to watch. She stomped one leg in front of her and then behind, swinging her arms to keep time with the beat. She tumbled to the ground, spun on her shoulder blades, sprang up and got light, her feet switching beneath her, her fingers fluttering like wings. Penelope marveled at their bodies, how much they were able to do. They were young and gifted, elastic, black. They seemed as far from death as it was possible to be.

When they were done, the dancers applauded themselves and encouraged the passengers to drop donations into an overturned fitted cap. Penelope looked at them, swaggering up and down the car, and she couldn't help but pray for them—*Keep them safe,* she thought.

When they passed her, she gave them all the singles she had in her purse. "Thank you, ma'am," said the girl with the braids, and it surprised her, at first—*ma'am*—and yet, it seemed right.

Back in Bed-Stuy, Penelope sat on the stoop, where there was plenty to distract her. Her thoughts were a thread that would spool endlessly if she gave them a start in the quiet of the house. She took in all the activity along the street: the cheers of children in a game of catch at the corner, the scrape of a scooter along the pavement, the cars stalling beneath the traffic light, the babble of men and women into their cell phones. The wind unsettling the trees, the white glare of the sun.

She didn't notice mother and daughter approaching until they were just outside the gate. They stood in trench coats and rubber boots, mirror images of each other, aside from their size, the colors of their hair. The mother carried a large potted plant, the green leaves higher than her head.

"May we come in?" Samantha didn't wait for an answer and pushed open the gate. "We heard about your mother. Our friend who helped you with the deed called DR this morning to speak with her. A man named Marcello told him everything."

"We're really sorry that she died," Grace said, as if they had rehearsed.

"After my mother died, our house was filled with flowers. Everyone kept sending us bouquets and wreaths, which was lovely, until they all started to rot. The house began to stink, and we had to throw away all those flowers. It was like losing my mother all over again."

"No one is going to send flowers," Penelope said.

Samantha lowered the terra-cotta pot onto the stoop. The plant was all drooping green leaves.

"Rhododendrons are tough—they can survive the cold, but they bloom in the summer. Pink and purple blossoms. They look tropical almost. We thought they'd remind you of your mother."

Samantha and Grace waited for Penelope to say something, but she didn't. She didn't want the Harpers' pity, even though they had been kind to her at the end, letting her stay in their house until the trip to DR, connecting her to the lawyer to help with the deed. But they weren't friends. What had brought Samantha here? A sense of neighborly duty? Some false connection they shared as fellow women, daughters? The etiquette of grief? Penelope didn't thank her.

"I'd like to say to you that no one should ever have to lose a mother, but, unfortunately, we all do. I wasn't much younger than you when my mother died. It's a nightmare, but you can live with it. It's for the best that our mothers go before we do. I couldn't see that until I had Grace."

"It isn't a nightmare for me. It's a nightmare for my mother."

It was a half-truth, the most she had said about how it felt to know her mother was gone. The loss was greatest for Mirella. She was the one who had found her place, who had learned to like her life, then had her self snatched away. What had Penelope lost?

Samantha smiled at her, meaningfully, a smile that was like a frown.

"You're much less selfish than I am then. More than anything, I felt bad for myself when my mother died. I still do. Losing a mother is like losing the most primal part of yourself—the most fixed thing you know about life on this planet."

"Like I said, we really weren't very close."

Grace listened to the women go back and forth, and she was blushing, as if she was embarrassed by all the talk of sympathy and death. She wouldn't meet Penelope's eyes. Maybe her dream of Penelope had been tainted by her status now as half an orphan, or maybe the weeks had worn away at the girl's fascination with Penelope. Perhaps the news of Mirella's death had made her newly aware that her mother would die one day, too, and she had decided to devote her attentions to Samantha. She was probably right.

Samantha explained the best place to plant the rhododendron. It would grow best on higher ground, somewhere the rainwater wouldn't pool. And she should get it in the ground soon—this was its growing season.

"We'll be heading home now. Say good-bye to Penelope, Grace."

"Good-bye, Penelope." The girl repeated after her mother, and Penelope said good-bye, too, without rising from the stoop. The women nodded at one another, and Penelope watched them walk away. The two Harpers with their arms around each other's waists, their hair swinging over their shoulders, as they went down Halsey Street. Penelope called after them.

"No car service?"

Samantha spun around. "We walked!" she called, and they went on north to Bedford, where they turned the corner and disappeared.

Jon arrived once his shift was over, gliding on his bicycle in the dark, unfazed by the sheets of rain falling over the block. His face was wet and serene, as he locked up the tires and frame to the gate in front of the house. He dragged a tarp over the bicycle then bounded up the stairs.

He kissed Penelope and they sat on the navy loveseat in the parlor. She covered them with a ratty blanket from her childhood that she had found upstairs.

"You bought a plant?" Jon gestured to the rhododendron in front of the fireplace, all filled with bricks. She shook her head and didn't say more. She didn't want to revisit the afternoon, the visit from the Harpers, or the hours afterward. She had called Willow Lake and Ralph refused to come to the phone, so she lay down in her new bedroom on the first floor with the lights turned off, and she felt as if a great time had passed since yesterday. She had spent her whole life in this house, in this dark little room. She had never lived in Pittsburgh, or in Providence, or on Greene. She had always been here. Her mother had always been dead.

"I brought you something," Jon said, and he produced a lump, wrapped in tissue paper, from his bag. Penelope withdrew two pale yellow ceramic cups. They didn't have handles, and they each had a visible seam along one side, as if two halves had been joined imperfectly. Penelope raised one of the cups overhead and saw two letters etched into the underside: *BW*.

"Did your mother make these? Bertha Wright?"

"Birdie," Jon said. "Nobody ever called her Bertha."

Penelope looked at the cups again, appreciated their even glaze, their weight in her hands.

"She used to take me sometimes to her ceramics studio in Lincoln Square. It wasn't cheap, but she paid for time whenever she could. She started putting these ridges in everything when she got sick. She said she'd spent years trying to make perfect, beautiful things, but that wasn't real—everything in life could be taken apart. Everything has a seam, and it's a lie to try and hide it."

"*Seams*," Penelope said. "Sounds like a show they'd have in some gallery in Chelsea."

"I know a lot of people wouldn't consider her an artist—all she ever made were salt shakers and bowls and pitchers, but her stuff is all over our house in Chicago. I think it makes my dad feel like she's still around."

"You never told me how she died."

"It was her liver. Cancer. How's that for fucked? My dad plowed through handles of vodka for years, and he's already outlived her by a decade. She wouldn't even drink wine at communion. Said it gave her headaches."

"She sounds like a saint."

"She was my mother."

Penelope thanked him for the cups.

"Everyone is bringing me presents," she said, and neither of them mentioned Mirella. "Tell me about the bar," Penelope said before Jon could ask her about her day. He indulged her.

The owner had been around at Sheckley's, spilling drafts, putting mixing spoons in the wrong cup, asking a dozen questions—had Jon remembered to check the icemaker for mold? Where did he keep the receipts from last night when he closed out the register? Had he set out the olives on every table? Olives were going to be the new thing at Sheckley's—pitted, marinated, fat green olives. He'd made a deal with Sprout to put them out in tiny bowls on every table with a little placard describing their origin, and their price per quarter pound at the shop. Penelope listened as Jon went on about the olives, how they didn't pair with beer, how bar peanuts were bar peanuts for a reason. He made her laugh.

Penelope brought out a deck of cards so they could go on with the evening, without any useless heaviness. She taught Jon a gambling game she had played with Ramona. It wasn't long before she was forgetting turns and playing the wrong cards, and Jon started to win.

"I guess you're a natural," Penelope said and left for her room. Jon followed her and climbed into bed beside her. The thunder was far off enough that the house was mostly peaceful, the rush of water in the drainpipes, and the smell of Jon: wet denim, smoke, industrial-strength dish soap.

"Did the Harpers bring you that plant?"

"How could you tell?"

"'Cause they're nice white people."

"My father wants to go to DR."

"That's no surprise either."

"It surprised me. She's already dead."

"Jesus, Penelope."

"She didn't even go to her own mother's funeral."

"Well, you don't have to be her." Jon reached for Penelope's hand. "I couldn't stop thinking about her today. I was setting out those little bowls of olives, and I wondered what Mirella would think of Sprout if she could see it. Whether she'd like the things there, since she's got such *elevated* tastes, or whether she'd hate it just on principle."

Penelope was shocked that Jon could spend the day thinking of her mother, whom he'd never met and never would meet. "She'd like it," Penelope said. "And she'd hate it, too. She never wanted the store to close."

Jon looked at her, squeezed her hand, and waited for her to explain.

"We had trouble with the store long before those Seattle hippies priced us out. There were good years and bad years, especially when I was little. One year when we were still living on Marcy, Pop fell behind on the rent. I don't know how much, but he'd sit up every night at our kitchen table with his head in his hands, going through piles and piles of paper. I didn't know what they were—loans or bills or notices or what, but I knew it wasn't good. And Mirella—my mother—she kept saying, *We'll find the money, we'll find the money, we'll make a way.* Even though she wasn't miserable then, not yet, I remember being shocked at how confident she was, when my father couldn't be. One day, one of the front girls called in sick, and Pop was in a panic—said he couldn't afford to open late, to lose even an hour of sales, so Mami and I went to help him sweep and set up. But before we went in, Mami led us around to the side of the building, and she pulled out this knife, a Swiss army knife. And she turned to us and said, 'This store is going to stay open. I know it. But no matter what, whatever passes, we will be a family.' And then she starts scratching into the brick her initial, just an *M* for her first name, and then she puts the knife in my hand, and helps me write out my initials. I must have just been learning my letters. And then my pop wrote his initials down, and he was all teary-eyed, and he kissed my mother—at least, I remember them kissing—and then we all went inside. My mother went back out there, after we were done inside the shop, and she retraced every letter. She wanted to make sure we'd pressed deep enough."

"You've never mentioned that."

"I don't have many stories like that."

Jon opened his mouth to speak, and Penelope cut him off.

"Don't start with any of that 'love' shit. My mother wasn't Birdie Wright."

"It's obvious, Penelope, that she—"

Penelope plugged her ears and started to chant: *I do not want to hear it, I do not want to hear it, I do not want to hear it.* It was childish, she knew, and she would have felt embarrassed if she didn't care more about sparing herself. She would rather Jon find her ridiculous than listen to him say again and again that her mother had loved her, that she had lived with the knowledge of it.

Jon quieted, and Penelope uncovered her ears. "Let's just go to sleep," she said and turned off the light.

"Jon."

"Miss Grand?"

"Do you still miss her? Your mother?"

He didn't answer right away, and Penelope felt scared, the darkness of the room coming down around her.

"Most days, it's not so bad. I even forget sometimes and go about my day for a while as if nothing is missing. But eventually I remember she's dead, and then it's bad, but not as bad as it was that first year without her."

"And your father? Is he all right?"

"He doesn't drink anymore, so it seems like he's better than he's ever been. It's hard to tell. He still talks to her. Out loud, like she's in another room and he just can't see her. He says he can still hear her voice when he needs to."

Penelope could hear Mirella shouting, as clearly as the rain, the creak of the old house.

"I don't want to keep my mother's voice with me."

"Then keep something else."

It wasn't long before he was asleep, and Penelope slipped her hand into the waistband of his jeans. She felt his skin thrum against her fingers: his heart. She slid one leg on top of his, her left calf over his right shin. Their linked ankles were an anchor, rigging them to the room and one another. It seemed to help, to touch him, but she still couldn't sleep. Her head was too filled with Mirella. *Mami,* she wanted to say. *Mami, stop.*

Penelope climbed out of bed and sat on her trunk. Her easel was still open, the clean cotton paper clipped to the top of it. There was a jar of drinking water on the floor, and all her supplies in a neat pile: the tubes of paint, her brushes, a palette knife, a rag to wipe everything off.

Penelope took up a filbert brush, her fingers curling to pinch the handle. She began by building stone. She left the edges of the paper blank and started near the center. She scumbled together white and blue, gray and pink. The wall began to form: grainy, dappled in light. The exterior of a house would never be this colorful, no matter how creamy the paint, or how bright the day, but Penelope kept going. She swept on the paint with thick, free strokes, as if the color were blowing out of her center, into her arms, her fingertips. She was emboldened and brought in yellow, switched to a fan brush to tap in even greater light.

She couldn't remember the color of the shutters or whether there had been shutters at all. She used the mop brush to swipe on white and gray to make the sill, and then two slender strips of indigo for curtains. Had there been curtains? If there had, they should have been indigo: dark and mesmeric. The curtains were cast open, but she did not want to paint inside yet. She moved to the garden.

She hadn't listened when her mother named the flowers; she hadn't taken them in with her eyes either. She had been elsewhere, wondering what would become of the two of them and trying to appear unmoved. She worked without any real memory, feeling her way through color: violet, blue, pink. She pressed her round brush down to make the petals, twisted her wrist around for the bud. The flowers swelled larger than scale, but what did it matter? A swipe of black for a stem, folds of yellow and green to make each leaf. She worked until she had filled the paper, the garden inching into the edges of the painting, rising up the wall, and onto the sill. The only empty space was where the windows should be. Penelope blew on the paper and considered the center.

She took up the mop again and brought together red and yellow and blue, then more yellow, and white. Where the windows should be, she painted only light: gold and orange and yellow, then rivulets of pure white. It took a few minutes to get the color right, and she inspected the painting when she was done. It was beautiful—hurried and loose and aglow. She could have kept it to remember the house in the residence in the north of the island, to remind herself of where she and her mother had once stood together, but she decided to give it away. She would take this to her mother, whether Mirella would have wanted it or not. She would take down one of those awful still lifes, and hang it in her house. She had never been one for words, and she considered it her best reply to her mother's last letter and question—*Have you found your life?*

The answer was obvious—*No*—and also, *Ya casi.*

20

SALIDA

They arranged for a flight in the late afternoon so that they would have enough time to get Ralph ready for the airport. When Penelope arrived at Willow Lake, he was already packed and in his wheelchair. His shirt was a serious plaid, his leather oxfords recently shined, his gray hair slicked back with tonic and parted on the side. He had a little suitcase filled with clothes, and a larger duffel bag with medical supplies, the wooden transfer board, washcloths, protein shakes, pain pills, a bedpan and a basin in case it became too difficult to get him to the tub or the toilet in Mirella's house. He'd taken the poppies out of the vase on the windowsill and wrapped them with a navy handkerchief into a bouquet. He held them in his hand.

As Penelope wheeled him out of his suite and down the hallway, the nurses called after him to have a safe trip. They waved as he passed, and Ralph gave each of them a wink. He'd charmed them all. She helped Ralph into the passenger seat of the taxi, and she sat in the back while he made small talk with the driver. It amazed her he wasn't more sullen, more silent. She let him have his normalcy. For a while, he was just a man in a car riding to the airport.

When Ralph told the driver the terminal number, he asked, "Flying international today?"

"First time," Ralph said.

"Where you going?"

"The Caribbean."

"Wow! That will be like paradise," the driver said, and Ralph didn't contradict him.

The driver brought out the luggage, while Penelope helped her father into the chair and onto the curb. The driver told Ralph to have a blast in DR, and Ralph nodded, arranged a blanket around himself in the cold.

They got through security fine, although Penelope was sweating the whole time, worried they would ask Ralph to get out of the chair, and that she wouldn't know how to help him. Once they were inside, he asked her to go buy him a cup of coffee, and she didn't want to leave him alone. He was reading the paper peacefully when she got back, and he drank his coffee, then said he had to use the bathroom. They found an accessible bathroom, and Ralph went in by himself. She stood outside the door, wondering if she was strong enough to kick in the lock if something went wrong. Soon she heard the flush, then water running in the sink. Ralph knocked on the door, and she opened it to let him out. He was shaking his wet hands.

"All that money for a ticket and they can't put a roll of paper towel in the bathroom. Pfsh."

They had some time to kill before their departure. At the gate, they were surrounded by Dominicans on their way home, tourists readying themselves for vacation, and they were somewhere in between. The sun was setting, and Ralph closed the newspaper, pulled a cell phone from his pocket.

"Where'd you get that?"

"Faye helped me order one online. It's in case we need anything. We can call Una from down there. It was Freddie's idea."

"You called Dr. Elias?"

"He had a right to know. He knew your mother. And it's smart, I think—to keep connected."

Penelope raised an eyebrow at her father and smiled. "We'll be fine," she said.

Ralph squinted down at his phone, tapping and trying to understand. Eventually, he gave up and put it back in his pocket.

"So that man you mentioned—her friend. The one who called. He won't be down there, will he?"

"Mami's neighbor? No. He's gone."

Ralph looked relieved. He went back to people watching, observing the new parents with their wailing infants, grandparents with children who kept wandering off, the childless middle-aged folks who had the space to read and eat, talk on the phone, while they waited to board.

"I wish I was going to see her, and not just her house," he said. "But it's something. How's her garden? You know, your mother, she had art in her bones, same as you. That's where you get it from. Her garden—that was how she drew. Do you remember what the yard was like when we first moved in? Just dirt and a square of cement? But she made it beautiful. Did she plant roses?"

"I can't remember."

"She always said she planted those for you. We thought for a while about naming you that, *Rose*, but your mother said it was too common. She liked Penelope."

"I didn't know."

Ralph gestured at the chipboard case Penelope had with her. He asked what was inside.

"I made a painting for Mami. I thought I'd leave it there for her."

"Is that right?" Ralph smiled. "Good girl now, Penny. Good girl."

Ralph said he was starting to get hungry, so Penelope unpacked some of the food Una had dropped off for them the day before. She had made macaroni and cheese, and green beans, roast beef, and her infamous potato salad. Penelope had foisted most of it off on Jon, but she had brought along the black cake, full of stone fruit and rum.

"I should go find us a knife."

"No, no, no," Ralph said, and he reached out his hands. He unwrapped the cake and tore off a hunk for Penelope, another for himself.

"We'll eat it just like this."

They sat quietly, as passengers at other gates began to line up to board. When he was done with his piece, his expression went sour.

"I can't believe she's dead."

Penelope didn't know what to say. She believed that her mother was dead, but she still couldn't fathom what it meant. The only way she had ever known her mother was through her body: the scrape of her fingers in Penelope's scalp the few times she had helped her wash her hair in the sink when she was a girl, the pudding scent of her cold face cream. The ringing of her gold bangles, the residue left by an eye pencil ground into her chin to create an artificial beauty mark. The crust of mud on her cutoff jeans. The flap of her red hair in the wind on the beach, her downturned mouth on the ride up the rocky side of the mountain. The impact of her fingers on Penelope's sternum that time in the kitchen. Penelope had long tolerated the idea of Mirella no longer being her mother, but she couldn't comprehend Mirella no longer being Mirella. She had always been herself, her own woman in her bedroom, in her yard, on her island. Her body had always been somewhere.

Ralph put his hand on Penelope's shoulder. "When she was alive, at least there was a chance," he said. "Even if most of the time we don't really know how to change. We can't hardly figure out how to love right. But there was hope. Now . . . Nothing is as final as death."

"Maybe not," Penelope said. "Look at Coltrane. Isn't he with us all the time?"

Ralph smiled as if it pained him. "And McCoy. Don't you forget McCoy."

Penelope pulled a pair of headphones from her backpack and reached into Ralph's pocket for his cell phone. She began to tap on the screen.

"What are you doing?"

She handed him an earbud, and he recognized the song immediately.

"Run it back, run it back," he said. "I want to hear it from the start."

They sat, awash in the turbulence of the piano, the way it rang in many directions. The saxophone sailed in, and they could hear the chant even before it was uttered. *A love supreme. A love supreme.*

They gave themselves over to the music. Ralph rapped on his chest, the additional percussion of his fist. The cymbals switched, the piano faded, until there was only the bass, deep, spare, the sound of sorrow. Penelope took her father's hand. She wanted to tell him who he was to her.

"Wait, wait, wait," Ralph said, holding up a finger to shush her. "Listen to this part, Penny. Listen." He shook his head from side to side, as if the music were too much, as if he could hardly bear it.

ACKNOWLEDGMENTS

My first thanks are dedicated wholeheartedly to my agent, Kristyn Keene. Thank you for your unwavering belief in my work, your editorial vision, and your commitment to getting this book into the world. I am also so grateful to my fabulous editor, Morgan Parker, who understood this project, and whose love for Brooklyn, black women, and our stories helped push *Halsey Street* further and deeper. Thank you also to Vivian Lee and Alexandra Woodworth, who saw this book through until the very end.

I'd have been lost without the generosity of dear friends and fellow writers who were willing to read *Halsey Street* and offer notes. Thank you to Elizabeth St. Victor, Bin Jung, Emily Helck, Meghan Flaherty, and Thomas Sun. I am deeply indebted to you all for your encouragement, friendship, and advice.

I started *Halsey Street* at Fordham University, where early versions of these pages passed through the skilled and generous hands of many writers: Kim Dana Kupperman, Meera Nair, and John Reed. I am also beholden to Christina Baker Kline, who taught me how to write a decent short story and told me it was time to start writing a book. I am also grateful to the many writers at the Columbia MFA program who gave me direction and support as I wrote this book: Sam Lipsyte, Matthew Sharpe, Stacey D'Erasmo, Victor LaValle, Rebecca Godfrey,

Ben Marcus, and Johanna Lane. I am thankful to my many colleagues at Columbia, as well, especially Michael Hafford.

I offer a special thanks to John Crowley, my first writing professor and mentor at Yale. John has believed in my writing for as long as I've known him.

I am grateful to my family for their love and support over the years: thank you to my mother, my father, and my brother, Luciano. I found the drive and audacity to write in part because of how committed you've been to providing me with both education and opportunities. Thank you also to my uncle, Adlai, who bought me at least two laptops and loaned me another—your generosity and kindness have been enormous gifts to me in my life. I also thank my aunt and uncle, Mayra and Edwin, and their children, for being devoted, consistent, loving family to me.

And my highest thanks I offer to my husband, Jonathan Jiménez Pérez, whose faith in me and in this book has never wavered. You have supported me and loved me in more ways than I can count. Thank you, Jonathan. This book is for us, for our freedom.

ABOUT THE AUTHOR

Naima Coster is a native of Fort Greene, Brooklyn. She holds an MFA in fiction from Columbia University, an MA in English and creative writing from Fordham University, and a BA in English and African American studies from Yale. Her stories and essays have appeared in the *New York Times*, *Guernica*, *Arts & Letters*, *Kweli*, and the *Rumpus*. Coster is the recipient of numerous awards and a Pushcart Prize nomination. A former editor of *CURA* and a former mentor of Girls Write Now, Coster is also a proud alumna of Prep for Prep, the leadership development program in New York City aiding high-potential minority students in public, charter, and parochial schools. She currently teaches writing in North Carolina, where she lives with her family. *Halsey Street* is her first novel.